SHADES OF BLACK

IN DARKNESS CAST

JONATHAN SHUERGER

Shades of Black: In Darkness Cast 2020 by Jonathan Shuerger

Cover illustration 2020 by Louie Roybal III

Cover design 2020 by Louie Roybal III

Map 2020 by Louie Roybal III

Interior design 2020 by Jonathan Shuerger

Ebook: 978-1-7352824-2-8

Softcover: 978-1-7352824-0-4

Hardback: 978-1-7352824-1-1

Published in the United States by Creative Grumbles, LLC.

Learn more about Jon's writings at www.creativegrumbles.com

To contact Jon, email him at jjshuerger@gmail.com

Kickstarter Edition

Printed in the United States of America

❀ Created with Vellum

CONTENTS

SHADES OF BLACK I: IN DARKNESS CAST

Prologue	3
1. Arrival	7
2. Quest	38
3. Basic	52
4. Warrior	69
5. Wolves	85
6. Ambush	105
7. Consort	129
8. Leavetaking	152
9. Ghosts	169
10. Servants	192
11. Weapons	210
12. Preparation	237
13. The Wall	253
14. Doom of Kings	279
15. Threat	315
16. Tomb of Rachna	348
17. Killing Ground	376
Epilogue	411

KICKSTARTER EXCLUSIVE SHORT STORIES

Son of Anak	421
Ashes	455
Acknowledgements	479
About the Author	481

Shades of Black: In Darkness Cast is dedicated to the warfighters of the 26xx field in the United States Marine Corps. This is for the 267xs (41s now), 21s, 31s, and 51s who swore the oath to serve, and either SL3ed gear at 1700 on a Friday or spent years in a windowless box explaining to the LT how many slash marks is appropriate on a classification marking. God bless us, every one.

Rah yut kill!

SHADES OF BLACK I: IN DARKNESS CAST

PROLOGUE
WARNING

There is no sound more heartbreaking than an old man walking through a field of his sons' skulls.

The rain makes them slick. My shoes, more suited to libraries and repositories of arcana, struggle to find traction on the gleaming bone. I lean on my staff heavily as I pick my way through the field of jagged skeletons, my breathing ragged, my tears masked by the rain.

So many.

Each skull grinning from the ground belonged to a man of Avalon. Some from Tabayla, some from Corland, others from the far-off mountains of Saradon. Their uniforms paint the ground like an artist's palette, a record of the impossible alliance of the nations of Avalon. Men of every race, color and creed, all coming together to face a lord of the Everlasting Dark. It had shaken the heart with pride to see them march out in the morning, a thousand flags whipping in the poisoned breeze and a thousand horns sounding the advance.

Then the day ended, and I saw that beneath our uniforms and the color of our skin, our bones are all the same.

That had been yesterday.

He did something to the rain. It tastes like an alchemist's laboratory smells, and has vastly accelerated the decomposition process. The flesh

*sloughs away from the bone like mud sluices away from rock in a stream,
leaving behind the broken ivory and iron. I suppose it is merely another of his
endless preparations for yesterday's battle, to keep the rot of a million corpses
from killing him where their blades failed.*

*He planned for everything, it seems. I find it more likely that he enjoys
the view.*

*I can see him, when I lift my gaze from beneath my sodden hood to the
peak of the Black Pyramid. Only when green lightning claws through the
sky, separating the false darkness from the true with a jagged spear of light,
can I see the shadow that pretends to humanity's form. He stands alone,
looking down on the abject ruin of a world with his eyes of ice. He stares at
the twisted bodies of tens of tens of thousands, and he does not blink.*

*He waits, Acheron's Bane sheathed on his back and his arms folded across
his darkmail. The twisted skeletons of Avalon's greatest warriors and
sorcerers lay around him, their skulls gaping at the broken sky. The bones of
drakes and gryphons decorate his fortress, discarded where they crashed after
he ripped them from the sky.*

He waits for more to come, and we have nothing more to send.

*My eyes sting from the rain, and I lower my eyes back to the graveyard
that threatens to steal my footing. Despite the downpour, my feet crunch into
the soil where I step, because the dirt can no longer retain moisture. The land
died months ago.*

*I cannot kill him, I know this. After the slaughter of yesterday, after
hearing the soul-shattering cacophony of hatred's masked champion
murdering Avalon's sons, I don't think anyone can. Not even my brother.*

*My brother. He is a flash of silver on the side of the Pyramid, and I can
hear him roaring in maddened grief as he pulls himself up the slick stones. As
Avalon dies, Valantian's soul dies with it. As the Scion, the protector of all
Avalon, he alone suffers the true weight of what the Everlasting Dark has
done. I cannot imagine his agony, nor how it must tear at his sanity.*

We have lost everything, and I weep.

*I write this now, muttering to my fey scribe as I stagger through the
bones, to warn anyone who may come after us. Anyone his purge has missed.*

Do not repeat our sins. We thought it dispelled by the strength of our

Light, but in truth, the Dark was only ever a candle's breath away. It lurks behind the skin of the world, and strikes from the crimes we thought buried.

I write this now, before I join Valantian on the altar of our ruin, to beg for forgiveness.

We are sorry. Oh, God, we are sorry.

—last testament of Gemelte Asirius, High Chancellor of the Magi, brother of the Scion

1

ARRIVAL

No one saw things as Gideon did, and he found he liked it that way.

The tiny village of Halcyon nestled at the foot of the mighty Ironback Mountains, far to the west of the continent, though not so far as to reach the sea. Farmers tilled their fields and raised strong children, who in turn tilled the fields when their fathers passed into the earth. Their crops sold well, and the town well-spoken of by the merchants who passed through. Their barns stood together in the town itself, arranged thus by the knight who had founded the village for ease of defense. The inhabitants remained content with their place in the Almighty's design, never thinking to go beyond their station.

Except Gideon.

Gideon stabbed his pitchfork into the sweet-smelling hay, but where an ordinary farmer simply saw provender, Gideon's mind blazed with images of glory. He was an orphan adopted by farmers no more; he was a soldier of Samothrace, caught in the awful wars to the East. His unit lay dead all around him, lost in the savage melee of the past hours.

His pitchfork transformed into a shining spear, and with a growl, he thrust it forward into a scabrous demon, one of the mythical invaders trying to break through the armies of Samothrace on the killing fields of Bel Farak. As his young muscles bunched, Gideon hoisted the shrieking monster upward, presenting it to the throne of God, and a bolt of lightning lanced down to incinerate the creature upon the tip of his weapon.

Gideon hurled the broiled carcass behind him, brandished his spear with a flourish, and roared, "Who's next?"

He jerked to a stop as he met the warm brown eyes of the woman he called his mother. Talia Halcyon stood in the open door of the barn, one hand on her hip, the other resting on her very pregnant abdomen, a wry smile on her face.

Gideon stumbled at the sight of her and righted himself awkwardly. He was fifteen years old, but already the size of an ordinary man and he still struggled to control his limbs. He stammered, "Mom, I, uh, I'm—"

Talia raised her hand and said, "I know. The long war against the hay continues. As long as it gets in the loft, I suppose that's all that matters."

Gideon grinned sheepishly. "Yes, ma'am."

She winced a little and put a hand to her swollen belly. "Oh, this one is *kicking*. Why must you kick me, I haven't even done anything to you yet!"

The widow glanced back at Gideon. "I'm going to go sit in the house for a few minutes. See if you can't vanquish this lot in time for supper."

Gideon dipped his head. "Yes, ma'am."

"And remember to drink your water."

"Yes, ma'am."

"And wash up before you come in. I won't have you covered in the intestines or whatever of your enemies in my house."

Gideon grinned. "Yes, ma'am."

No one expected him. That was the point.

The warband had ranged far this season, penetrating Samothrace's steel-clad battle lines to tear at the exposed hindquarters of the empire. From the barren east, he had driven his raiders, bypassing vast prairies and rich farmlands, holding them obedient to his vision with an iron hand. Now they stood on a hill far to the west of the tainted lands of their birth, weapons held in their fists, shackles ready to cast upon the slaves of Samothrace.

It required singular vision to wait so long, patiently bypassing easy prey to stab and rip where the enemy thought himself safe. His men hated him for his patience. For his vision.

Aganyn smiled.

Below him, the village bustled about its daily activities, completely ignorant of the monster surveying them. Examining them. *Judging them.*

The wind gusted through his black robes like the malice from his soul.

He spoke.

"Make them suffer."

As soon as his words hissed through his lips like a malignant fog, fifteen Jahennan maidens stepped forward and daubed thick warpaint onto his warriors' bodies, inscribing hellish runes that seared the eyes to see. Huge chests bare to the biting cold swelled like mighty bellows and exhaled in growling huffs. Clouds of steam chugged from their mouths and noses as thoughts of the bloodshed to come coursed through their minds.

He, their employer, their *master*, stalked before them. His soulless eyes, their irises bleached the color of milk from staring at the searing secrets of the damned, drilled each one to the ground.

"Make. Them. Suffer."

Nostrils flared wide. Arms wrapped in muscle like bands of steel flexed, trembled. One warrior could not contain himself and shouted hoarsely, *"Destroy!"*

In one smooth motion, inhumanly fast, Aganyn, servant of Gehenna, inquisitor of the Lord of Thorns, gripped the warrior by the throat and squeezed with terrifying strength. Veins in the doomed man's head bulged out, as if trying to escape his skull, and his knees buckled beneath him.

Aganyn snarled softly, yet he ensured that every warrior heard him. "No. Not destroy. Suffer. Like *this*."

The inquisitor hissed a dark syllable, and the barbarian mercenary choked suddenly, his eyes wide. His mouth fell open, but no scream would come out.

His fellows did not move, except to avert their gazes from the atrocity in front of them. Hardened warriors of Gehenna all, even they had no wish to watch the thing eating their comrade's eyes.

It took ninety seconds for the man to finally die, and Aganyn let the corpse slump from his grip to the earth. Goosebumps prickled his flesh as he silently offered the sensation of the man's last moments to Gehenna's distant throne.

The warrior's pain was only an appetizer for the agony to come.

WHEN GIDEON HEARD ELYN SCREAM, he dismissed it out of mind. That idiot girl was always screaming about something. She just wanted attention, and she got far too much of it.

He jammed his pitchfork back into the stack of hay and heaved another forkful in front of the horses, his back feeling little strain. He had been working the Halcyons' farm ever since the knight and his wife had adopted him four years before. When Sir Armand died five months ago, he shouldered the man's burden of the farm without complaint.

Gideon's body equaled many grown men in size and had grown hard with the years of labor. He knew the girls in town spoke admiringly of his build and sharp green eyes; he suspected his meddling mother had a good deal to answer for in instigating that situation, though she denied it vociferously.

He did not care. Girls and their drama were not something Gideon needed in his life. He had enough to occupy him with the work on the farm and the battles of his dreams. He swiped his sweaty mop of tawny blonde hair out of his eyes and readied his pitchfork for another stab, putting Elyn's manufactured panic out of his head.

When Fordred, the blacksmith, screamed, Gideon's head snapped up. Fordred *never* screamed.

He stepped outside, pitchfork in hand, and came upon a scene from Hell.

Barbarians with the blood-runes of the worshippers of Gehenna on their chests thundered through the village, hurling torches into the thatched roofs as they laughed raucously. Already, plumes of fire reached into the sky, and columns of black smoke billowed all around.

Elyn ran screaming through the center of the village. Even as she ran, a mounted warrior revolved his arm around his head and snapped it forward. Elyn's legs swept out from under her, and she hit the ground hard, her legs wrapped in a bola trailing a line of rope back to her attacker. The raider lashed the rope to his saddle horn and hauled on it, jerking Elyn back toward him. She screamed again, clawing at the earth for help. The raider laughed.

Slavers.

The empires of the world paid their expenses in human currency and washed the dirt from their streets in human blood and tears. But they were supposed to be a world away from here.

A hoarse sobbing cry rose from the smithy. Gideon's wide eyes glanced that way reflexively, and immediately, he wished he had not. Three of them forced Fordred's head toward his own furnace, roaring in laughter at his begging as a fourth pumped the bellows for the flames. They were burning his face off.

Elyn screamed again, and Gideon moved.

"Hey!" he shouted. The raider holding Elyn's rope twisted toward him.

Gideon brandished his pitchfork toward the barbarian. "Let her go!"

The man brayed a laugh and wheeled his horse toward Gideon. The warrior spurred his mount to a gallop, spittle spraying from his mouth as he raised his sword above his head and angled the ragged tip at the boy, still dragging the screaming girl behind him.

Gideon's mind refused to register the hundreds of pounds of horseflesh and bellowing barbarian bearing down on him. His mind ignored fear and sense, instead reaching for Armand's stories of warfare, and how to stop a charging horseman with a spear.

Gideon threw himself forward, planted the base of his pitchfork into the dirt and ducked, wrapping himself around the handle.

It was like getting hit with a cliff. A savage impact jarred Gideon's skull and smashed into his ribs, and he flew several yards to crash into the ground. His tongue flamed with pain as his teeth clamped down on it, and Gideon choked on the thick taste of blood in his mouth. His...everything...hurt.

The stories didn't say it hurt...

The barbarian's horse thrashed nearby, screaming and trying to kick away from the killing tines lodged in its chest. The motionless body of the rider sprawled beyond it, neck cocked at an impossible angle.

That should have been me.

The thought burned through the haze of pain, and a fleeting prayer of thanks flashed through his mind. Setting his hand against his ribs, Gideon forced himself to his feet, grimacing at the sudden stiffness of his body.

Elyn sobbed on the ground nearby, and Gideon limped over to her, pulling his knife to saw through the bola wrapping her ankles. A few swift cuts, and Elyn's legs were free.

"Go hide in the fields. Stay low," he said, and Elyn nodded quickly. She ran off behind the barn.

More bolas whipped through the village, dragging friends to the ground. Lassoes and nets fell in all directions, casting the chains of slavery onto people he had known since birth. Everywhere, the screams of family and the diabolical laughter of the raiders filled the air.

What do I do now?

Widow Halcyon would be alone in their home, scared, hands folded over her swollen abdomen as she shielded her unborn child. If any of the raiders entered the house...

The thought of that nightmare banished his pain and forced him to his feet.

The house was just ahead.

HIS MOTHER LOOKED UP, fear warring for control as Gideon staggered into the hut. "Oh, it's you! What is happening? Are you all right?"

Gideon scanned the hut and answered, "Slavers. Jahennans."

A hand rose to cover her mouth, the other instinctively covering her unborn child.

One glance told him that other than being scared, she was fine; Gideon moved past her toward the fireplace. There, mounted above the stone, rested the iron sword of Armand Halcyon, knight of Samothrace. Not a ripple of taint or a patch of rust marked the blade.

His adopted father had defended the lands of men for decades against raiders and monsters with this weapon. He had died with it clamped tight in his fist only months ago, coughing his way into a grave dug by a Sheolin assassin's poisoned blade. It was the closest thing to a holy relic Gideon had ever seen.

On the final day, Armand called Gideon to his bedside. Gideon had come hesitantly, feeling woefully undeserving of last words from such a warrior. The gruff knight considered the youth with his steely eyes, rimed with grit and watery from the venom snaking its way through his veins.

"Gideon," he said. "Look at me, boy."

Gideon had met his gaze then, the weight of the dying man's stare almost pushing him back. Sir Armand had been a forceful man in life; on the banks of the river Death, he seemed ferocious.

"Take care of your mother, lad," Sir Halcyon rasped through the phlegm in his lungs. "She's yours to protect now. She took care of you, now you take care of her. Anyone comes to take advantage, you take this sword from the fireplace, you stand in the door, and you don't move or be moved until she's safe. Am I understood, Gideon?"

Gideon stared at the blade above the mantle now. In the months since Sir Armand's death, Gideon touched the blade only to wipe dust from collecting on its sacred edge. To practice with such a relic felt the worst kind of sacrilege.

Outside, the sounds of terror and savagery rose. Women sobbed, slavers roared and children shrieked.

Gideon's resolve hardened, and his fingers closed around the hilt of the Halcyon blade.

"Understood."

FLAMES REACHED high into the air, as though trying to flee the madness below. The screams continued, punctuated by cracking whips as the slavers corralled the farmers and their families into milling groups of sobbing men and women, shackling them together in long roped lines while shouting obscenities at the helpless villagers and inflicting their individual sadisms on their captives.

Aganyn stood apart, his lifeless eyes seething. There was much suffering to be had here, yes, but nothing that one did not find every day, nothing fit for his master, the Architect of Suffering. A horde of Mammon's mutants could achieve as much, and without traversing the continent.

He sighed. An inquisitor could do better.

Shouts descended from the northern hill, and Aganyn turned to see an improbable sight. Gorak, a savage of little brain, stumbled back from the doorway of a nearby hut, clutching his midsection in horror. Aganyn caught a glimpse of a foot of gleaming iron protruding from the man's back before it disappeared out the way it came. An instant later, a gleaming arc slashed through the man's neck, and Gorak's head and body parted company.

A man—no, a boy, but large for his age—stood in the doorway, feet planted, shoulders squared. He clearly meant to deny entrance to the hovel.

Aganyn raised an eyebrow, and even as his lips framed the curse that would kill the hapless hero, even as the demons writhed nauseatingly in his flesh as he invoked their power, the teachings of the *Liber Cruciatus* flashed through his mind.

--Every man suffers in equal measure to another, save for two: those who give life and those who preserve it. The suffering of such souls is exquisite, for they suffer not their own pain only, but of all those around them. The wise servant of the Architect will give heed, and as a preparer of fine delicacies will select and mix only the ingredients of soul-torture that will produce a masterpiece fit for the Lord of Pain.--

The daemonic syllables died stillborn on his lips. The warlock considered for a handful of seconds, then gestured brusquely.

"Bring him to me. Alive."

GIDEON KICKED the slaver's sagging body out of his path, flicking a long lock of blonde hair out of his eyes. More of the barbarians had seen him, as had that man with the dead eyes, and he swallowed hard, squaring his stance. Heroes in stories did this all the time. The Jahennan inquisitor pointed toward him, snarling something gutturally.

At the last second, just before the first screaming savage hefted his axe for the killing blow, a thought flashed through Gideon's mind.

I hope those stories were true.

Time to stop thinking.

He caught the downward sweep of the axe and directed it toward the earth. His return cut slashed the man's throat clear to his spine. A roaring barbarian hurled himself forward, two wildly slashing swords scissoring in front of him. Panic provoking response, Gideon squeezed his eyes shut, gritted his teeth and thrust forward, his sword aimed at the man's chest. Trying to block the unexpected attack, the warrior cross-blocked the sword up into his own brain-pate.

Gideon jerked the sword out and span it once in front of him.

I'm alive.

A swell of excitement rose in his breast. If he continued like this, he could defend the doorway well enough. Maybe this wouldn't be so bad...

The sword itself rebelled against him. The handle flashed white-hot, hissing in Gideon's palm before he dropped it with a yelp. Gritting his teeth in pain, Gideon looked up in time to see a hulk of a man stepping in front of him with an upraised fist.

Pain.

Blackness.

"WAKE UP, BOY."

Slowly, the murky tunnel cleared and the world came into focus. Gideon groaned as his head pulsed like a hammer was trying to beat its way out of his skull.

Before his bleary eyes, the scarlet robes of an Inquisitor of Gehenna resolved into clarity. Judging by the size and weight of the medallions and charms hanging from his neck, a well-favored one. The man fingered a fiendish chainwhip bristling with spikes and glass. His eyes, as milky as that of a blind man's, never left Gideon's own.

Oh, God.

Beside the silent warlock stood the mountain of a man who had put the hammer in his head. Gideon's scorched hand reached for his sword instinctively, vainly.

"So."

The voice grated against reality, void of any shred of pity.

"You, alone of all these cattle, wish to play the hero."

The barbarian at his side grunted derisively; the warlock ignored him.

"Do you know who I am?"

Gideon surged against the heavy hands on his shoulders, managing to gain his feet and coming almost to eye level with the demon-worshipper. "Didn't know pain addicts got names."

The corner of the once-man's mouth turned up ever so slightly. "We do not. At least, not the ones we were born with. By the time we pass through our final trial, our previous lives have been scoured away, leaving only that which is pure."

The inquisitor's voice dropped to a whisper, vile in its blasphemous reverence. "When we stand, raw and bleeding before the Wailing Throne, the Master of Pain himself looks upon the faithful, those pure enough to survive the lashes and the racks, and he gives us a new name, written in down in blood and glory for the ages."

The sorcerer focused on Gideon. "He named me Aganyn, prophesying that I would be the first to see such power as this world has never known. Do you know the name?"

Gideon could not have answered if he wanted to. The shock of the name coursed through his body like lightning, blanking his mind, freezing his blood and closing his throat. His bright blue eyes stared into the empty abyss of the fallen man's soul, even as his mind refused to accept that Aganyn the Damned stood before him.

What is he doing here?

Aganyn smiled. "I see that you do. Excellent. So rewarding to know one's work is appreciated in his own time."

The brute next to him grunted something too guttural for Gideon to understand, but Aganyn, clearly drawing on years of experience to understand the man, nodded. "Yes, bring Abram. The sight of what he could have been will be...bracing."

The man nodded and gestured to another slaver, who jogged away.

His mouth tasted like iron and salt. Gideon grimaced and spat, his stomach roiling as he saw the ropy strand of blood drooling from his bottom lip. His head ached, his tongue was practically screaming with pain and his sword hand was scorched and blackened, weeping blisters just beginning to form.

At least my nose isn't broken.

That was something.

Aganyn waited a few moments, observing the captive before him until Rosh returned with his ward. Abram was nearly the same age as the young man on his knees, but far thinner. The boy's eyes, far too old for his age, sunk into his skull, and he could not quite keep the trembling from his hands.

Aganyn could glimpse through his charge's tattered shirt a bloody patchwork of scars. Good. The boy continued his study of the arts of agony through self-flagellation.

Yet...

The inquisitor squinted. Some of the scars appeared haphazard.

Abram came to stand before him, shoulders slumped. The trembling worsened.

Aganyn let the silence stretch for a moment, relishing the boy's growing fear while also despising it as unforgivable weakness, before he spoke.

"Abram."

Abram bowed stiffly. His scars must have pained him as the skin of his back pulled taut, but no expression crossed his face. That, at least, the boy remembered.

"Your flagellations are out of alignment with the pain channels. You lack focus."

Abram kept his gaze rooted to the ground as Aganyn stepped behind him, not allowing any tone to creep into his voice. "My lord, I sought to strike harder in order to increase my enlightenment. I lost control of my flail."

Aganyn raised an eyebrow at his student's statement. Without warning, his hands shot out and gripped the boy's back, thumbs spreading the skin of the lacerations wide. To Abram's credit, only a faint 'mmmmm' of pain escaped his tightly pressed lips.

For long seconds, Aganyn probed several wounds with his rough hands, studying his student's handiwork with a critical eye.

Finally, the warlock leaned back and rasped, "Your enthusiasm is commendable, young initiate. Yet in your exuberance, you have fallen prey to a common error among the followers of Gehenna. Here," he jabbed a thumb into a deeper cut on Abram's back, "and here, you have struck hard enough to cause damage to the holy vessels of pain, diminishing their capacity for sensation."

Abram, tongue bleeding from where he had bitten it, choked, "And without sensation, we are nothing."

Aganyn nodded, pleased with his student's recitation. From his belt pouch, he pulled a leather strap with strange thorns studding the length. "I cannot fault you for your zeal. Take."

The demon-worshipper tossed the vicious lash to his protege, who snatched it out of the air greedily. Had he been capable, Aganyn would have smiled at Abram's almost unseemly eagerness.

The lad at his feet, however, did not see the value of this moment. "What is he so happy about?"

Aganyn answered while watching Abram twine the new lash with the others, "The addition of a new lash to an acolyte's flail means another step along the path to the shedding of self. This particular lash bears the thorns of the bloodfire bush. Each stripe with his flail will now burn for hours, enhancing his suffering and bringing him closer to the truth."

The boy glared at him with disgust. "And that is..."

Aganyn turned to face him, the corners of his mouth twitching upward despite himself, and breathed, "All is pain."

Around him, the barbarians bowed their heads and droned, "All is pain."

Still staring at his captive, Aganyn gestured, "Bring the slaves. I wish to show a thing."

GIDEON KNEW he was going to die. The Acolytes of Gehenna were fanatics and torturers, raiding villages and towns for victims and sacrifices to their dark god, the Architect of Suffering.

Strangely, the thought of his own death failed to shake him. He only hoped he met it honorably, with no cowardice to stain his soul at the end. Like the stories.

But when the line of shackled slaves stumbled to a halt before the damned inquisitor, his hands began to shake.

Folks he had known his entire life huddled together, their faces tear-stained and grimy, the women and small ones crying softly. Many of the men joined them in weeping, either in anger or horror. The rest tried to shield their families from the hulking barbarians that lashed out with stinging whips or crushing blows.

Halcyon's widow stood in the line with cruel iron shackles on her wrists, cradling her belly gently. They had already fitted her with the slaver's collar, and the heavy yoke bowed her thin shoulders, absurdly oversized for her small frame.

The instant he saw her so callously treated, a shock ran through his body, rushing through his veins till Gideon gritted his teeth with the intensity of it. The portion of his mind able to retain reason noted with some alarm this new emotion, and tried to warn it away, desperate to preserve its existence.

It was like spitting into a hurricane. Never in his life had Gideon desired to kill a man more than at that moment. His breath became harsh in his lungs, and his hands clenched and unclenched at his sides.

Before he realized it, a ferocious prayer had formed in his mind. *God.*

One.

Give me just one of them.

A second later, the one Aganyn had called Abram glanced at him, sneered and kicked at his stomach.

With a growl of hate that surprised even him, Gideon doubled over, trapping the acolyte's foot into his gut and twisting savagely. With a cry of alarm, the initiate pitched to the ground, pinwheeling his arms for balance.

Gideon rolled to his knees over the other teen and powered his fist into Abram's face. More than a decade of fieldwork-hardened muscle slammed into the acolyte's jaw, breaking teeth and splitting his lip.

Then it hit again. Again.

Enormous hands covered in hair ripped Gideon off of the bleeding boy, pinning his arms to his side even as he raged, still trying to reach his target. Through the fury pounding in his head, Gideon could hear uproarious laughter, and he exploded again, thrashing in the barbarian giant's steel grip. He only succeeded in making them laugh harder.

The acolyte named Abram staggered to his feet, one hand cupping his broken jaw, the other pointing at Gideon as he shrieked, "Kill him!"

Abram's eyes went wide at the sudden burst of pain as the shattered bones of his chin ground together, and he howled anew, falling to his knees, which set the slavers to greater heights of hilarity.

Several raiders imitated his girlish squeals and sobs, and one man fell over into the dirt, holding his sides as he roared his amusement.

Aganyn stalked over to his crying protege and gripped him around his purpling jaw with an iron hand. As the bones grated, Abram's eyes went wild, but the fear of his master overcame even his pain. His voice tight, Aganyn rasped, "Control yourself, boy, and offer your pain to the god of agony."

He turned back to Gideon, still grinding Abram's jaw. "We do not serve the darkness through the precepts of Mammon, sating endless hunger. Nor do we kill for death's sake, as a Sheolin priest. We honor a far more refined intellect than that, so do not believe that you will earn a merciful death from your actions."

Gideon glared at him, spitting, "I don't want your mercy, demon!"

Aganyn dropped his acolyte and strode to the line of slaves, speaking as though Gideon had not. "Had you studied your *Liber Cruciatus* in depth, apprentice, you would know that while a certain visceral enjoyment may be extracted from torturing such a courageous individual, such pleasures are banal and fleeting, fodder for the less educated, such as these servants here."

He gestured with blackened fingers toward the savage brutes beside him. "But when one is old and can do naught but reflect back on his time of service, what shall he say? 'I remember how I tortured that great man' or 'I broke her will in seven hours'? I, Aganyn the Damned, say no."

He paused in front of certain slaves, grasped one by the chin and turned her head from side to side as though she were a horse for sale. The warlock tutted in disappointment and continued.

"Such is not a sacrifice fitting for the Master of Pain. No, to truly distinguish oneself in the eyes of our lord, one must exercise a degree of…creativity."

Aganyn's dark eyes locked with Gideon's on the last word, and the boy's blood ran cold. A dark horror uncoiled in his gut, as he realized that every ear, barbarian and townsperson alike, had turned to hear the words of the inquisitor with rapt attention.

"And so I will not lay a single brand to this lad's skin. Not a lash, not a thorn, not a cross word. But I *will* break him, and his suffering will be wine of a superior vintage on the tongue of He Who Sits on the Wailing Throne."

One of the barbarians ventured, "How, great one?"

Aganyn turned and smirked. "He is a hero. Heroes must protect."

With a striking motion, quick as a viper, Aganyn spun, jerked Talia Halcyon out of the line, and slammed a clawed hand into her lower belly, penetrating, lifting and crushing with the blow.

Time froze.

His mother's eyes bulged in shock. The air exploded from her lungs in a terrible groan as she collapsed to the ground, arms hugging her abdomen in a belated attempt to protect her unborn child.

Aganyn, hand drawing back, still curled into that dreadful claw, stepping back as the stricken woman folded at his feet.

Abram's wide-eyed gaze, taking it all in with lips slightly parted, his short panting breaths of excitement.

Gideon did not even know he was screaming. His young body surged against his captors with desperate strength, actually breaking loose of their vise-like grips before the surprised brutes adjusted their holds. His feet clawed at the ground, digging furrows into the soft earth as he *willed* himself to be at Talia's crumpled body.

He could hear his own stricken shrieks echoing off of the mountains, waves of denial and anguish combining and slashing through his soul with relentless agony.

One thought pierced the cacophony in his mind. *I failed.*

Aganyn the Damned closed his eyes as he laid a gentle hand on Abram's shoulder and whispered, "Now *that*...is suffering."

MINUTES PASSED, stretched into years. Gideon lay in the dirt on his stomach, spent and hoarse, the knee of a slaver pressed down upon his back. His mother wept on her side, rocking back and forth as she clutched at her stomach.

Aganyn stood next to Abram, arms crossed, his black clerical garment wafting in the wind. Gideon heard him speaking quietly.

"Be certain when performing Rupturing Bowels to strike low and penetrate toward the target's diaphragm. The more crushing the blow, the more deformed the fetus, and when the female passes the detritus, the pain shall be renewed..."

Helpless with the grief and rage rushing through his system like a flooding river, Gideon closed his eyes.

God.

The single word was so choked with betrayed hurt, it was an effort to think it.

How can you allow...this?

Aganyn took a step back then forward, thrusting with clawed hand as Abram awkwardly copied him.

I thought you could see this.

I thought you would know.

Why can't you stop it?

The widow rolled onto her back, sobbing into the sky. Gideon clenched his eyes shut, unable to watch her anymore as he thought one last forbidden thought.

Do you even care?

He instinctively banished the unfamiliar thought, but it rushed back, battering his faith with the evidence before his eyes. He had been taught his whole life that the Father cared. All the stories said so.

A traitorous, blasphemous voice whispered to him.

Would a caring God allow this?

Gideon groaned. The urge to give in overpowered him.

Face it. The stories were wrong. There is no all-powerful invisible fairy of a god standing ready to save you from evil.

Gideon shook his head in weak denial at the insistent voice.

Look. This is what the gods do. While you pretend to be a hero and pray to the nothing in the sky, this is where true power lies.

Embrace it or live under its heel. There is nothing else.

And for a terrible instant, Gideon wavered.

To believe or not to believe...

To cast aside a life's worth of faith and embrace this reality, or hold true to some *deluded fanciful naive notion* that God cared.

I refuse.

Within his shattered soul, something hardened, as though an emotional jaw clenched in determination

I will not accept that this is all there is. I will believe you, Father.

Save us...

AGANYN CONSIDERED THE DAY, and felt a warm glow of satisfaction with the results. Abram had learned many valuable lessons; he would be ready to join the Inquisitorial Scholastica soon. Suffering had been dealt, both in quality and quantity. Gehenna's unholy name had been written in blood, wrenched out of sacrificial victims in screams and praised under the open sun.

Yes. A good day.

Aganyn turned to his second to order the slaves moved out when he hesitated. The words died in his mouth as he detected something... subtle. Infinitely subtle. Foundational.

Something had just shifted.

He glanced at the boy on the ground. Seconds ago, his eyes had held the look of the crushed, broken, and defeated. Aganyn's victims all looked that way when he finished with them.

Not anymore, with this one. The boy's gaze was expectant, as if anticipating something.

A distant tremor moved through the air, kicking up a small gust that whispered past his ears. A rumble sounded in the distance, from the west, and Aganyn turned quizzically toward the sound. One of the stars over the mountains seemed...brighter, almost as if it were approaching.

He glanced back at the boy and met the cold fury in his emerald eyes. The young man had the look of a wronged man watching a prisoner meet his fate at the headsman's axe.

Uncertainty sank its claws into him for an instant, and he shook it off angrily, breaking away from the grim judgment in that look.

The chieftain Rosh came to him, something like fear in his eyes. "My lord?"

I am no superstitious savage swayed by tricks of the weather!

Aganyn sneered at the man. "It is nothing more than wind and thunder. Cinch your loinstraps tighter or find me a *man* to lead."

The brute bristled at the insult, but sullenly stepped away.

Another rumble, an explosion this time. Louder. Closer.

Aganyn squinted at the strange star. It *was* growing brighter.

What in the name of the Three Thrones is that?

And larger.

That is not a star...

In the blink of an eye, a star burning with hellish fury barreled overhead, ripping the very breath from their lungs with the force of its passage, leaving a long trail of fire behind. An enormous thunderclap shook the insides of every human being beneath as the air rushed back in its wake, the two fronts crashing together like two mighty armies on the charge. The falling star roared as it fell, zeroing in on its diminutive counterpart still rooted in the earth.

With a titanic collision, the comet smashed into the mountain, shearing half of the stalwart peaks off completely and powdering the remainder. It punched straight through, impacting on the ground beyond the mountain and throwing every man standing to the earth.

The two barbarians had been standing on Gideon's shoulders with their boots, one with his knee on Gideon's back. When the earth bucked beneath them, however, it hurled them from their feet and into a pile of stone masonry nearby, cracking their skulls silently. The quake did not discriminate between inquisitors or slaves, but cast them all down in its rage.

The ruin of their mountain protected them from the fury of the burning meteor, deflecting the destructive force and causing it to flow over and around the village, though it howled like the battlecry of God Himself.

The shaking and roaring continued for long seconds, unmanning the burliest warrior and caused them all, savage and slave alike, to clutch one another and cry out in fear.

Of them all, only two were without fear. Aganyn snarled as he lay prone, gripping the rebellious earth in an attempt to stabilize his position.

The second was the boy. Aganyn glanced at him sharply in the cacophony and though the lad clutched at the ground to steady himself, his fierce gaze never left the helpless inquisitor. Once he knew that Aganyn saw him, his lips moved silently amidst the destructive cacophony around them.

I asked for this.

Aganyn glared back, teeth bared, clawed hands clutching the ground. It would take more than an assault of the sky to fell Gehenna's mightiest servant.

As suddenly as it began, the noise and shaking stopped. The silence itself was almost as deafening as the blast. A thick curtain of dust hung in the air, obscuring the warlock's vision and clogging his throat. Coughs and cries for help echoed in the gloom.

One of his warriors tried to stand, but his knees failed him, weakened by the trauma, and he fell back to the earth.

So they remained on the ground, breathing hard, calling out to various heathen gods and trying to regather their strength. Thirty mighty warriors and an inquisitor, reduced to the level of the slaves, unable to stand, lying or kneeling in various abased positions.

It was unconscionable.

It was not *right*.

Crunch.

Crunch.

Crunch.

Crunch.

Aganyn's mind struggled to process what he was hearing. He, Aganyn the Damned, Inquisitor of Gehenna and recipient of the sole prophecy spoken by the Master of Pain in more than a thousand years, *could not even stand*, and yet somehow, someone's boots crunched the broken ground in even, controlled steps.

With each footfall, chainmail clinked. A slight cough echoed through the gloom, along with a casual clearing of the throat.

Aganyn lifted himself to his knees, managing to get one foot beneath him. Unholy spirits writhed in his flesh as he dragged strength from them and poured it into his limbs. Familiar nausea wrenched his gut, and the shock of it caused him to fall to his knees yet again.

As he knelt, a shadow appeared in the fog.

The first thing he saw was black. Aganyn's eyes were irresistibly drawn to the unfathomable darkness that wrapped around the man's form in fading tendrils, rendering him ghostly, ethereal.

A shade.

With an effort, the inquisitor blinked and refocused, realizing that the darkness wreathing the stranger was nothing more than black chainmail, but so black that all light that fell onto its surface could not reflect, could not escape.

The second thing Aganyn saw were his eyes. They were a light blue, like ice from the northern regions, so cold and intense that they seemed to be afire. They pierced everything they saw, and when they fell upon him, Aganyn felt himself almost impaled upon the spear of his regard.

Wresting himself away from the power of the man's stare, Aganyn noticed other features. A single weapon, a curved blade, rested in a black sheath across the man's shoulders. His white hair fell to the middle of his back, gathered with a clip depicting a stylized raven. His hands and feet were sheathed in the same dark mail as his body, and a simple hooded black cloak hung from his shoulders, halting at mid-calf.

The man stopped a few yards from the assembly. His eyes flickered like hidden flames, and they continuously wandered over the landscape, like an animal out of its lair surveying its surroundings. A bird chirped nearby, and the stranger's head cocked slightly to the side, almost quizzically.

The sight of this behavior bled away the weakness in his knees, and Aganyn rose to his feet, gathering his poise and power to him with the simple gesture. On his own feet, in the quiet aftermath of the devastating assault, the dark stranger no longer seemed a threat. Aganyn had seen such behavior in new acolytes as they entered the dungeons of Hinnom for the very first time, wide eyes taking in every fresh detail, trying to fit themselves into the surreal strangeness around them.

This man did the same.

Aganyn grunted in amusement as his men rose around him to face the newcomer. He turned to the prone boy and rasped, "This is what you asked for?"

Chuckling harshly, he turned back.

The stranger was gone.

Aganyn blinked. Where did he—

A low crunch sounded from his right, and the inquisitor turned to see a huge bare-chested warrior named Aric sag to his knees, eyes dulling, blood spilling from his mouth. His spear was missing.

"What...?"

A malicious whisper slashed through the air just by his ear, and he jerked away instinctively as the crump of collapsing armor and a grunt exploded from his left. Another of his men clutched in horror at Aric's spear, now protruding from his own abdomen and pinning him to the ground like an insect ready for examination.

Aganyn glanced around furtively. There was *nothing there.*

Rosh reacted first. "To the horses!" he roared, the veins standing out in his neck, and the barbarians bellowed in response, trying to banish their fear with rage. In a milling horde, roughly twenty burly slavers rushed for their animals, miraculously still tied to their posts and terrified.

Abram tried to run with them, but Aganyn slammed a hand onto his shoulder, his milky eyes narrowed, trying to pierce the fog. He rasped, "No, apprentice. Watch first."

A swift-footed tribesman named Ord broke free of the pack by a good ten yards and launched himself onto his horse with a single leap. It was an impressive jump, one very few warriors could repeat, and the heart of every slaver who saw him lifted at the inspiring sight of Ord rearing his horse back, axe slicing through the air in defiance.

Until the stranger killed him.

Aganyn saw it happen. Ord was still rearing back in his saddle when a dark shadow leapt up toward him. Ord could not even scream as the stranger arced over him like a raptor from nightmare, *over* the rearing horse's head, and ripped the man out of his saddle by his throat.

The killer landed into a crouch and slammed Ord's skull into the ground with a thud, fracturing the back of the man's skull and pulping his brain. The slavers were only just beginning to arrest their forward momentum because *no one can do that* when the stranger darted forward and snatched Kril away into the fog, leaving only the man's screams with them.

At his side, Abram's breath came short and fast, and for once, Aganyn did not fault him. This man killed his men with the ease of a hawk slaughtering doves. They had not just failed to scratch their murderer, they had yet to swing a weapon.

Several warriors made as though to pursue into the fog, but Rosh barked hoarsely, "No! Stay *together*, by the gods, or he'll kill you one by one!"

As if to punctuate the chieftain's command, Kril's screams abruptly ended.

The warriors instinctively drew together in a circle, eyes darting everywhere as the fog seemed to draw in closer. Seconds were passing, each one dragging out for an eternity as they strained their eyes, their ears, their minds for any sign, *anything*, that the killer was nearby.

All Aganyn heard was dark laughter.

GIDEON SPRAWLED ON THE GROUND, within yards of the Gehennan warlock. The inquisitor and his protégé remained frozen in place, only Aganyn's lips working as he intoned blasphemous incantations. He was as blind as the rest of them.

He could barely see the group of frightened barbarians as they slowly circled, desperate to find their killer. One of them, the big one called Rosh, bellowed into the dense fog, trying through savage bravado to banish the phantoms he saw in the clinging mist.

Patience.

Gideon froze. That thought had not come from his mind.

It had a foreign taint to it, almost as if another man's tongue had grown within his mouth and spoken the word. It felt intrusive. Repulsive.

And it continued, every word spoken with sinister intent.

All men fear judgment. The darker the sin, the greater their fear.

Gideon felt paralyzed. He knew, he just *knew*, that somehow he heard the thoughts of the killer's mind. The voice in his skull was dark, refined, controlled.

These know more than most, for they have allied themselves with the damned. These, above all, are familiar with the fires of perdition that await their bartered souls. Their knowledge alone condemns them to far greater torment.

The group grew agitated with the absence of activity in the wake of their comrades' deaths. Some began to edge toward their horses, while others glanced back at Rosh, uncertain. Their unity fractured.

Patience. Allow them their fear. Make them cower before the fog of the unknown wherein lies their death, and the shadow that heralds their final judgment. Let them fear the dark and the fire. Soon, they shall know nothing else.

The voice rasped now, infecting Gideon with a hate foreign to his own heart.

See the dawning of comprehension upon their faces as they realize the imminence of their end. Enjoy the games fearful souls play, the desperate bargains they attempt to stave off their own oblivion. Most of all, savor their pathetic denial of the inevitable as they clutch to retain something they never before appreciated or understood.

A chilling chuckle echoed through Gideon's captive mind, becoming audible, just as he saw a shadow slowly rising from the ground in their unknowing midst. It coalesced with deliberate lack of haste into a nightmare with eyes of burning sapphire, hand sliding forward to reach for one of their number.

Whatever fool penned that patience was a virtue...never indulged in the vice.

. . .

AGANYN WATCHED, disbelieving, as the stranger tore Rosh off of his feet and snapped his neck with a brutal wrench. His fellows reacted with shock, twisting to confront the newfound threat, but far, far too slowly. By the time their eyes focused on the shadowy killer, his clawed hands slashed through the air, sending two slavers staggering backward with weeping rents where their throats used to be.

Unable to retain their courage with their champion dead and the windpipes of their comrades clenched in the mailed fists of a wraith, the circle broke.

Barbarian warriors scattered in all directions as the black warrior flicked his wrists casually and dusted the palms of his hands together.

Aganyn, gut clenching as demons poured their power into him, summoned an orb of flame in his hand and roared, "He is one man! Kill him!"

With that, Aganyn hurled the potent sphere at the newcomer, grinning fiercely through his nausea as the devastating energy burned through the air. Such a spell had burnt great holes within phalanxes of shielded men.

The orb struck the black warrior with a clap and exploded, dousing the area around him with roaring flames and staggering the man forward.

Aganyn grinned ferociously. No matter what he thought himself to be, this newcomer could not hope to withstand the sheer might granted to an inquisitor of Gehe-

With a sudden intake of wind, the flames raging around the warrior sucked into the dark depths of his armor and vanished.

The stranger turned to Aganyn and locked his icy gaze on him.

In a panic, Aganyn reached out and subsumed the minds of his fleeing warriors. Demonic power writhed in his veins, but Aganyn clenched his teeth against the agony and crushed his warriors' wills with ruthless focus, replacing their impulse to flee with the unstoppable urge to kill. With a precision they had never before experienced, each warrior turned and charged the black stranger with no thought of survival.

Only when the first had reached him, swinging his axe with every intention of bisecting his target, did the killer draw his sword.

The blade was a lance of darkness as the warrior sidestepped and whipped it across the slaver's throat. A shriek erupted as the man fell.

Aganyn blinked. Dead men could not utter sounds, much less force them from cut throats. The blade flashed again, and another dead man screamed. As the stranger slew more of his warriors, he realized that it was not they that cried out.

The timbre changed with every slash. The pitch with every thrust.

The black sword screamed like a banshee choir as it killed Aganyn's men.

When the last of his tribesmen collapsed to the ground, victim of the shrieking sword, the newcomer examined the blade, his eyes seemingly lost in contemplation for a few seconds. The wails increased in pitch, and Aganyn swore to himself that he could hear the terrified cries of his own men joining the chilling chorus of screams. As though waking from his reverie, the man shook his head and sheathed the dark blade, silencing the horrible cries of the damned.

Breathing hard, the inquisitor thrust forward with both hands, expending all of his power to call the roots of the ground to wrap around the stranger's limbs and hold him fast.

The roots did not stop the man's approach in the slightest. They withered, fell to ash and blasted into powder before the heavy tramp of his boot scattered them to the winds.

Drained by his expenditure, Aganyn could only collapse to his knees before the dark warrior, who regarded him for a moment with disdain.

After that moment, he held up his hand and a familiar orb of flame guttered to life. With a deep, cultured voice with a hint of foreign accent, the stranger spoke.

"You dropped this."

Aganyn stared at him. It had taken him twenty years to learn that spell, more to harness the winds of destructive energy. And even then, he had never been able to hold it for more than a second. Such force had to be released or it would melt through the caster's own hand.

Yet here the stranger stood, with the exact spell hovering gently in his palm, with no harm done.

Aganyn whispered, "What are you?"

The stranger kneeled down, still holding the orb, and gripped Aganyn's head by the hair. "I am your bane, demon worshipper. You think that because you begged hard enough and whored your soul away, you have power? You could have been something that the Fallen Ones themselves feared, and yet you chose *this* pathetic existence, living off of the kitchen scraps of cast-out exiles. Your kind disgust me."

As his grip tightened on Aganyn's hair and arched his head back, the orb began to burn more fiercely. "I find it despicable that vermin such as you infests this world, filling it with your...*submission*."

The sphere was spinning fiercely now, its light flashing across Aganyn's face as a charging sound began to build. Aganyn stared at it with horrid fascination, waiting for it to overload with the power being dumped into it, but it continued to build until a miniature sun blazed in the palm of the man's hand. With undisguised hate, the stranger growled, "I am judgment. I am extinction. I am Ashkelon, the last Avala, and those abominations you pray to, I prey *upon*."

In the instant before he thrust the supercharged sphere into Aganyn's chest, a single thought, a memory of a prophecy, flashed through Aganyn's mind, existing for less than a second as his body ignited from the burning torrent boiling his blood to steam.

You will see power...

GIDEON SQUINTED against the churning maelstrom of fire engulfing the inquisitor. His skin felt the heat even from this distance, yet the black silhouette stood unmoving, stark against the screaming inferno at his feet.

By rights, the man should have been unconscious from the agony already. *High pain tolerance*, Gideon thought grimly.

Without warning, the burning warlock lurched to his feet, limbs wheeling about him in flames, and dashed into the hills, vanishing into the dust until all that remained of him were his cries of horror.

Without a word, their savior, the man calling himself Ashkelon, turned and walked away.

Grunting against the pain in his side, Gideon limped as fast as he could to catch up to the taller man.

"Thank you, lord, for saving us," he called out.

The stranger stopped and turned. Ice-blue eyes knifed into Gideon as the silhouette regarded him, almost as a lion with a kill might regard a coyote.

"What makes you think I saved you?"

Gideon blinked. Of all the responses he had imagined, that was not it.

Ashkelon cocked his head to one side. "Your village has been annihilated, and the vast majority of your men are dead. The remainder are either too old, too young or too cowardly to be of any use. Your crops are ash in the wind and your animals are dead or fled."

He pointed. "From the height of the six stalks of grains that survived, I would assume you are a month away from harvest, or would have been. What part of this constitutes salvation for you?"

Gideon opened his mouth, then closed it.

The stranger arched an elegant eyebrow. "I am waiting."

Stubbornly, Gideon jutted his chin forward. "We are still free. We have you to thank for that."

The man glanced around pointedly. Fires raged on bare earth from the sorcerous conflict. The bodies of farmers and barbarians mixed where they fell on the ground. The fields were black where they did not still burn and the air choked with ash. It looked like a volcano had gone off.

Gideon swallowed, hard.

Ashkelon looked back and smiled. "You are welcome."

He turned to leave, but Gideon called out, "Can you not stay and help us, hero?"

Pausing, the stranger shook his head slowly, disbelievingly. "Your definition of heroism is as skewed as your perception of salvation if you believe I am such a person. Again, boy, I did not come here to save you."

Gideon persisted, "But you did."

The stranger grunted, "In passing, perhaps, I prolonged your miserable lives long enough to starve or freeze in this wilderness. Such is the reward of freedom, I suppose; you had best enjoy every second."

Gideon had trouble understanding half of the words the man said, and the accent made it worse. Stoically, Gideon repeated, "Help us, *please*."

"I will not. The sparing of peasants' lives as a result of a minor indulgence in killing a demon worshipper does not confer responsibility upon me to sustain those lives. I came here to seek out the great heroes of your world and engage them in...conversation."

This last he said with a sardonic smile.

Gideon blinked. "We have no great heroes."

Ashkelon chuckled. "I have been here less than ten minutes and seen a stripling make demands of a dark sorcerer for the sake of his people after surviving a slavers' raid commanded by a man under the sway of the powers of Hell. I believe that the law of averages dictates that there be others like you."

Gideon was almost shaking with his *need* to get this man to help. The stranger sighed. "Very well. Take your people and walk that way."

He pointed east.

"The wind has carried the dust and its poison away from the waters in that direction. Many of the animals will also have fled in that direction, and likely congregate at the water there. Your journey will be arduous, but leave the injured and the old and you should survive."

Gideon glared at him. "We will not do that."

The sorcerer smiled. "Then die. I do not care either way."

He turned away and began walking, ironshod boots crushing the ash beneath his feet. Gideon squinted. "That's the other way. The opposite direction of what you told us."

The stranger did not even turn. "You seek life and the means to continue it. We differ greatly in that respect."

"YOU DROPPED THIS."

2

QUEST

This is disappointing.

The old refrain echoed through his mind as Ashkelon glided to the side, easily avoiding the hacking lunge of his doomed assailant. The wretch cried out in feigned battle rage, as if he had any idea what pure rage *was*, and backhanded his axe toward Ashkelon's midsection.

Ashkelon sighed and stepped deeply to his right as though in the midst of a waltz. He watched the axe blade swing wide to crash into the stone wall of the tower, spraying chips of metal and stone across the spiral staircase. Off-balance as the man was, Ashkelon stepped forward and thrust his palm into the man's shoulder, spilling him down the stairs in a clatter of armor.

No harm done. Yet.

Out of breath and gasping, the soldier pushed himself to his feet and charged up the stairway, his ill-fitting armor hampering his progress. This man obviously served as some kind of captain, by the useless ornamentation on his imitation silver armor. He was also three levels below the rest of his men, and likely on his way out of the tower when he ran into his current foe.

Ashkelon shook his head, waited patiently till the man reached him, and kicked his shoulder.

Down the stairs, the coward crashed. After his limbs finally stopped flopping over one another, Ashkelon waited for the would-be hero to get up. And he waited.

Nothing moved but the man's chest as he struggled to draw breath while lying face-down on the floor.

The corners of Ashkelon's mouth turned down. "By the Dark, this world is pathetic."

The soldier lifted his head and stared at Ashkelon, chest heaving. "I can't...I can't beat you. You're too..."

Ashkelon stepped down the stairs slowly, his darkmail clinking with every footfall. "Yes, I know. Competent. Fast. Articulate. As a general rule, if you cannot speak your mind in one breath, do not bore the rest of us."

The captain fell into instant silence. He did not reach for his weapon.

Ashkelon sighed again. "Are you getting up or not?"

The soldier paused, weighing the best answer that would allow him to continue his flight.

Ashkelon's eyes narrowed at that.

"Your parody of existence is now over. On your feet or on your back, it makes no difference to me."

Ashkelon lifted his hand before him, and a nexus of thrashing darkness swirled to life in his palm. The soldier's eyes widened in shock, and he began scrabbling backward, moaning, "No, no, please..."

Fear had a certain flavor to it. Ashkelon fed the spell in his gauntlet with a mix of fear and his own revulsion, adding emotional energy in doses with the sensitivity of a chef seasoning a steak.

"Consider this mercy."

Ashkelon thrust his hand forward in a claw and launched the dark orb, ribbons of black trailing back to his eyes and mouth. The nexus itself punched into the screaming soldier's chest, and while no results were immediately visible, the spiritual effects were disastrous.

Faint blue energy coursed along the dark strands back to Ashkelon, who inhaled and drank it as though it were a rare wine. The nameless coward collapsed to his knees, his skin drying, wrinkling, flaking off even as his muscles rotted on his bones. The shrieks faded to hoarse gasps as his vocal cords grew brittle and his lungs failed.

If anyone alive had remained in the room, they would still hear faint screaming echoing from the strands and believe with horror that the sorcerer consumed the man's soul.

Unfair, and to be honest, simplistic. Ashkelon had no ability to consume a soul, *eternal's* definition being what it was. But life energy...that was something altogether different.

The predators of Hell that men called vampires effected a crude version of this ritual by feeding on the blood of their victims. Ashkelon had taken the method, dispensed with the feral components and theatrics, and refined it to this catastrophic version.

Ashkelon's spell simply released all of the life energy in the man's individual cells and passed it through a conduit back into Ashkelon himself, replenishing his own. Any scholar of science with the appropriate equipment could do the same. The screaming itself was only a by-product of the energy displacing the air as it flowed back into the caster.

Nothing Hell-born or evil about it. Ashkelon merely collected the man's waste energy, in this case the entire man, and recycled it to better purpose. It served infinitely more use than leaving a rotting corpse on the ground.

Yet no one will thank me for my efforts at conservation.

The thought pleased him. His laughter ringing off of the stone walls, the Onyx Mage strode back up the stairs into the tower to continue his search, leaving the soldier's desiccated body on the floor to stare in silent horror.

In his ascent, Ashkelon came across more bodies, killed in more mundane, widely accepted ways. Sword slashes, stab wounds and claw rakes appeared to be the order of the day. Society preferred such wasteful slaughter to his own method.

Ashkelon shook his head at the unending predictability of it all as he walked. As far as strongholds of evil went, this one was fairly standard. A moat of fire, bestial and demonic minions of the lower orders, dungeon after dungeon with macabre implements of torture and a sense of pervasive darkness that sucked at the soul: standard issue for the warlocks of Sinai.

He should know. In the last five years, he had visited a good number of them.

Ashkelon sighed deeply, sinking into a mild state of depression. No innovation remained, just a series of defective copies of copies, reading the same books again and again for secrets that had never been there.

The same imagination also lacked in the forces of false Light. Flashy silver armor without a mark on it, newly-forged swords hawked at a premium from cheap street vendors, forced battle cries from pitifully young throats imitating fairy tales in a vain attempt to manufacture courage...

His black soul ached for Avalon, in days long since past. Days when a lone warrior, bearing the scars of a hundred wars, stalked through the endless stairways, throwing down demon after demon without a trace of fear, girded in righteousness, the unthinking hatred for evil his only defence, his courage a mere afterthought.

Sigh. Days worthy of darkness...

But this...

The world of Sinai, as the inhabitants called it, demonstrated a singular lack of anything Ashkelon might call heroism. For the last five years, he had stalked the main continent, walking the shadows of its kingdoms. The primary bastion of men called itself Samothrace, a city of towers and palaces situated on a bay. Armies marched from its gates in constant succession, always toward the east.

He had found nothing remarkable in the place. It was Man's greatest city only because it was the last to be consumed.

To the east, he had searched the hellscape of Barak Fel. Sulfur rose in wisps from the trenches as men fought and died in whole companies against siegebreaker beasts and heaving masses of slaves. He found nothing worthy of notice in that desperate war, either. By his reckoning, that stalemate would end within months, and not in humanity's favor.

Far to the east, straining to break through Samothrace's defense lines, the devastated lands of the Three Architects. Three exiles from the Celestial Rebellions had fallen here, and the lost and damned gathered themselves to their banners.

Sheol, Architect of Death; Gehenna, Architect of Suffering; Mammon, Architect of Hunger.

Ashkelon's lip twisted at the memory of pacing those vile lands and seeing the sycophancy of its citizens. It irked his dark soul to see humanity in servitude to such abominations.

Avalon had...extradited...its supernatural refugees generations before. Ashkelon had personally seen to many himself. The fact that the men of Sinai struggled to do so rankled.

He stepped over a man's body, his nose wrinkling as he did so. Unwashed, yet awash in liquor. Given to his own vices, and come to punish another man for the same.

Let them both rot. Ashkelon was here for neither.

The crashes of combat echoed down the stairs. Metal struck metal, the sound ringing off the stone walls of the keep and mixing with snaps and snarls from summoned denizens of the underworld. Ashkelon's ears attuned to the clamor with the experience of centuries, parsing the disparate sounds and categorizing them appropriately.

One combatant, wielding sword and shield. He was beset by beasts and a handler, if the whip cracks were anything to go by.

It would end soon, by Ashkelon's judgment. Whatever soldier had made it to the chamber above had done well to make it this far through the tower, particularly after the evident incompetence of his fellows, but mere seconds remained in that life story.

Ashkelon shrugged slightly, his expression more disappointed at this waste of time than anything else, and turned away.

A voice lifted above the hellish cacophony, a war-shout apart from the roars and curses otherwise filling this pathetic keep.

The sound of it arrested Ashkelon, causing him to turn back and consider the sound.

In Ashkelon's considerable experience, men made many different sounds before they died. The spectrum ranged from silent sighs to full-throated shrieks, with sobbing, weeping, babbling, moaning, whining, gasping, snarling and a hundred other expressions a man's soul might vomit in his final seconds.

This one, though.

The timbre of the voice was something apart from the ordinary. The voice held fear in it, itself an indication of sanity, but tempered by anger. Furthermore, the sounds of the strikes of his weapon indicated discipline, rather than panic or savagery.

A beast screamed, and the voice roared in triumph.

Ashkelon stared up the stairs, his skin prickling with the sound. Surely not...

Memories surged unbidden of a hundred battlefields. On each, a shout echoed through eons in defense of humanity itself against the exiled predators beyond the veil of material reality. As each hero banished another twisted invader from Hell, that shout marked the victory of the righteous. It erupted from the mouth of the warrior fighting for his life above.

It was the first of his kind Ashkelon had encountered on Sinai, and he had killed enough of them to know what one sounded like.

The snarls grew louder, snapping Ashkelon out of his reverie. A cry of pain exploded from above, bitten off in gritted teeth.

At the sound, a cloud of shadow billowed around his jaw, snapping into solidity as a war-mask encasing the lower half of his face. His features shrouded, Ashkelon stepped into the shadow striping the wall next to him and lunged up the crumbling staircase toward another, crossing ten yards in the blink of an eye. Upon reaching that shadow, he leapt again, the sound that of a bitter wind howling through a cave.

The shadow walkers had been myths among Ashkelon's own people. They could strike from anywhere a shadow was cast, cross unimaginable distances in no time at all, and still remain hidden from pursuit. Worshippers of the Everlasting Dark, they had been; destroyed or imprisoned by the champions of the Light in ages past.

All but one.

Shedding the darkness for the light once more, Ashkelon burst from the mouth of the stairway into a circular room filled with opened cages.

Kennel.

Wolves with sickly yellow eyes weeping sulfur jerked toward him at the intrusion, and a beast-like mutant bearing various signs of self-mutilation brayed in alarm.

Ashkelon's gaze raked across the room. He assessed and dismissed the corrupted monsters rushing toward him; their diminished souls would soon no longer clutter this mortal realm. He searched instead for the one he had spent years loo—

He found him.

A young man stood at the opposite end of the room, near the stairway to the master's throne room. The pack of wolves slunk towards him, ears back and fangs bared. He stood tall in the face of the demons, his stance square. His armor had nearly shredded from his broad frame, and his shield bore nicks and gouges from heavy use. His long blonde hair hung loose, a sweaty thatch that whipped around his face as he looked from foe to foe.

He lunged forward and slammed a broken blade into a wolf's ribs. As the creature shrieked and fell, claws scrabbling at the stones, another of the pack leapt onto his shoulder from the side.

Ashkelon expected him to die. Most men would have fallen to the ground from the impact, trying to keep the creature's snapping jaws from wrenching their throats out. Disappointment welled up within him.

The soldier twisted and slammed the creature against the wall, roaring as fangs like knives punctured his shoulder before the wolf collapsed to the floor.

That shout again.

The *Light* in those flashing green eyes.

Before Ashkelon, a hero spat to the side, lifted his broken sword at the ready and faced death with flint in his soul.

To Ashkelon, trapped in this world of pitiful grey mediocrity, he shone like a newborn star.

Beneath the sorcerer's mask of shadow, an involuntary smile

tugged at his lips and swords of ice sprouted from his fists. The novelty of the smile only broadened it further as he stalked forward into the pack, sweeping his blades out to his sides like scythes.

It truly was a day of firsts. He had never saved a hero before.

WHEN THE STORM of darkness erupted into the room, Gideon sighed. It was one more bad thing to add to the Bad Day.

They had him backed into a corner, the hounds of the Crowfather prowling toward him and more coming. Armand Halcyon's sword now extended only eight inches beyond the hilt, the rest still sticking out of the mouth of some twisted thing two floors down.

He had refused to run when the rest did. He had seen the remains of the woman the Crowfather's demons had fed upon.

I'm not leaving without justice.

Derision had curled the lips of his companions as they fled. Even in their cowardice, they found breath to mock the "pretend knight".

Now he stood on the last floor before the Crowfather's sanctum, more by virtue of his stubbornness than anything. His size also helped; Gideon probably weighed two or three stone more than the next man, all of it hardened first by farm work, then soldiering.

It seemed, though, his luck had run out. He did not think his size was going to do anything to the sorcerer emerging from his conjured darkness, eyes glittering like sapphires above a black half-mask.

Now was as good a time for a quick prayer as ever.

Lord, please receive my spirit.

Swords of ice extended from the shadow man's fists, angling out to his sides.

And I hope you have good hands, because I think I'm coming home fast.

The venomous thorns on the paingiver's lash hissed past Gideon's ear, and he snapped back into the moment. He jerked his head to the side reflexively, dodging the poisoned weapon and dropping his shield down to catch a hellwolf as it tried to crush his knee in its maw. His shoulder ignited with pain from the bite there, but he gritted his teeth and forced the pain away. The beast clawed at the boss on his shield, snarling as its demonic claws shredded the wood away.

Shouting, Gideon stomped his armored boot into its jaw, snapping yellowed fangs out of its mouth. The demon yelped and fell backwards, scratching at its face and squealing.

Gideon took a breath and set himself as ten hellwolves with gleaming yellow eyes stalked toward him. Behind them, the sorcerer stalked forward, raising his icy blades in salute.

This would probably not take very long, but by the Almighty, Gideon would not enter Heaven's gates without a last fight.

He smashed his shattered sword against the boss of his shield and bellowed, "Who's first, then?"

He was not expecting an answer, which is why he jerked when something whispered into his mind, *Save the rhetoric. This shall be over swiftly.*

Gideon jerked at the voice in his head. Memory layered across his vision, and he saw the dark sorcerer with new eyes.

"Oh, no. Not you. Not here."

The skin around the man's eyes crinkled with a hidden smile, and the voice answered, *Believe me, I am as amused as you that I am here to help.*

In a shadowed blur, the sorcerer rammed his left hand blade into the unsuspecting handler's neck and twisted, snapping the blade off. As the corpse fell to its knees, the killer who had called himself Ashkelon clenched his fist and wrenched it backwards.

Every hellwolf tore off of its feet with a surprised howl, away from Gideon and directly toward the black mage. Ashkelon's remaining blade of ice slashed twice, and he cut apart two of the creatures in mid-air, carving through the tainted meat without resistance. Acid blood showered around him, yet not a drop touched the dark lord as the bisected wolves flopped to the floor.

The survivors crashed into the far wall, their claws scraping at the stone as the hell wolves sought purchase.

Ashkelon dipped his head slightly toward Gideon. *Greetings.*

His eyes widened in both recognition and mild surprise, and he cocked his head to the side. *Again, it seems.*

Ashkelon's back faced the wolves rising from where he had thrown them. The pack snarled and leapt forward.

Ashkelon swept to the side, speared a wolf in mid-air and slammed it into the ground, shattering his second blade into fragments of skittering ice as he pounded the demon into the floor. Claws and fangs snapped at where he stood.

You are taller than last I saw you.

Gideon watched as Ashkelon lunged and gripped a wolf by the skull and spine, lifting the hapless creature above his head. For half a second, lightning coursed through the creature, lighting it from the inside, and thunder cracked in the room as the smell of ozone and burnt hair flooded Gideon's nose.

Ashkelon rammed the corpse into the mouth of its packmate and kicked both animals back. He twisted his wrist as both creatures hit the ground, and the body of the burned hellwolf contorted of its own volition, snaking around the body of the living wolf and squeezing like a python. Bones snapped in both demons.

The remainder of the pack backed away, ears flat and whimpers just beginning.

A bit late for that, I think.

The killer snapped his fingers, and each surviving wolf dropped from sight as their own shadows swallowed them whole. The sorcerer sighed and rubbed at his jaw, the black mask dissipating into smoke at his touch and revealing the lines of his face.

He turned back to Gideon and held up a finger. "I believe I know the answer, but I must ask to be certain. Do you remember me?"

Gideon lashed out with his shield, throwing it forward in an arc to drive the iron rim into the side of the sorcerer's head. A groggy sorcerer could not focus to cast.

His shield met nothing but air. Ashkelon sidestepped the blow easily, his almost-smile never leaving his face. Gideon stumbled a bit, but recovered enough to send the shield back along its course with a roar, again trying to bash the sorcerer in the head.

Ashkelon thrust his palm forward and stiff-armed the shield, halting the blow before it could gather any strength. With a deft move, he kicked out Gideon's leg and sent the soldier crashing to the floor.

"I see that you do."

Gideon twisted around on the stones and stabbed upward into Ashkelon's groin with the shard of the sword in his hand. Ashkelon caught the blade in his palm, the iron refusing to penetrate his gauntlet, and twisted the blade out of the young man's hand.

"Enough," he said.

Rolling to his feet, Gideon again swung his shield toward Ashkelon's head, leading with the boss. The sorcerer blocked it with his forearm and sighed audibly.

"The same attack again? You require instruction more than I believed."

And he destroyed Gideon's shield.

ASHKELON'S HAND stiffened into a claw, and he raked down across the surface of the shield. Darkness flared from his fingertips as it dragged furrows through the wood, and the shield exploded into shrapnel. Gideon staggered back a step, his eyes wide but judging from the balling of his fists, undeterred.

Ashkelon raised his eyebrow. "I suppose I should find this stubbornness is a virtue, but for now it wastes our time. Calm yourself."

The boy attacked anyway.

This time, Ashkelon used no sorcery. He slapped the first fist away and struck him in the stomach with his palm. His elbow swung up to crack under the man's jaw, then swung back with a powerful backhand to slam him spinning into the wall. Gideon sagged to the floor, dazed from the precise blows.

Ashkelon stood over the downed man, bemused but patient. "Have you finished yet? I would rather not kill you as I did your companions."

Bleeding from nose and mouth, Gideon glared up at him. "If you really killed my friends, then you are going to want to kill me, too."

Ashkelon smiled again. "Do not threaten me, apprentice. Bravado accomplishes nothing, and wastes time when action will do so much more. Besides, the cowards who left you to die are not what I understand to be friends."

Gideon squinted at him. "'Apprentice'? What are you talking about?"

Ashkelon considered the soldier for a moment, thinking how best to phrase his thoughts. Squatting down next to him, Ashkelon said, "I have a proposition for you. You will bind yourself utterly to my service for the duration of your apprenticeship, and in return, I will give you what you desire most."

Gideon lifted himself to a seated position, his armor scraping as he scooted away from the sorcerer. "And what do you think I desire most?"

Ashkelon gestured around him at the fallen hellhounds, the twisted bodies of cultists. "You wish to be a hero."

Gideon opened his mouth, but Ashkelon cut him off. "Spare me the requisite protests of false humility; I know you better than you know yourself. I imagine you are here to remove the master of this tower, likely in an attempt to spare some commoners his predations upon them?"

The soldier answered slowly. "Yes, something like that."

Ashkelon's tone turned hard. "You did not even make it to his sham of a throne room. But for my intervention, you would have died in a demon's doghouse, remembered only by the mutants gnawing on your bones. Accept my tutelage, and I can prevent such a fate."

He had Gideon's attention, albeit against his will. "How?" the boy asked.

Ashkelon seated himself upon the ground, the shadows pooling around him. "I am a master of Death. I have been inculcated in the doctrines of the Everlasting Dark, which includes more than a few studies of the Light. More relevant to you, I have faced thousands of heroes and sinners of every persuasion, whether mage, knight, scholar, assassin, or warlock, and slain them all. Train under me, and I will teach you everything I have learned over generations of conflict against the finest champions Heaven and Hell have to offer."

Ashkelon drew Gideon's broken sword from the ground and fingered the shattered metal. A solid weapon, well-made, lacking any magical properties. Absently, Ashkelon summoned the missing fragments into his other hand and began to fit them together.

"I would like to train you to be a killer beyond compare. I will take the raw material that you are and forge you into a weapon that both the Dark and the Abyss will learn to fear."

Gideon watched with wide eyes as Ashkelon fused the weapon back together. Ashkelon's gauntlets pressed against the metal shards, and wisps of shadow escaped from the cracks before they sealed together, leaving no evidence the blade had ever been broken.

Ashkelon offered the weapon back to Gideon. "At the risk of sounding arrogant, my craftsmanship is second to none. Will you accept my offer?"

Hesitantly, Gideon reached out. His hand wrapped around the hilt, but his eyes never left Ashkelon's.

At last, he glanced away, toward the stairway and said, "I can't, yet. The Crowfather still has to…"

Ashkelon clenched a fist and intoned, *"Jakle."*

ABOVE HIM, Gideon heard someone start to scream. The voice spiraled higher and higher, increasing in desperation until it shrieked like a tea kettle. A second later, a titanic explosion rocked the tower, knocking dust and decorations from the stone walls.

Gideon gripped the stones as the tower's skeleton groaned around him from the fearsome blast. When the noise faded, Ashkelon repeated, "Will you accept my offer?"

Judging from the shudders of the tower, Gideon thought it a safe bet that everything above this floor was dead.

He glanced at the sorcerer sitting beside him. Something vicious lurked in the man's striking eyes, a caged madness flickering like a flame. Gideon had the distinct feeling that the man saw him more as components than a human being.

And yet, demons, sorcerers and soldiers lay strewn in his wake. Gideon's shoulder burned like fire from the bite he had taken, and his muscles ached from the battle through the tower. Ashkelon did not appear to have exerted himself *at all.*

Oh, Lord, I am actually considering his offer. I do want to be a hero. What do I do?

His own words from five years ago, directed in spite at the hellish enemy who had brutalized his mother, rose within in his memory.

I asked for this.

He pressed his lips together. He could hear his mother now, hands on her hips, saying, "Either pray specifically, or be thankful for the answer you get."

Taking a deep breath, Gideon offered his hand to the sorcerer. "If you can make me a better fighter, then I accept...master."

Ashkelon smiled, this time without humor. "Your first lesson, then."

Eight inches of ice burst through Gideon's ribs and tore his lungs in half before lancing into his heart. His breath withered in his chest as cold spread through his torso, clawing toward his shocked eyes, where black clouds gathered. Gideon did not feel his body slump against the floor, nor his blood draining from the awful rent in his chest. Rather, he felt his *self* begin to fall, swirling around a great well of darkness like a leaf in a drain.

Ashkelon's voice remained conversational, though it seemed to come from a great distance.

"This is called...death."

Gideon could not speak, though he tried. His murderer leaned over him, his smile the only thing he could see through the shadows taking over his vision.

"You should get used to it."

And the darkness took him.

3

BASIC

According to the ancient Scriptures, hidden away by the Signovencium Church and known only by rumor, the Everlasting Dark ruled the cosmos first.

Within its realm, vast storms of night crawled across space, blacker than the void itself, hiding monstrous leviathans of unfathomable hunger. By their power, chaos was sustained and life could not take hold.

Then, at the command of the Almighty, Light burst forth across the savage domain, driving back the void dragons and establishing an oasis free of the claws of the Dark.

Within this harbor, God planted a garden. He formed man and woman of the dust of the ground, carefully shaping each and every part into a being in His image. His final act was to breathe into His creation the Breath of Life, conferring upon humanity its eternal soul.

Breath. I need more of it.

The thought flicked through Gideon's mind as he staggered backward, sinking to one knee. His mind screamed at his lungs, ordering them to fill themselves with oxygen, but they could not obey.

His new master's mailed fist slamming into his diaphragm had seen to that.

Ashkelon crouched in front of Gideon and slapped him lightly on one cheek. "Focus. Understand what you are feeling. Comprehend it. Measure it."

His icy eyes narrowed. "Now get past it, and never fail again."

Air. I need air.

Familiar blackness invaded the corners of his vision as Gideon's body heaved at the motionless air, trying to overcome the invisible death gripping his lungs in rigid stasis.

A backhanded slap lit Gideon's face on fire with its force.

"Do you think that your enemy will have compassion on you?"

An iron boot thudded into Gideon's flank, but he managed to lurch to the side, robbing it of much of its force.

A bite of air seeped into his lungs, flushing his blood with new strength.

Ashkelon kicked again, and Gideon managed to sweep his forearm at it, knocking it away. *There, you bitter old man. I blocked it...*

The sorcerer's boot did not come to rest. Instead, it slashed back in a blistering hook kick that Gideon did not block.

GIDEON CAME TO LEARN, over the course of several weeks, that mercy did not rank among the virtues of Ashkelon.

Actually, Gideon remained unsure if there were any virtues of Ashkelon, unless cruelty, ferocity and ruthless discipline could be counted as such.

In those terrible months, Gideon suffered more than he had in his entire life. Every waking moment was spent fending off savage assaults, launched without notice or provocation. Ashkelon would attack him when he slept, when he ate, when he relieved himself in the forest.

And he was not permitted to fail.

Ashkelon's fiery blue eyes locked with Gideon's as he loomed over him, snapping, "Your focus is slipping. React with the appropriate counter next time."

Gideon groaned from his prone position on the ground. "You...did the wrong strike. Not the one you were teaching me."

Ashkelon barked a sardonic laugh. "You think this is a dance, where each partner will act at the appropriate time as expected? Shall I delicately clasp your hand while whispering sweet nothings into your ear?"

Anger flared in Gideon's breast at the mockery, but he swallowed it, knowing it to be pride. "No, master."

Ashkelon's eyes burned with intensity. "Combat is not a dance. We do not take turns, and we do not fight as expected by our enemies. We fight without pattern. We snap bone, rupture organs and tear out throats. We do anything necessary to kill our enemies and strike fear into their allies, because death incites terror. Terror produces hesitation. Hesitation means weakness. Weakness..."

Gideon took a deep breath, calming himself. "Invites death, master."

"Now get up and do something unexpected for me for once, such as countering adequately."

He did not.

ADDING TO HIS MISERY, Gideon was forced to provide for his own needs. He scraped roots out of the ground with filthy fingers, built his fires out of scattered brush and fallen limbs and even resorted to wolfing down the grubs beneath fallen logs.

Once, Ashkelon allowed him to hunt. In his former life, Gideon had relished the quiet and isolation of hunting. He found nature soothing, away from the noise of people, and he had spent many hours alone with his thoughts as he prayed and meditated upon the legacy of Armand Halcyon.

When Ashkelon offered the opportunity, Gideon leapt at the chance.

It proved a mistake.

The silence of the forest provided some respite from the sorcerer's acidic presence. Gideon sighted down his arrow at the doe grazing in the thicket, slowing closing one eye. Waiting for the perfect second to release...

A harsh voice hissed in his ear, "Close that eye again, and the crows will feast upon it tonight."

Gideon jerked reflexively, firing the arrow wildly as the shadow stalking him from his blind side reached for him. As Ashkelon slammed him into the tree to punish him for his trespass, Gideon glimpsed the doe fleeing into the woods.

That night, he sat shivering by a weak fire, forbidden to sleep til he had crafted a quiver of arrows to replace the single shot wasted. As his chilled fingers fumbled over the shafts, Gideon thought back to that deer and despite his situation, flashed a brief fatalistic smile.

Keep running, he willed the beast.

Keep. Running.

THE SUFFERING Gideon endured at Ashkelon's hands was not the worst part of his ordeal. None of the beatings, deprivation, scorn or punishments could match the true horror of what the sorcerer did to him.

The most awful part of his training occurred whenever Gideon failed, and Ashkelon killed him.

Gideon's fingers slipped as they clutched at the hilt of the sword jutting from his chest. They were slick with red blood, a deep crimson. Life-giving crimson.

His. Both the blood and the blade.

He collapsed to his knees, still clutching at the Halcyon family sword levering his ribs open with every shuddering breath. His graying vision lifted to see a nightmare striding toward him, hand lowering from a blade cast.

Ashkelon gripped the handle of the blade and kicked Gideon in the chest, jerking the sword a full forearm's length out of his body. With a quick flick and twist, Ashkelon cleaned the blade of Gideon's blood, spattering his fallen body with a hot rain.

The dark mage clenched his fist, his blue eyes cold, and Gideon gave a hoarse gasp as the lips of the chasm cut into his chest pulled. If breath had been available, he would have screamed in indescribable agony as his organs sewed themselves back together inside of his body, obeying the sorcerous imperative compelling them to function once again. Bones and skin reformed, choosing to rebel against nature rather than Ashkelon's cruel will, and the crimson pouring from his chest reversed its course, fleeing back into his veins. With a final wrenching spasm of bone reknitting, Gideon's wound closed and air flooded his lungs.

As he gasped on the ground, Ashkelon's dark voice invaded his consciousness. "Your failure is not its own punishment. When you fail, those you profess to protect suffer, as well. If you fall in battle, Hell will advance over your corpse and tear into the weak behind you. Their screams would be the final sound to accompany your failed soul to the Halls of the After."

"And so you taste of this black chalice. You will sup at the table of the doomed, that you may know the fate of those you would fail. I will bring you back from the threshold of Death, until such time as I determine you have no further value. At that time, my apprentice, you may die."

He was tired.

No, *exhausted.* Reduced to a worthless scrap of humanity by the horrors inflicted on him. Gideon was sleep-deprived and malnourished, nerves forever on edge lest the psychopathic sadist catch him off-guard again.

If Gideon failed, Ashkelon beat him to death. Burned him. Speared him. Drowned him. Shot, strangled, stabbed, exploded, exsanguinated, eviscerated, and decapitated him. He was boiled alive, pulled apart, crushed and poisoned.

Failure.

He died every day for weeks. He endured the soul's sickening tumble into Death dozens of times from sunrise to sunset, and at night, it was *worse.* Ashkelon murdered him in his sleep without provocation, sliding a knife into his throat simply because he could.

Failure.

Gideon died on his knees, on his feet, on his back, his stomach, face and side. His body thudded into the dirt with a crash of mangled armor over and over again.

Each time, Ashkelon snarled the same word as Gideon fell into the blackness of Death.

Failure.

ON THE MORNING of the eightieth day, as the sun broke above the tree line on the Ironback mountains, Gideon snapped.

Ashkelon was delivering one of his dark sermons as Gideon performed push-ups in the tatters of his abused armor on jagged rocks. His palms were slashed and bleeding from the serrated stone as the sorcerer's voice droned on.

"Banish the thought of pain. Refuse to allow its dominion over your mind. Pain paralyzes, paralysis is weakness, and weakness..."

Ashkelon held up a finger, one elegant eyebrow arched in a gesture of mild contempt as he awaited his pupil's inevitable response.

Gideon threw his sword.

He was not even aware of the decision to do so. His hand whipped to the scabbard mounted on his back, the blade rasped as it escaped the sheath, and Gideon roared as he rocked back on his knees and hurled the Halcyon blade with both hands at the source of his torment.

Ashkelon's eyes widened in surprise as the shining sword sliced through the air toward his chest. He slapped the keen edge aside just before it skewered him where he stood, and the blade sparked as it skittered over the razor-sharp stones.

"You seem angry."

Gideon's boots pounded the earth, tossing flecks of stone as he charged, shoulder lowered and mouth open in a wordless bellow of hate. He tackled Ashkelon clean off of his feet, the smaller mage grunting at the impact of Gideon's mass. His master landed on his back with Gideon already rocketing a bleeding fist at his head like a boulder from a trebuchet.

Just before Gideon creamed Ashkelon's sharp features, just before glorious satisfaction flooded his veins, darkness exploded around him and his fist pounded into soft dirt.

Not Ashkelon's smug face. Not even something that made a satisfying sound, like wood or stone.

The faint *piff* of punching dirt.

Gideon turned to glare at Ashkelon standing a few yards away, nonchalantly dusting himself off, and he howled in frustration.

Ashkelon glanced at him and smiled, an arrogant smirk that only infuriated Gideon more.

Gideon stabbed his finger at him and screamed again, his entire body rigid and shaking as he channeled all the hate, rage and pain of the past weeks into a single primal bellow directed at one man. He would be speaking with a rasp for days, but *he did not care.*

The roar lasted for a few seconds, while Ashkelon waited patiently for the noise to stop. It did, eventually, trailing off pitifully as Gideon's lungs failed to continue projecting his discontent at Ashkelon.

Ashkelon spread his hands and opened his mouth, but Gideon snarled at him, "No. Shut up. *Shut...up.* I don't care. I don't want to hear it."

Ashkelon furrowed his brow and repeated, "You appear to be upset."

"*Upset?* You have starved me, robbed me, beaten me, deprived me of sleep and *killed* me, and you think I'm *upset?*"

"Those things make you angry."

Gideon actually struggled to articulate a response to this level of density. "Whah—*yes.* Yes, Ashkelon. Yes. Mm-hm. Those things make me angry. Enraged, actually."

Ashkelon considered him. "And you want to stop those things?"

Gideon stared at him for a moment, hands planted on his hips, chest heaving. "Yes. Of course I do, you maniac. Who wouldn't?"

"Would you stop them from happening to someone else?"

Gideon paused. "Why are you asking me that? Of course I would."

Ashkelon nodded once, briskly. "Walk with me."

He turned and walked away, his darkmail cloak whipping behind him. Gideon followed behind, a terrible idea curling up in his gut that Ashkelon knew *exactly* when he would break.

Tilting his head, Gideon could just make out a woman's scream over the wind. Staggering up a short hill, he crested the top to see a settlers' covered wagon on the road. Bandits surrounded it, tearing women and children from each others' arms. Two men shouted hoarsely, brandishing makeshift tools as weapons. They already bled as the robbers laughed.

Gideon's heart pounded as his gaze flashed back and forth across the scene.

At his side, Ashkelon folded his arms and said, "Without a doubt, the males will be killed and the women kept alive for as much sport as they can provide. If the children survive to reach the market, they will be sold as slaves to the highest bidder, who will use them as they see appropriate."

Gideon's breathing pattern accelerated, and he glanced from Ashkelon to the scene before them.

Ashkelon gestured almost wearily. "I give you permission to save them from this fate."

Gideon hesitated, watching for the trap. He took a step forward, and froze immediately when Ashkelon spoke again.

"Or..."

Ashkelon clenched his fist and black smoke pooled in the air around his hand. "...I can command that these stones be made bread."

The aroma of hot bread fresh from the baker's hearth flooded Gideon's senses an instant before his eyes beheld the reality. A board groaning under the most delicious supper Gideon had ever seen unfolded itself for him at Ashkelon's feet. A large turkey leg dripped its rich juices onto a plate crowded with roasted potatoes. A flagon of water stood by a twin flagon of wine, and a fluffy pastry filled with baked apples and cinnamon sagged under heavy cream.

Gideon's mind blanked. His mouth flooded with saliva, and his instincts roared at him to ignore the screams, ignore everything and dive into the succulent banquet awaiting him. A low groan escaped him before he could bite it back.

Emotionless, arms crossed, Ashkelon was neutral. "You may either try to save them, or satisfy your hunger. You have time for one choice."

Go to. You deserve it. People die everyday...

Ashkelon watched him carefully, as Gideon seemed frozen for a split-second.

You need your strength. What good are you without food, anyways?

What good ARE you?

Gideon's fist clenched.

"Where is my sword?"

The words choked out of his dry throat.

Ashkelon cocked his head. "Again? I could not hear you."

Gideon looked at him, away from the food he so desperately needed, opened his palm and said it again, "Sword."

With a slash of purplish-black, Ashkelon pulled the gleaming Halcyon sword from a rent in the air. He held it out to Gideon—then set it on the small banquet table. He stepped back, face impassive.

Gideon walked forward and gripped the handle of his sword. He did not spare the food a second thought, because *hesitation means weakness.*

Ashkelon raised an eyebrow and asked, "Nothing? Not even an apple for the fight?"

Gideon's eyes were cold and hard as he lifted his sword and stared down the blade at the carnage beneath him.

"I have what I need."

THE FIRST BANDIT was still laughing when a lance of iron ripped through his chest and tore his heart open.

The second turned at the sound of his comrade's body hitting the ground. He, at least, saw his killer.

The third dropped the woman struggling in his arms and actually got his own sword up before Gideon's blade hammered into him, knocking him backward.

Gideon did not stop moving. He barreled forward and rammed his blade through the brigand's chest, twisting and jerking it back even as he spun to cut again at the enemy nearest him, who was only just turning to meet the threat.

The flat of Gideon's blade slapped the man across the face, spilling him to the ground. Two more rushed him, weapons raised.

As they pounded toward him, Gideon felt the training of the past weeks take control of him. His concentration divided, almost as if there were now *two* Gideons.

One lived in the eternity of a single second, dispassionate, detached, noting each vulnerability in turn and selecting the appropriate strikes to expend the least energy while reaping the maximum benefit.

The other felt time rage around him like a hurricane. He fought in a whirlwind of ringing steel and roaring heartbeats, never stopping, never relenting because *weakness invites death.*

The resulting gestalt was a Gideon who could see every weakness of his foes and gloried in exploiting them. The bandits had no concept of what they faced.

His sword deflected both incoming strikes and slammed into the chest of the first before tearing back out to slash the throat of the other. The bodies had yet to impact the ground before he angled himself for the charge of their companions. The thugs shouted in anger, brandishing their weapons in threat as they rushed him.

Gideon barely noticed the threat. His mind had already processed the deaths of the first three and worked on the remnant when their blades reached him.

Every capacity for hesitation had been squeezed out of him over the past weeks of torture. All softness, all inefficiency, all *weakness.* Ashkelon's brutal lessons took hold, and suddenly, the bandits' own hesitation was glaringly apparent. Wasted movements. Sloppy guards. Lazy openings. Every mistake Gideon himself had made and paid for in life's blood.

Ashkelon's words echoed in his thoughts.

All I see is weakness.

He caught a blade on his vambrace and slapped it aside, ramming his fist into the man's face. With Gideon's size behind it, it likely fractured the man's skull as it pitched him backward.

The bandits' eyes widened, and Gideon charged.

Gideon flitted between falling blades like a dancer. He did not even feel like he was hurrying as he crunched a foot into a bandit's groin while simultaneously arcing his blade to hamstring the man's companion trying to flank him. His sword flashed back and ended both men in a series of looping cuts.

For a brief instant, he caught sight of the wide-eyed gazes of the settlers as he deflected a blade over his head and crushed the bearer's throat with a spearhand. They watched, open-mouthed, as he fought an entire gang of reavers, spilling their bodies across the road.

How am I doing this?

He caught sight of Ashkelon standing on the hill, arms crossed. He watched his student execute his training.

What did you do to me?

Gideon thrust and slashed, his Halcyon blade weaving an impenetrable web of iron before him. The bodies of the slain tumbled away, slumping across one another in death, til there remained only one.

The final bandit swung his axe wildly, his eyes wide with horror. Gideon side-stepped the attack with a terrible calm and slammed his elbow into the man's chest, pitching the man off his feet even as Gideon reversed the grip on his blade and rammed it into his spine.

Gideon's lungs pumped like a forge's bellows, his blood pounding in his head. His body struggled to meet the punishing demands Gideon had placed on it. His vision blurred, and he found it difficult to remain standing. He was weak, drained, and ravenously hungry.

But still he stood, and he had not failed.

An hour later, the grateful family departed, their strength restored by Gideon's abandoned feast.

Ashkelon came to stand beside him as he stood with his arms crossed, sword cleaned and sheathed on his back, watching the survivors dwindle into the distance.

Considering his decisions.

Ashkelon broke the silence. "How do you feel?"

"Hungry," Gideon answered honestly, grimacing at the rumbles in his gut, "But somehow full."

"Really."

Gideon turned to glare at him. "Man shall not live by bread alone, the Scriptures say."

Ashkelon said nothing to that, but offered him a pouch. Gideon hesitated, but his hunger forced him to accept the bag. It contained two small loaves of brown bread, several strips of dried meat and a large apple. As Gideon registered the surprising contents, Ashkelon held out a waterskin.

Gideon blinked several times at the unexpected kindness, trying to force the stinging in his eyes back. After the endless cruelty and hatred, this simple gift put him on the edge of an emotional breakdown. He had to take a number of deep breaths to control himself, hating himself for being so weak in front of Ashkelon.

Ashkelon glanced away, giving his student his space. "Sit and eat slowly. The fruit first. It will satisfy your immediate need for strength."

It was not a feast. It was barely even a meal. But…

It is enough.

Without a word, Gideon obeyed.

Regarding him as he ate, Ashkelon spoke. "You have passed the first test."

Gideon glanced up from his meal.

The sorcerer continued. "You have sacrificed your satisfaction of your basic needs to provide them to complete strangers. Starving, exhausted and abused, you overcame temptation in order to thrust yourself into a dangerous situation where you were outnumbered, and you triumphed."

"Out of all the men I have seen on this world, you are the first to deny his own needs for others."

Gideon forced himself to keep chewing. *Who knows when I'll get food again?*

But he listened.

Ashkelon looked into Gideon's eyes, almost into his soul. "I find you valuable. If you continue under me, I give you my oath that I will make you into a true hero of the Light. I will not rest or stop until you are the finest example of humanity's defenders. You will confront suffering and misery like no other, and stand fast before them. You will do battle with demons of Hell and monsters from the Abyss, and you will overcome."

Gideon stared at him, his cheek stuffed with apple, and finally asked the question that had been burning a hole in his mind for weeks. "Why? Why are you doing all this? Why are you training me? Why do you want a hero so much?"

Ashkelon crooked a half-smile. "You would not like that answer."

Finally smiling himself, Gideon said, "I don't like most of what you say. Answer the question."

The sorcerer considered him for a moment before answering. Finally, he said, "Because, when at last you stand ready, you shall kill me."

GIDEON STOPPED CHEWING. The world itself fell silent at Ashkelon's words.

He spoke around his mouthful of apple. "What?"

Ashkelon sighed and said, "Continue eating. I will explain, as I can."

He seated himself cross-legged on the ground and steepled his fingers before his face, his cold gaze examining Gideon. After a moment, he asked, "Why were you in the tower where I found you?"

Gideon tore a chunk of bread away from the roll and answered, "We were there to kill the Crowfather."

Ashkelon shook his head. "No, that is what you were there to do. I want to know *why* you were there."

Gideon gestured helplessly. "Because he was evil."

"A trait you yourself lack entirely."

Grimacing at the dry rebuke, Gideon shook his head. "No. I have evil within me."

"Then what drove you to end his life before taking your own? Or that of another evil warlock's in his place?"

Gideon looked at Ashkelon blankly, unsure how to respond.

Ashkelon sighed. "Did he have direct villainous influence upon your life? Was this evil man threatening *your* family? *Your* lands? *Your* people?"

After a moment, Gideon shook his head. "No, he was not. We came from another region."

Leaning forward, Ashkelon transfixed Gideon's gaze with his own. "Then why target *him*?"

Gideon realized where this was going and winced slightly. "Because that is who we were being paid to kill."

Ashkelon's eyes glinted with satisfaction, and he leaned back. "Exactly. In the place of pure motives, greed. In the stead of justice, profit."

Gideon felt distinctly uncomfortable. "We took pay, yes, but we destroyed evil when we found it."

"You mean, when it was pointed out to you by a customer with heavy bags of gold."

A trifle defensive now, Gideon shot back, "Fighting men still need to eat."

"And you ate considerably better after making a kill, until necessity drove you to seek another," Ashkelon retorted. "Your hungers ruled you, not justice."

Gideon opened his mouth, but Ashkelon cut him off. "You were not acting the part of a selfless hero, my apprentice. You were a mercenary, a mere sword for hire. An expendable commodity to be bid upon and haggled over. Though possessed of a high personal standard of morality, you compromised it to put food in your mouth."

The bread lay heavy in his mouth. Gideon found it difficult to swallow the lump.

Finally, he answered, "It was the only thing I could find to do."

Ashkelon considered him. "At last, honesty. Go on."

Gideon did not look at him, but instead stared into the skies. "This was the only way I could find to stop evil men from doing what happened to me. The man who recruited me promised to give me armor, enough to eat, and a good war to fight."

Ashkelon chuckled. "And you believed him."

Gideon grimaced. "I was younger, and a little more naïve. It was a gray area."

Ashkelon considered him a moment, then sighed. "A gray area. I cannot tell you how much I hate that phrase."

"Why?" Gideon asked.

"A gray area assumes that there is a middle ground between darkness and light. Gray is *not* a color. It is white, dirtied with a small amount of black, and deceived that it is an acceptable compromise. Men say that true purity cannot exist, and therefore gray is more realistic."

Gideon shrugged. "This is the world we live in."

Ashkelon looked at Gideon. "I reject this notion. Everything not pure white is just another shade of black."

Gideon pointed at him with the heel of his bread. "You claim to judge the actions of good men? *You?* You're responsible for dozens of murders that I have witnessed personally, and all of those were me!"

Ashkelon's eyes flashed coldly. "I know what I have *seen*. I know what ideals the champions of the Light purport to uphold. It is likely that I can recount the names of more heroes who have died by my blade than you have ever heard of, and yet they were all flawed by darkness in some way."

Gideon did not back down. "Oh, come on, master! How can you expect a man, any man, to be perfect? If that were the case, none of us, including you, could measure up."

Finally Ashkelon grunted and turned away. "It is too much, perhaps, to ask purity of purpose for the entirety of one's life."

A wry smirk creased his face. "There is only one Valantian."

Gideon furrowed his brow. "Valantian? I don't know that name."

"You would not. He was not from this world," Ashkelon said, then smiled wryly to himself. "You could say, however, that he was my hero."

Gideon blinked at that. "I'm sorry, *your* hero?"

Ashkelon looked back at him, his eyes shining coldly. "Imagine a world shrouded in the Dark, as billowing clouds of black roil in the sky and strangle all life. Call it sin, if you will, or chaos, or evil. Men light candles or hold torches to hold back its cruel inevitability, but they are fools. When their torches begin to fail, when their candles gutter and flicker in the night, that is when you can see them begin to reason within themselves. They say, 'my blackness is not as black as the blackness over there', and they claim that they are more righteous, that they are more worthy of honor and praise. Soon their perceptions are governed and dictated by the night around them, as they begin to judge the world according to the laws of the blind."

Ashkelon sneered. "So the people of Avalon huddled together to tend dying fires and congratulated themselves on the sparks they produced, hoping that these pathetic flashes of light would dissuade the gods of murder and that the fangs of the Dark would choose someone else. But the Dark knows its own. It sees the darkness in man and recognizes it, is drawn to it. There is no gray in the Dark. The end of man was nigh."

Gideon leaned forward and asked, "But?"

Ashkelon nodded. "But Valantian. In the endless fog of the Dark, Valantian Asirius was a blazing star, burning the darkness away wherever he walked. He was granted great gifts by the Light, almost searing the eyes of those who beheld him. A tireless champion of good, the Scion of Avalon itself, he defied the night and forced it back with sword, shield and fury, breaking the armies of evil and forcing them to hide in fear. It was because of him that the Dark lost its hold on my world. Him, and his brother Gemelte."

"What happened?" Gideon asked.

Crossing his arms across the unnaturally black plates of his armor, Ashkelon answered, "The Dark found a champion of its own."

Ashkelon glanced away, and Gideon saw his eyes grow distant as he remembered. "When I arose from the shadows, I took the Avala off-guard. I snuffed out their fires one by one and left them to the brutal truth of the night they had deluded themselves into believing no longer existed. In a rage, Valantian came against me, and we fought. We fought for years, decades, neither able to overcome the other. He was everything that was honorable and right in man, and I was everything…else. The very values of good and evil clashed together, consummating on the peak of my fortress."

"And you lost. That's why you're here." Gideon took another bite of his food. "Because Valantian banished you?"

Ashkelon sighed, and for a moment, Gideon was struck by what seemed to be regret in the sound. "That…is not wholly accurate."

Gideon waited, but Ashkelon left the question unanswered.

The mage rose to his feet, his dark cloak swishing, and said, "Finish eating and take your rest. You have much to learn, and tomorrow, your training begins in earnest."

He walked away, leaving Gideon with his food.

Gideon stared after him for a moment, before muttering to himself, *"Tomorrow's* in earnest? What have we been *doing?"*

4

WARRIOR

I t was the nature of the beast, to practice swinging and blocking and moving with a heavy weapon until one's arms burned hot and the weapon trembled from exhaustion. Gideon could remember days past in his mercenary unit when he would collapse on his bedroll, hardly able to pull a blanket over himself, but content with the day's hard work.

Ashkelon, however, had taken that good, proper, familiar feeling and elevated it to soul-shattering fatigue. Gideon had never been so tired in in his entire life. He didn't think *anyone* had.

By his estimation, Gideon had performed more sword drill than a battalion of soldiers. His arms felt like someone had hung lead weights from them and forced him to do six hours of sword drill a day for weeks on end. It was appropriate that they felt that way, because that was *precisely* what happened.

Every morning, the mage encased Gideon's arms in a heavy black metal, then instructed him in the sword styles and masteries of dozens of cultures, guiding him through hundreds of ritual movements called forms. Invariably, Gideon could only hold up his arms for the first hour, struggling to learn the flowing styles of long-dead monks or the brutal chops of the barbarians of the plains. Then, inevitably, his arms would begin to sag, his technique would falter, and he was reduced to swinging with dead limbs, desperately trying to match Ashkelon's serpentine motions throughout the complicated forms being demonstrated.

Only after Gideon could no longer raise his arms would Ashkelon draw a blade out of smoke and duel him.

GIDEON STAGGERED BACKWARDS, desperately heaving his blade two-handed to deflect Ashkelon's flickering blade. The Halcyon family blade just barely caught the edge of Ashkelon's sword and nudged it just enough to cause the blade to lop off a lock of Gideon's sweat-drenched hair instead of the entire head.

Too exhausted to arrest the blade's path and withdraw it to a guard, Gideon turned with the blade and launched a heavy horizontal cut at Ashkelon's midsection.

Unfortunately for him, Ashkelon had foreseen the attack, which was a surprise to no one, and stepped into the blade's arc. Ashkelon's forearm blocked the hilt while he sharply punched Gideon across the jaw with the pommel of his weapon, then whipped the blade back around to rest at Gideon's throat.

Gideon sagged. *Dead. For what is probably the twelfth time in an hour.*

The sorcerer pulled the blade back and raised an eyebrow. "Do you require rest? Your bladework is suffering."

Gideon rubbed his eyes on his shoulder, since he was unable to lift his arms, and cracked his neck. "I don't know what you're talking about. I actually hit your sword that time."

Ashkelon inclined his head sardonically. "So you did. Well done."

Gideon blew out his breath and hefted his screaming metal-encased arms to put his blade *en garde.* "Again?"

Ashkelon saluted him with his blade and answered with a slight smile, "Again."

NOR WAS the training limited to weapons only.

Gideon parried Ashkelon's thrusting speartip with his blade and ducked the butt-end as it lashed out for his head. The sorcerer spun to deliver yet another stab, but his student had stumbled backward out of range. Immediately, Ashkelon lowered the spear. "You concede the advantage when you retreat."

Disbelieving, Gideon laughed harshly. "Did I miss something? I had an advantage?"

The Onyx Mage ignored the sarcasm. "You could have closed the distance when my back was turned. Your aggression would have tipped the balance of the fight in your favor."

"But then you would have done something else and killed me anyway. What does it matter?"

Ashkelon leveled a chilling glare at him. "It *matters* because you would have seen my response to your attack. It *matters* because you would have learned something new, instead of wasting our time while you willfully ignore the lessons of the past. It *matters* because you would have been doing everything in your power to overcome your opponent, rather than conceding momentum because you think yourself a seer of all possible futures."

Shamed into silence, Gideon swallowed.

Ashkelon did not stop. His words spat from his lips with venom. "There are enough threats out there that you will not know how to fight. There will be no drills to help you discover the weakness in your enemy, when at last you meet it. You will be confronted by the unknowable, and it will thirst for your blood. At those times of deadly ignorance, all you will have is your indomitable assurance that you will be victorious. Your faith, Gideon, formed in these days of tedious reaction to knowable threats. Faith formed through knowing that *every* time a weapon sought your life, you reacted with all of your might, and wrested the initiative away through sheer force of will."

The sorcerer sneered. "Do you think you are a hero simply because you wear armor and bear a sword? I have seen heroes kill with rocks, clad in rags, starving and on the verge of death. Against all odds, they advance, striving to further the cause of righteousness for another day."

His voice shaking slightly, Ashkelon stepped forward, clenching a fist before him. "Heroes *believe*. Against reason, against evidence, against their instincts, they believe. They know that right will win, even when they know it can't. They are empty vessels filled to the brim with this impossible contradiction."

Ashkelon stabbed his finger at Gideon, eyes blazing fiercely. "*That* is how a lone man confronts an army of screaming savages, fitting his last arrow to the string with a laugh contemptuous of death. *That* is how a doomed rearguard meets their end with a hymn of victory on their lips. When surrounded by the Everlasting Dark, when the candles of false hope have guttered out and the fangs of demons glisten wetly with their ageless hunger, the just continue to live by this insane, hopeless, *glorious* faith."

For a second, the two of them remained, eyes locked on one another's, one clad in dirty iron, the other draped in shadow.

At last, Ashkelon said, "Therefore it might behoove you to react to these knowable threats with a modicum of that same faith, if you are not willing to be a disappointment to all those who worship the title *hero*."

As Gideon lifted his aching arms and brandished his tarnished sword, the thought came unbidden to his mind.

Like you.

Ashkelon slung the spear around his head and drew it back, sliding the rough haft through the curve of his thumb and forefinger of his forward hand til it rested just below the spearhead, tip angled toward Gideon. "Now stop wasting mankind's last moments of life, and fight like you believe."

ASHKELON'S REBUKE NEVER LEFT him. His cutting words echoed in Gideon's soul, infecting his dreams, his meals, his prayer. He threw himself into his training, practicing under Ashkelon's merciless gaze and further by himself. His mind, formerly barricaded against the deluge of instruction, opened fully to accept and absorb.

He crawled through mud, dragging a "casualty" with him as arrows borne of magic sliced through the air above him. Dirt and grime darkened his skin, and his muscles ached as he gripped the heavy tree trunk and dragged it a few more inches. He gripped his sheathed family sword by the blade, trying to wrestle with the log one-handed while not dropping the weapon. Gideon had died enough times for that particular sin.

It did not matter that the task seemed impossible. Above him, merciless darkness walked, watching.

"Faster," Ashkelon commanded. "Do you not care that this man lies near death? Or is all that praying a facade to hide your true weakness?"

Gideon gritted his teeth, adjusted his grip, and hauled the log a full foot forward with a groaning snarl, his bicep screaming at the strain.

Sweat poured over his face, washing grit into his eyes. Gideon spat a thick wad of spittle into the muck and gathered his legs underneath him for another push.

Only a mile to go.

"Faster," Ashkelon demanded.

IT TOOK WEEKS. Months, even. Endless pain and drill, followed by endless pain and drill. But Gideon began to suspect something.

He suspected he was getting better.

Without warning, Ashkelon complicated his drills, including more and more advanced techniques in the routines. Oftentimes, Gideon would stand, muscles taut, ears perked, waiting for Ashkelon to bark out the name of a routine. As soon as he sprang into the lethal movements of that particular form, Ashkelon would change the routine, forcing Gideon to flow into the alternate form seamlessly.

His blade became as familiar to him as his arm. Ashkelon took to stealing Gideon's sword at every opportunity and killing Gideon with it if he succeeded. As a result, Gideon ate with his father's weapon leaning against his knee. He slept with the weapon, curled around the sheath protectively to prevent Ashkelon's theft. He did not so much as relieve himself without the sword on his person.

A few weeks past, Ashkelon began to cheat in their duels. The first time, Gideon deflected a sword thrust and tucked his foot behind him, spinning into a lateral cut that would have torn a normal man in half. *I got him this time*, flashed through Gideon's mind. But the ironwood haft of a melee spear blocked his blade, and Gideon had to recoil from a blitz of flashing thrusts and slashes, desperately defending as Ashkelon assaulted him with an entirely different weapon conjured from the ether.

The day before, Ashkelon forced Gideon to spar him blindfolded, then somehow made him weightless. As he thrashed in panic, rising toward the sky, Ashkelon slammed his mailed fist into the side of the the his head, spinning him about with no hope of halting his momentum. Then the madman restored nature's order... and nature gave Gideon a concussion.

It was impossible.

It was hopeless.

It was really, *really* fun.

Gideon could not help it. He woke up grinning fiercely at the challenges of the day before him, though his body ached as if he had been pressed in a vise.

Today, his arms were trapped at his sides with vine from some kind of plant monster from Ashkelon's imagination, he was half-blinded and choking from a poisonous pollen burst and he was fairly sure the thing was trying to eat him, but as he juked and dodged its whipping fronds, Gideon grinned like a fiend.

I'm going crazy. He's making me crazy.

The thought made his smile bigger. He kicked out at one frond, ducked and rolled under a spray of thorns, which apparently it could also fire at him with a hiss of compressed air, because what plant would be complete without its own supply of compressed air, and came up face to face with the primary pod, a giant pink bulb that had *teeth* for some ungodly reason.

His hands were tied, its plant limbs were about to wrap him up and drain the blood from his twitching body, and what was left of him would probably nourish the thing's little plant babies.

Gideon did not hesitate.

ASHKELON PRESSED the poultice of foul-smelling herbs and chemicals to the side of Gideon's face, careful to leave him a nostril to breathe through, and asked, "A headbutt. You decided to strike a sicarian mankiller...with your face."

There was about a quarter inch of one of Gideon's lips that could still move. "It sheemed like a good idea at da chime."

Ashkelon placed another poultice across the puffy, warty, blood-red mass that was Gideon's face, and said, "I am going to have educate you with better ideas. The swelling should go down in about an hour. I will brew you tea to flush the toxins out of your system. You will not enjoy that."

"I hink my faysh ish melching."

"That would be the mankiller's poison activating your nerve endings. I am told it is a remarkable sensation."

"Eh. Oo should chry it."

"No, thank you. I am one of those rare individuals who learns from the pain of others."

Gideon huffed, the best he could do for a laugh. "Ere j'lenty to learn here."

Ashkelon actually smiled. "You did well, my apprentice."

"Chaught him a leshun he wo' forget. Dish ish da world of *man*."

Ashkelon chuckled and patted him on the shoulder. "Take your rest. You will be fighting it again tomorrow."

The sound Gideon made blurred the line between a whine and a pitiful cry. Then a huffing sigh, and the warrior said, "Wifout da head'utt."

"Ideally."

SPARKS SLASHED off the Halcyon blade as Gideon parried Ashkelon's backhanded attack. Thankfully, the screaming blade remained sheathed and mute on the sorcerer's back; according to Ashkelon, the cursed steel would blast his simple sword into bits of skittering metal.

The conjured blade that Ashkelon bore twisted and warped in his hands, becoming a two-handed warhammer arcing toward Gideon's skull. He sidestepped the swing, and the head of the hammer cratered the ground with a thud. Gideon kicked at the head of the hammer, fouling Ashkelon's retraction of the weapon, and lunged forward, taking advantage of the split-second of vulnerability the maneuver had granted him.

The dark sorcerer met his attack with a squared stance, deftly dodging the first two stabs of Gideon's flickering blade. The warhammer transformed and split into two short curved swords, deadly in close quarters.

Gideon gave him no space. His adopted family's ancient sword lashed out like a viper, forcing Ashkelon to parry with both blades. Gideon rode with the force of the deflection and cut back, his response tearing the swords from Ashkelon's hands.

That did not mean Ashkelon was beaten; the memories of the sorcerer's countless hand-to-hand victories added even more speed to his follow-on strike. Gideon roared as he shouldered Ashkelon back and hacked at him, his weight squarely behind the strike, his sword angled toward Ashkelon's midriff.

Unable to dodge the blistering attack, Ashkelon dropped one foot back to brace himself and crossed both wrists before his face. Gideon's sword smashed into his black darkmail bracers and the power behind the strike staggered his master back a single step.

One step.

Time froze, and for just an instant, Gideon's soul exulted in the solitary stumble of Ashkelon before one of his attacks. It was not a dodge. Not a tactical retreat designed to fool him into over-extending. An honest-to-God stumble because Gideon had hit the pitiless warlock too hard and too fast for him to recover.

Over the heavenly choirs singing glory in his soul, he heard the faint sound of history screaming for his attention.

Realizing his mistake, Gideon lunged into a kick, but his pitifully short second of triumph had given Ashkelon all the time he needed. Ashkelon shifted to avoid the kick and ducked to drive his mailed fist into Gideon's groin. Gideon doubled over with an explosive groan of pain and betrayal, just in time to meet his master's knee to his forehead. His sword ripped out of his hand and he found himself staring into Ashkelon's burning eyes with his own blade gently kissing his throat.

Gideon closed his eyes and sighed. "I almost had you."

The blade left his neck. "If that is what you wish to believe."

"You almost fell. I almost made you fall."

Ashkelon grunted in amusement as he returned Gideon his sword. "A single step backward does not a fall make, apprentice."

Gideon took his blade and swung it a few times, loosening his wrists as he retorted, "No. You're not taking this away from me. You stumbled back, I saw it. Admit it. Admit it, you miserable, heartless monster. I *almost* had you that time!"

Ashkelon smirked and embarked on a slow-paced circle of his apprentice, hands held behind his back. "Ah, yes, almost. I have heard of this concept, of attempting but not attaining one's goal. It must be an acrid experience to have come so close to success, but have it snatched away so cruelly. Even the word itself sounds disappointing. *Almost.* It leaves such a bitter taste in the mouth, don't you think?"

Gideon narrowed his eyes. "You're mocking me."

The smirk widened to a teeth-baring smile, which on Ashkelon, looked disturbingly reminiscent of a wolf's snarl. "Then I suppose, if I were in your situation, I would take my *almost* and improve it to a performance worthy of more than a miserable, heartless monster's mockery."

The rush of anger energized Gideon. His swordhand rotated once more, and a grin broke out on his face as Gideon realized he wanted nothing more in that instant than to wipe that smug smirk off of that insufferable pale face. A low growl of pleasure escaped his gritted teeth, and Ashkelon's eye brow arched. Lowering himself to a fighting stance, the sorcerer hissed, "*There* he is. There's the warrior I wish to see."

Gideon cracked his neck, still grinning. "I hope you're ready, master. You're going to eat dirt in a few seconds."

"Hmm. Words."

Sparks sprayed onto the hard ground as the blades of mercy and murder clashed once more.

THE CHILL CREPT in that night with icy fingers. Ashkelon seemed immune to its touch while Gideon lay on the ground, shivering. The sorcerer was seated cross-legged, facing away from him, elbows on his knees as he held his bared sword at eye level, the blade parallel to the ground. Ashkelon stared at the weapon as it screamed back into his face.

Gideon wrapped his thin blanket tighter around his body and tried to block out the choir of the damned. Yet Ashkelon's seated figure occupied Gideon's thoughts, robbing him of rest.

His mother had spoken of men like this. "Soldiers get hurt," she had said, "And most of the time, you can't see where the wound lies. It stays with them for the rest of their lives."

It was the same every night. Gideon would collapse onto the ground, half-dead with exhaustion, and Ashkelon would draw his sword and hold it before him, meditating upon the screams. His black half-mask would coalesce from the smoke and conceal his features, masking his thoughts as his ice-blue eyes searched his blade.

What makes such a man? Who was he, Father, before he became...this?

A heavy sigh escaped Gideon.

"Praying?"

He rolled over at the sound of Ashkelon's voice. The sorcerer had spoken over his shoulder, his eyes never breaking their gaze upon his blade.

"How did you know that?" Gideon asked.

A grunt of amusement. "Some of my...experiments...sighed as they prayed. I used to annotate the sounds human beings made as they passed through various stages of despair. It may interest you that it would seem no one was listening."

Faint contempt put an edge in his tone. Gideon propped his elbow under him as he regarded the dark warrior before him.

"You don't believe in God."

Ashkelon remained still, his back betraying nothing of his thoughts to his apprentice as choirs of the lost shrieked in his hands. At length, he asked, "Do you know what this blade is?"

Gideon did not answer. His master required no response from him for these tales.

Ashkelon continued, his eyes locked on the killing edge of his weapon. "The master swordsmiths of the Avala were peerless in their craft, before the Dark took them. They forged marvels of engineering and science, placing the dominion of Avalon firmly within the hands of men. But in all their number, only the starsmiths truly *created*."

"Each one apprenticed for thirty years before forging his first sword. As a recruit, he would swear an oath on the day of his apprenticeship to serve the starsmiths with his life, whether he passed or failed. The attrition among the candidates baffles the mind; only one in a hundred might pass his master's scrutiny over three decades of training. The rest were cast out, relegated to menial servants or common blacksmiths, enslaved, the losers in the ultimate gamble."

Ashkelon's voice dropped to a whisper. "But if a man succeeded, Gideon, if he was deemed worthy by the masters, he, on the final day of his apprenticeship, could approach the Anvil of Avala, and there offer himself as a living sacrifice. A winged spirit would appear before him, and ram the burning Blade of Eden into his belly. The heavenly fire would boil his blood as it scoured him, testing his purity. If the candidate survived his trial—and most did not—if he were deemed pure by the celestial being, the spirit would gift him with a secret from Above, with which he could forge a single sword."

Gideon blinked. "One sword?"

Ashkelon closed his eyes and a small smile tugged at his lips. "Only one. The love of his life. The swordsmith, filled with the flame of Eden, would work upon the Anvil of Avala, under the watch of the mighty spirit, spurning food, water and rest until his masterpiece lay completed before him."

"They called their creations starswords."

"Tempest Wing, Sunspire, Drakesplitter—each blade the only one of its kind in the universe. Swords of surpassing beauty, crafted with celestial gold and gems from the deepest reaches of the earth—they had *souls*, Gideon. As such, they were without price. The starsmiths gifted them as they willed, to the individual or bloodline they believed most worthy of their life's work."

"This was no small gift. The bearer of a starsword could pierce the minds of men and know their hearts better than they did themselves. The bearer of a starsword saw the future of kingdoms, the secrets of emperors and the very will of God. Kings impoverished their own nations for the merest chance of possessing such a weapon. They often sent the strongest of their sons to apprentice to the starsmiths, hoping against reason that one might overcome the trials and grant their line a starsword."

As Ashkelon spun his tale, images swam before Gideon's eyes, almost as if the sorcerer weaved the story into physical form with nothing but his words. It riveted him in place.

Ashkelon went on. "The last to ascend the Stairway was called Acheron. He was the last to speak to the winged spirit, and the last to use the fabled Anvil of Avala. He was a musician, his soul vibrating with the music of the spheres, and the spirit took his passion as a material for the blade. Under its tutelage, he forged a starsword, yes, but also a window to Heaven itself. The music of the Celestial City flowed from the blade, capturing the wills of the hearers. They called it *Hamdalithien*, the Song of Heaven."

His story paused. Ashkelon's forehead creased, almost as if in pain, as Gideon watched a featureless man bearing a blazing sword step before a crowd, all of whom without exception tumbled to their knees before him, entranced by the song of the sword.

"But Acheron, witnessing his sword's power, became covetous. They say that his soul blackened in that moment when all bowed before him, and he declared that no other deserved a blade from the winged spirit. He demanded that they build a temple to house the blade, and within a few short weeks, Acheron installed himself as the

High Priest of the Shrine of the Starsword. With the starsword's power, wealth flowed into Acheron's coffers. He married a princess from every realm, tying them all to his newborn cult."

"The kingdoms fell into idolatry, as Acheron commanded them to worship the starsword he had created. His demands grew more and more costly as his lust for power and wealth grew, until at last, men rebelled."

The images swirled, resolving into a council of kings pointing at a robed man with a staff of office and a tall miter. Faint accusations echoed until the robed man brandished the sword, his face contorted with rage.

"Acheron declared that the starsword was angry, that it had seen their treacherous hearts and spoken to him of it. He swore to slay every king in turn til the traitors were found. He raised his sword to kill, but the entrance of a stranger stayed him."

A hooded man in beggar's robes and a gnarled walking stick stepped between the furious priest and the cowering kings, hand raised gently.

"With a quiet yet firm voice, he condemned Acheron for making the gift of Heaven into an idol, daring to state that Acheron had proved himself unworthy of the rank of starsmith. Before Acheron could strike him down, the stranger offered a contest. If he could prove that Acheron's heart was black with evil, Acheron must surrender the blade to him."

"With a laugh of scorn, Acheron rashly accepted, for who could dare to judge Acheron? His holy blade rent the very air as it swept toward the hooded stranger's neck."

"Before Acheron's blow landed, however, a terrible shadow intersected the starsword's path. *Hamdalithien* shattered into a thousand shards of starmetal, its song forever silenced. Before Acheron's horrified eyes, the winged spirit itself towered over the humble beggar. This time, however, it did not bear the fabled Sword of Eden, but a blade forged from the Everlasting Dark itself."

Ashkelon turned to face Gideon, his black blade still resting in his palms. The same weapon held in the hand of the titanic being standing in a pillar of flame.

"Intoning the same litany as the day Acheron stood before it for judgment, the spirit speared Acheron with the blade, and this time, he was not found pure. The betrayer screamed as his soul, stained with sin, was torn from his body and cast into the void, into the realm called the Outer Dark. But his last cry did not fade as his soul fled; it keened still from the blade, trapped forever as a memory."

"The beggar proclaimed to the kings that the name of the sword would ever after be *Acherlith*, or Acheron's Song. The rune for its name can also be read *Deathscream*. Its existence is to serve as a warning, to caution humanity against placing any creation, however beautiful, before the Creator. Every life that the blade takes will echo from its killing edge as an eternal reminder of Heaven's horror at Acheron's treachery."

Ashkelon held out his sword for Gideon to see. "This is Acherlith, forged from the darkness beyond reality. It is not a starsword, shining with light and beauty, but a voidblade, tearing all light from its presence and the life from its victims. When I rose from the Dark, I found it in the deepest dungeons of Avalon and claimed it for my own. Since that night, it has counted the tale of my murders and sung them like a herald to my victims. Everyone I have ever killed, every soul I have torn from a fragile mortal, howls from this sword every time I draw it."

Gideon's eyes widened. So many voices rose from that length of nightmare-black steel. He might as well have tried to listen to the sea and count the droplets that made up the waves.

Ashkelon grunted in bitter amusement. "Most men can try to hide from their sins, Gideon. Most can shroud them in self-deception, convincing themselves that they are good. But not *me*."

He thrust the blade before Gideon's face.

"Listen. You can hear their lives summed up in their last cry, their stories condensed to a single sound at the moment of their death. Every night, I hear them: criminals, family men, champions and footmen of Heaven and Hell, all screaming their last words, begging to be heard. I cannot escape *my* sins, for they are ever before me."

Ashkelon's voice grew rough with passion, his fist tightening around his sword. "How many screams do you hear? How many shriek from Acherlith's damned blade for mercy, release or vengeance? How many more *have* to die before Someone deigns to answer them?"

With growing trepidation, Gideon watched as Ashkelon rasped his hate through clenched teeth. "So ask me again if I believe in God. Ask me *again* if I believe He will answer the prayers of those He claims as His children. Any god who would stand by and watch as I murder so many of his people is worth less than the empty worship he receives."

Ashkelon stabbed an accusing finger at his apprentice, voice hoarse with emotion. "If He cared at all, *Valantian would have won.* God's most righteous servant would still be alive and he would have *stopped me* before I..."

The sorcerer cut off abruptly as Gideon lifted his gaze from the wailing sword and stared at him.

"What did you *do?*" he whispered.

For an instant, Ashkelon's knuckles went white on his sword, and Gideon was startled to see terrible vulnerability flash through the sorcerer's eyes. His lips parted slightly, and a ragged sigh, barely audible, almost weeping, escaped him, even as the howling from the blade swelled and intensified, threatening to swallow the sound.

Gideon grunted and took a step back as he felt a raging tempest of emotion spill out from Ashkelon to claw at his spirit. It was an eternity of rage, focused by a terrible oath that should never have been spoken. It was the aftershocks of an endless war waged alone against the Divine. It was an entire epoch of killing, of hate, of a quest for dark vindication, and in the end...

Grief.

Emptiness.

Ash.

For a moment, Gideon knew what it was to be Ashkelon.

But that moment ended. Growling, the Onyx Mage wrenched

control back over his spirit. Familiar darkness crept over his face, solidifying into his black half-mask as his eyes narrowed to slits of glacial blue. The tidal waves of hate and grief smashing against Gideon's soul silenced abruptly, reined in once more by Ashkelon's titanic willpower.

Coldly, through the shrieks of countless souls, Ashkelon hissed, "*I won.*"

The dark warrior turned away, again raising Deathscream's unholy length before his eyes, again listening to the immortal cries of his victims.

But the young man heard the rest of Ashkelon's sentence, the part he had bitten off before it escaped his lips.

And I wish I had not.

Softly, Gideon asked, "If you don't care, then why listen to them at all?"

Avalon's murderer did not answer immediately , and Gideon had not been expecting him to. He wrapped his blanket tighter about him and made to lie on his side, but a faint whisper held him.

"Because prayers should be heard."

5

WOLVES

The fires were dying.

Just hours before, the flames had roared, crackling in their hearths as they glutted on hardwood, belching sparks into the jarl's hall. Diligence and need kept such fires burning, and in times past, the fires of the Wolves burned hottest of all. When Old Man Winter reached out with greedy fingers, the flaming claws of the Wolves scalded him and thrust him back into hiding.

In times past. But now the fire was dying.

Anya Helsdottyr glared at the smoldering coals, her dark eyes flashing as they insulted her with the metaphor they personified. *Can we not even stoke the fires when a guest comes? Do we not even* pretend *anymore?*

The little light that the fire cast revealed the scene before her. A thin man shivered before the imposing figure of her father, the jarl of the Vulfenkind. The peasant's face was lined with care, but hope brought some light into his eyes.

There was none in her father's.

"No."

His low voice, her favorite sound when it did not betray the essence of what it was to be a Wolf, rumbled with the devastating response.

"You will have to look after yourselves."

The petitioner blinked, confusion creasing his brow. Wolves never turned down their serfs' requests for protection. It was unprecedented. "But...but, my lord—we are *farmers*—we cannot fight *spiders* with *pitchforks*—"

Shadows pooled in the crags and recesses of Heimdall Fangthane's face as he sat upon his throne of carved oak. "I did not ask for your chosen profession, headsman, nor is it my oath to compensate for the consequences of such decisions."

Other Wolves stood about in the throne room, still as stones, all shrouded in shadow. *As if they could hide from their shame,* Anya thought bitterly.

The village headsman swallowed. Hard. "*Please,* my lord—we cannot fight these demons alone."

The jarl leaned forward, and the light of the meagre flames glinted in his eyes. "You have your answer, headsman. I will not bleed this pack for your lack of foresight."

Her father raised his voice, ensuring that every Wolf heard his iron will. "No Wolf will ride to Estvik. Now take yourself and go. Spend your own blood before asking that we spend ours."

Anger kindled courage in the petitioner's heart. The headsman of tiny Estvik opened his mouth, willing to dare the wrath of the jarl. Anya knew what his words would be, for they snarled within her own soul.

This is your oath! This is your purpose! You are Wolves!

But Skald Greymane, the grizzled keeper of the sagas of the clan, stepped forward from his place and rested his scarred hand comfortingly on the headsman's shoulder, cutting him off. Quietly but firmly, Skald murmured, "No is no, lad. Best be on your vay."

Tears of despair and disappointment beginning to fall, the crushed headsman allowed Skald to gently guide him out of the longhouse. The acrid stench of betrayal thickened the air as their guest departed with a last look of hurt. His thoughts were clear to all.

How could you...?

Once the stricken peasant was out, the Wolves glanced at one another, but none dared raise his eyes to their jarl.

You cowards...

Anya's fiery temper flared and she let her disgust be known.

"Pah!"

Jarl Fangthane glared at her, and his voice sounded like boulders grinding against one another. "Do you have something to add, *daughter?*"

His tone made it very obvious that she did not, as did his stormy glare. Many lords and warriors wilted before the furious gaze of Heimdall Fangthane, unwilling to risk his legendary wrath.

But there was a reason the elders had surnamed Anya "Helsdottyr".

"I have one question, Father. What are you all looking for, when you look at each other?"

There was no answer to Fangthane's daughter as she stalked the center of the room, her eyes flashing, her wild black hair whipping behind her as she snapped her gaze from Wolf to Wolf.

"Are you looking for Wolves? Because I know I am, and I don't see any!"

A rumble of discontent met *that* statement. Heimdall slammed his fist into the armrest of his throne and snarled, "You go too far, daughter."

Anya met his smoldering gaze with her own. "And you don't go anywhere! Even *dogs* defend their hearths, Father! What are you defending from the comfort of your throne?"

Her father's nostrils flared and his jaw clenched. She was spitting thoughtless words she would later regret, she knew this already. She was taking shameless advantage of his love for her and embarrassing him in front of his warriors. But years of enduring this slow death was too much for her anymore, and the words kept spilling out of her.

Teeth gritted, Heimdall snarled, "I am defending my *pack*! I do not needlessly spend their blood at the whim of every crying farmer and milkmaid that crosses my threshold."

Anya snapped back, "And when did we begin to fear bleeding?

What Wolf dreads old Skald singing the story of his mighty death, with the bodies of his foes piled around him? Why do we now fear such glory instead of this slow wasting away, this *hiding* in our lair as we die from disease and old age?"

Warriors were starting to wince. Wolves lusted for glory, and their desire began to war with their duty to their liege as her words stirred them.

Heimdall knew it, too, because he felt the same in his own heart, and he roared his frustration at her. "*You know why!* We do not have the blood to shed, not anymore! We do not have the axes to lend to lesser men. Our strength has been bled from us from a hundred cuts and we are *dying!*"

His last words echoed across the longhouse, leaving a silence so complete one could almost hear the smoke of the dying fire wafting through the air.

When their jarl spoke next, his voice broke with the pain of its utterance. "We are the wounded wolf that limps through a wilderness without prey. If we are to survive, then the Pack will heed my command. No Wolf hunts, no Wolf dies. We rest. We restore. We survive."

Many heads bowed, heeding and hating his words at the same time. But not Helsdottyr.

She stared at the remains of what was once a roaring fire and spoke. "You are right, Father. We *are* dying. And we die a little more every time a peasant from Estvik leaves our hearth without hope."

Anya turned from the dying fire and stalked toward the bearskin door, her heart breaking as she heard her father call her name.

THE COLD CLAWED at Anya's face as soon as she ducked through the bearskin of her father's lodge into the outdoors. It was good. It kept her tears from breaking through her defenses.

Serfs smiled at Anya as she stepped into the common ground between longhouses. They were used to her kindness and bright smile, but she found she could not summon it today. Not when she and the Wolves they served failed them so completely.

She swept her gaze across the majesty of the Wolves' lair, the stone fortress Hammarfall. Fenced by a tall stone wall at the fore, a mountain at the back and ringed with spear throwers round about, the Wolves had little to fear if they remained slouched in their cave. Their stores would see them through any siege, if any of their enemies had had the patience for such a thing.

No, we will be fine.

Her mood grew more bitter as she saw Skald helping the headsman onto the nag he had ridden here. With kind words and wise advice, the Wolf ancient attempted to soothe the wounds inflicted by the merciless jarl of Hammarfall. For once, however, Greymane's rough humor failed in its intent. There was no comfort to be had for the disconsolate man. His disappointment would turn to bitterness on the road, and at the end of his trek home, Estvik would hear nothing but the cowardice of those who claimed fearlessness.

The people of Estvik could not flee, for the winter would kill them as surely as the demons of the forest. They were trapped with nought but a flimsy palisade, better suited for keeping out cattle than invaders, to prevent the insidious death crawling toward them.

He would ride back to a ruin to be, his mind filled with images of the massacre to come. His heart would tear within him from the aching pain of impending loss, unable to prevent his imagination from showing him the faces of his sons and daughters as they died.

The screams of his beloved. The smell of ash on the wind.

The same fate that awaited them all while Wolves remained in their lairs, their fangs rotting and falling out, til at last it reached them, too.

Anya felt a single savage tear trickle down her face, hot against her skin, and she swiped it away angrily. *No. No tears for something not yet lost.*

The princess glared at the broken peasant and squared her shoulders.

If her father deemed the male seed of the Vulfenkind too precious to squander in defense of his people, well, there was no shortage of wombs that could wield bow and spear.

"Ow! What are you doing?"

Anya tried to pull away from Skald's rough hands as he bent her head in front of him and checked her scalp like a chimp picking fleas from a companion. Her horse stamped impatiently, saddle only half-strapped on, as the warrior manhandled her like a child and berated her with his heavy accent.

"Checking for head vounds. I am thinking bull has kicked you in head for you to haf come up vith this plan."

"Ah, enough, Grandfather! I am going. You cannot stop me."

Skald Greymane stepped back from her and eyed her. Literally eyed her. One of his eyes was milky-white, burned beyond hope of healing in the same fire that had roughened his voice. The same fire he had saved her from as a babe.

Usually, a crude leather patch concealed the orb, but when the cantankerous old Wolf wanted to make someone uncomfortable, he took it off.

"You think no, small-fang? Vhen all feeble Skald has to do is raise voice in alarm and your father sends twenty Volves to track you down vithin single mile and drag you veeping back to hearth? This sounds like stopping you to me, but maybe I am old and know no better than an emotional vench."

Anya hesitated. He was right. All the giant story-teller had to do was shout. So she switched strategies.

"No, Grandfather, you know better. You know everything."

Skald pulled back, wagging his finger at her. "Oh, no, you don't. I know vat you are up to. You are fooling no one, tiny princess."

Anya graced him with her bright smile, the one she always used on the ancient warrior because it always worked. Many were intimidated by Greymane's scarred visage, but Anya knew that underneath the leathery skin and ragged tears in his flesh beat the softest heart in the chests of men. She had only to flutter her eyelashes and smile sweetly, and the Wolf would practically twist *himself* around her little finger.

Her arms slowly slipped around him and she lay her cheek on his barrel chest. "But I love you so much…"

"You are vorse than pit viper, I svear!"

Anya pouted, because it also always worked.

Skald raised his eyes to the heavens and slumped, defeated. "They are going to exile me for this, this time. I vill be alone and cold in vilderness because my great heart cannot resist one little girl's sad face."

Anya rested her chin on his chest and grinned at him. He gave up faster every time. "I really do love you, Grandfather."

"Ach. And do not call me grandfather! I am not so old, nor vould I haf permitted brat of mine to go so long vithout good beating!"

She reached for the hanging straps on the saddle, but his next words stopped her. "Also, I am coming."

Anya turned, refusal on her lips, but Skald's weathered face remained resolute. "If you think I am letting favorite granddaughter vander off by herself vith such romantic foolishness fluttering in tiny head, then head vound is vorse than I think. So mighty Skald is coming. Somevone must keep an eye on you, little she-volf."

Anya relented to his brand of affectionate abuse. No Wolf was more faithful to his family than old Skald. She was glad he was coming.

"And vhen ve return, you vill tell the jarl that I resisted mightily against your viles, little Anya."

Anya grinned and affected his accent. "Oh, I vill tell him, old vone."

"Ach! Vhere is respect for gray head!"

THEY RODE OUT AN HOUR LATER, supplied for a week's journey, a fiery warrior princess and an ancient storyteller.

Helsdottyr bore her bow and a full quiver of arrows fletched with hawk feathers. Two more quivers hung by her legs on her saddle, ready to deliver their deadly shafts in case the quiver on her back emptied. On her waist swayed two long daggers the length of her forearm, handles wrapped in leather for grip, the blades curved and viciously sharp. A small hand-axe lay strapped to her thigh, reassuring in its familiarity. It was the only thing she had of the mother she had never known.

Skald Graymane's great hammer hung across his back, its huge steel head weathered and nicked from a lifetime of battle. Standing upright, it reached the height of a grown man, and if swung in anger, was capable of crushing a fully armored knight's bone cage.

As a child, Anya had sat at his feet and heard stories of the Vulfenkind overcoming impossible odds in the defense of right-eousness. Every battle left a scar on the grizzled veteran, every lost friend another line of care in his craggy face. Each story had been told to Wolf cubs as Skald leaned on that mighty warhammer. As fearless Vulfen heroes struck their demonic foes, he would slam the heavy head into the ground, the metal clang of it punctuating his stories and adding brutal realism. Anya would gasp every time, her vivid imagina-tion and Skald's mastery of his craft recreating every battle in perfect detail.

Anya smiled, unable to admit how comforted she was merely by Skald's existence. The man told the stories of Wolves, weaving their deaths into epic tales to inspire their comrades and descendants to further deeds of renown. Yet here he was, venerable, ancient and deserving of a rest by the hearth, choosing instead to suffer the cold in his aging bones to follow his adopted granddaughter in her youthful mistakes and bring her back alive.

Men like this come once an age.

Of course, that did not stop the complaining...

"Ach, vy do you short-tooths not choose to do the stupidness in summertime? Then Skald's bones vould not ache so."

Anya grinned and called over her shoulder, "Close your mouth, grandfather. The hot air will warm you."

"You are like a voman! Vhat does voman know of voes of mighty Skald?"

She laughed, the clear sound of her voice lightening the somberness of the wintry forest.

Skald cracked a smile, his eyes gleaming. "I like you better this vay."

Anya glanced at him. "What do you mean?"

"Laughing like this. It has been long time."

Sadness touched Anya's heart. She turned back to the trail, seeing the tracks of the desultory peasant an hour's ride ahead of them. She sighed.

Before she could sink into depression, Skald's gravelly voice broke into her fugue. "You are too young to lose hope, little Anya."

She snorted bitterly. "Hope, grandfather? What hope do I have? There are how many of us? Fifty? A hundred, with the graybeards and cubs?"

Skald shrugged. "Times are bad. Ve take losses. Such is the vay of a varrior's life."

Her temper flaring, Anya retorted, "But I am 'not a warrior'! I am a *woman.* Do you know what Father told me the other day?"

"I haf feeling I am about to find out…"

Anya spat the words. "He is offering my hand in marriage, grandfather, to the entire Pack! I am going to be bid upon like some cow on market day!"

"Vy do vomens alvays choose cows? Vy not jewelry, or art, or veapons? These are all pretty things that are sold in markets, but they choose *cows.* This is trap, I am thinking…"

Anya ignored his grousing, continuing to vent. "He would have me sold to the likes of Feros, or Fyrss, condemned like a common criminal to grub about the house and sire cowardly children—"

"This is not vhat criminals do…"

"—so that they, too, can hide with their fangless father when the horns blow for heroes and learn to ignore the cries of the defenseless in favor of their own worthless survival because '*every Wolf is worth ten lesser men*' and '*we must think of our own*'! Pah!"

Skald laughed. It was infuriating.

"Breathe, small-fang, *breathe.* Things are not so bad as you say."

Anya scoffed. "And how is that, old one?"

Skald's rumbling voice grew serious, stilling her outbursts. "Because in spite of lashes your childish tongue tears into his soul, your father does right thing by Volves, young one. You think him covard? *You?* A young girl-pup vith clean fangs?"

Anya opened her mouth, but Skald beat his breast, his voice roughening with passion.

"Jarl Fangthane has killed more demons with pinky toe than entire brood of ungrateful Volf-pups! Vhy, vonce I see Heimdall, vounded, vhen all others retreat, consumed vith the murder-fog, take up broken axe and slay minotaur champion to break whole herd. By himself! But now he is jarl, and he must listen to little girl-child call him covard. Skald thinks maybe he has perspective you lack. Skald thinks maybe Anya Helsdottyr should learn to keep teeth together."

Anya's face reddened from the rebuke, and any other man would have endured her famous temper. But not Skald. Her anger drained more quickly than it could build in the face of his disapproval.

Her shoulders slumped. "I cannot help it, grandfather. I don't think; I just feel and act. I am a bad daughter."

Skald grunted in sympathy. "Ach, do not be sad, now, little Anya. You suffer from stupidness of youth. Is normal at your age. Vhy, I remember vhen young Heimdall, not yet jarl, challenge Jarl Brood-slayer and entire council to kill-circle because they say he has to vait vone year before marrying your mother. Vone year! They say he vould never amount to anything, because he could not control temper. Now he is jarl. Is this not so? I say it is so. I vas there."

Anya had to smile. The story was true. It was one of her favorites.

"Besides, lovely small-fang, you are *both* right. Jarl Fangthane is right to keep Volves alive to fight, and Anya is right to remind him of Volves' purpose. I, being as vise as I am, believe answer lies in middle of path. Vait and see. Vhen ve return to Hammarhold, and Jarl Heimdall is done beating little girl-child like dirty hearth-rug, you vill see pride in a father's eyes that only daughter has grown up brave and strong, just like her mother. You vill see. I am never wrong."

Chuckling at the old man's boasts, her heart lighter, Anya replied, "I will not be the only one being beaten, grandfather. You're here, too."

"Ach, who vill beat mighty Skald? I bend them all over knee vhen they vas cubs, I vill do it again. And then be exiled. Forever. Because I get no respect."

Anya's laughter rang through the forest again.

ANYA'S good humor stayed with her all the way up to the first words she heard drip scornfully from an Estvik-born mouth.

"And what business do *Wolves* have here?"

Anya's mouth dropped, and she stared, speechless, at the response of the low-born peasant manning the gate to Estvik's wooden walls. Anger flashed in her suddenly, and she drew in what Skald called "dragon's breath", ready to roast the man alive where he stood.

Quickly, Skald answered, forestalling Anya's savage retaliation before it could start. "Ve vere invited."

The peasant scoffed. "You *were* invited, that is true. But Estvik has other allies now, more reliable than the promises of Wolves. You can run back to your cave."

Skald grinned. It was not a smile.

"I am liking you, and vay that you speak to mighty Skald and volf-jarl's daughter. Vat is name?"

The chubby commoner stood straighter, as if he could approach anything near to the sheer mass of Skald. "I am Bartholomew."

Skald grunted. "You haf cheek, Bartholomew of Estvik."

With the creak of saddle leather, the giant warrior lunged forward and gripped the hapless gate-guard's jaw, jerking him forward close enough to breathe in Skald's snarling breaths. The friendly grandfather disappeared, leaving behind the hulking killer considered so dangerous by his brothers that he was trusted with their death songs. When all others fell to blade or sorcery, Skald Graymane lived, often tearing his foes to pieces in revenge of the fallen. His massive frame was draped in the skins and furs of countless kills, with the fangs and claws of only the mightiest beasts and darkest devils clattering on his armor, bearing terrifying testament to his prowess.

This was the Wolf who dragged the trembling Bartholomew closer to his milky eye, and with teeth still bared, his voice dropping to a leopard's wet growl, said, "If tiny man vants to keep cheek on face for tiny vife to kiss, tiny man vill get out of mighty Skald's vay."

Not surprising, after Skald released the man's skull, the guard scrambled out of their way.

As they urged their horses past the sweating fat man, Anya pouted, "I could have done *that*."

Skald grunted dismissively. "You are princess. I am old man. Better to act like princess than react like peasant."

Anya scowled. "Next time, *you're* the princess and I am the Wolf."

Grinning suddenly, Skald fluffed his long grey hair and fluttered his eyelashes at her. "And but for accident of birth, vat beautiful princess I vould be. I haf missed calling."

His absurdity cracked Anya's anger like a blow from his hammer, and she had to turn away to hide her smile, muttering, "*Stop*, Grandfather. You will scare the children."

Skald threw back his head and roared with abandon, filling the tiny town of Estvik with a warrior's carefree laughter. The peasants scurrying around them shot fearful looks as his mirth broke the tense quiet of the village, and a baby, startled by the loud noise, began wailing in its mother's arms.

Anya looked at Skald pointedly as the mother shushed the child. "See? You scare children."

"It is not Skald's fault that Estvik pups are so sensitive!"

As they rode further into the town, Skald muttered, "Though perhaps qvestion of *vhy* they are so sensitive should be asked."

Anya had to agree.

The inhabitants of Estvik huddled together in tight groups, and when in the cold light of the open, hurried furtively from cover to cover. No one was without a blade of some sort; even the children bore tiny knives, some of them obviously intended for use in the kitchen. Voices were low, hushed, hard to hear above the winter wind.

Skald's one good eye flicked from sight to sight in the village, rapidly assessing the situation they had entered. He took a deep breath and blew it out slowly. "This is not right, little Anya. These men of Estvik do not act like people safe behind valls; they act like...*prey*."

Anya asked quietly, "Grandfather, where *are* their men?"

His eye rested on a single building with a larger chimney than the others, with many horses tied outside of it. "Vhere men go to drown fear."

As always, Skald was right.

Anya stepped inside the tavern and immediately felt lightheaded from the combination of heat, body odor and alcohol that washed over her like a hot, fetid wind. She stepped to the side, nose wrinkling, trying not to gag.

Skald, on the other hand, stepped in and took in a deep breath, eyes closed in bliss. A smile tugged at the scars on his face. "Ah, do you smell that, small-fang? That is smell of *man*."

"Praise to the Almighty that I am a woman, then. I need to leave."

She tried to turn to duck back out through the door, but Skald chuckled and blocked her escape. "Now, now, little princess. You vanted to go on grand adventure and fight for downtrodden. This is vhere downtrodden are. Here, ve find out vhat Estvik fears."

Anya glared at him suspiciously. "You just want a drink, don't you?"

Skald put a hand to his heart. "You vound old man vith baseless accusations."

Anya put her hands on her hips, cocking her head.

"Fine, that is not *all* I vant! I vill only drink to be courteous! Good ale loosens tongues, and men talk more when they are not the vones buying."

Anya snorted. "If you get drunk, I am tying your foot to your horse and dragging you all the way back to Hammarfall."

Skald scowled playfully at her. "You are too young and pretty to nag old man so."

Smiling sweetly, Anya retorted, "Flattery will get you nowhere."

The old man grinned. "Ach, maybe not, but you, on other hand..."

Anya blinked, suddenly wrong-footed. "What?"

Skald's eyes twinkled. "Ve are gathering intel, little Anya. Skald is old volf, and vhile old volf can drink ten Estvik men under table vhile singing tales of glorious victory, I vill not be...appreciated like you."

"*What* are you talking about?"

Still grinning, Skald gestured broadly, taking in her entire figure. "You haf assets. Use them."

"What—no. *No!* How can you say that?"

The wily veteran chuckled and bumped her further into the room, mocking her. "Oh, ho, *now* ve are good girls? *Now* ve cling to virtue? I think not, small-fang. If ve vere good girls, ve vould be vith father, meekly obeying like proper daughters. But no. Ve are not at varm hearth of loving father. Ve are in smelly tavern, having adventure. So go. Have adventure."

Dragon's breath gathered in Anya's lungs, but Skald punctured her building outrage when he shrugged and said, "Or go home and be good girl. Mighty Skald vill be varm either vay."

Anya's lips paled to white, she was pressing them together so hard. Her nails dug into her palms as she clenched her fists in frustration at Skald's impossible choice. Finally, she rolled her eyes, sagged and growled, "Fine!"

"That is vhat Skald think small-fang choose. Relax, little vone. Mighty Skald vill save you if you get in too much trouble. So go. Haf fun vith adventure."

Repressed laughter shaking his giant frame, Skald shoved past her and spread his arms wide, calling loudly, "First man to buy ale to steal chill from old man's bones gets first pass at young beauty!"

The entire tavern shifted as one to behold the beauty in question, and under so many glittering pairs of eyes, Anya Helsdottyr suddenly felt very much like the lamb that had wandered into a wolf pack's lair.

. . .

Out. Let me out.

The thought played over and over again in Anya's mind as yet another pathetic sot sauntered casually by her table and flashed what he obviously believed to be a winsome grin.

No, it would not have been so even if you had teeth, old man...

Her breath hissed out as the dejected drunk slunk away.

Two minutes. She would give that battered old hound two more minutes, and then she was going to drag him out of there by his gnarled ears, poisoning the well on her way out, because *Almighty preserve us if these inbred swine actually manage to breed—*

A tankard appeared in front of her, and Anya closed her eyes, praying for either patience or a plague. Preferably one that killed quickly and targeted only *men.*

When she opened them, she arched an eyebrow and said, "You... are not a man of Estvik."

The man standing across the table in front of her bowed low, his hair gleaming in the flickering firelight. Anya had never seen such beautiful hair, silky and soft, brushed and obviously washed often. Its luscious dark curls cascaded across his shoulders, shining with oils. He was garbed in bright finery, clearly expensive, with puffed sleeves and pants that billowed as he moved. A wide-brimmed hat matching the rich blue shade of his outfit rested in the hand that swept out behind him as he bowed, ostrich feathers swaying at the motion. His other hand rested upon the ornate hilt of a jeweled rapier belted at his hip.

His voice flowed like honey, cultured and refined, every word pronounced to perfection. "Thankfully, I am not, milady."

The man rose, his oh-so-delicate voice massaging her ears with its softness. "If it please you, may I sit? I find most of the company in this...establishment...to be much less preferable to that of a lady's."

She could see why ordinary women would swoon over this man. He was flattering, educated and obviously high-born. He spoke with the honeyed words of a poet. He was doubtless a master at telling the soft lies that every woman craved.

A Wolf's daughter, however, was not an ordinary woman.

Anya crossed her arms and sighed. "Well, you *are* prettier than the others, I will grant you that."

Her careless response, from the looks of it, was not expected. Both of his finely manicured eyebrows shot toward the ceiling, and the man looked rattled for a moment. "Ah, I'm sorry?"

Anya laughed, well aware of her rudeness and wielding it like a fiendish weapon. "Yes, you most certainly are. Is that your actual hair, or have you harvested some poor mop's crown to hide your shiny pate? I would be careful, pretty man, or else the proprietor of this... establishment...might ask for your assistance in cleaning his floor."

She finished with a deliberate smile, enjoying the apoplexy that passed over the nobleman's face.

Something, though, nagged at the back of her mind, reminding her of every single other time she had spoken so rashly. Those times had never ended well.

Apparently, today would be no different.

Chairs scraped on the floor as armored men slammed their suddenly-forgotten drinks onto tables. Daggers rasped and swords loosened in their sheaths. Without looking, Anya became acutely aware of over thirty angry men rising to their feet, and cursed herself silently for somehow missing the fact that they were all wearing the same color of burnt orange.

The injured party smiled at her, but all courtesy had fled his face. It was the smile a snake might display, as it slowly looped its coils around its victim and crushed it to death. "Very amusing, for a savage princess."

Anya blinked, and the fop laughed delightedly.

"Oh, you thought yourself unknown? Delicious. You see, I'm here training a batch of the King's finest and I promised this dear subject of the Crown," he gestured carelessly toward the back of the room, "that my men would stand at his walls in defense of his quaint little hamlet. In return, he promised *you.*"

Her keen eyes knifing through the gloom of the tavern, Anya followed the direction of his hand and spied the jilted headsman of Estvik, sneering at her predicament.

This is the last time I help anyone.

Anya returned her gaze to the nobleman and crossed her arms. "And who are you, to command a regiment of paper men? My old grandfather could easily see this floor clean by mopping it with them."

The dandy bowed again, this time much more sarcastically. "Why, I thought you'd never ask. I am Sir Leopold of the House of Blietzer, loyal captain of the King's Takeshi and master of his recruits."

Anya's heart skipped a beat.

Takeshi. The King's bodyguards. The most lethal warriors in the realm.

But Leopold of House Blietzer had not finished. "These paper men, as you have so blithely put it, are the most recent recruits in training for placement within the Takeshi Order. Among the finest soldiers that have ever held blade, in my august opinion. It is the sacred duty of myself and Sir Kyuza over there to train them, and in the end, select who shall join our exalted ranks."

A shorter Eastern man, his hair pulled back into a warrior's long queue, dressed much more simply than his companion, glided forward. His voice was hard and cold. "Your words bring dishonor on our house, woman. You will make restitution."

Surrounded by a room of men who had had too much to drink and were fairly sweating testosterone, Anya had a fairly decent handle on what form that restitution would take.

Leopold smiled his viperous smile again. "Me, first, gentlemen. The privilege of rank and such."

As a rumble of lecherous amusement rolled through the gathering crowd, one more chair pushed back. Two Takeshi recruits, too busy leering at her to pay attention, were suddenly tossed aside like leaves as a giant mass of a warrior took hold of their shoulders and *heaved*. He shook the floorboards as he stalked toward the Takeshi captain, shoulders set, head low. Anya let out a deep breath of relief as Skald growled, "Vy cannot small-fang ever *keep. Mouth. Shut.*"

Anya rose to her feet and glanced around as he took a stance behind her. There were still thirty of the realm's finest soldiers to deal with, not to mention the two lords. And both her and Skald's weapons were securely stowed on the backs of their horses.

Horses standing outside, prancing on the moon for all the good they were doing them.

She muttered, "I am sorry, Grandfather."

Skald did not take his eyes off of the Takeshi in front of him as he grumbled, "You are alvays sorry. Try smart instead of sorry some time."

The one who called himself Leopold drew his elegant rapier, the well-oiled blade whispering out of its scabbard. The Easterner Kyuza bared an exquisitely worked dagger, worked with beautiful calligraphy and symbols.

Both weapons were obviously expensive, the work of master artisans, paid for by the King's gold and only granted to those capable of ending life with the same artistry displayed by the blades.

Skald suddenly chuckled and spread his hands, turning to grin at the hostility around him. "There is no need for this. Please forgive young girl's stupid mouth. She is not right in head. She does not know vat she says. Vat voman does?"

Anya glared at him, but concentrated on keeping her teeth together. She had done enough damage so far.

Leopold snickered and replied, "No, old one, there is every need for this. You see, I've heard of your barbarian order. If I'm not mistaken, it was the Wolves who used to keep safe the person of the King."

Skald went silent, all cheer vanishing from his face. Of course he knew; he was the lorekeeper of the Pack. He recalled every glory of the Wolves as well as their every shame.

Leopold did not stop, pacing with a finger to his lips. "Yes, it is coming back to me now. You savages actually *lost* that position, did you not? Yes, due to rather, oh, how would one put it delicately, *gross incompetence?*"

Skald exhaled slowly before he spoke. "Speak carefully, King's man, before you mock names of heroes who died far from family and hearth for people not their own."

The fop laughed snidely. *"Heroes? Is that what you savages call them? Your Wolves rode out to kill some ludicrous myth of a demon lord, and got themselves ambushed and killed to a man. Every last one of them! What heroes they must have been!"*

Anya winced at the sound of bone cracking. Still clenching his fists, Skald whispered hoarsely, "Not all."

Lord Kyuza looked up at that and narrowed his eyes thoughtfully, but Leopold continued as if Skald had not spoken. "Thankfully, the King recognized the worthlessness of you beasts and elevated proper men to their station instead."

The rapier swished in the air as the Takeshi captain flourished it, gloating. "Now, I would be remiss in my duties if I did not help you Wolves out of the predicament you put yourselves in."

Kyuza stepped forward, saying, "Captain, perhaps we should—"

Leopold cut him off with an imperious gesture and the warrior fell silent as the captain continued, "Be silent, my lord Kyuza. When we return their lovely princess to them, perhaps she'll bear a half-Takeshi into their dirty hovels and give some decency to their pathetic blood-lines. A sort of headstart on a *comeback*, if you will."

As his soldiers laughed, Skald's face paled with rage, and he trembled as he whispered, "You have no honor, Takeshi."

The old warrior spat the last word like a curse, and Kyuza winced as though he had been struck. But Captain Leopold merely laughed and replied, "Well, not yet, anyway."

The lord raised a hand and his cohort tensed to spring, blades gleaming in the firelight. He smiled again and hissed, "Not until I've taken *hers.*"

The Takeshi's hand twitched forward. His falling hand meant a tidal wave of armed soldiers surging forward to drag them down, to kill Anya's faithful guardian and do much, much worse to her.

But his hand never fell.

Something kept it locked in place.

A mailed fist wrapped around the nobleman's shuddering wrist, squeezing viciously to paralyze the hand. Leopold winced at the ungodly strength of the grip, himself no weakling, but suffering nonetheless. Slowly, the fist turned, forcing him to turn with it, bringing his gaze to meet blazing green eyes glaring through a thicket of tawny blonde hair.

Captain Leopold of the King's Takeshi flinched back as Gideon Halcyon snarled, *"That*...will not be happening."

6

AMBUSH

If the light that is in you be darkness, how great is that darkness...

He stood a good distance outside the village walls, draped in the shadows of frozen trees, listening to the silence of the black. Though Gideon had pressed him to enter the hamlet with him, Ashkelon had declined firmly.

In truth, though he would admit it to no one and barely to himself, Ashkelon considered it very likely that he would not be able to adequately interact with mortal humans. For years beyond counting, they had been nothing but chattel to him, fodder for the armies of righteous princes and infection vectors for his plagues.

To hear them laughing...singing...*sharing...*

The sorcerer grunted in derision.

When has there been anyone to share with?

A little-used, almost forgotten piece of him whispered back.

There was one.

Though he was alone, Ashkelon shook his head slowly.

She was...long ago.

That does not make her less real.

A shift in the silence interrupted the inner dispute and redirected his attention. Only one as attuned to the Dark as Ashkelon could have sensed it.

His head snapped up, and his pale eyes narrowed in search.

The wind changed first, still bone-chilling cold, but now bearing the taste of poison. It blew from the north.

Within moments, Ashkelon could sense the tiny creatures in the earth fleeing, crawling frantically through the soil. Birds took wing above him, eclipsing the light of the moon with their panicked retreat. Even the trees seemed to sense the danger, and with creaking trunks, leaned away from the ghastly menace.

Something unnatural was coming.

This would not ordinarily have irritated Ashkelon to the extent that it did now. But Gideon was still in town.

The boy had been gone almost half an hour, supposedly gathering information from the locals. The epithet applied to this region, the somewhat theatrically-named Spiderlands, had peked Ashkelon's interest weeks before as he had considered where next to take the young man's training.

No doubt, Gideon was bantering with the locals and swilling the local poison, taking solace in common humanity's company for a few brief moments, blissfully unaware of the evil creeping toward the town.

This is why I despise *banter.*

His ancient memories laughed in a lilting feminine voice. *You're just no good at it.*

He sighed in irritation, patience wearing thin with the persistent interruptions of the past. The boy's time was up.

Ashkelon was coming to get him, before the crawling in the forest worsened.

THE GATE GUARD opened his mouth to challenge the dark stranger, but Ashkelon had no wish to speak to anyone, much less a commoner with too many chins and too few active brain cells.

"Be silent."

Darkness coiling within him, he thrust out a hand with fingers curled to a claw. The man's eyes widened as an invisible force jerked him from the ground and hurled him within his gatehouse with the sound of wood breaking. The shadow stalked past, ignoring the hapless guard as he moaned plaintively.

Ashkelon's piercing eyes burned coldly in the night, searching the town for his apprentice. Behind him, the town gate slowly closed, the gatekeeper clearly unwilling to permit additional visitors to the burg.

There.

That must be the tavern. It was the only two-story building in the town, one floor for the vice of drunkenness and one for the sin of fornication. Ashkelon's lip curled in disgust at the indignity of having to enter the establishment.

You are going to pay for this, Gideon.

Ashkelon did not even bother to actually touch the door but blasted it open with a thought.

Let me find you with some peasant wench...

A man crashed into him.

Ashkelon sidestepped sharply and twisted to one side, letting the man's momentum bleed off into another direction. His attacker crashed into the frost-hardened ground and stayed there.

Bright colors, inexpensive make, coarsely woven. Military uniform.

Ashkelon sighed as his analysis led to one inevitable conclusion. He glared into the tavern's door, his cold eyes glinting in the black.

Everywhere that boy goes...

A BOTTLE SMASHED against the lintel of the door, spraying foul-smelling liquid everywhere. Bodies struggled in the low light, milling around a single focal point, where, as Ashkelon expected, Gideon fought like a madman.

The young man never stopped moving, cannoning his fist into one soldier's face to break his teeth while also deflecting a chair from braining him. Gideon snapped his fist back, turning the movement into a blistering elbow that cracked against the chair-wielder's skull and sent him reeling. Completing the turn, Gideon buried his foot into a soldier's stomach and slammed both fists onto the back of his head as the man doubled over.

Rising above him, a giant clad in furs with a silver mane and one eye roared, hefting a screaming soldier completely above his head to hurl him into a knot of rushing attackers, bowling them over and crushing a table to splinters. A ferocious woman fought next to the giant, crunching her foot between a man's legs, gripping his head and throwing him away behind her with one graceful movement.

They were holding their own so far, but weapons were coming into play. Gideon was already bleeding from a number of slashes, but there were several weapon fragments scattered about the floor, giving testament to Gideon's adherence to Ashkelon's teachings.

One thing to be grateful for, I suppose. He's paying attention.

Ashkelon planted his hands on his hips and shouted above the racket of cursing men and cracking pottery, "When you claimed you were gathering information, it did not occur to me that you would be beating it out of the locals."

Somehow, in the midst of choking a man into unconsciousness in the crook of his arm, Gideon managed to look apologetic. "I'll be with you...in a moment...master!"

Ashkelon tilted his head forward, just enough to dodge a thrown plate that ruffled his hair as it sliced through the air to shatter on the wall behind him.

"This is ridiculous."

The one-eyed giant palmed a soldier's face and bashed it back against the wall, shaking the building. His unfortunate victim slumped to the ground, limbs askew and eyes rolling back in his head.

Oblivious to the combatants around him, Ashkelon complained, "You are not even killing anyone."

Gideon deflected a dagger thrust with his vambrace and pinned the weapon to the bar, slamming a hammer fist down onto the wrist holding the blade. The knife-wielder screamed, dropping his weapon, and Gideon backhanded him, sending him sprawling to join all of the other motionless silhouettes on the floor.

"It's not...that kind...of fight!"

Ashkelon pinched the bridge of his nose, closing his eyes wearily as he said, "One must wonder, then, *why* you are fighting at all."

"I will be more than...happy to discuss it with you...*at length*... when I'm done!"

Ashkelon sighed and glanced around. There were still at least twenty men on their feet.

"I am not waiting."

The shadows seemed to suck in towards Ashkelon, collecting at his feet in a black puddle before exploding out, snatching the feet of every man in uniform and jerking them away from Gideon and his two companions to crash into the walls.

Stepping over a groaning swordsman, the Onyx Mage released the shadows, which snapped back to their natural places with a hiss, and fixed his cerulean glare onto his apprentice.

"Now you are done."

ANYA KEPT one eye on the men picking themselves up from the blast of sorcery, and one on the spellcaster himself. She had never seen shadows do that, spell or no.

Skald put his hands on his knees, mouth open and panting for breath. "Boy fights good, no?"

Anya snorted derisively and shrugged. "Pah. He is no Wolf."

Truth be told, she *was* secretly impressed by the blonde fighter. His courage and strength, not to mention surprising skill at arms, had saved them from being overwhelmed in the beginning seconds of the fight.

His green eyes were captivatingly fierce, too, but she was not telling Skald that.

Skald grunted in amusement. "Ach, he is not Volf for sure. Tiny Volf started fight. That vone almost finished it."

"We would have been fine," Anya said far too quickly.

Skald stood upright again, groaning. "Not likely, but then again, Skald is mighty still. Even if bones creak and ache like ship at sea."

He stepped toward the blonde fighter and the dark interloper, and Anya asked, "What are you doing?"

"Saying thank you. It is thing polite people do. You vould not know."

Ashkelon raised his eyebrow. "You attacked the captain of thirty men…over a woman?"

The man had said one sentence, and Gideon felt the narrative slipping out of his control.

He resented that.

"They were threatening her. I intervened."

Ashkelon took a small step to look pointedly past Gideon. "You *do* see that there is a giant protecting her?"

Gideon closed his eyes and let his head fall back in frustration. "Yes, master."

"So then, I suppose, I am sure the *attractiveness* of the aggrieved party had no bearing on your decision to intervene."

Gideon gritted his teeth. "No, master, I did not even notice."

A booming voice with a thick accent spoke behind them. "Vat vas that?"

Ashkelon answered without hesitating. "My apprentice was saying that your ward was not attractive enough to earn his notice."

As Gideon's mouth dropped, the one-eyed warrior roared in laughter, beckoning behind him and gasping, "Small-fang! You hear this? Boy is saying you are *ugly*!"

Gideon turned in time to be impaled with the daggers stabbing out of the young woman's dark eyes as she stalked forward.

"That's…not what I said," he offered lamely.

Still chuckling, the giant clapped him on the shoulder, staggering him. "All is vell, boy who is brave. I am mighty Skald, and I say it is honorable man indeed who vill fight Takeshi varrior—" at this his laugh threatened to overcome his words, "—for so *ugly* a voman!"

The old man called Skald collapsed into a chair, his mighty frame shaking with fresh gales of laughter as Gideon was impaled. Again.

As the battered warrior wiped tears of mirth away from his eye, Ashkelon glanced around them, seeing the wobbly soldiers he had cast away beginning to climb back to their feet, pulling weapons close and eyeing them murderously. He sighed.

"Did you not tell me that you were a better choice to gather information?"

Gideon closed his eyes. He felt suddenly tired.

"Yes, master."

"Why did you tell me that?"

Resigned to his fate, Gideon answered, "Because I thought the people would react...badly...to you."

Ashkelon made a show of looking around the room and spread his arms expansively.

"Well done, apprentice, you have certainly gained their trust. I am sure we will learn everything we want to know, now that a proper rapport has been established."

Gideon sighed, also seeing the rising platoon, and answered honestly, "I'm not sorry. It was the honorable thing to do."

"When you stand amidst the mass graves of thousands, ask the shades, as I did, what they think of honor," Ashkelon groused. "Their answers might surprise you."

The Takeshi captain, hair mussed and askew, pointed his rapier a trifle uncertainly at Gideon, and the young man cracked his neck as he answered, "I'll be sure to do that, master."

Ashkelon shook his head at Gideon's obstinacy and growled, "You have no time for this."

Gideon glanced at him, furrowing his brow. "What are you talking about? I have plenty of time."

"There are heroic deeds elsewhere."

Scoffing incredulously, Gideon gestured around him. "There are thirty angry men with swords who want to rape or murder us, and not necessarily in that order. What else could be more heroic than this?"

"Perhaps repelling the cult army currently besieging the city."

Gideon blinked at Ashkelon's nonchalant declaration. "What, *now?*"

Ashkelon tilted his head, considering before he answered, "It might as well be."

THE TOWN of Estvik was not large, really a collection of ten or fifteen structures clustered around a central fountain and ringed by a stout palisade built of logs. A single gate, locked and kept by a somewhat nervous-looking guard, allowed access in or out.

All of this meant that the little town was reasonably defensible, especially with a company of the King's men manning the walls.

Unfortunately, the King's men were not on the walls. They were resolving unfinished business.

Imperious scorn dripped from Captain Leopold's voice. "No, it won't be that easy for you, I'm afraid. You're not running off into the woods like a thief while the King's Takeshi scramble about in response to an attack that seems...rather *invisible*, actually. There is honor to be satisfied, after all."

Gideon fumed as the surrounding soldiers laughed, the point of the nobleman's rapier held under his chin. "You want to duel *now?*"

Leopold squinted and put his free hand to his cheek. "Oh, dear, I do apologize for any lack of clarity."

Lord Kyuza stepped to his captain's side and muttered, "There is something in the forest. Perhaps we should deploy—"

A protracted yawn interrupted him. "Nonsense, my lord Kyuza, this won't take long. And it will be good for the recruits to see how a Takeshi protects his honor."

The fop turned back to Gideon and raised an eyebrow. "You're going to need a *blade*, I'm afraid."

Do as he says.

Gideon glanced over at Ashkelon, and muttered through gritted teeth, "I thought we didn't have time."

Be swift.

Looking back at Leopold, Gideon nodded once, curtly.

"Ah, see here, Lord Kyuza? You can get some culture out of these country swains as long as you apply suitable motivation."

The rapier dropped, and Gideon pressed his lips together in frustration as he moved toward his sword, hung on a rack outside the tavern.

The barbarically-dressed pair were next to their horses, strapping on weapons and armor.

Skald grinned at him. "Fighting Takeshi?"

Gideon did not look at him, but pulled his sword out of the rack. "Yes."

The elderly giant glanced at his charge. "Out of curiosity, do you know vhat Takeshi is?"

Gideon grabbed his helmet and slipped it over his head. "No."

The woman fixed him with a glare of pure venom, then tossed her hand in the air. "Pah!"

She stormed toward the gatehouse, slinging a bow onto her back, her hair tossing angrily behind her.

Gideon watched her go through the T-shaped slit of his visor. "What did I say this time?"

Chuckling, the one-eyed giant slapped a hand on his shoulder. "Vat does man ever need to say? She is angry because she is voman, and so even she does not know vhy."

Skald glanced over at the Takeshi champion, slicing the air with his rapier with lightning-fast stabs and parries in a stunning display of skill. "Maybe she is sad that you die so young."

Testing the edge of his humble blade with his thumb, Gideon sighed and muttered, "It would not be the first time."

Skald looked back at him, appraising him with his single eye. "I hear story in such a statement, and old Skald loves stories, especially of underdog. Is veakness. Tell me, vat is under-pup's name?"

Gideon smiled. *Under-pup.*

"Just Gideon."

"Ha! You give much to old tale-veaver to vork vith, just-Gideon. I choose deed-name for you, that vhen I sing of you and your courage, you may be known among the Vulfenkind by hero's name."

The great man held out his hand, and as Gideon reached out to shake, clasped it in a warrior's grip, wrist to wrist.

"Now go. Make dead champions jealous of glorious end."

Unable to stop smiling at the old man's dark humor, Gideon returned it with interest. "You first, old one."

SKALD BROKE the grip with a bark of laughter and watched the young man who called himself just-Gideon stride back to the duelists' circle. Shaking his head and grinning still, he shouldered his mighty hammer and crossed the village square over to Anya, who stood waiting impatiently by the gate, testing her bow string.

Without looking at him, Anya stated, "You let him fight."

It was not a question. Skald cracked his neck before he answered it. "Is not mine to let. Choice belongs to each man."

She tugged her string back, a trifle angrily, Skald thought. "The Takeshi will kill him."

"Body is not in grave yet, small-fang."

Anya glared at him. "No one can beat a Takeshi, grandfather. Not in single combat."

Skald shrugged. "And so it vas said of demons, before Vulfen come. Blonde cub may surprise you. It vill be as God vills."

Her gaze fell upon the young fighter in the battered armor, watching him roll his shoulders and rotate his wrists to loosen up, then upon the captain of the legendary Takeshi. Anya shook her head slowly. "God does not will this."

The old man grunted. "That is as may be."

A spark of wickedness lit Skald's eyes, and he leaned in close to Anya, his gravelly voice lowered to a wicked whisper. "But is nice to look at, eh?"

Anya broke her stare with unseemly haste and shoved Skald back as he chuckled. "Get on the wall, Grandfather. You match-make like an old woman."

She slung herself onto the scaffold set just under the top of the wall. Still cackling, Skald trudged up the stairs with his heavy tread. "Oh, vhy so defensive, small-fang, eh?"

"I'm not being defensive!"

GIDEON SQUARED his stance and inclined his head toward the garish swordsman. "I'm ready."

Smirking, Leopold replied, "Oh, I'm sure you are. Lord Kyuza, if you would consent to officiate?"

The easterner stepped forward, a single long curved sword hanging on his back and a shorter matched dagger at his hip. His beard was black, waxed to a fine point just past his chin but not long enough to give purchase should combat descend to grappling. His eyes were dark and serious, his voice the same.

"These are the rules. The insulted party has issued challenge, and by Takeshi law, the challenge can only be ended by the challenger."

Gideon stared at him. "We duel until he says different?"

Kyuza's face might have been set in stone. "Captain Leopold has fought in over fifty affairs of honor. All of them have ended in death."

Gideon took in a deep breath and let it out slowly. "Wonderful."

"I only tell you this so that you know there will be no mercy, and that you will not disgrace yourself with a coward's hope as you meet your fate."

Gideon looked him in the eye, one eyebrow climbing. "Why do you care?"

The small Takeshi bowed slightly at the waist. "Not all Takeshi have forsaken honor, young man. I would have you die with yours."

Turning on his heel, Lord Kyuza stepped to the outer rim of the dueling circle. His expression betrayed nothing.

Gideon sighed and spread his hands. "Has anyone considered that I might not die?" he complained.

CAPTAIN LEOPOLD BLIETZER of the Takeshi Order knew exactly what he was: a beautiful killer.

His stance was balanced to perfection, his weight distributed evenly, counter-balancing the elegant rapier held *en garde*. His height and long limbs granted him a reach several inches beyond most men's. His build was slight, yet strong; the perfect balance of muscle to mass.

The lustrous locks that usually fell down his shoulders and back were wholly natural, not an artificial affectation as worn by many of the Royal Court. In Leopold's mind, his hair served as a tangible reminder of his innate superiority, a right granted by birth. Even now, tied back to prevent obscuring his vision, the weight of his hair pressed on his back pleasingly, a token of his station.

As far as skill was concerned, House Blietzer had provided only the finest of dueling instructors and tactical tutors for their only heir. Had this backwards savage studied under the likes of Chatelaine? Montague? Van der Strout? The tutelage of dozens of grand masters and dueling champions fairly sang from Leopold's every movement, their knowledge distilled and perfected to create a single luminous being with a lashing tongue of silver.

Leopold's sword was the envy of emperors, an ancient rapier set with priceless gems and gilded with white gold. The crest of House Blietzer had been sculpted into the looping swirls that protected his sword-hand. The blade itself was folded royal steel, forged by the King's own smiths and presented as a gift to his most loyal and valued retainers. It was a reminder that House Blietzer's continued favor in the eyes of the King depended upon its ability to end his enemies.

His muscles contracted sinuously as he paced the outer rim of the dueling circle, coiling languorously like pythons around his bones, ready to explode with violence. Leopold's physical perfection had drawn remark from the King himself, who had elevated him to the rank of captain of the Takeshi merely to delight in Leopold's artisan approach to killing.

In short, the scion of House Blietzer was captain of the Takeshi because he could entertain the Royal Court.

No other man could murder with such elegance. Such poise. Such style.

Leopold sunk further into his stance, sighing sensuously as his awareness heightened to the needs of personal combat. *This* was the only reason to be alive.

Not breaking his gaze from the peasant's startling green eyes, the King's sanctioned killer called out confidently, "Place your bets, gentlemen. We're playing for seconds and strokes, per usual."

SKALD SHOOK HIS HEAD GRIMLY. "Is foolish to believe fight is von before blades clash."

Next to him, Helsdottyr scowled. "What is he doing, chopping wood?"

Looking to the object of her complaint, which, no surprise to an old man, happened to be the young man named Gideon again, Skald grimaced. "Ach, come on, lad! Vhen I vas sticking out *neck* for you?"

GIDEON STOOD STIFF AS A BOARD, gripping his simple iron blade as tightly as he could to drive all blood from his knuckles. His knees were hardly bent at all, in sharp contrast to his opponent's coiled stance. Within the confines of his helmet, his eyes tracked Leopold's blade, following the flashes of light, rather than the set of the shoulders and hips that governed movement.

In short, he was doing everything wrong.

A trickle of sweat tracked down his spine.

Hold.

ASHKELON NARROWED his eyes as the dandy circled the obviously petrified Gideon. Suddenly, a lunge faster than any serpent and a flash of silver, and Gideon recoiled, covering his eyes, stumbling backward and hacking with his sword at empty air.

Snickers of contempt erupted from the circle, and a satisfied sneer twisted the Takeshi's face as Gideon over-reacted and attacked, chopping stiffly with his blade and leaving openings in his defense a chariot could drive through.

The skin around his eyes creased as Ashkelon gave the tiniest of smiles.

"*WHY ARE YOU DOING THAT?*" Anya fairly bellowed as the young man retreated from a simple stab, flailing with his sword.

His single eye squinting with suspicion, Skald watched as Gideon stumbled over a stone into the circle of mocking men and was promptly shoved back toward the Takeshi.

"He's toying with him, Grandfather!"

Something clicked in Skald's mind, and the old man inhaled deeply as comprehension swelled. "Yes, small-fang. Yes, he is."

GIDEON WAS SWEATING HARDER NOW, just barely deflecting the rapier flickering toward him. Any moment now, the nobleman was going to get tired of playing with him and end it.

Hold.

Just a little longer.

KILLING with theatrical flair was what Leopold did best. Every attack that the champion launched provoked a fresh wave of laughter from his admittedly sycophantic coterie as the peasant heaved his sword about him in a panic.

He took to hooting like a monkey with every stab, his eyebrows raised and his expression one of idiotic wonder. This humiliation evoked further laughter from the recruits, but nothing from the commoner but gasps for breath.

Disappointing, really, and tiresome. The boy's performance in the tavern had led him to expect more.

Out of the corner of his eye, Leopold could see Lord Kyuza's disapproval in the cast of his face, the set of his stance.

Watch carefully, Kyuza. This is why I am Captain and you my hanger-on.

The switch from humiliation to execution happened in the time it takes for an eye to blink, and the Takeshi's sword sped to take another life.

GIDEON SENSED the change in his opponent, the altering of his intent, the lethality of his purpose.

Now.

Time froze as the lessons of Ashkelon hissed through his mind.

Sin is the gateway of death, and deception the gatekeeper.

If you must kill, deceive. If your opponent is inferior to you, feign weakness. If superior, conceal your strength.

Remember that the first sin was the lie.

The second was murder.

HE WAS NOT THERE.

Leopold's sword, usually unerring in its aim, pierced empty air as his opponent twisted to the side like a snake. A vambrace of humble make slapped his rapier to the side. Acting on instinct, he bent his elbow for an automatic return strike, but the peasant closed the distance, his palm slamming into the back of his elbow and over-balancing Leopold forward.

Then the peasant's fist crushed Leopold's jaw. He actually lifted off of the ground with the blow, stars exploding behind his eyes. He felt his perfect jawline shatter under the impact, and he pitched backward, shards of teeth spewing from his bleeding mouth.

All trace of the bumbling farmhand had disappeared, and Leopold looked up, his vision hazed by pain and concussion to see the emotionless faceplate of the warrior who had bested him.

The warrior not breathing hard anymore.

He tried to get up, but sharp metal tugged at his neck, and the captain froze as he felt his skin part under its gentle kiss.

Gideon's voice was cold as winter's claws. "You should yield."

The sword pressed further, drawing blood.

Dropping his gaze, Captain Leopold, unparalleled swordsman, heir of House Blietzer and Master of Recruits of the vaunted Takeshi, did the hardest thing he had ever done.

He *submitted.*

HER JAW FELL open and Anya gaped unabashedly like a schoolgirl.

"How did he do that?"

Skald's eyebrows had climbed to his hair line, and an incredulous laugh shook his mighty frame.

"Hyva! I tell you this! Old Skald is alvays right!"

He threw back his head and howled into the night sky, his breath leaving his body in an aggressive roar of triumph that shook the night with its ferocity.

HIS HEART still pounding hard in his chest, Gideon removed his adopted father's sword from Leopold's neck and spoke to the now-silent circle of Takeshi soldier-recruits. "Honor has been satisfied. Deploy your men on the walls and prepare to defend the town."

He hoped his voice sounded steady.

Lord Kyuza, eyes glinting with newfound respect but otherwise expressionless, quickly stepped around Gideon and assisted his captain as the man clambered to his feet, unable to speak for the pain in his fractured jaw. The Easterner took Leopold's arm across his shoulders, supporting the man's weight. The nobleman's sword remained firmly clasped in his other hand.

Glancing at his master before speaking, Kyuza said solemnly, "It will be done. The Takeshi will fight."

Gideon nodded, acknowledging the warrior's promise, and turned away to look at Ashkelon.

Exposing his back.

· · ·

LEOPOLD stiffened imperceptibly as the young man arrogantly turned his back to his vanquished enemy.

You baseborn mongrel, I will teach you to scorn a Blietzer!

Leopold planted his free hand on Kyuza's face, shoved the smaller Takeshi warrior away and whipped his blade back and up to eye level. The point hovered in the air for less than a second as Leopold visualized the path of the sword. The rapier would drop slightly and then arc back up, slipping into the junction between skull and spine to carve into the brainstem.

Death would be immediate.

Leopold's lip curled into a contemptuous sneer as he began to step forward to drive his blade into Gideon's brain and execute the most satisfying murder of his career.

STUPID, stupid, stupid! Gideon's mind railed at him.

It was too late to turn, defend, dodge or even cry out. Only the barest beginning of an anticipatory wince creased his eyes, the slightest tensing of his shoulders as Gideon started to brace for the strike.

Yet the expected blow never fell.

In the years to follow, no matter how many times Gideon recounted the death of the Takeshi captain, his mouth would dry and an involuntary shudder would rack his body.

Leopold's foot would not move. Some kind of vise clamped it in place. Involuntarily, he strained to lift it forward and when it still refused to move, he looked down.

It might have been more merciful had the nobleman *not* done so.

A spider's head the size of a large melon protruded from the ground, trying to envelop Leopold's foot with its drooling maw, mandibles clenching and unclenching spasmodically around its prize as it adjusted its crushing grip. Beady black eyes gleamed hungrily from under a forest of short bristly hairs, and it made a sound like a man gagging as it worked the trapped limb farther into its distended gullet.

Leopold looked up into Gideon's shocked eyes, inhaled deeply and screamed.

THE DOOMED man's shriek broke the paralysis gripping the scene.

Gideon threw himself backward as the earth exploded upward around the stricken Takeshi and monstrous segmented limbs ripped themselves from the ground to wrap around their prey. Leopold had time for one more scream of anguish before the gargantuan arachnid jerked him underground.

Ashkelon's voice whispered furiously in Gideon's mind. *GET OFF THE GROUND!*

Gideon did not have to be told twice. The warrior sprang to his feet, felt the earth shift beneath him, took two bounding steps forward and hurled himself with the strength borne of fear toward the boarded porch of the tavern.

Cold dirt showered him as another clutch of legs erupted from the ground where he had lain not seconds before. The grossly swollen head of another spider eyed him and hissed in inhuman fury at his escape from its ambush.

Others were not so fortunate. Peasants screamed in terror as monsters burst from beneath their feet and dragged them into holes like gaping mouths in the land. Their sobbing cries were only muffled when they vanished beneath the earth.

One soldier-recruit was fast enough to throw himself away from his would-be devourer, but the spider simply crawled further out of the ground and coiled its body, legs shaking like tightly-wound springs. Faster than sight, it lunged forward to latch its mandibles into the man's thigh with a sickening crunch. It jerked back, the spider heaving its shrieking prey back toward the rent that had issued it, its victim screaming and gouging furrows in the torn earth as he was dragged away.

He managed to halt his progress for a moment when his bloody fingers gripped a root firmly anchored in the ground. It did him no good as the spider crouched and cracked his body like a whip, ripping his fingers free of the root and hauling him weeping into the damp darkness.

Apprentice.

Gideon could not move. *How do I kill that it's not possible it's eating him God please I don't want to die not like that—*

Gideon!

Flinching from the force of the sorcerer's will, Gideon whipped around to see Ashkelon step onto the killing ground, locking eyes with his apprentice.

Like this.

The earth exploded at his feet. With a casualness belied by his speed, Ashkelon sidestepped and swept Acherlith out of its sheath to shear through the forest of limbs that reached for him, reducing the clutching legs to a collection of slime-spewing stumps.

Still halfway out of the ground, it was the spider's turn to scream as its claws clattered down around it. Without even looking at the beast, Ashkelon whirled gracefully and slashed downwards, cleaving the monstrosity's head perfectly down the center. Ashkelon completed his turn to end facing his apprentice, just as the butchered creature toppled slowly behind him, stumps spasming and trying to curl beneath its body.

He locked eyes with Gideon again, and inclined his head a fraction.

They die as all creatures do.

Gideon stared at Ashkelon for a second, standing alone in the midst of monsters, beckoning him to come.

Trust me, Gideon. You can kill spiders.

Irrational fear had hold on Gideon's limbs. That, in the end, drove him to reach for his shield.

Rising slowly, Gideon stepped onto the torn ground, muttering breathlessly, "I can kill spiders."

Yes. You can.

.   .   .

ANYA WHIPPED another arrow out of her quiver as she planted her foot onto the head of the monster trying to climb up to her. Dodging a spear-like limb of hardened chitin, Helsdottyr tried to kick the spider free, but its claws were dug into the wood of the scaffolding.

Her temper flared hot at its resistance, and with her typical forethought, Anya yelled in fury as she leapt full-on to the beast, catapulting them both off of the wall. As the spider hit the ground, her leather-clad knee smashed into its mouth, breaking one of its mouthclaws off with a spray of white ichor.

Cursing herself for an impetuous fool, Anya rolled forward, narrowly evading the creature's legs as they tried to trap her onto its body in a ghastly embrace. She exited her roll with bowstring already drawn to her ear and put first one arrow, then another into the thrashing spider she had just escaped. Then another.

As she poured one arrow after another into the dying creature, her mind chanted, *I hate these things I hate these things I hate—*

An ear-splitting screech sounded from behind her, and Anya spun to see another spider reeling from the hammer strike that had saved her. Skald ducked several stabbing limbs and swung his mighty hammer in an arc from low to high, the iron-banded steel connecting with the creature's chin in a devastating uppercut. The powerful blow lifted the spider completely off the ground, upending it and exposing its grotesque underbelly.

With a savage roar, Skald turned once more and corrected his hammer's arc into a lateral swing, punching the hammerhead completely through the monster's exoskeleton and crushing it against the log wall of the stockade. The spider practically detonated against the wall from the force of the titanic blow, drenching the old Wolf in dripping slime. Skald reeled in disgust, spitting.

"Ach, it is in mouth! I am blaming you, small-fang, for jumping off perfectly good vall like happy goat!"

Anya flashed a grin as Skald complained, even as she scanned the scene of the battle.

There were perhaps eight spiders left alive, and the shock of their attack had passed. The Takeshi soldier-recruits had evacuated the center of the town, climbing to the walls to escape the treacherous ground. Anya could see Lord Kyuza shouting at his men, reforming their discipline even as he helped to pull men up to the walls.

Two spiders prowled below the men they hunted, hissing and spitting, but long spears and angry shouts kept them at bay. There would be no feeding there.

Over a dozen holes pocked the surface of the ground in Estvik. They were large; large enough to accommodate the bulk of the monsters who burst forth from them.

Plenty large enough for the cultist brotherhood that even now began to boil forth from the depths.

"Grandfather?"

Skald hawked another glob next to him once more in revulsion. "Vhat?"

"I think we should get back on the wall...."

His one eye glared at the invaders, and a single word passed his lips like a curse.

"Venans."

This time, Skald spat in sheer revulsion, as though the name itself were as repulsive as the spider slime, and Anya understood why.

The fanatics clambering out of the ground were traitors to their own kind, slaves to dark idols. They drugged themselves into stupors, lay down in hallucinogenic fogs and injected themselves with exotic venom, seeking deeper connection to the spiders they worshipped. Their skin was tinged the yellow-green of disease from the poison in their systems, their eyes wild with insanity and their faces sticky with drying mucus.

The Venan cultists bore scraps of armor and a motley array of weapons, scavenged from those they managed to waylay and kidnap or from those fallen warriors the spiders dragged back to their dens. They attacked with wild screams and maniacal laughter, always stabbing like lunatics, seeking to overwhelm their prey with the strength born of madness.

Venans were not warriors. They were cowards, murderers, babystealers, cannibals and oath-breakers. They stole women from their houses as men worked the fields, and days later, the search parties would find their mutilated corpses in the forest, if they found them at all.

His voice deadly grim, Skald growled, "Onto vall vith you, happy goat."

Anya had time to blink before the giant lifted her up and bodily hurled her onto the ledge she had so recently abandoned. Her stomach impacted the edge of the platform and she gasped as the breath exploded from her lungs.

Skald shook his grey mane, spread his feet and settled into his stance, brandishing his mighty hammer with a feral gleam in his single eye. One of the Venan invaders noticed the veteran warrior by the gate, raised his weapon and shouted. Ten of his fellows turned at his call, the firelight shining from the poison on their blades.

The corner of Skald's mouth turned up.

Anya swung her legs up onto the platform and shouted down, "Grandfather, quickly!"

Without looking at her, the Wolves' bard replied, "And let small-fang's heart-throb take all the fun?"

Anya's brow creased.

What is he...?

She saw.

UNITY.

Back-to-back, the soldier and the sorcerer faced their foes. Half a dozen spiders the size of horses crouched and hissed around the two figures, one clad in beaten iron and the other draped in shadow. At least three dozen murderers and rapists cackled madly at the sight of the imminent feast of their salivating gods. More scrabbled from the holes torn in the ground.

Gideon flexed his arm inside the grip of his shield. His eyes darted amongst the horde with concern. He had no idea how they were going to kill all of these creatures.

Ashkelon spoke first, his arms crossed over his darkmail breastplate as if there weren't a legion of foes two arm-lengths away. "Apprentice?"

His face hidden by the T-shaped visor of his helmet, Gideon turned his head a fraction to acknowledge. "Master."

The young warrior had no idea what Ashkelon would say. Probably something about the music of death and how Gideon should relax so he could *"dance to the song of slaughter"*, or some soliloquy on tactics and vulnerabilities...

Ashkelon gestured to the wall, beyond the mass of writhing limbs and drooling pagans. "There."

Gideon obeyed. Standing on the wall, safe from the treachery of the ground, villager and Takeshi alike looked down on them.

Only the two of them remained on the ground.

Ashkelon tapped the packed dirt with his foot. "Never allow it to pass from your memory that this is ours. These fiends," he encompassed the clutch of horrors with a single sweep of his arm, "would take that from you. They cannot abide the memory that Man was given the dominion of the earth over them."

Gideon nodded, the slightest tilt of his head. He exhaled slowly, the truth of Ashkelon's words setting his blood afire.

His eyes locked back onto the nearest spider in front of him. It was a monstrous creature, its black carapace knotted with chitin growth and streaked with yellow slashes on its bulbous abdomen. Acid drooled from its mouth with a sibilant hiss, and its eye clusters gleamed with awful hunger.

Gideon sank to one knee, and set his sword to lean against his shoulder guard. His eyes never left the unthinking hate of the abomination before him as he took a handful of the packed earth. The dirt clung to his gauntlet, and a small stone scraped against the mail. He lifted it to his nose and inhaled deeply, smelling the richness of the land given to the children of Men.

The spider shrieked at him in unthinking fury.

Ashkelon drew Acherlith from its sheath, drowning out the cacophony of the living with choirs of the dead. "We alone stand on the ground granted to us by birthright. Whether Light or Dark, this place is ours, and not the feeding ground of a failed angel's pets."

A low growl escaped Gideon's helm as he stood, brandishing the Halcyon blade. The spider snarled back.

"You alone stand of the children of Light on this patch of ground, deeded to Man at the dawn of time. As others watch, you fight to keep what is yours."

Sacred earth crunched in Gideon's grip as he clenched his sword.

"Today, my student, you stand as a hero."

As the first spider leapt, Gideon could not help but grin under his helmet.

He grinned like a fool.

7

CONSORT

The spider marked black and yellow had no name, nor any kind of personality. It had hunted men for over a century, dragging them into burrows to drain them dry of their fluids and take the bounty back to its ravenous kin.

It had killed dozens of men, many that were equipped like the one standing before it. Their weapons never mattered. Every man flinched back from it when it lunged at them.

That was why, for the first time in its existence, it felt shock when this one broke its face.

GIDEON'S SHIELD crushed into the monster's mandibles and drove it backwards, its legs scrabbling for purchase against the force of his charge. He powered into it, teeth clenched, as his sword swept out to chop through another monster's foreleg and sever the claw.

Hemorrhaging pus and ichor from its broken mouth, the recipient of his first strike screamed and lunged, its fat body heaving against his shield. A wave of foul reek washed over him, gagging him with its noxious odor. Gideon slammed his shoulder into his shield and his feet churned a furrow into the soft dirt as he pushed back against the beast's frenzied strength. Legs, covered in fine hairs and topped with twin tines, lashed around the edges of his shield, trying to get at the meat behind the metal. With a roar, he lifted his sword and hacked down. The weapon sank into the creature's body, splitting it open and releasing the rancid stench of its intestines like a furnace blasting heat.

Two more, from the sides. Gideon jerked his sword from the spider's heaving thorax, parried their spearing legs with both sword and shield, and stomped onto the wounded spider's head. It cracked like an egg under his boot, splattering ichor out onto the cold earth.

Grimacing at the slime soaking his foot, Gideon ducked a clutch of limbs scything toward his neck and swung his sword at the attacking monster. The spider lurched backward to avoid the blade, but Ashkelon hit it with a fistful of fire and blasted its front half into a cloud of burning shrapnel.

Almighty, I'm tired.

As dozens of screaming cultists hurled themselves at him, Gideon snarled in denial and fought. Crude picks, dull axes and stabbing limbs savaged his armor as he turned killing blows into glancing misses. His arms and back burned from every exertion, pouring rivers of of exhaustion into his muscles, but he did not relent.

Hefting his shield to shoulder level, he surged forward and punched the rim into a charging Venan's mouth. Teeth exploded from the wretch's face as he flipped over from the power of the blow.

Disaster, always waiting in the wings, chose that moment to strike. One of the arm-straps of Gideon's shield, sliced halfway through from the spider's claws, broke loose from the force of the hit. Dropping his shoulder instinctively to catch the unbalanced weapon, Gideon felt his world shatter as a blistering impact slammed into his head through his fallen guard.

Dazed and reeling, Gideon stumbled back as his attacker, an ebony brute wielding the femur of some sort of saurian, roared in triumph and swung again. The titanic blow caught his cheekguard, already deformed from the earlier impact, and tore it off along with half of his helmet. A rusted pick slammed into his breastplate, driving the wind out of him, and a trio of howling cannibals bowled him over into the dirt, scrabbling for his neck and eyes with ragged fingernails.

Gideon tried to fend them off, but the broken shield hampered his left arm. He flailed with his sword, but the Venans pounced on his arms to pin them down, hissing and laughing to one another in their foul tongue.

One beckoned toward something he could not see, and Gideon's gut wrenched as something clamped onto his foot with hot, wet breath.

Searing light burned his vision, and heat flooded his lungs as the air shrieked like a boiling tea kettle. The pressure on his foot vanished, and Gideon's eyes sprang wide at the sight of a shadow blacker than black lifting a spider off of the ground with spiraling strands of violet lightning. The monster convulsed as the jagged threads of energy snapped and cracked through its insides.

Its worshippers lunged for him. Ashkelon dropped his hand and the creature smashed into the ground, steam seeping from the edges of its exoskeleton. With peerless grace, the sorcerer weaved between the clumsy strikes of the Venans, first the bone-club, then a chipped obsidian axe. His black blade lashed out to open the axe-wielder's neck to the spine even as he stepped into the ebony giant's guard. As the cannibal reeled, Ashkelon clamped his palm onto his tattooed forehead. His eyes flashed cyan, and with a screeching crack, he blasted the back of the Venan's skull clean off, blinding his companions with the contents of his brainpan.

Ashkelon's eyes were like burning sapphires set above a mask of shadow as he regarded Gideon's struggle, and a dark laugh erupted from his lips.

Gideon butted one of his attackers back with the scraps of his helmet and snarled, "What is so funny?"

"Forgive me. I am ever entertained when a paragon of virtue dies on his back in the mud with petty scum rummaging through his pockets."

As the mage's laugh rose above the battleground, Gideon's eyes narrowed.

He arched his back violently and scissored his legs, wrenching his limbs free of his captors. The first Venan collapsed as Gideon's sword punched into his heart, the second following him after Gideon rammed his gauntleted fist into his windpipe. The last tried to run, but Gideon hooked his ankle with one leg, kicked out the back of his knee with the other and rolled onto the screaming murderer's back as he fell. The cannibal died with eight inches of iron in his spine.

Gideon rose to his feet, jerking his sword out of the Venan's corpse, and glared at Ashkelon. "Sorry to spoil the show."

Ashkelon grinned at him with something approaching amiability. "Someday, perhaps."

Turning from his master, Gideon spent a single second evaluating the battle. The Venans had ceased springing from the spider tunnels, but there were still dozens of them within Estvik, embattled with the Takeshi and the town's inhabitants.

A sudden screeching howl cut through the screams and the clamor of metal crashing against metal. Gideon grimaced against the grating shriek, feeling the bones of his skull shudder at the sound. For a breath, the combat halted, the defenders unsure of what the ungodly cry portended.

As one, the Venans broke away from their individual battles and flooded in one direction, directly toward the still-closed gate of Estvik, where a single aged Wolf leaned on his hammer.

"PAH! Come, you filthy dogs. Mighty Skald has strength enough for you all!"

Skald roared as he whipped the heavy head of his warhammer about him and slammed another clutch of Venans aside in a welter of poisoned blood and breaking bone. His gray mane plastered to his skull with sweat, and every swing burned more than the last, but years of battle had seasoned the Wolf like gnarled oak. The hundredth enemy flew back with as much force as had the first, as would the thousandth.

"And so you vil all die!"

The old warrior twisted and brought his hammer down, smashing a cultist to organic ruin. The cannibal's brothers launched forward, knowing that Skald could not get the hammer's head aloft in time.

Skald growled and punched the haft of his warhammer forward, the six-foot iron shaft easily turning the Venans' eager blows aside. Expert punches like sledgehammer blows dropped each demon-worshipper like bags of grain, buying the giant enough time to heft the warhammer again.

"As if vise Skald does not know vhat you are thinking! Pah!"

"Grandfather!"

Arrows slashed past his ears, and Skald turned, heedless of the Venans to his back or the darts hissing through his hair.

"Vhat is it, small-fang? Skald is being very busy, and has no time for telling bedtime story."

Anya scowled even as she loosed arrow after arrow into the horde behind Skald. "Get up here, you doddered idiot, or they will kill you!"

Skald chuckled and turned wearily back, but not before answering, "I think not. You are calling me nasty names."

Before Anya could retort, the screeching cry drowned her senses. Her teeth gritted against the force of it, and she collapsed to one knee, holding her head. The cry lingered for a few seconds, then cut off, the silence that followed almost as deafening.

Then the Venans came.

Over fifty of the debased wretches poured toward the gate, overwhelming Skald and slamming him back against the hardened wood as they scrabbled at the gate mechanisms.

Anya screamed, *"Grandfather!"*

GIDEON MOVED.

As soon as the silver-haired veteran vanished beneath the cannibal tide, Gideon charged, alone, his feet pounding through the churned earth toward the gate. He lowered his shoulder and hit the first Venan in the small of his back, cracking vertebrae and hurling the smaller man out of the fight. His shield arm whipped across his body, and the broken shield smashed two cultists' blackened teeth from their infected gums. Without pausing, Gideon took his sword in a two-handed grip and hewed a cultist's head from his shoulders.

The force of his charge unbalanced the horde, and dozens of men staggered in the packed mass. Gideon powered forward, using his size and momentum to pierce the horde, splitting it up the middle. In such close quarters, Gideon punched with his elbows and the hilt of his family sword til he stood above the bleeding Wolf.

In the second before the horde regained its balance, Gideon beat back all four of the Venans clawing at the struggling storyteller. Even as Skald's massive hands clamped onto Gideon's belt for support to rise, Gideon slashed back and forth in a wide arc, clearing a space around the gate.

With a grunt of effort, Skald hauled himself to his feet, wiping blood from his grizzled brow and grasping his warhammer. "Ah, just-Gideon! You have come to steal old man's thunder?"

Gideon parried another three swipes from the snarling Venans and punched one back into the crowd, speaking between grunts. "It looked like you were having too much fun by yourself."

Skald brandished his hammer before him, slamming a line of wretches back with the haft. "You are being kind to not let elder walk in red snow alone. I vill speak of you to High Host vhen ve reach their Halls."

As the press surged in, Gideon grinned fiercely, his sword twisting about him with sprays of sparks as he deflected axes and knives. "Red snow? Is your heart giving out in the excitement, old man?"

Just before the horde swallowed them, Skald laughed and bared his teeth in turn. "Let old Volf show you how dying is done."

I should let you die.

Ashkelon watched his protégé smash frothing cannibals back, his armor hanging in tatters from his bleeding frame. Gideon's suicidal assault had permitted the fallen warrior to regain his feet, but accomplished nothing more than offer up his own head on the plate.

Still, it had been inspiring.

A lone warrior in ragged armor, lunging into a crowd of debased monsters with a broken shield, a cheap sword and a cry of anger on his lips—it brought back memories. Memories of an unstained time, when men with pure hearts and clean hands forced evil back into the Dark.

The sorcerer's head inclined in respect. He had thought those men fools at the time, as they died in unthinkable numbers for transient gains. He had never considered that he would one day miss them.

Hm. The longer one considers the great canvas of the past, the more one finds the subtlety in the brushstrokes that produce its beauty.

A fascinating line of thought. One worth discussing with his apprentice, should he survive.

Ashkelon sighed as his thoughts concluded in an annoyingly obvious necessity. "What I must do for conversation...," he grumbled as the ice of his eyes caught flame.

THE VENANS SCREAMED.

To be fair, they had been screaming the entire time, but now the pitch shifted. Shock, pain, despair, pleading: they replaced the tone of murder.

The gate no longer stood. It could not withstand the force that the dark stranger had brought to bear within the span of a single second.

Anya saw his eyes ignite, and the monstrous segmented legs from two of the spiders around him wrenched out of their thoraxes with sprays of ichor. A flick of a dark gauntlet, and sixteen improvised spears tore into the pack of Venans like bolts from siege ballistae, the air cracking like thunder in their wake. Two, three, even four cannibals at a time were spitted on the limbs and driven into the gate like insects on a board.

Even as she leapt for the wall section, the gate blasted off its hinges under the colossal impacts. Anya hit on her side and rolled, arrow fitting to the string even as she rose to a knee.

Only two figures remained standing in the destruction, covering their eyes with their arms. Demon-worshippers writhed mid-air around them, offered up like grisly trophies on the amputated limbs of their idols.

Anya lowered her bow in relief as the men dropped their arms, and the grimy features of Skald and the blonde soldier came into view.

SKALD WINCED and picked at something on his hand. "Ach. Please ask master to vatch aim next time. I have splinter in hand."

Gideon lifted his sword to reveal that half of the blade had snapped off, and sighed heavily. "I'll do that."

The dust around them thinned, allowing torchlight to illumine their surroundings. Gideon could begin to see the walls and shattered gate around him clearly in the bright light.

He frowned. It should not be that bright. "Skald..."

The old warrior was not looking at him. He was looking behind him, into the woods outside the gate. A fey look filled his eyes.

Gideon's shoulders sagged. "I don't want to know what is out there, do I?"

The Wolf shrugged. "That depends on vhat young man seeks in life."

Closing his eyes, Gideon cracked his neck and loosened his shoulders. "What do I seek? I seek love, long life, a hot meal, a *nap*...."

Skald's face was as impassive as granite. "Vell, none of that is behind you."

Gideon turned. As the dust settled slowly, shapes resolved out of the blackness of the woods. Hunched, gibbering wretches wielding flint knives crawled alongside arachnid demons the size of horses. These spiders were colored differently, with bright streaks of red and yellow painting their carapaces.

An army.

His voice caught slightly. "There are...a lot of them."

With a great sigh, Skald lowered himself painfully to a piece of wreckage. "Aye."

Gideon closed his eyes wearily. "So all this was an advance force, just to open the gate."

The veteran Wolf squinted his one eye and scratched at his chin. "Very likely."

"The gate is now open."

"Aye."

Rubble crunched behind them, and Gideon turned to see Lord Kyuza, filthy, spattered with the blood of human and demon, step beside him. His dark eyes narrowed at the sight of the force arrayed against them, and the same weariness in Gideon's eyes reflected in the Takeshi lord's.

Great shadows loomed out of the forest as giants fifteen feet tall wielding monstrous bone-clubs strode forth, their poisoned skin reflecting the firelight of the tiny town that defied their advance. Cultists and spiders skittered around their ankles as they stomped toward Estvik.

At some unknown signal, the horde stopped, perhaps a thousand feet from the gate. The only sound to break the silence was heavy, ragged breathing from hundreds of fevered throats.

Gideon pressed his lips together in a grim line. "How many do we have left?"

Kyuza spat something bitter on the ground and gestured behind him. Perhaps a score of Takeshi recruits in their dirty orange and a handful of Estvik's bravest men joined him at the gate, all ragged, all bloodied, their eyes bright in their begrimed faces.

They were all looking at Gideon.

They expect me to lead them.

As realization dawned on Gideon's face, Skald chuckled and said, "Since they know you, you defy death. Vhy does it shock you that vhen death come for them, they look to you?"

Eyes wide, Gideon shook his head. "No, no, no. This is a mistake. I'm just going to get them killed."

Kyuza glanced out toward the legion of cannibals and demons, then back at Gideon. A faint smile pulled at the corner of the warrior's mouth as he put a hand on Gideon's shoulder and answered, "We can die on our own. We just want to blame *you*."

Gideon raised a wry eyebrow and answered, "How very Thracian of you. Make sure the blame does not fall on you."

That touched something in the doomed men, and a few smiles broke out.

Kyuza grinned back at him. "See, you do know us."

Skald chuckled loudly and slapped Gideon on the back. Laughs rose from the men around them, free and full.

There is something to the sound of a man's laugh when he is ready to die.

A foot stamped on the boards of the rampart above them, breaking the moment, and Anya Helsdottyr scowled down at them, her black eyes flashing. "What is so funny? You could be planning, or doing something useful besides standing around and 'sharing the moment'!"

The men quieted, chastised. Skald squinted at Anya with his one steel-grey eye. "Small-fang, you are loved with all of Skald's great heart, but even I think your bow is strung too tightly."

The statement caught Gideon at the wrong moment. Before he could prevent it, a great laugh erupted from his chest, explosive and echoing in the silence. Unfortunately, he was the only one of the group to laugh, and he could not stop. Slowly, her glittering black eyes narrowed to cat-like slits. Gideon quickly began coughing, anything to cover the peals of laughter still rocking his body.

With regal slowness, the Wolf maiden took her bow and very pointedly fit an arrow to the string, tugging slightly to ensure a good fit. Gideon looked away, back toward the enemy. Where it was safe.

He muttered to the chuckling men around him, "Well, at least this can't get any worse."

At the center of the horde, a dull horn brayed, and the front ranks parted to reveal the army's commander.

For a moment, the gathered men fell speechless, until Skald murmured, "Vhy vould you say such a thing *out loud*?"

HER NAME WAS JA'A.

Time had long since devoured whatever clan who had given her the name. Many claimed that they hailed from the land of her birth, deranged survivors raving in their last moments about a path of famine slashing through the breadbasket of the north.

If Ja'a herself had told the story, the tale would have been of a fisherman's daughter, born in the kingdom of Peylon in the north of the island of Girattar, cast out to starve when her father discovered her mother's infidelity. Shunned by her clan, she scrabbled insects from the ground with her thin fingers, and consumed flowers where she could find them. She grew wizened and ghastly, but managed to remain alive, though perpetually on the edge of starvation.

Her only friends were the spiders whose webs she harvested for sustenance. Seeing her crooning to the tiny creatures, the villagers named her witch and drove her from their lands with savage beatings and the casting of stones.

As she lay in a cave, weeping and near death, a powerful spirit discovered her, and her unceasing hunger pleased him. In the arms of that bitter god, Ja'a found love and acceptance. She swore herself to Mammon's service, and in return, he made that service undying.

Days later, her village vanished. After a week, all trade ceased out of the kingdom of Peylon. The other kingdoms of Girattar staggered, then collapsed under the weight of refugees fleeing the advance of a creature with noxious light burning in her eyes.

When Girattar fell silent, the kingdoms of the continent burned the bridges to the island. They set a watch, sinking all vessels that fled. They paid a terrible price in innocent lives reaped, salving their tattered consciences with the knowledge that the dread hag of Peylon had been contained.

Ja'a did not know how long she wandered the Faminelands of Girattar, forever burning in her terrible hunger but not consumed.

But her lord cared for her. He did not forget her. He would not forsake *her*.

Coming to her on wings of fire, Mammon bore his adoring disciple to a new land, a land of Men who hungered, and commanded her to bring them to him.

Ja'a did not know the full extent of her lover's plans. She did not care. It was enough that she hungered, and that through her deprivation, her god was pleased.

FROM THE MIDST of the horde, she stepped forth. Her feet and arms were bare, despite the frigid cold. Rags clung to her emaciated frame, and her grey hair hung in ragged clumps over her face. Despite the green tinge to her skin, she appeared human, until one noticed the appendages sprouting from her shoulders and dragging on the ground behind her feet like a bride's train. They resembled the wings of a bat, stripped of membranes or skin. Like skeletal fingers, or the legs of a spider.

Hulking warriors flanked her, their swollen bellies pushing through great suits of bronze warplate. The bloatguard carried rusted axes, hooks and clubs, and they followed their mistress with heavy shuffling steps and droning chants. For her part, the inhuman horror leading the army paced with quick, jarring strides, like a bird, wringing her hands and darting quick glances at the fallen gate.

From the distance, the defenders of Estvik could hear her raving, her voice dry and cracked like a charred corpse.

"No, no, no, why are they still alive? They are not *supposed* to be still alive. They should be starved, yes, starved of breath. Then I can do what my lord asked, yes, I could, but I can't, because these ones are still alive."

She stopped suddenly and stabbed her long, talon-like fingernail toward the gate. Her eyes burned sickly yellow as she shrieked, "*Why are they still alive?*"

A keening moan went up from the masses, and the men at the gate glanced nervously at one another.

Gideon saw the darkness shift out of the corner of his eye, and without taking his eyes off of the creature before him, asked, "What is she?"

Ashkelon stood next to him, arms folded over his chest. "Demons appear to act no differently on your world than on mine. They often take mortal women as consorts, imbuing them with supernatural power drawn from their own essences. They also produce twisted offspring, monsters and nightmares to plague humanity and further the demon's ends. This one seems to prefer spiders."

Skald grunted. "Ve did not know she vas real. Ve name her Ja'a, Whore of Mammon."

Gripping his broken sword tightly, Gideon asked, "Can it be killed?"

Ashkelon gave him a wry smile. "*I* have slain them."

Gideon glared at him. "Oh, good. That's helpful."

The young man glanced at the men around him. "Does anyone have any ideas?"

Something twanged above them, and the creature called Ja'a reeled, a wooden shaft embedded in her chest. A gasping shriek ripped from her lungs, and Ja'a wrenched the arrow out with a welter of black blood. With a snarl, she cast the arrow at her feet, and fixed her sickly gaze on the defenders.

She growled one word. "*Feed.*"

The horde roared and charged, cannibals and spiders rushing forward in a pounding mass, desperate for the warm flesh within the palisade.

Gideon snapped his gaze up to Anya Helsdottyr, who stared back at him brazenly, bow in hand. Her chin lifted in defiant challenge. "There. Do you know what to do now?"

Skald sighed and heaved himself to his feet, bringing up his warhammer and grinning. "Do not let her vords vound you, young pup. Small-fang is just jealous of attention you are giving to other voman."

Swift as lightning, Anya snatched an arrow out of her back-mounted quiver and put the dart into a lumbering giant's eye. The giant sagged and collapsed, crushing a score of Venans beneath his bulk. Even as she reached for another arrow, Anya called down, "Oh, yes, grandfather, I will make sure to dress myself like a painted tramp from Samothrace so that I please him."

Gideon found himself unable to look away from the warrior

woman. Her hair whipped and thrashed behind her as she loosed arrow after arrow into the charging hordes, her dark eyes blazing like stars as she raged against the darkness before them. She scorned the cold, choosing to enter battle bare-armed and bareheaded.

She is absolutely beautiful.

The head of Skald's hammer shoved into his back, jarring him from his reverie. The grizzled veteran grinned at him. "Army first, lad. Then real fight."

Gideon grunted, and shook his head to clear it as he started walking forward absentmindedly. "Right. You're right."

Skald's eyebrow raised slightly as Gideon strode forward, swiftly transforming from awkward farm boy to...something else. The lad did not even look to see if anyone joined him on his advance. The walk became a jog, the broken sword lifted, the jog broke into a head-long run, and the first Venan flipped over backwards with shattered iron in his throat.

Gideon parried the follow-on attacker and rammed his shoulder pauldron into the wretch's face. As the Venan staggered back, jaw broken and bleeding, a hawk-feathered shaft slashed over Gideon's shoulder and hit the Venan in the chest.

Beautiful.

Ducking another lunging attack, Gideon scooped up a fallen weapon and hurled it end over end to brain a screaming cannibal and knock him off of his feet. A giant drooling poisoned froth from his misshapen mouth staggered forward, breaking the arrows hissing continuously into his chest. Gideon grimaced and readied himself for another charge, hoping aggression might off-balance the fiend.

A mighty roar sounded behind him, and Skald Greymane thundered past, warhammer wheeling around his body to smash the giant's knee and pulverize the bones within. The giant brayed and stumbled back, clutching his shattered joint, and Gideon threw his broken sword, burying Halcyon iron under the mutant's chin. The giant's head snapped to the side, his eyes rolled back, and with a low moan, the creature crashed into the ground.

Another wave of several dozen cannibals rushed forward,

screaming dark hymns as they came. Gideon sighted on one naked brute with serpentine tattoos curling across his flesh, while to his right, Skald hefted his hammer for a mighty cross-swing. They braced for impact.

The man with tattoos launched himself forward with a cry, but a spear thrust over Gideon's shoulder and took the frothing cultist in the pelvis, halting him mid-air. The spear twisted and jerked backward in a welter of blood, and Gideon stepped forward and cracked the wretch's skull against the ground.

Yelling battle-cries of their own, the Takeshi met their foes on the open field. The impact of the charge knocked the emaciated cultists off of their feet. Spinning and leaping, the recruits of the King's Guard crashed through the disordered ranks of Venans, reaping a terrible slaughter with their bright swords and sharp spears. The cultists twisted and toppled in droves as the superior training, weapons and size of the King's guard slaughtered them en masse.

Lord Kyuza fought at their head, a sword in each hand, the blade in his left much shorter than the long curved sword in his right. His face was set in a terrible mask of focus and fury as he spun through the ranks of the corrupted. Every motion harvested a life as the whickering blades cut through all they touched.

Skald's great hammer never stopped moving. The iron-banded steel smashed skulls, splintered bone-cages and blasted chitin and ichor back into the Venans, while the Wolf wielding the dread weapon sang a terrible incantation of woe on the souls of the slain.

Too many of them were dying. Rather than overrunning the defenders in a single wave, the Venans found themselves in the killing field, and their courage snapped like brittle sticks. They flooded back toward their mistress, hands raised to ward away the relentless barrage of arrows the Wolf-maiden sent whispering through the air to kill their captains, blind their giants and slay their idols.

At the forefront of the maelstrom, Gideon Halcyon laid about him, his green eyes flashing, fighting with stolen weapons, stones and his mailed fists. No bladework could outmatch his skill, no insanity-born rage could overcome him. Giants pounded their great clubs into nothing but earth, and confusion reigned on their slack countenances as their life gushed from terrible wounds rent into their veins.

The army was breaking. Gideon could feel it. The Estvik force scythed through the center of the Venan mob like a reaper through wheat. The mistress of the horde lay just before him, shielded by her titanic bloatguard.

Skald roared, "Not too far, boy! They vill surround us!"

Gideon hesitated.

Arrows pitched Venans off their feet around him, and Gideon could hear Anya yelling, "Fall back, you brainless fools!"

Even in the heat of the battle, Gideon knew they were right. As the fleeing Venans reached their mistress, something bolstered them. Their veins distended in their faces and arms, and they turned back to face the defenders with something sulfurous burning behind their eyes.

They were rallying. If the Takeshi penetrated any further into the Venan army, the reforming cultists would cut them off and destroy them. Already, the flanks of the army reached past the Takeshi onslaught, clawing to enter the gate and ravage the warm meat inside the walls.

Gideon sucked in a breath to call for retreat—

And shadow whipped past him.

Like a dark wind, Ashkelon scattered the rallying Venans like leaves. Acherlith howled as it looped in great arcs around his body amidst blasts of lightning and flame. Gideon squinted as the sorcerer seemed to flicker in and out of time, here one instant, elsewhere the next, always killing. The Venans stumbled, unable to find the sorcerer before his black blade lashed from another quarter and stole their screams from their mouths.

Shadow-walking.

Even in the midst of shouting and slaughter, Gideon blinked. That thought...was not his.

Tentatively, cautious in his own mind, he asked, *What?*

Every man carries a gateway to the Dark with him, hidden in his shadow. Ashkelon learned to use those gates a long time ago.

Gideon did not know how this voice entered his mind, but as he watched, he saw what it spoke of. Ashkelon would slaughter three or four with sweeping sword strokes, then vanish into the shadows. An instant later, he appeared within another group to strike again. His sword never stilled, the screams never silenced, and the blood continued to stain the ground black.

The voice continued, refined and intelligent. *It was a rare thing on Avalon. It surprised me the first time I saw him do it, but one should expect no less from the avatar of the Everlasting Dark.*

Ashkelon's teeth bared in a feral snarl, and his silver-white hair lashed around his face as he killed. A ball of fire spat from his palm and exploded in a clutch of Venans rushing toward him, hurling blistered bodies dozens of yards with the force of the blast. Snapping tendrils of lightning streamed from his fingertips, crawling up the seizing body of a giant and cooking it alive.

For an instant, his gaze settled on Gideon, and Ashkelon snarled, "Go. Kill her!"

Skald powered his hammer into the flank of a struggling spider and sent it flying across the battlefield. He backed away, calling, "Gideon! Now! Fall back now! Ve have to defend the gate!"

Kyuza, fighting now with one sword and dragging a wounded recruit with the other hand, cried out, "To the gate! Back to the gate!"

A titanic explosion stole his words as Ashkelon blasted another patch of the battlefield, raining blood and bodies. His cerulean eyes blazed as he shouted, "Do not heed them! What matters the lives of a few wretches if you can kill a Consort? Kill the leader, and this army will break!"

Gideon looked at her, hefting his stolen axe unconsciously. Only her bloatguard stood between him and Ja'a.

I can end this. I know I can.

Ja'a stared back at him, a smile starting to spread across her face. He heard her hiss, "Yessss. Come to me, hero. Come."

Several bloatguard lumbered forward to engage his master. Ashkelon rammed his voidblade completely through the breastplate of the first, then tore the blade up and out of the creature's neck, still bearing the armor on his sword. The bloatguard collapsed, shorn almost in half, and with a slash of his blade, Ashkelon whipped the breastplate off like a discus to decapitate a second.

"You will save more lives through her death than will be lost in that thankless hamlet today. Focus on your prey. Kill. Her."

Gideon glanced back at the town and saw the Venans streaming around the field of death Ashkelon had created. They dashed for the gate, where the Takeshi and Skald struggled to reform and deny them entry. Gideon thought of all the innocent lives within, pressed his lips together and shook his head.

"I'm sorry, master. I can't."

As Ashkelon bellowed in the silence of his soul, Gideon fell back from the battlefield, leaving his master alone.

ASHKELON WAS SO surprised and furious at the sight of his apprentice's retreat, he actually stopped killing for a moment. Acherlith fell to his side, its ebon blade hissing with steaming blood. In the midst of a besieging army of monsters and lunatics, scant yards away from its demonic commander, Ashkelon took a breath to compose himself, before he ripped a fiery mountain from the bowels of the earth to devour the sons of men and Hell together.

The demon fighters eyed one another warily, unsure how to proceed.

He let out a long breath, feeling his rage cool to a simmer. "Very well. If you would have it your way, then you may do it your way. Alone."

The sorcerer sheathed his sword. One of the Consort's champions roared a challenge and powered forward, slaughterhooks swinging.

Ashkelon shot him a glare of pure hatred, and his eyes flared like blue suns. The top half of the bloatguard vaporized and exploded. Scraps of armor sliced through the air amidst a rain of slime as the creature's waist and legs tumbled forward. The other guardians flinched, then looked back at their mistress uncertainly.

Ashkelon held up a hand that he slowly clenched into a fist. "Do not bother," he growled, "I no longer care."

His darkmail cloak swishing behind him, the sorcerer strode out of the horde.

No one tried to stop him.

GIDEON SKIDDED to a stop at the wreckage of the gate. Kyuza and Skald were helping a man through, arms slung over their shoulders. As they eased the man to the ground, Skald clapped Gideon on the back. "Good to see you living, just-Gideon. You vorry old man so vith your antics."

Gideon looked around, assessing the defensibility of the gate. "How are we doing?"

Shrugging, Skald answered, "Vell, half of us are dead, the other half vounded, the enemy is regrouping and mighty Skald is hungry. Old men should not die on empty stomachs."

Gideon glanced at him. "If it's that important, I guess we can find an apple or something for you."

Skald sniffed. "Vhat kind of last meal is this? Vould prefer roasted boar leg."

Cutting off Gideon's reply, a feminine voice called out to him, "Warrior."

Gideon glanced up to see Anya standing on the rampart, looking down at him. For some reason, that made him flustered. "Uh, yes. Thank you, by the way. For the, uh, arrows. The arrow...shooting."

Sweat trickled down his back under his armor. *Arrow shooting? You are going to die alone.*

She raised an elegant eyebrow, and her dark eyes bored into his. "What would you say if I told you I was trying to hit *you?*"

Gideon rubbed the back of his head and tried, "Um, thank you for missing?"

The corner of her mouth quirked upward. "Hm. Well, you remained in the midst of the enemy. I could not hit you for all the foes you fought."

Wait...was that a compliment?

Anya turned away from him before he could think of anything sufficiently coherent to say in response. She tossed her hair over her shoulder and said, "And you are welcome, Gideon, for the arrow shooting."

Saving Gideon from the need to speak anymore, Lord Kyuza stepped to his side and said quietly, "We need to prepare. They will come again. Will the dark one stand with us?"

Gideon closed his eyes wearily and sighed, "I would not count on him. He's...probably upset with me."

He opened his eyes again. "All right. We hold the gate. Get the men who can fight together. No one gets in."

Nearby, Skald suddenly took a long sniff of the cold winter air. A great smile, like the rising of the winter sun, broke out on his face, and he roared, "You heard the boy! Not single vone of these flesh-eating vermin vill touch hair on Estvik child's head! You have vord of Skald!"

The battered defenders stared at the giant veteran, the sudden change jarring. The Wolf hauled a villager to his feet, almost yanking his arm from his socket and laughing. "Ha ha, up, man of Estvik! You do not vant to be on duff vhen victory comes, take Skald's vord on that!"

A look of confusion spreading across his face, Gideon glanced at Anya, who seemed as off-put by Skald's behavior as the rest of them.

Skald saw it. "Oh, vipe smile off lips, you baby-fanged cub. I know vhat you are thinking. You are thinking old Skald's mind has snapped like dry branch. Vell, let me tell you, there is nothing more dangerous than old Volf ready to meet his God!"

Skald whipped up his hammer and planted himself between the gateposts, his eye bright and glaring, stance wide. Talismans clicked and skulls rattled as he shook himself, teeth bared in a death-defying grin.

"Boy. Come."

Still glancing at Anya, Gideon jogged to the veteran's side. He cast his gaze over the besieging army, which began to move toward the village again.

His voice low as a whisper, Skald said, "There is actually vone thing more dangerous than a Volf ready for Death's halls."

The storyteller threw his head back and howled into the night sky, the force of it enough to freeze the horde in their tracks. The howl lasted long and loud, terminating in a wet growl.

For a moment, silence. The the Venan army rumbled forward once more.

Then another howl answered Skald.

And another.

And another.

Skald grinned as a chorus of savagery rose from the woods around the horde, and as the first shadows leapt from the mists to bury their axes in poisoned flesh, he snarled, "*Volves.*"

From both sides of the army, huge warriors clad in furs ripped into the Venan horde, howling like beasts. The flanks recoiled in shock as first twenty, then a hundred of their number died in the first seconds of the ambush. Ja'a's emaciated followers flew like straw in a windstorm as the Vulfen slammed into them with reckless abandon.

Gideon could see Ja'a snarl to her bloatguard, and their diseased horns began to sound a retreat. Skald began to laugh, his mighty frame shaking with defiant mirth, and he roared into the horde, "*Heimdaaaaaall!*"

Horses bearing Wolf warriors thundered toward the gate of Estvik, cutting off any hope of an attack on the town. A chieftain almost the size of Skald reined in his horse only when he stood in the gate itself, bearing an axe on his back that looked capable of shearing a horse in half. The horde of Mammon melted back into the night, and the chieftain shouted, "Let them go. We secure the town, then we hunt."

One of his retinue nodded swiftly, lifted his horn, and blew a long clear blast over the battlefield. As answering horns acknowledged, the chieftain dismounted, leather creaking and armor clanking. Skulls of his own rattled against his warplate, and his eyes, strangely familiar, pierced through Gideon, assessing him for weaknesses.

Gideon felt very uncomfortable under that stare.

Fortunately for him, the chieftain shifted his attention to Skald, who grinned insouciantly.

"Hello, my jarl."

The chieftain did not return the sentiment.

Fists clenching, Jarl Heimdall Fangthane of the Wolves stalked toward his storyteller and growled, "Where. Is. My. Daughter?"

WOLF MAIDEN

8

LEAVETAKING

Jarl Heimdall could shout very loudly when he put his mind to it. Throughout the battles of the Wolves, his voice rose above the screams of dying men and demons, above the clamor of crashing steel and sounding horns. His throat was raw and scarred from bellowing orders in the heat of battle and cursing the eyes of his enemies.

Therefore, when Heimdall roared his daughter's name, everyone in Estvik and possibly all the realms of Men heard it.

"Anyaaaaa!"

Heimdall allowed his daughter innumerable liberties. Since the day of her birth, they two had weathered the hardships of raising a family without a wife and mother. He had persevered with a will of iron, seeing her through the confusion of childhood til she flowered into a shield-maiden of Wolves. She knew when she could push his limits, and when to put her teeth together and submit.

From the look on her face, she knew today was one of the latter instances.

"Here, Father."

She dropped down from the ruined rampart of the gate, landing lightly. Her bow hung across her back, and though streaked with demon's blood, his daughter did not appear hurt.

For an instant, relief flooded Heimdall's heart. An instant only, then his face screwed up in rage again, and he stalked toward her, his cheeks reddening. Wolves, veterans of a hundred battles or raw youngbloods, hurried to clear his path.

"Never has any man had a daughter so disobedient, so disrespectful as you! What did I tell you to do?"

Anya started to speak, "Father—"

He cut her off, speaking in the language of the Hammar. "*I said, stay!* I commanded you to stay! And now the Hammarhold lies empty, our lair bereft of its warriors, because the honor of my Wolves would not allow any of them to stay behind while their jarl searched the wilderness for his brat!"

Anya dared to lift her eyes for a second. "Father, Estvik needed our help—"

Heimdall turned from her and gestured grandly at the ruin of the town. "Oh, I can see *that*, daughter. Within a day of your arrival, Estvik is burned to the ground, much like the respect of my warriors for their jarl."

He twisted back and advanced on her. "You disrespect me in the Lair, you disobey my commands, and now one of my fiefs lies in ashes. Rebellion leads to destruction, daughter! My rivals will ask, how can Heimdall Fangthane protect the lands of the Wolves if he cannot even control his own hearth? How many challenges would you have me fight?"

Hot tears sprang unchecked to Anya's eyes. "Father, that is not fair!"

Heimdall, lost in his temper, scoffed at her and threw his hand up in the air. To Skald, Anya and every Wolf present, it was a familiar gesture, one he commonly employed to express his frustration. He had never struck his daughter, nor any of his warriors, especially not with anything as insulting as a backhanded slap.

There was, however, a man present not familiar with Heimdall's mannerisms.

A thunderous impact rocked the lord's chin and blacked out his vision for an instant. The sheer force of it sent him spinning to the earth, and blood pinked his gums, flooding his mouth with the taste of iron. Around the ringing in his skull, a single thought coalesced through the fog in his mind.

Someone...wants to die.

Heimdall rolled to a knee and got a good look at the man who had just signed his own death sentence. Every Wolf present had frozen in place, one in the midst of biting an apple. They all stared at the young man in tattered armor standing between the Wolf Lord and his daughter, fists clenched. Death of his own stared out from the warrior's eyes.

Chest heaving, the man growled slowly, "Stay down."

Anya's mouth hung open, and she grabbed at his arm frantically. "No. No, Gideon, stop."

The one called Gideon shook his arm free, his eyes not leaving the massive warrior. "He will not hurt you. I don't care who he is."

Heimdall stood funereally slowly, and Gideon jabbed a finger at him and snarled again, "*Stay. Down.*"

Skald tried to step forward, but Heimdall lifted a hand, his dark eyes inscrutable as he indicated the ravaged town around them. "You challenge me, boy? Here? Now?"

Bleeding from a hundred cuts, his eyes bright against his filthy skin, Gideon glared right back. "Take another step and find out."

Heimdall cocked his head slowly, considering this Gideon with a detached air, as a butcher might consider a hog. For a long moment, he said nothing, breathing steadily through flared nostrils. At last, he spoke, his voice grating like the opening of a stone coffin.

"Skald...draw the circle."

Skald closed his eye wearily and lifted his face to the heavens. "Ach, jarl, boy does not know what he is doing."

The lord fairly snarled, "Then he dies ignorant!"

Anya pushed past Gideon, emphasizing every syllable, "*No, Father! He does not know.*"

Uncertainty flickered through the boy's eyes. "Know what?"

Before she could answer, the jarl stabbed his finger at Gideon, "Know wh—are you daft as well as suicidal?"

Gideon glanced at first his daughter, then Skald. "Why?"

Heimdall spoke slowly, as if to a child. "Are you or are you not invoking the Rite of Challenge for my daughter's hand?"

MOMENTS LATER, the warrior they named Gideon leaned against the fragmented palisade, rubbing his temples slowly, trying to come to terms with the magnitude of the mistake he had just made as Heimdall's daughter and storyteller pleaded for his life.

"For the last time, Papa," Anya groaned, "he was just protecting me!"

Skald chimed in, his weathered face earnest. "Aye, jarl, he vas excited. Battle still pounded in his veins! Also, he does not vant her at all! He even said she vas ugly. I hear it!"

Anya glared at the old warrior. Skald ignored her.

Jarl Fangthane squinted at her suspiciously. "You seem passionate enough about saving this young warrior, daughter. Enough to warrant me splitting his skull for entirely different reasons."

She planted her hands on her hips. "First, you want to sell me to the Pack like a wheel of cheese, then you want to put an axe in the first man to fight for my honor! Which is it, Father, because I do not know!"

"Aha, so he *does* want you! He dies!"

A frustrated growl erupted from Anya's lips, and she yelled, "Papa, you are impossible!"

She stalked away, her hair lashing behind her in her fury. Anya leapt onto her horse, and the surprised animal whinnied at the unexpected mount. Seconds later, the two of them thundered out of Estvik's shattered gate.

With a great sigh, Heimdall watched her go, his weathered face creased in contemplation. "She likes him, doesn't she, old one?"

Skald shrugged. "She is voman, so who can say, my jarl?"

The Wolf Lord grunted. "Don't spare my feelings, storyteller. Speak the truth, as you are meant to do."

Bowing in acquiescence, Skald answered, "Vell, since ve are speaking truth now, there is much to like in the boy."

Heimdall glanced at him. "You approve?"

"I have but vone eye, my jarl. I have seen him but vone day. Both are filled vith his courage and skill at arms."

Turning his gaze to the battered young man, Heimdall grunted. "So, he is brave. What, then, are his deeds?"

An involuntary grin stretched Skald's face. "Vell, first there vas barfight..."

GIDEON LOOKED out into the darkness, searching for his master. Ashkelon had not been seen since the end of the battle.

Since Gideon had disobeyed his command.

He did not know what Ashkelon would do about his refusal to abandon his fellow defenders to slay the demoness. Uncertainty wormed through his gut, and he felt like a child awaiting a father's chastisement.

Then there was the matter of the voice.

Exhaustion blurred Gideon's vision, and he winced, feeling the aches of a day of constant battle settle into his joints. An involuntary smile tugged the edges of his lips upward as he thought, *Well, whether the Wolves kill me or Ashkelon, I might as well die well-rested...*

Turning from the darkness, Gideon moved toward the fires, where Lord Kyuza arranged billeting for his men. Gideon laid out his bedroll next to soldiers who mere hours before would have gladly killed him, but now welcomed him as a brother and gave him a place close to the fire.

He stripped what little armor remained on his frame, kicked off his boots, pulled his blanket up over his head and fell asleep as soon as his head hit the crook of his elbow.

. . .

THE BLACK PYRAMID *seemed to swallow the sky as it leeched the land around it dry. The soil crunched under Gideon's feet, giving off the reek of old death. Emerald lightning flickered through the sky as sulfurous showers stung his skin. The hissing rainfall increased to a downpour, washing away the dead earth around him to reveal thousands of leering skulls.*

Gideon gazed in horror as the acidic thunderstorm revealed a field of moldering bones and rusted armor. An entire war's worth of the dead lay scattered and broken before the structure, whole generations of the fallen sacrificed to its naked ambition.

At the pinnacle of the cursed ziggurat, waiting atop a flight of black stone stairs, Gideon could just make out a solitary figure with its arms crossed and face shrouded, standing silent sentinel over the desolation.

Waiting.

In a flash of verdant green, Gideon found himself standing atop the pyramid near its master, looking down on the valley. It was Ashkelon, as he thought. The shadow warrior seemed fixated on the field below him, his startlingly blue eyes piercing the cloying mists, his white hair blowing freely in the poisoned wind.

A gentle exhalation escaped him. "At last."

Gideon looked, and there, dashing across the field of the dead, was a man. His eyes burned with zealous fire, and light gleamed from his silver plate as the warrior charged alone toward the Onyx Mage, a titanic sword held low in his mailed fists.

"Aj-gelun vyl ivaras!"

His voice, noble and furious, echoed across the dead plain, and his heavy boots pounded the black basalt as he raced up the pyramid. His breath sawed in and out of his lungs as he vaulted the high stone stairs, stumbling in his mad rush to come to grips with the silent figure awaiting him.

A brilliant blue flash, and another man, a scholar by his appearance, snapped into reality alongside the silver warrior. His hand caught hold of the warrior's shoulder pauldron and pulled him to the side, arresting his dash. The warrior shook free, backing away and snarling, "Do not try to stop me, brother. This is for Avalon."

The scholar moved to block his path, his voice shaking with passion.

"Valantian, Avalon is dead. Losing yourself to vengeance will not bring back its people, nor raise its white towers again from the ashen earth."

The warrior called Valantian spat, "I am the Scion, Gemalte! The children of Avalon were my charge, my responsibility, my life! That black whoreson has left me with nothing!"

The man called Gemalte shook his head sorrowfully. "No, brother, there is more to you than this. We are more than the vengeance of those who died fearing the Dark. If we had served the Light as we should have, the Onyxian would never have risen. The death of Avalon is ours to own."

His chest heaving, Valantian looked back to the dark figure standing near Gideon. His voice dropped to a low growl, intense, almost pleading. "If you were ever my brother, then get out of my way. Let me kill him. Please."

A tear tracked down the scholar's cheek, and he shifted his ornate staff to a two-handed grip. "I will always be your brother, Val. I will go with you to whatever end."

Valantian nodded, and the two of them turned together to face the black sorcerer gazing at them from the summit. The warrior took a deep breath, and as the brothers charged the devil killing their land, he roared a single accusing word in the tongue of judgment.

"AJ-GELUN!"

GIDEON JERKED awake when something heavy and metal struck his ankle. His blanket crackled as the morning frost flaked away, and Gideon struggled to focus, his dream vying with reality for his concentration.

His bleary eyes caught sight of Ashkelon walking away without a word, his black cloak swishing behind him. He glanced down at his ankles, and saw his family sword, reforged and whole, lying on his foot.

Gideon gripped the hilt. Tears sprang to his eyes at the sight of his adopted family's blade, and he blinked them back, feeling foolish and hoping Ashkelon did not see.

"Thank you," he called out after his master.

Ashkelon ignored him.

Gideon sighed and pressed the blade to his forehead. A dark thought leapt to mind. *Better to wake up with my sword on my foot than in it.*

Little things mattered.

Glancing around, he saw the Wolfjarl Heimdall and Lord Kyuza speaking together, with Skald and a few other Wolves standing nearby. Gideon lifted himself to his feet, groaning at the unbelievable number of aches he possessed, and managed to stagger over to the small gathering.

The Takeshi noble saw him and welcomed him with a small bow of respect. "Good morning to you, lord Gideon."

Feeling somewhat awkward, Gideon half-bowed back and grimaced as something twinged in his back. Rising slowly from the bow, he answered, "Good morning to you, captain, but I am no lord."

Heimdall glared at him. "That leads me to something else. What exactly *are* you, because I am told the word 'boy' fits poorly. If I believed half of what this senile old man weaves about you, I would send you to cast the Three back to the Abyss and let myself go to fat."

Gideon glanced at Skald, who winked back. "Uh, just a farmboy turned soldier, lord," he said.

The Wolf Lord eyed him, and his voice dropped to a low growl. "Do not lie to me. You are something. I would know what it is."

The fur-clad warriors around him stirred, and Gideon began to feel surrounded. "I am not special, lord. There was a need, and the Lord has given me the gifts to fill those needs."

Heimdall sighed, and the burgeoning menace seemed to drain out of him. He closed his eyes, as if weary. "Of course you are not special. You only fought a company of the King's Guard with your bare hands to save my daft daughter, bested the King's dueling champion, fought burrowers on open ground, saved my daft storyteller from his own stupidity and convinced a paltry handful of men, your *enemies*, mind you, to charge a demon Consort and her cannibal army, all in the same day. What in Freya's unshaven legs could be special about you?"

Gideon winced and gestured helplessly. "It sounds like more than it was, lord."

The jarl rubbed his jaw. "You hit like a drunken boar, and yet when your deeds are boasted of, you blush like a maid. You are right, Greymane. This one bears watching."

Skald grinned and scratched his beard. "Skald is alvays right, my jarl."

"Don't let him near my daughter. She'd like him, and I don't want to deal with killing him right now."

Skald's grin grew. "I like him, too, jarl."

In spite of himself, Heimdall chuckled. "Well, keep it between you two, old man. I don't want to deal with *that*, either."

A low murmur of amused growls and chuckles went around the circle, then died down. Heimdall grew serious. "Despite the best efforts of the King's men, for whose sacrifices we give thanks—", he indicated Lord Kyuza, who bowed in acknowledgement, "—Estvik is lost to us. The gate is splinters, and most of its men are dead. The survivors will go to the Hammarhold until we have crushed Mammon's vermin. This is my will."

Nods all around, except from the village headsman, who looked very small and defeated. Heimdall glared at him. "You have no voice here, little man. You would have sold my daughter to an evil man for evil use out of spite. You are fortunate she feels no ill will, else I might leave your bones for Mammon's hordes to pick their teeth."

Slowly, listlessly, the headsman nodded.

Heimdall turned from him. "Estvik's people leave today. My warriors and I shall remain here to burn the bodies and curse the remains. Words of woe shall be spoken so that evil may fear to return to Estvik."

The jarl gestured toward the surviving Takeshi. "You are welcome to join us in our hearth. Pass the winter with us, king's man, and be warm at our fires. You have earned such hospitality as we can offer."

Lord Kyuza bowed again, his expression serious. "Your offer is kind, great jarl, but I must return these recruits to the capital.

Samothrace has need of Takeshi to keep it safe from threats such as this, and these have now earned their place."

Heimdall nodded. "Then go with honor, King's man."

The Takeshi bowed once more and turned to Gideon. "You are welcome to travel to Samothrace with us. The King values skill and courage such as yours."

Gideon smiled and shook his head. "You have my thanks, lord, but I would see this through. Besides, I am yet an apprentice, with much to learn of my craft before I may be of service."

Kyuza nodded. "As you wish. Should you ever visit the capital, seek the hall of the Takeshi. You will find welcome there."

"I will do it."

Lord Kyuza moved past him toward Skald. "Elder."

Skald rested both hands on the haft of his warhammer and leaned on the weapon. "Aye?"

The Takeshi bowed once more to the venerable warrior. "Our warning to the King demands speed. We cannot see to the bodies of our fallen."

Skald nodded, understanding immediately. "Aye."

Kyuza's eyes burned with intensity. "They died far from family and hearth, for a people not their own."

Skald Greymane straightened then, and all beheld a glimmer of the true majesty of the battle-sage of the Wolves. His voice grew husky and his single eye blinked repeatedly. "The valor of King's men shall be heard vhen the Vulfenkind ask for deathsongs. Their deeds shall be heard in saga of Estvik, and ve shall bring our sons to their graves vhen they ask to know of courage and honor."

Bowing once more, Lord Kyuza turned from them all and gestured sharply to the few surviving recruits. Perhaps ten, all that remained of the Takeshi force, lifted their swords in quick salute to Gideon and the Wolves, and followed their lord onto the long road south to civilization.

A heavy hand slammed onto Gideon's shoulder, and he turned to face Heimdall. The great Wolf peered at him. "So the apprentice will stay until all of our enemies are slain for us, eh? And what does his master have to say about this?"

"Nothing. Nothing at all."

It was not Skald or Gideon who answered the lord of the Wolves. Ashkelon himself emerged from the shadows, Acherlith sheathed on his back. At his advance, every Wolf present instinctively bared his teeth and gripped the hafts of their axes. Darkness emanated from the bitter sorcerer, chilling the air about him with an air of palpable threat.

Ashkelon stopped a few yards short of them, his icy gaze fixed on Gideon. Mist coiled about his limbs, and his voice held a deadly calm. "We will do as my apprentice wills."

Heimdall growled a question as he faced off against Ashkelon, nostrils flaring in challenge. "Greymane?"

Skald shook his head and answered quickly, "He is not enemy, my jarl. I think."

Ashkelon finally shifted his attention from his apprentice to stare at the Wolf lord. "Do not let your taleweaver deceive you. I would kill everyone of you with a thought, if the inclination so took me. Be grateful that it does not."

Shock fell on the assembly at the bald arrogance of the threat, broken when one of Heimdall's Wolves roared and charged forward with his axe.

Skald shouted, "No!", grabbing the man's weapon and hurling him back. The mighty veteran lunged ahead and stood with his feet planted, hands up, holding back the Wolves' snarling advance.

Heimdall glared at him, his face purpling in fury. "What is this, old one? Who is this rag of arrogant filth to think he may threaten me in my own fief?"

Skald kept his one-eyed gaze respectfully downcast, but he pleaded, "My jarl, do not do this! He is a changer of the fates."

"A boaster *and* a witch? All the more reason to kill him!"

Skald slammed his palm into his chieftain's chest and forced him back. "Jarl! *He does not boast vhen he speaks.*"

Heimdall hesitated. "What?"

Skald exhaled slowly. His hand did not budge from Heimdall's breastplate. "The strength of darkness is great vith him. He makes shadows kill and demons scream. It is beyond the Pack, this thing that you vould ask."

The jarl held his warrior's gaze, searching for uncertainty or deceit in his grey eye. There was none.

Speaking slowly, with forced calm, Heimdall asked, "Boy. Is your master a danger to my people?"

Gideon paused for an instant, looking at Ashkelon warily. He saw nothing but detached disdain in the man's cold eyes. Gideon shook his head. "Not unless you make him one."

The Wolf chieftain shot a fierce look back at Ashkelon, who awaited him with a cool expression, one eyebrow arched in faint expectation. "Very well. Apprentice, you have my countenance. You may sleep at my fire and fight with my pack, but your master will provide for himself. I may not kill him, but neither will I welcome him."

Ashkelon dipped in what might have been seen as a bow. "The hospitality of Wolves."

Heimdall turned to his warriors. "Feros, Fyrss. You will travel with Elder Greymane and the people of Estvik. Ensure that they reach the hold safely."

The two warriors nodded sharply and moved toward their horses. Gideon glanced at Ashkelon, who gazed back at him impassively. *I guess I'll make the decisions.*

"Jarl, with your permission, I will travel with them as well."

Heimdall appraised him shrewdly, then nodded. "An extra sword will not be amiss. Go."

"And I will go with him, also."

The Wolf lord turned to see his daughter step forward, bow slung on her back. Her arrows she had replenished from the stocks the Wolves had brought with them. He raised both eyebrows and asked pointedly, "*Him?*"

She hastily added, "*Them.* I will go with them. The people of Estvik."

Heimdall continued to regard her, his eyes narrowing thoughtfully. "Really?"

Anya lifted her chin unconsciously, meeting her father's challenge. "Yes, really. I can organize the relief supplies they will need and find hearths for them to dwell in. Is this not the work of a she-Wolf?"

Her father did not believe a word of it. "Yes, it is, and honorable labor, indeed. Greymane, you will go with my daughter. You will stay by her side, so that she does not stray. You will make sure she goes to the hold and *stays* there until I arrive."

Skald lifted a fist to his breast. "You have my oath, jarl."

Heimdall eyed Gideon. "And don't let her near that one."

AN HOUR LATER, the survivors of Estvik began the trek to the Hammarhold. The train of shuffling peasants, creaking carts and braying livestock snaked through the broken battleground, bypassing the twisted bodies of men and monsters. The grim remnant of Estvik's population watched Jarl Fangthane's warriors pull corrupted corpses onto blazing pyres, spraying sparks into the cloudy sky with every body they cast on the flaming logs.

Gideon walked beside Skald's horse, dwarfed by both the man and the horse. Seeing Gideon's interest, Skald leaned down. "They burn bodies to kill eggs."

The young man glanced at him. "Eggs?"

Skald nodded. "Aye. Ve learn this after ve lose Notodden. The varriors of Notodden slay Venan raiding party and mount them as trophies. Days later, Notodden is consumed."

Gideon stared. "The Venans take spider eggs *inside* their bodies?"

"To them, is vorship. They give body as sacrifice to hungry gods, and in return, they believe they are fast, strong, invincible. Is vhy they look so sick, and smell so rank."

Gideon shook his head as he watched the bodies burn. "What convinces a man to do that to himself?"

Skald shrugged. "Some men lose their vay, just-Gideon."

The caravan began to enter the forest, and Gideon pursed his lips, looking at the trees around them. He could see no further than fifty yards, due to the density of the forest.

Skald clicked his tongue. "You are vorried, young man?"

Gideon glanced at the train of oblivious civilians behind them. "The Venans are still out there and now these people are exposed. It makes me uneasy."

The one-eyed veteran clapped him on the shoulder. "I vill tell you story of the birth of the Vulfen, and perhaps you feel better."

Gideon raised an eyebrow. "All right."

Skald leaned back in his saddle and began his tale.

"Vonce upon time, long ago, people of the northlands vere plagued vith raids from a powerful varrior tribe, the Vulfenkind. They burned and pillaged along the rivers and shores of the continent, and prayers vere offered to the Almighty to save His people from the fierce hunger of the Volves. Vone day, Volf chieftain, Jarl Brakstad Stonebreaker, approached Hammarhold vith longship."

Skald's eyes closed as he recalled the tale. "Their hair vas stiffened vith the grease of bear fat, and their faces painted with the blood of priests. Their ships sailed up Great River vith black sails, proclaiming death to their prey. Vhen Brakstad beached his dragonship on the rocks of Hammarhold, he say no vords. Vithout battlecry, he vaulted the side of his vessel and stalked toward Hammarfall with his varriors, axe in hand."

"But no arrows greeted Jarl Brakstad Stonebreaker. No panicked mob of men seeking to bury the bite of axes in Brakstad's brainmeat. Just single old priest, leaning on staff made from fig tree."

"Brakstad heaved great sigh. Only vone puny man to defy Jarl Stonebreaker? Vhere vere the varriors? Vhere vere the men to challenge a Volf Lord and make his blood to sing vith danger and death vonce more? No, now all flee before Vulfenkind vith vater in their veins, and only vone at death's door bars his vay. Brakstad hefted his axe vith sorrow. He vill honor last brave man of the northlands vith quick death. A varrior's death."

"As jarl approaches, old priest looked into varchief's eyes and said vone thing. 'Keep my sheep.'"

"Brakstad stopped. He did not think he heard old man in good vay. 'Vhat?' he growled."

"'Keep,' repeated old man, 'my sheep.'"

"Brakstad looked from old man to see city of Hammarfall behind him. He knew that old man meant people of city, those cowards hiding in closets vhile old priest speaks for them. He sneered. 'I am Jarl Brakstad Stonebreaker,' he roared, 'varrior-king of the Vulfenkind! I burn hearths of kings! I break the spears of the doughty! I am a volf, not keeper of bleating sheep!'"

"But old man showed no fear in Volf Lord's anger. In that moment, even vith murder black in his mind, Jarl Brakstad began to doubt. He asked qvestion vithin heart. 'Vhat do I keep? I burn. I kill. I take. Yet vhat vill I take to halls of the afterlife vhen the deathfrost rimes my brow? Vhat more than the souls of men vill burn bright in the darkness of Forever?'"

"In that moment, brazen horns blew, and Jarl Brakstad turned to see hills darken with shambling, groaning hordes of Sheol, Architect of Death. Hundreds of corpses, bereft of their noble souls, lurched toward the city, led by dread murder-priests to slake their dark god's thirst for blood of men."

"The Volf's eyes videned, and he looked back to old man, who for last time vhispered, 'Keep. My. Sheep.'"

"Brakstad could have left. He could have taken his varriors and sailed, raiding only veak and easy targets. But old man's simple vords took hold of Volf Lord. They lodged like barbed arrows in soft meat of his heart, and he knew that to tear them free vould leave his spirit to bleed out and die vithin him."

Skald met Gideon's eyes. "No man can live vith dead soul."

"His axe rose, and his varriors tensed. They expected to see smile of his axe bite deep in old priest's chest. They expected to see the dark spray of lifeblood fountain into the air, and hear the death-rattle as life-breath pushes through hot blood filling his mouth. The chief's axe flashed forward, bright against snow, but it vas no killing blow to cut the strings of men. It vas signal—to *charge*. The mighty chieftain thundered past old man, a terrible roar bellowing from his lungs at last as he carved the first shambling corpse in tvain vith single blow."

"In that day, Jarl Brakstad Stonebreaker met the Sheolin murder-priests in pitched battle and broke them. The varriors of the Volves savaged the demon's armies and tore throats from his priests, and even the most bloodthirsty of the Vulfen found his lust for battle sated."

Skald stroked his beard, bringing his story to a close. "After that day, Jarl Brakstad brought his varriors to the Hammarhold, and they learned of the Almighty from the old priest. They named him the Volfherd, the vone who brought them in from the long night to sleep at Master's fire."

"Since that time, the Vulfenkind fight for those who cannot. Ve prowl these lands, alvays ready to tear the throats from those who do evil. Even demons fear to prey upon the sheep of the North, for these sheep are guarded by Volves."

Skald gestured to the caravan behind them. "So let them come. Ve are Volves. Ve may keep the Master's sheep, and ve may sleep by His fire, but ve haf not forgotten the night from vhich ve came, and our teeth are still sharp."

One of the Wolves riding nearby grunted derisively. Casually, Skald twisted to regard him. "Young Feros, you do not agree?"

The Wolf Skald called Feros shrugged, the bone ornaments twisted into his black dreadlocks clicking together. "That story might impress the farmboy over there, taleweaver, but true warriors are not swayed by your fairy tales."

Skald drew himself up and turned the full force of his eye on the warrior. "Those *fairy tales* are the song of our people, vhelp, and the lifeblood of our clan. Now I am thinking ve need another scouting of the voods. Just to be safe."

For a breath, it seemed as if Feros would defy Skald's command, but in the end, the Wolf tugged on his horse's reins and galloped for the front of the column. The other Wolf assigned to them quickly rode alongside him, and the two disappeared into the mists.

Gideon watched them go. "What was that all about?"

Skald sighed. "Those two are brothers, evils seeds planted by traitorous father hanged for his crime. They grew up believing in nothing, and since becoming varriors, seek to become masters of all around them. They are dangerous, but vith our losses, jarl must take every axe."

Gesturing helplessly, Gideon asked, "Then why do they care about *me?*"

Skald scratched at his throat. "Because they vie for Anya's hand, and now they think you are contender."

A stone dislodged under Gideon's foot, and he stumbled. Awkwardly righting himself, he glanced automatically ahead to see the jarl's daughter riding at the front of the column, sitting tall and proud in her saddle with her bow on her back.

Trying to cover his misstep, Gideon asked, "So why do they want her? I mean, not that she's not desirable."

He winced as he said that last word, and resolutely kept his gaze forward as a slow grin spread across Skald's face.

"Vell, Feros and Fyrss vish to rule the Pack. Since Heimdall has no son, whoever vins the Helsdottyr claims the Vulfenkind by marriage-right."

Gideon sighed. "Oh. Politics."

Skald inclined his head. "It is stench in nostrils of God."

Rolling his shoulders to loosen the aches and trying to look at everything but the warrior princess swaying in her saddle in front of him, Gideon muttered, "Well, I won't be here long enough to be a problem for them."

Skald grinned even wider. "Ve shall see."

9

GHOSTS

Four hours later of trudging through dense wintry forest, Skald finally raised his fist and called a halt. The survivors of Estvik eagerly dropped their burdens, and faint complaints wafted through the woods, borne on the smoke from a dozen crackling campfires.

Swiftly and silently, Feros and Fyrss built the fire for the Wolf warriors, while Anya seasoned and prepared a quick meal of potatoes fried with bacon. Skald settled his great bulk down next to the fire with a theatrical groan, eliciting an indulgent smile from Anya and a scrap of sizzling meat. Seeing Gideon hang back, Skald gestured. "Just-Gideon, come. Varm yourself at fire."

The two brothers glanced at one another, then at Gideon. Fyrss spoke first. "And who is this to sit at the warrior's fire?"

Gideon stopped, and Skald narrowed his eye. "He is my guest. I say he is velcome at my fire, and so he is, *boy*."

Anger began to smolder in Feros' dark eyes. "It is my fire also, *old one*, and I have seen no record of his deeds beyond what you say, a tired taleweaver known to exaggerate for his favorites."

Anya's dark eyes flashed, and she snapped, "So speaks the courage of men who arrived *after* the battle."

His face tightening, Feros growled, "Watch your tongue, woman.

Perhaps we have fallen as far as you say, if Wolves have to share a meal berated by rebellious wenches and stammering farmers."

Skald's hammer slammed into the earth before Anya could retort. "Enough!"

The silver-maned veteran gestured sharply toward Gideon. "If you doubt stranger's prowess, challenge him and have done with it. Otherwise, do not veary old man vith talk lacking deeds."

Feros moved to block Gideon's path to the flames, his eyes filled with contempt. "Well, farmer? Either step into the circle, or back away from my fire."

Gideon looked the Wolf up and down, noting his wide shoulders and powerful build. It matched his own.

"I have nothing to prove to you," Gideon said, "and I am tired and cold. This is not worth fighting over."

Fyrss stepped to his brother's shoulder. "So find another fire."

Gideon shook his head in frustration and almost turned away, but out of the corner of his eye, he caught Anya looking at him. As soon as he glanced toward her, she looked away. Her face had fallen into a strange impassiveness, as if the standoff held no interest for her.

Do not walk away, young man. She is watching you.

Gideon blinked. The voice again, the same as earlier. It did not hold the distinctively bitter bite of Ashkelon's sendings; instead, the voice was gentle and kind.

Tentatively, he reached out. *Who are you?*

A friend. All will be revealed in time, but now you must focus on the two fools here, and the young princess pretending not to care what happens to you.

Gideon blew out his breath slowly. *One day, my thoughts will be my own...*

The gentle laughter of an old man echoed in his mind. *Few indeed are those who may claim that.*

His sword rasped out of its scabbard as Gideon sighed. "Where are we doing this?"

· · ·

SKALD CIRCUMSCRIBED a ritual circle in the hard earth of the forest, roughly ten strides across. Upon seeing the drawing of the circle, a small crowd gathered.

He spoke as he dragged his warhammer's head through the cold dirt. "Rules are simple, just-Gideon. Fight vith blade. Fight vith fist. Fight vith honor. Fight til first blood is spilled or til line is broken. Only then is grievance satisfied."

The veteran completed the circle and stepped out. "You stop when I say stop, or I vill put hammer through gut for disrespecting grey head. Begin vhen both are in circle."

Without hesitation, Feros entered the circle, his dark eyes predatory, his axe gripped loosely in both hands. "Come on, dirt-tiller."

Gideon sighed and stepped into the circle.

Immediately, Feros lunged forward, his axe whipping around his body in a devastating lateral slash meant to eviscerate Gideon where he stood. Most men would have stumbled back out of the circle to evade the swing, forfeiting the contest. Most men had. It was Feros' favored technique, and how he had risen so far in the Wolves' esteem.

But most men had not been trained by a mass-murdering sadist. Gideon's iron caught the axe just below the head and lifted it over his head. Meeting no resistance to his all-or-nothing attack, Feros staggered a single step, only to feel something bite at his neck like an insect.

His hand flew to the stinging, and came away striped with red.

Gideon shouldered his sword and sighed. "Are we done now?"

Feros glanced at Skald, who grinned and shrugged. "Vhat? You vant to say you vere not ready?"

The younger Wolf spat. "There is no satisfaction here. Any man can get lucky once."

"Any man except you," Anya called out, and Feros' face reddened as the crowd laughed.

"Again!" he roared, "Unless the farmer is a coward!"

Skald gestured expansively. "As you vill."

With a savage warcry, Feros feinted, sweeping his axe toward Gideon's thigh before reversing the attack into a chop at his neck.

Unfortunately for the raging Wolf, Gideon predicted the trick. He stepped into the attack, caught the axe with his right hand, pivoted and hurled the surprised warrior to the ground, disarming him with one smooth motion.

An instant later, Gideon stomped on Feros' wrist, pinning the limb to the dirt, and his sword flashed down to rest in the thrashing warrior's tear duct. The crowd gasped, and Feros suddenly stilled. In the silence, Gideon looked down at him. "Do I need to draw blood, or is this sufficient?"

Skald grinned, his eye shining with mirth. "Is up to him. Feros? Vhat say you?"

Feros' hate-filled eyes flickered to Gideon's, and Gideon raised an eyebrow and twisted his sword slightly. With pain tugging at his face, Feros growled, "I yield."

"Good."

The sword eased from his eye, and Feros lifted himself to his feet, swatting away Gideon's proffered hand of assistance. Gideon shrugged at the Wolf's rudeness and tossed his axe to Fyrss. "You. Do you need to get anything out of your humors? The circle is already here, so we might as well do this now."

Wariness dominated the Wolf's eyes, and he shook his head curtly. "My brother spoke for both of us. I will abide by the decision of the circle."

Gideon inclined his head and turned to the crowd. "Is there anyone else with a grievance, or can I go warm my hands now?"

The crowd chuckled and clapped appreciatively, til a single drawn-out word cut through the noise.

"I."

Of its own volition, the crowd divided, leaving the path open for a shadow standing with blades formed from hate and ice. Gideon's heart chilled with dread as Ashkelon advanced toward the circle, his searing gaze never leaving his student.

Before Gideon could stop him, Skald frowned and said, "Very vell, fate-changer, rules are sim—"

He never had the chance to finish. Ashkelon lashed out with one blade, and Skald jerked back, narrowly missing a cut throat. The sorcerer ignored his surprised oath, one blade held before him in a low guard and the other sweeping out behind him. With a silent prayer screamed to the heavens, Gideon leapt to meet him.

No one there, not the peasants, not the battle-hardened Wolves and according to Skald, not even the angels, had ever seen two mortal men move so fast. The blades of ice and iron flickered, darted and slammed into one another dozens of times in the blink of an eye. Sparks and shards of ice sprayed from every contact.

Ashkelon's left-hand blade arrowed toward Gideon's heart, and the young man twisted away and smashed it to ice chips with his palm. Chainmail forged in the underworld and stained with sin slashed around the sorcerer's body as Ashkelon lashed out in a flying kick, hooking his heel under Gideon's ear and blasting the warrior out of the circle.

His eyes wide, Skald started to say, "The contest is ov—"

Shaking his head groggily, Gideon raised his sword and managed to blurt, "Stay back!", as Ashkelon stalked toward him, a fresh sword freezing in his hand. Gideon shoved the nearest peasant to him away before his master fell upon him again.

The swords of ice rained down relentlessly on Gideon, battering his guard, freezing his flesh. The swords shattered like glass and refroze as the dread warrior hammered them on Gideon again and again. His breath came in short gasps as Gideon staggered back from Ashkelon's assault, parrying and deflecting with increasing desperation.

Frostbite seared his forearm as Gideon slapped a sword away, and he grit his teeth through the pain. "Master...I am *sorry*..."

In answer, the swords scissored together, and Gideon lunged back, falling to his backside and rolling to avoid being cut in half. Ashkelon gave him no space, sword strikes slicing the air around his apprentice as Gideon managed to parry or avoid each freezing blade.

Rolling back to rise to his feet, Gideon's foot snagged a root, and with a strangled cry, he pitched backward. His back slammed into a tree, and before the young man could recover, Ashkelon closed the distance, backhanded Gideon's sword from his grip and sank his blade in Gideon's chest up to the icy hilt.

Faintly, Gideon heard splinters burst from the back of the tree. Roaring filled his ears as his lungs froze in his chest.

Gasps of horror erupted from the crowd as the sorcerer twisted his blade and snapped it off with a wrench of his arm.

Sweeping his warhammer high over his head, Skald roared and charged, his face thunderous with wrath. Ashkelon thrust his palm toward the oncoming warrior, and a wave of invisible force catapulted Skald off of his feet and into the crowd. Lightning flickered dangerously in Ashkelon's eyes as the Wolf struggled to rise, and Anya rushed over to Skald, as much to prevent him from trying again as to check on his condition.

Turning back to Gideon, Ashkelon spoke at last, his voice a low hiss. "Look at you. Writhing like a beetle stuck to a board. You disgust me."

He could form no words, just a long *nnnnnnggghhh* as his lungs desperately tried to inflate around the bleeding canyon in his body.

Ashkelon paced before him, waving his groan away. "Spare me your insipid excuses. You ran. I paved the way for you to slay the mistress of a *demon lord*, and you fled at the moment of truth. For what? To share a moment of brotherhood with dregs?"

The sorcerer stepped close, his pale features mere inches away from Gideon's. "You, alone of all these pathetic wretches, had the skill and tactical flexibility necessary to kill the whore. I can understand the storyteller, shackled by the memories of the brothers he failed with his survival, or the Takeshi slaves, oathed to defend the subjects of a king too distant to care. Let them die to lengthen the lifespans of diseased peasants. But *you...*"

Ashkelon punched his other sword into Gideon's ribs, sneering as Gideon's eyes widened. "You were to be more! I have spent months elevating you beyond these commoners and their temporal concerns. You are a warrior of righteousness, trained to the exacting standard of evil. You were to be everything the Everlasting Dark hungers to confront, an unyielding avatar of justice in an eternal conflict. You are *not one of them.* You are judgment incarnate, and yet at the hour of your duty, when darkness bellowed your name into the night, *you turned back."*

Blood bubbled from Gideon's lips as Ashkelon continued. "You are unworthy of your forebears, and the mantle which has been passed to you by countless bearers of the Light. They would cast you from their ranks with scorn on their faces, writ by the magnitude of your failure. I should let you die where you twitch, a sad disappointment to both the Light and the Dark."

Anya cried, "Just stop it, demon!"

Ashkelon jerked around to face her, his eyes blazing with fury. His voice growled low with threat. *"What* did you call me?"

Anya stood, shoulders back and chin raised in defiance. She walked toward the sorcerer and planted herself between the dying Gideon and Ashkelon. "You heard me. No man would act as you have. Only demons are so heartless."

Fighting back the blackness stealing his sight, Gideon reached out, trying to grip her elbow and pull her away. Anya glanced at the touch, then looked back at Ashkelon, her voice going soft. "Even now, at the gate of Death, he tries to protect, as he did at the gate of Estvik. Where you would have left us to die, this man sacrificed personal glory to stand with strangers. So, yes, I name you *demon*, an inhuman monster to be cast into the darkness alone to burn in its sins."

She looked Ashkelon up and down, contempt twisting her beautiful features. "What else would you be?"

Ashkelon gazed at her, his expression revealing none of the thoughts within him. Gideon slumped, losing his grip on reality and beginning his tumble into the black.

"Very well."

THE WORDS WERE SO QUIET, they were almost inaudible. Anya opened her mouth, but no words came. A force battered her backwards, toppling her to her backside beside Skald.

Ashkelon squared off in front of Gideon, his eyes raking over his apprentice's still form. Power began to radiate from him, the air shimmering as if it rose from desert sands at noon.

The sorcerer began to chant quietly, intoning words the witnesses strained to hear. He lifted his hands, palms facing Gideon, and placed them over his heart.

Lightning crackled on his gauntlets and flesh sizzled. Gideon's eyes snapped open in shock and his mouth opened in an agonized scream, his back arching against the unyielding wood of the tree.

Ashkelon had not yet finished. Almost not seeming to hear his apprentice's cries, Ashkelon gripped the shards of ice lodged in Gideon's chest and pulled, the broken blades sawing out of his ribs. Gideon tried to collapse, but Ashkelon slammed him back against the tree with one hand and intoned a deep droning incantation, almost a hymn. Ashkelon's eyes gleamed silver-blue and Gideon shouted again, trying to buck away from his master's grip.

With the sound of cracking bone and the smell of cooking meat, Gideon's wounds reknit themselves at Ashkelon's will. Sinew snaked across Gideon's ribs even as the bones re-fused. Gideon gritted his teeth to quiet his screams, but strained moans escaped his lips as he bowed, shaking, over the black claw clamped onto his chest.

At last, when Anya thought Gideon could not possibly suffer any more, Ashkelon released him, and the warrior pitched onto his face in the dirt.

Looming over his gasping apprentice, Ashkelon growled, "So then, *man*, live another day. Bask in the air that fills your lungs and the comradeship you share with fellow men. But when the day darkens and the sun hides her face from you, when all you can hear are the shrieks of your children being eaten alive by creatures too terrible for words, you will weep when you remember you could have saved them all."

The sorcerer stepped over Gideon and strode into the forest. Just before he passed Anya and Skald, he stopped. Anya's heart chilled within her breast as his cold eyes fell upon her, and the sorcerer clenched his fists at his side, fury tensing his dark frame.

"Never."

Hate shook his voice, but on hearing it, Ashkelon clenched his jaw. Anya could see the muscles working as he fought for control of himself. He spoke again.

"Never...call me *demon* again. Transgress a second time, and I shall show you a fate befitting a daughter of Hel."

Anya swallowed reflexively as Ashkelon stalked into the forest.

Skald shouldered past her to reach the resurrected warrior struggling to rise from his knees. Reaching under the young man's armpit, Skald heaved Gideon to his feet, even as his other hand pulled a blade sheathed at his wolfskin belt. His steely eye searched Gideon's as the knife hovered just below his diaphragm.

Gideon met his gaze and firmly put a hand on the blade. "It's me."

Skald's eye tightened. "I have killed shieldbrothers before, revenant, to save them from necromancy's vile hold. If you speak false, I vill not hesitate to end you and free the boy's soul."

Looking into his pained glare, Gideon believed him. "Grandfather. It is me, not a ghost."

Anya looked into Gideon's eyes, also. They were hard, but not soulless. The sorcerer had invited no wraith to possess the boy's body. Pressing his lips together in a thin line, Skald sheathed his knife. "Now you vill tell Skald how many."

Gideon winced and prodded his aching chest. "How many what?"

Skald ground his teeth, and Anya froze. She had never seen her grandfather this angry before. "Boy...," he warned, "This is not first time you have died. How. *Many.*"

The warrior shrugged free of Skald's embrace and staggered slightly before recovering his balance. "I'm not sure."

He bent to recover his blade from the cold earth, and they heard him mutter, "Whenever I fail."

The bones in Skald's hand cracked, they gripped his warhammer so hard. The veteran was breathing deeply, his shoulders heaving with the effort to contain his rage. "Vhy? Vhy do you endure this vicked man?"

Gideon knelt and tested his sword's edge with his thumb. He seemed to consider Skald's question. "An orphan lives off of the generosity of others. For my entire life, I dreamed of being a hero, of the looks of respect such a man would receive just for walking into a room. When men looked at me, I saw outright contempt, at *best* pity. When it came to it, I could not even save my own mother. Then he came."

He pointed his sword toward the forest where the dark killer had disappeared. "Do you even know what he is? He is the Enemy personified. He is the villain in every story ever told. Ashkelon is everything dark, cruel and lost. Mercy for its own sake does not occur to him."

Anya gestured after Ashkelon. "And this is the man you would take for your example?"

Gideon lowered his head, one hand clenching. "*Who else?* You were born Wolves. You are already heroes, with stories and songs singing about your courage. I have nothing but the memory of my mother's death."

Skald shouted angrily, "Ve do not learn like this, Gideon! This is evil!"

Gideon cut him off. "Just like the Dark and everything in it, Skald. The enemy had no mercy, either, and when I failed before, it was the innocents slaughtered, not me."

His voice broke, and Gideon struggled for control of himself. "Ashkelon may be a vicious tyrant, but he cares enough to see me succeed. He cares enough to ensure that I can't accept failure. He doesn't pat me on the head or rub my back, whispering that I did the best I could. When I fail, he kills me, so that I know exactly what the stakes are. Best of all, when I fail under him, *I* am the only one who dies. And I'm getting better."

Skald opened his mouth again, but could find nothing to say to Gideon. Anya stared at him, searching for something, anything, to say to turn the warrior from this terrible path.

Gideon did not give either of them a chance. "So I will die as often as I must. I will give my last breath to defend the innocent, and if Ashkelon brings me back, I will give it again, and again, and again."

Gideon's iron sword rasped into the sheath on his back. "Now, I will find him and I will thank him. I will thank him for being pitiless, so that I know the price of failure. I will beg him to take me as his student again, and when I face the Darkness for true, it will find no weakness in me."

THE FOREST SHIVERED as a shadow tore through the trees, chased by screams and whispers.

Just stop it and help him, demon!

Ashkelon's face twisted at the words. His pale hair whipped about his head as he snarled, "How dare they?"

The fortresses are fallen silent, my liege. The Demon of the East has taken them and every soul within.

Back, scourge of the Dark! Get back to the Abyss that spawned you!

You may have triumphed today, son of shadow, but Hell knows your name, and it will come for you.

Ashkelon's breath came fast as he fought the whispers clawing at his mind. Acherlith thrummed on his back, the soul-memories within surging against their prison. Ashkelon's teeth gritted against their rising screams as the ghostly impressions of skulls leered from the ground.

The worst of it was the hallucination. Everywhere he looked, a Man stood amongst the trees, shrouded in sackcloth. He stood and watched with golden eyes, a silent angel of judgment, waiting.

Demon...

Ashkelon's teeth bared in a feral growl. *You do not judge me.*

The whispers rose again.

What kind of hellspawn poisons CHILDREN?

May the Everlasting Dark devour your soul, monster!

The sorcerer swept to his left, trying to shake the relentless avatar and the ghosts shrieking at him. The sky hung grey and dark above him, pregnant with the judgment of the universe upon him.

Demon...

The sorcerer snarled, "Be silent!"

Demon...

"Leave me alone!"

What else would you be?

Screams rent the cold air. Ashkelon jerked, a chill of dread racing through his veins that he had succumbed to madness at last.

But no. These were real screams, torn from the throats of the living to echo through the forest. He could feel their souls gasping into the ether from a nexus of life force nearby.

Ashkelon twisted and dashed toward the source of the screams, a familiar refrain, desperate to escape the ethereal demands of the lost and the unyielding gaze of the hooded figure.

GIDEON LEFT the encampment behind him, breaking into a short jog. He grimaced as his freshly reknit bones shifted, but he ignored it. Every time Ashkelon brought him back, it always hurt.

Next, you will say that just means you are alive.

Quick as a viper strike, Gideon whipped out his sword and lunged to the side to avoid any attack. Nothing but the silent trees and new-fallen snow greeted his eyes.

The voice murmured in his mind once more, sounding amused.

Put it away, sir knight. I mean no harm.

Gideon's voice was hard as stone, and he did not put the blade away. "Show yourself."

I will. Try not to kill me. Again.

A chuckle echoed in Gideon's mind as yards away, a faint golden glow formed. It grew quickly, coalescing from motes of light into the ghostly representation of an old man leaning upon an ornate staff. Symbols and writing Gideon did not recognize embroidered the elder's robe.

Gideon did not lower his sword. "I know you. You were in my dream. At the Pyramid."

Small details could not escape Gideon's heightened senses, thanks to Ashkelon's merciless instruction. When the elder did not take a breath to speak, Gideon noticed. His gaze hardened.

The ethereal figure held up a hand, slightly shaking with age. *I am no threat to you, Gideon, adopted son of Halcyon.*

"I'll be the judge of that. How do you know me?"

A smiled tugged at the corner of the old man's mouth. *Frankly, young man, I would not, but for your association with the Onyxian Mage.*

Gideon pursed his lips. "The Onyxian Mage...Ashkelon?"

The ghost nodded. *We did not know him by that name. Not then.*

Gideon's forehead creased in confusion. "Who is 'we'?"

We, the people of Avalon. The first victims to taste the edge of the Dark champion's bitter vengeance. The voices you hear wailing from his black blade are ours.

Gideon's sword lowered. "Avalon? Is that...Ashkelon's home?"

The ghost inclined its head in acknowledgement. *I am sorry to interfere in this world's affairs, sir knight, but I must. For the sake of your civilizations, I bring a warning to ward away the fate that lies in store for you.*

Gideon pointed at him. "You know me, but I do not yet know you. Name yourself."

Of course. Please accept my apologies. It seems the state of death has eroded my courtesies. My name is Gemelte Asirius, and it was I who sent the dream.

RATHCHUK WAS A SMART ONE. He had deep thoughts. He could remember all kinds of things the priests said.

Hunger is not just the void in a man's gut when he craves food.

It is the purest state a man can achieve.

It is a surprise to no one that man is a creature of needs, beholden to his lusts. In opposition to this, beasts succumb to their lusts, fighting and consuming one another in their pathetic instincts to survive just one more day. But man...man is the apex.

So the bitter lord Mammon teaches his devoted children. A man can endure hunger, and in so doing, overcome his base nature and reach an ascended plane. Want becomes the vehicle that elevates a wretched soul to the level of the angels, who neither eat nor need.

To keep hunger sharp, however, and prevent the sacred reminder from sinking to a dull ache the robs the mind of clarity, one must whet it with gluttony, the other extreme of the sacred scale. One to balance the other. And so Ja'a, the Blessed Lady and Consort of their master, gave the country of the Wolves to her emaciated slaves with a free hand.

"Go, my children. Go and feed. With every mouthful of faithless flesh you feast upon, rain praises on your sweet master. Your loving lord. Your *god*."

And they went, and fed.

Rathchuk the Swallower bared his filthy grin at the twisted wretch opposite him in the Wolf-server house and snarled in warning. Polluted saliva dripped from his black, infected gums and slapped wetly on the wood floor. The other, a mere acolyte of the Marrow Suckers coven, screeched and flinched away, but stubbornly refused to retreat.

No one should refuse Rathchuk. He was a Blessed One.

Angling his head back, Rathchuk allowed the cretin an unobstructed view of his Blessing, since maybe he didn't know. To prove his namesake, he swallowed noisily, his throat working hard to force a phlegmy gobbet down his gullet. The challenger swallowed, too, with less effort and more fear.

Good. Cower before Rathchuk, little creep.

Rathchuk the Swallower could swallow so loudly because his lips could not close all the way. His lips could not close all the way because the nasty healers of the Lord of Hunger himself had ripped out all his pathetic before-teeth and implanted gnashing fangs an inch long in their place. They declared him *chosen*, a Blessed One! Him!

Goron Fingercruncher had not believed at first. He had tried to withstand the will of the gods, but Rathchuk had made him believe. He believed good when Rathchuk swallowed him and his sons without chewing.

Now they all believed.

He struggled to form words through his lovely fangs. "M-mine, little creep! This one being for Rathchuk! Not dirty creepers!"

A whimper escaped from the under the bed they stood over, quickly muffled by a fleshy hand. The sound perked up his ears, and a moan escaped his lips. The Wolf-servant girl-child's sweet voice made Rathchuk's mouth water all over again, and he wiped his chin with the back of his filthy arm.

Young, and tender, and juicy, and...

"Boss!"

Rathchuk gave a frustrated whine-snarl at the shout of the stupid Marrow Sucker who had intruded on his reverie. He stuck his head out the window of the Wolf-servant house and snapped, "What is it! What is being so important as to interrupt the great Rathchuk in his hunger!"

The stupid Marrow Sucker dipped quickly in obeisance. "Man coming! Has noisy sword!"

Rathchuk snarled again. So stupid. "Swords don't make noise, stupid! Swords are quiet, like you should be instead of interrupting Rathchuk!"

The stupid Marrow Sucker shifted from foot to foot, his useless arms dangling at his sides.

Stupid.

Rathchuk sighed loudly. "Very well. Great Rathchuk will come and kill dark man with the not-possibly noisy sword. Then you all see how mighty Rathchuk is being."

His stupid servant squeaked and scampered off, wailing for the tribe to assemble. Rathchuk turned back to his breakfast, only to see the scrawny wretch trying to sneakily reach and take what was Rathchuk's.

Rathchuk pounced forward, gnashing his fangs, and the wretch jerked back and ran.

Stupid. They all were stupid. He should eat him next, maybe, after the Wolf-servant girl-child.

And bring his snack with him. He was not trusting creeps.

NOTHING BUT DETRITUS HERE.

Frustration bleeding from his soul, Ashkelon stood on a hillock overlooking the broken gate of a town gutted by cultists. His eyes raked across the ruins, seeing the bodies, split open like ripe fruit, sprawled across the slate steps of burning homes. Cannibals looked up from their feeding, filthy knives and shards of obsidian gripped tight in their grimy fists.

They were just vermin. Nothing capable of sustaining the furious release that his soul craved.

A sharp glance behind him, and he saw the shrouded Man with the golden eyes, arms crossed. He had yet to see the apparition move a muscle, yet it stalked him like a shadow.

Acherlith vibrated in his sheath, the shrieks within the blade battling to breach their prison. Ashkelon drew the black blade and winced as the screams of billions trapped between the realms flooded the quiet forest.

It was not the volume that made him flinch, nor the fear, hate and pain in their shrieking voices. As always, it was their innocence. The wrongness of their deaths battered Ashkelon's conscience like waves in a hurricane. They should not have died. The Light should have saved them.

Demondemondemondemon...

His spirit stiffened against the onslaught. Ashkelon curled his lip and aimed his cursed weapon at the hooded Man, sighting down the length of the wailing blade. The voices shrank back, the accusations ceasing as the darkness in Ashkelon gathered and swelled.

His eyes blazing with skyfire, he spat through clenched teeth, "If it bothers you so much, perhaps you should have stepped in then. Besides, none of these screaming ghosts were truly righteous, no matter how they claim otherwise. There are none good, and I will not give credence to any claims that I kill for base pleasure."

Ashkelon made to turn away from the rabble gathering below, disgusted with both himself and them, til a sound plucked at his hearing. Higher-pitched than the infernal squeaking and giggling of the demented horde in the town square, the sound was a note apart from the cacophony of Hell-worshippers.

A girl. Terrified. His gaze found her, struggling in the grip of a black-jawed monster. Alone amidst the gibbering—

—*morass of darkness, swallowing me and drenching me in its cold embrace—*

—cannibals, trying desperately to free herself from—

—*chains. Far too heavy for my childish wrists, dragging me to the metal floor of my cage—*

—the grip of the black-gummed champion. Her eyes locked onto the—

—*noble visage of a knight, stopping on his journey to observe the mine—*

—dark spectre standing in the forest, looking into the ruined town. Through ratty black tresses, her eyes begged and her mouth soundlessly pleaded—

—*don't leave me—*

Memory moved his mouth with hers, and Ashkelon felt the ghost of ancient disappointment, the harshest betrayal, slash through him again.

The sorcerer felt the gaze of the Man stabbing into his back.

As it was then, so it is now. That knight had no idea of the hidden price of minding his own business, so long ago.

Ashkelon glanced back, and saw the apparition's head tilt to the side.

And now here you are.

Ashkelon shook his head with glacial slowness and his gauntlet tightened on the hilt of his cursed sword. Darkness and screams swelled around him in a thunderous tide as he exhaled slowly.

"Not. Again."

THE DARK MAN'S sword *was* noisy.

It was yelling, yelling like the Wolf-servants had yelled when Rathchuk had descended on them like thunder from a storm.

Rathchuk furrowed his wise brow. Yelling swords were strange, but there was only one of them, and the wielder was talking to himself. Sometimes Rathchuk talked to himself also, but that was because no one else was as smart as Rathchuk. It was why he was Blessed.

The crying girl-child tried to pull her arm away from his grip, but Rathchuk held his snack with the strength of a thousand girl-children. His strength was such that the girl-child shrieked in pain, and his lips stretched into a grin as he gloried in his divine power.

The dark man started at the sound of the girl's cry, and Rathchuk's pleased grin began to disappear.

Mutters began to rise around Rathchuk from his servants.

"Why does his eyes glow?"

"Sword's *loud.*"

"Why is glowy-eyes walking this way? He is only one meat..."

Rathchuk became angry at their cowardice. He whirled on them, shouting, "You are all stupids, all of you! He is one man-meat, and we are Mammon's Suckers of Marrow. I am being his Blessed One. How Blessed does you think he is being? He only has glowy eyes and noisy sword!"

One of his stupid servants raised his palsied hand.

Rathchuk turned on him, still holding his crying girl-snack. "*What is it, stupid?*"

The Marrow Sucker pointed shakily, and Rathchuk turned back to the dumb man-meat.

He was gone.

The forest had turned blacker than the blackest black-thing, pressing into the shattered gates of the town, creeping like smoke along the ground. The air turned heavy with weird pressure, popping Rathchuk's ears as his Blessed jaws gaped at the transformation. The woods looked like a roiling cloud, blocking out the cold light of the weak sun as it glowered down at the servants of the Hungry God.

And it was *breathing.*

As HE JOGGED through the forest, following the broken snow trail of Ashkelon's passage, Gideon struggled to come to grips with his companion.

"You are saying that you are from Ashkelon's home, which is on a different *world* than this one?"

The ghost calling itself Gemelte trailed after him, never out of breath, never breathing.

Indeed. What did you think Ashkelon spoke of when he said 'my world'?

Gideon shrugged. "I thought he was speaking metaphorically. He does that."

Your ignorance is understandable, given your society's grasp of science and the cosmos.

His breath panted evenly from his mouth, blasting puffs of mist from his mouth as he ran. "You say you're trapped in Acherlith with the others. So how can you talk to me? Have you escaped, somehow?"

The hesitation was slight, and any other man might have missed it, but Gideon did not.

The soul prison you call Acheron's Bane thrives off of death energy. Every time the blade takes a life, a window opens into the prison. You, however, have been slain a number of times, yet your soul has been held back by Ashkelon's will. I observed that the windows remain open longer as Acherlith battles the Onyxian for your soul. When the time came, I was ready.

"So why talk to me? Why not run away?"

The ghost chuckled. *I am a spirit without a body. Rather than roam the barren wilderness of the soulscape, bemoaning my fate, I choose to help you change yours.*

Gideon's legs churned through the snow up an embankment. "Really? And what is my fate?"

The humor faded from Gemelte's disembodied voice. *To die as we did.*

The young warrior continued to struggle up the hill. "And how did you die?"

As Gideon crested the rise and beheld the ruined village, the ghost murmured, *See for yourself. He's doing it again.*

THE SERVANTS of the Outcast Ones had, no doubt, seen many terrible things in their lives. They had seen men, women and children sacrificed to the hungers and fetishes of bitter false gods, slaking some unfathomable thirst for vengeance on the kingdoms of Man.

Hell they knew, or so they thought. Death, on the other hand, was an entirely new and visceral experience for them.

Ashkelon arrowed out of sentient darkness, his blade shrieking like a raptor released from its cage. The eyes of every wretch in the town lifted to behold his ascent, the dark avatar of judgment come to punish them for their sins.

He slammed down next to the fanged champion and threw Acherlith, the howling sword spearing into the Venan nearest to him and pinning the mutant to a doorjamb. His eyes flashed as he assessed the recoiling warband at the speed of thought, while the blade began to drain the life from its victim.

Ashkelon could easily kill every twisted slave in the town, but the girl provided a layer of complexity to any assault. He could almost hear his apprentice bleating about protecting her young sensibilities from the horror of the massacre Ashkelon was about to perpetrate.

In the fury of lightning that was his cognition, Ashkelon conceded the argument his student never had the opportunity to make. *What is the purpose of protecting innocence if innocence is itself destroyed in the process?*

He altered his tactics accordingly.

Time resumed its normal passage. The cannibals nearest the impaled Venan stared dumbstruck at the screaming shaft of black metal sucking their comrade dry. Ashkelon pivoted and slammed a hammer fist onto the arm of the black-gummed champion holding the girl. Bones shattered in the man's wrist, and he opened his distended mouth wide to give voice to his pain.

The sound might echo in her memories. By the Dark, this is complicated.

Ashkelon backhanded him across the cheek, and mutated fangs burst from his weeping gums from the sheer force of the blow. Ashkelon whipped around and kicked the crying champion with enough power to rupture several organs within his body, particularly targeting the diaphragm.

Rathchuk the Swallower died facedown in a pig trough, his Blessed jaws full of slops, his final words a gasping wheeze.

As the warband reeled from the death of their champion, the girl stared at her dark savior with wide eyes. Ashkelon turned to her and for an instant, hesitated. *I do not know what to say. I have never saved anyone before.*

He could almost hear Gideon's laughter.

Gruffly, trying to conceal the unexpected awkwardness, Ashkelon held out his hand and commanded, "You will not fear me."

It only took her a second to make up her mind. Ashkelon did not know what he had been expecting, but it surprised him all the same when she rushed forward and wrapped her thin arms around his waist, burying her face in his hip. Ashkelon let his darkmail cloak fall around her, wrapping her head about the ears with his arm to shield her from the cacophony of the dying, and clenched his other fist.

Acherlith tore from its now-desiccated victim with a wet rip and hung in the air, its lethal edge dripping with polluted blood as it awaited its master's command.

The Venans looked from Ashkelon to the cursed sword and back, the faintest realization dawning in their yellowed eyes. One even began to take breath to implore him for mercy.

As if.

Ashkelon dropped his hand. His sword vanished, moving too quickly for the eye to follow as it circumscribed a single vicious arc around its master. There was a sound like the tearing of wet cloth, then Acherlith slapped into his waiting gauntlet.

One after another, the Venans slumped or fell apart, some managing to whimper faintly before the weapon hungrily devoured the last of their ability to scream.

Before releasing his ward, Ashkelon sheathed the wailing blade, muting its unearthly howls, as he assumed the child would find it unsettling. He allowed his cloak to fall away, freeing her sight, and stepped away.

At least, he tried to.

She refused to let go. Tenaciously, the girl clung to him like a second skin, matching his backpedaling steps with her own. Ashkelon could feel the very uncomfortable sensation of her cheek snuggling into his hip, as if she were drawing *comfort* from touching him.

It was unsettling. It was repulsive. Every fiber of his being demanded that the contact cease immediately.

"You are safe now," he tried. "You may let go."

Nothing.

He tried command.

"Release me."

She was having none of it. The child remained attached, like a stubborn tick.

It was one of the very few times in his life Ashkelon began looking about for help.

GIDEON MADE his way down into the ruins of the town, Gemelte still drifting behind him. It was remarkable simple to track Ashkelon. All you had to do was follow the screams.

The bodies of the townsfolk lay mingled with the fallen Venans, the innocent joined with the corrupted in death.

To the Devil's Blade, we are all the same.

"Your people had a lot of names for him," Gideon growled as he picked his way through the corpses.

The Dark plagued our people for centuries. We did not know it was one man for many years; hence, the multitude of distinctions.

Glancing at him, Gideon asked, "Centuries? How old is he?"

Gemelte spread his hands helplessly. *I was the greatest scholar of Avalon. I spent years studying and searching all texts of the Everlasting Dark to find his name, his age, his homeland, all to no avail. It was commonly believed that the Dark, in vengeance for the losses suffered to my brother the Scion, formed him itself and unleashed him upon us.*

Gideon halted, scanning the town for signs of Ashkelon. He wrinkled his nose at the sight of a black-jawed mutant with broken teeth. "Did you not agree?"

I believed nothing without evidence I could see. Gods, demons, even the human soul: I was a skeptic of all.

Gideon grunted in wry amusement. "Well, looks like Ashkelon settled a couple of those for you."

The ghost inclined his head. *The point is conceded.*

Gideon finished examining the pattern of bodies and muttered, "Well, I think he went that way. You ready to see him again?"

Gemelte drifted back. *I believe it for the best that he not know I escaped. He might attempt to imprison me again, and I would rather lend my wisdom to you instead.*

Gideon sighed, letting his head hang to stretch the muscles of his neck.

You are handling my presence well. I expected more resistance.

His neck cracked, and Gideon groaned in relief. "Did you know that I used to be a farmer?"

What of it?

Gideon chuckled ruefully. "It is just that before Ashkelon came, I used to fantasize about these things. Ghosts, dark sorcerers, heroes fighting demons. I always secretly wanted them to be real, so that life would be more interesting."

And?

Gideon moved forward, leaving the phantom Gemelte behind. "I miss when things could surprise me."

He stepped around the corner of a building and stopped dead.

Next to a ruined fountain, Ashkelon stood, his body stiff as a board and his arms held out from his body. Gideon's eyes widened as he saw the little girl, maybe nine or ten years of age, hugging his waist for dear life and peering suspiciously at the newcomer.

Ashkelon sighted him and breathed a faint sigh of impatience mixed with relief. "Apprentice, at last. Get over here. It won't let go."

Raucous laughter rang out through the forest.

10

SERVANTS

I n a large tent in the midst of the Mammonite encampment, surrounded by baying lunatics and snuffling beastmen, an art critic waited for his audience.

Abram focused on the sheet of human skin arrayed before him. Under the wide brim of a weathered hat, his dark eyes flicked this way and that, taking note of the whorls and creases in the flayed parchment, the hundred tiny signs that marked events in the wearer's life like the rings in the trunk of a tree.

"Does my flaymaster's work meet with your approval, inquisitor?"

A faint smile tugged at the scars on Abram's face, and he turned on his heel smoothly to face Ja'a, the Satiatress, beloved Consort of Mammon.

Pretty titles for a fallen angel's whore.

Abram kept such thoughts masked behind a demesne of detached politeness and answered, "The work is adequate, lady, though lacking in essence. A Jahennan would seek to keep the subject alive so that the victim's agony might be continuously inscribed on its skin, line upon line, and precept upon precept."

Ja'a tilted her head and crooned, "Are you a fleshreader then?"

Abram inclined his head in a shallow bow. "As a pastime only. To my regret, I lack the necessary time to devote to the path of the flay-master. The more one considers the pains inflicted on human flesh, the more one learns of the human condition. It is said that the greatest of the Order can see the skeins of the future writ on a victim's skin, as his pain aligns with the agony of the human race."

Her filthy bone-wings dragging behind her, Ja'a stepped beside Abram and considered the human canvas draping the frame. "So you do not approve, then?"

Abram shook his head. "This work is without life. It speaks nothing to me."

Ja'a slipped him a sidelong glance, her eyes bright with the vigor of the insane, and she said, "So, the Jahennan art is dead. I find that this speaks a great deal to me."

Abram's smile did not reach his eyes, and he gestured toward the shadowed recesses of the adjoining compartment of the tent.

"I see you are composing a Mammonite piece as well, lady."

Ja'a swept her ratty locks aside almost prettily, and said, "Really? Thank you for noticing. Just a couple of dogs I found in the woods. They followed me home."

Abram tried to keep a wince from his face. The two gaunt speci-mens stretched on the racks looked very little like human beings any more.

Ja'a looked back at them with something like affection. "I'm thinking of adopting them."

Abram squinted at them. "How are they so...?"

The consort waved a hand demurely. "My lord is the God of Hunger. He told me once that men are ruled by their needs, and that to break a man's will, you have only to leave him to his lusts."

The inquisitor grunted. "That should take more time than this."

She shrugged. "You know little of Mammonite sorcery. I have touched their appetites and increased their cravings. Their bodies have consumed themselves to feed a rapacious hunger they have never before experienced. Either they will break, or they will die."

Ja'a looked at him. "Men always break."

Time to change tacks.

Nodding in feigned acknowledgement, Abram said, "I'm sure they do. Have you had time to consider my lord's proposal, lady?"

Ja'a crossed her emaciated arms and moved further into the great tent as she asked, "Your lord? Surely you speak of Gehenna, the Master of Agony?"

Abram followed her, careful to leave space between himself and the unstable demoness. He tread on dangerous ground here.

"My mission is in service to mighty Gehenna, of course."

Ja'a scoffed. "Your words writhe in your mouth like a python's coils, inquisitor. Do not lie. You have abandoned your god for another. A *man*, no less."

Abram kept his voice neutral. "You misunderstand. The Hand does not command our worship, only our loyalty."

Ja'a made no such effort. Disdain dripped from her voice like venom. "The 'Hand'. A vain and arrogant title."

Abram replied, "Lord Carcharoth *is* the chosen vessel of the Three. Your own lord, mighty Mammon himself, has blessed his ascendance, granted him command of the Mammonite forces about the Altar of Hinnom, and imbued him with a portion of his power."

Ja'a could contest none of those things, and she knew it. Abram continued, relentless. "Carcharoth has taken ragged warbands of scattered worshippers and forged them into an army the equal of any Samothrace can muster. Fires burn along the entire border of the eastern realms as Sheolin, Mammonite and Jahennan warriors fight not as the disparate warbands of times past, but a single united Legion of Hell."

He stepped closer to her, risking her ire. "Carcharoth wishes your aid. The power of the Consort of Mammon would swell his armies to a tide that would drown the lands of the infidels in a wave of hunger, pain and death. With you and the World Eater at his side, *nothing...*"

A faint hiss was the only warning he had, and Abram leapt back, barely dodging the tips of her fingerclaws as they sliced before his face. Ja'a's yellow eyes gleamed with mad fury, and she screeched, shaking the air with the power of her demonic wrath.

Abram cursed under his breath as bloatguard shouldered into the tent, hefting massive axes before their distended bellies. A single blow from any one of the swollen giants would cleave Abram in half, and the urge to reach for the poisoned rapier at his belt grew to a terrible itch.

Ja'a crouched in front of him, snarling and spitting like an enraged feline. Ropes of saliva sprayed from her lips as she shrieked, "Your treachery is laid bare, adulterer! I could have respected you if you had been true to your master, but instead you fornicate with a blasphemer!"

Abram tried to speak, but Ja'a was incandescent and would have none of it. "You speak your honeyed lies because of the World Eater, and it belongs, ever and only, to Mammon, lord of the lands of men. I should kill you where you stand for your sacrilege."

Abram's tone grew hard. "Watch yourself, consort. I am the emissary of the Hand. To strike at me is to strike at him, and through him, your god."

The demon queen glared at him, her breath coming in panting growls. Her deformed guardians edged forward, their rusted blades held at the ready.

Finally, Ja'a hissed, "*Mammon* is my shield."

She tossed her chin toward Abram. "Kill him."

The bloatguard rumbled forward as Abram drew his rapier. Steel rang against corroded iron as the Jahennan inquisitor lashed out with his envenomed blade, driving the massive guardians back as his free hand tugged out his excruciator lash.

The weapon was the same Abram had trained with under Aganyn, but with many more lashes bound into the handle, tokens of the trials passed on his path to full inquisitor. The various strands bore poisoned thorns, hooked barbs and metal weights, all designed to acquaint the excruciator's victim with the agony relished by Gehenna. The lashes uncoiled menacingly at Abram's feet before leaping forward with a flick of his wrist.

The lashes snaked around a bloatguard's neck, parting his flesh with sickening ease. The mutated man's eyes widened as his blood turned to fire in his veins, and his rusted axe clanged against the ground as he desperately tried to prise the torturous whip from his throat.

Abram jerked the lash back, tearing pieces of flesh from his victim and yanking him forward. His rapier whispered through the Mammonite's fatty neck, splitting arteries open, and the Jahennan inquisitor kicked the body toward the other bloatguard. His lash flicked behind him, ready to agonize again as Abram held his rapier out, warding off his assailants.

He stood tall before his would-be assassins, and called out a single word before they swarmed him.

"Ursus!"

The bloatguard nearest the heavy fabric of the tent never saw what killed him.

Something thundered through the side of the tent, its shoulder lowered like a ram. It hit the hapless bloatguard in the middle of his back and swept its arm out, shattering all of the guardian's vertebrae and launching him through the roof of the tent to smash out of sight elsewhere in the encampment.

The bloatguard's companion fared little better. A black greatsword the length of a spear hacked down into his shoulder and ripped clear through armor, flesh and bone to lodge in his pelvis. The invader wrenched his weapon back with a savage twist and the Mammonite practically exploded with the force of the exiting blade.

The bloatguard got their first look at their attacker.

Even hunched over in a feral crouch, the invader dwarfed Ja'a's bloatguard, themselves taller than most men. The Mammonite elite took a step back involuntarily, their minds rejecting again and again what their senses screamed at them. His arms, bare and stitched with rippled scar tissue, rivalled the trunks of most trees in size. Patched plates of armor crusted with old blood scraped together like rusty knives over his massive frame and a heavy bear pelt draped his shoulders. His eyes, red and crazed in his battered horned helm, gleamed like coals from the forge.

"Is that—?" Ja'a asked. She seemed struck by the legend before them.

Abram nodded, his own voice breathy with awe. "The last Slaughterlord of the Tor Kayn."

Her voice escalated to another shriek. "By the gods, *kill it!*"

A blast of air huffed from his helm, half anticipation, half aggression, and the slaughterer blurred forward, hacking left then right to catapult two more bloatguard back in welters of blood and toxic entrails. At last, their dull senses acknowledged the threat to their mistress, and the bloatguard surged forward, rusted axes chopping ponderously.

It was difficult to see the slaughter in the darkness of the tent. Abram saw only flashes of movement, but the *sound.* Skulls powdered and spines cracked. Gore spattered the canvas walls as though a butcher hurled buckets of blood.

The last bloatguard to die buried his axe in the invader's side, the first—and last—telling blow of the engagement. The giant *growled*, a bass rumble Abram felt in his chest, and jerked the Mammonite closer to wrap the bloatguard's head in the crook of his elbow. He crunched the man's head with a single flex of his bulging arm, and Abram winced as the Mammonite's head crackled like a crisp bread crust. His body sagged, and his hands fell from the axe still lodged in the slaughterer's side, but his killer was too far lost in bloodlust to care.

Bellowing to vent the furnace of fury boiling his blood, the warrior wrenched the guardian's skull free of his body. Still screaming, he snatched the corpse by the ankle, whipped it bodily up into the air and smashed it against the ground.

After four consecutive impacts, Abram stopped hearing bones crack.

When the body began falling apart like an abused bag of refuse, the creature—for it could not be a man—hurled it aside, ripped the axe from its ribs, lifted its arms to the sky and roared, shaking the air with the force of its pain, rage and hate. Entire armies had given voice to their aggression with less power.

Panting heavily, the creature cast its smoldering gaze about and sighted Ja'a. A volcanic rumble started within its chest as it stalked toward the consort.

Alone of the Mammonite servants in the tent, Ja'a stood her ground before the monstrous warrior, claws splayed and noxious power pooling in her slitted eyes. The titanic servant of Carcharoth stood twelve feet tall, towering over the wasted demon consort, but she did not flinch back. For an instant, Abram entertained the fantasy of how an encounter between the two champions might end.

But such a duel was not Carcharoth's command.

Reluctantly, he said, "Enough."

The Tor Kayn ignored him. Ja'a snarled and her bone-wings arched from her back to angle towards it.

Abram added force to his voice. "Ursus, in the name of Carcharoth your master, *stay.*"

The killer halted in his tracks. His seething red eyes remained locked onto the consort's burning yellow orbs and his breath snarled raggedly from his helm, but at the name of Carcharoth, he stayed.

Now, with the ruin of twelve elite warriors painting his armor and dribbling from his fingertips, the light of sentience returned to his eyes and the barbarian snorted. When he concentrated enough to form speech, it sounded as though each word had to escape a dungeon crafted from thorns and hate.

"I obey."

Abram stepped forward, winding his excruciator lash back up and taking care to step around the piles of ruined mutants. "My lady, I'm not sure you ever met the Slaughterlord when you were in Mammon's court."

Ja'a's eyes widened in recognition as she stared up at the giant. "*You....*"

Ursus remained silent, glowering down at the consort, awaiting Abram's word. Abram grinned and shook his head. "He never speaks of his time there, but I've often wondered if you encountered one another."

Abram glanced at Ursus. "Before Mammon cast him out."

Ja'a spat. "My love betrayed no one! He betrayed him!"

She stabbed her clawed finger into Ursus's face. "You *left!*"

Ursus growled, a rumble dredged from the depths of Hell, and

Abram shook his head. "I've seen the records, lady. The Tor Kayn tribe killed for days in the War of Blood. Mammon used them again and again against Samothrace's hardest targets. On the tenth night of fighting, when the Thracian heavy horse broke the minotaur herds and threatened to slaughter all, the Tor Kayn died to the last to throw the cream of Samothrace back."

"Out of the wreckage of thousands of men, only Ursus emerged, bathed in blood and wearing the skull of Knight Lord Kerrington on his belt. Yet when he dragged his broken body to Mammon's throne to offer him the trophy, he found the gate to the Halls of Hunger barred to him. The Tor Kayn had been annihilated, and therefore being no longer useful, forgotten."

Sneering, Ja'a turned away. "Why would the great Mammon concern himself with failed slaves?"

Bones popped as Ursus clenched his fists. Abram could feel the rage beginning to radiate from his frame.

Abram chuckled. "And now we see the fallibility of our gods. Had Mammon embraced Ursus, had he shown gratitude for the sacrifice shown by such noble servants, he would have gained a champion like no other. Yet instead he heeded the words of jealous advisors. The cowards of the herds repeated their betrayal to save themselves, blaming the Tor Kayn for the disastrous defeat."

Ja'a sneered. "I heard the story. He renounced the gods and dwelt in the wastes north of Hinnom. He killed *everything*, where it hailed from Hell or Samothrace. He gathered dozens of failures and apostates to his banner, stealing worshippers from the true pantheon."

Abram grinned. "And he did so very successfully. Not one of the Three dared admit the toll the Sons of Ursus took on their forces, lest they appear weak."

His laughter died and Abram grew somber. "Until Carcharoth."

Ja'a hesitated. "What did he do?"

Abram gestured briefly and said, "He learned of Ursus. He heard of his rejection by the gods, his pain at his betrayal. A day later, spurning armed escort, he walked into the wastes armed with nothing but his hands. Eight days later, Carcharoth returned to the Altar with Ursus and before the mightiest lords of Hell, Ursus bent the knee and swore his fealty. Not to the gods who abandoned him, but to the *man* strong enough to defeat him."

Abram turned his hard gaze on Ja'a.

"This is the lesson, lady, and Ursus your example. Carcharoth has given us and thousands like us the way forward. Free of the mistakes of Heaven's bitter exiles and united in hatred, we *will* overthrow the kingdoms of men and claim our birthright. We *will* break humanity to our will, and once we stand united as a race, neither the gates of the Celestial City nor the lords of Hell will be able to stand against us."

Abram crossed his arms and inclined his head toward her. It was not a gesture of respect. "This meeting was a test, to see if you could overcome your slavish devotion to your god and stand among the champions of the free. This initial test you have failed. Count yourself fortunate it is not the only one."

The consort hissed in reply, "And who is it that would judge me? Traitors? Blasphemers? I spit on you and your tests. The gods themselves walk among us, and instead you would call a blistered corpse 'master'?"

The Jahennan paused, momentarily wrong-footed, and Ja'a smiled. "Oh, yes, inquisitor, I know the truth of the failure wrapped in black rags, and the boy who served as his acolyte. How long did it take you to drag poor Aganyn's charred remains across the continent to the Screaming Throne?"

It was Abram's turn to feel spikes of anger, yet he tamped them down with an effort. He said, "You know nothing of what you speak. My lord Carcharoth was not broken by his marring; he has been elevated by it. His suffering has raised him from the level of base mortality to savior of humankind. He is no longer who he was."

Ja'a snorted in derision. "I am sure that is what he has told you. I merely find it ironic that the champion of those who betray the gods would not himself have lived without their blessing."

The demon queen regarded them for a moment, then waved a clawed hand. "You and your slave may remain with us. Witness the power of Mammon's loyal servants and perhaps, if you beg sufficiently, you and your outcasts will be permitted to return. Mammon is merciful, and he is always in need of…strong souls."

This last she said with a lingering stare at Ursus.

Abram narrowed his eyes. He had not expected such a reversal.

What games are you playing at?

Lacking any other response, he nodded graciously and turned to leave, but Ursus remained in his place, gazing stonily into the depths of the tent. Horrible groans sounded dully from within.

Ja'a noticed his stare and giggled shrilly. "Do not tell me the beast appreciates art?"

With the sound of boulders crushing together, Ursus growled, "Are they strong?"

The consort smiled sickly and teased her limp hair with a claw. "They were already among the mightiest of predators before my hunters found them in the forest and brought them to me. I am merely reversing their domestication."

She looked back at the twin figures lying twisted and contorted in the darkness, shivering in the dark. "Soon, they will forget all that they were, overwhelmed by the ravening of their own nature, and I will show the Wolves the unfettered power of the Architect of Hunger."

Ursus grunted, unimpressed. "Your touch makes them weak. I will test."

Ja'a's yellow eyes glittered. "We shall see. Perhaps you will join them."

His piece said, the titan stalked out without another word.

Abram remained for a moment, concealed within the entrance of the tent, watching the Consort.

The woman cast her gaze to her projects, and her eyes glowed pale yellow with affection as she stepped back into the dark. She padded softly over the ground, as if careful not to disturb her children's rest.

She bent low over them and crooned, "You hear him, babies? Grow up big and strong for mummy. You have wolves and giants to slay."

The demon queen knelt between her newest sons and gently

wiped the sweat away from their foreheads. They shuddered feverishly at her touch.

"Get your rest now, children. Your time is coming."

Lost in a fog of tormented dreams, Feros and Fyrss writhed in obedience.

GIDEON'S TEETH ached with the cold. The frigid wind had frozen his gums and cracked his lips, but he could not stop grinning at the sight before him. Some joys were just worth the pain.

Just ahead of him, Ashkelon marched through the forest, his darkmail clinking as he forced a path forward. Snow crunched underfoot and branches creaked overhead as the arctic wind blew gently through the woods.

Gideon chuckled out loud. Ashkelon glanced over his shoulder at his apprentice and said, "I find your joy in this situation unseemly."

"I find your sticking swords in my chest unseemly," Gideon retorted. "You're getting no sympathy from me."

Ashkelon sighed and turned back to face forward.

Three paces behind her savior, a little girl diligently dogged his steps, carefully placing each tiny footfall into the prints in the snow left by Ashkelon's boots. Her name was Saima, and to Ashkelon's visible discomfort, she refused to be apart from him for any length of time.

Any.

The trio crested a rise and Ashkelon exhaled in relief as the column of Estvik survivors, led by Skald, came into view. "At last."

He turned to the little girl and gestured imperiously toward the convoy. "You may now return to your people."

Saima eyed the fires, then shook her head quickly, her black hair whipping around her face.

Ashkelon blew out his breath forcefully. "Child, *please* go back to your kind."

Instead, she darted forward to wrap her arms around Ashkelon's thigh. Ashkelon stumbled back a step from the impact, clenched a clawed hand into a fist and fired a searing glare at Gideon. "Apprentice...*do something.*"

Gideon shook his head. "Ashkelon, for heaven's sake, do you really not understand what is happening?"

"I am to be plagued by some miscreant's errant spawn for eternity in exchange for a momentary lapse in judgment."

Gideon crossed his arms. "Do you even know what a hero is?"

Ashkelon narrowed his eyes. "Shall I raise up the bodies of the thousands I have slain?"

He chose to ignore that. "What a hero is to *us*, then. Whatever you may think of them, master, heroes are not isolated destroyers. They do not hunt evil and eradicate it wherever they find it so they can move on without consequences. If they were, they would be no different from you."

Ashkelon remained silent, little girl fastened firmly to his leg. "I trust there is a point to this lecture?"

Gesturing, Gideon pressed on. "Heroes do not just destroy evil; they replace and suppress it by encouraging good to rise in its place. A hero connects with the people he saves. Their welfare concerns him and occupies his thoughts."

"That sounds tiresome."

Gideon gave a wry grin. "Yes, Ashkelon, it is. That is why God has given strength to the mighty, so that they might bear the burdens of the weak."

The sorcerer scoffed, "According to your definition, heroes must lead unbearably mundane lives."

Gideon shrugged. "It might seem so to you, but it is of immeasurable value to common people, especially children."

He gestured to Saima. "Look at her, Ashkelon. She lives in a world at the mercy of monsters and devils. When she was terrified and utterly helpless before them, you intervened. You struck like an angel from heaven and saved her from everything her nightmares ever held. Is it any wonder that she can't bear to be apart from you?"

His lips pressed into a thin line, Ashkelon looked down at the quiet girl.

Gideon's voice grew soft. "Every time she faces fear, she will remember you. When imagined monsters gather around her bed at night, she will remember the magelord who leapt from the darkness, who cared enough to embrace her in the safety of shadows and slay her dragons. Like it or not—and believe me, I don't—*you* are her hero now."

A low hiss escaped Ashkelon's mouth. "Poetic, apprentice. Inspiring, even, to addled fools enamored of romantic fairy tales. But I did not save this child to gain her adoration. I saved this child because if she had survived her trial, she might have become me."

Gideon squinted and said, "I don't understand."

Glancing away, Ashkelon snorted in something like disgust. "As a child, I was condemned to a terrible fate to pay a debt incurred before I drew breath. One sworn to the Light could have intervened to save me. For convenience's sake, he declined, and I was left to find my own way in the Dark."

Ashkelon turned back and spread his arms to encompass himself. "This was the result."

Gideon considered him for a moment. "I am sorry for your pain, but I think you are wrong."

"Am I?"

Gideon nodded. "The darkness did not twist you until your savior abandoned you. I think that if you cast her away, you invite the same fate on her that you sought to divert."

His eyes narrowed in thought, Ashkelon looked down upon Saima, who gazed back at him with large brown eyes, chin resting on his thigh. She was small for her age, and thin. Her skin bleached pale by the weak sun of the north, flecked with spots of pink where the cold nipped at her cheeks.

Saima stared back at him, saying nothing.

Gideon felt the gentle hand of Gemelte touch his thoughts. He started in surprise at the revenant's action, and suddenly Gideon heard whispers echoing through his mind.

Quietly now, Gemelte whispered. *We do not want him to know that I am here.*

Gideon managed to refrain from nodding, and he relaxed enough to let the foreign memories fill his senses.

He saw, overlaid across Saima's face, that of another child lost in darkness. Through the bars of a metal cage, a man in armor similar to Gideon's own turned to walk away, fading into the black.

A whisper drowned out all others.

Don't leave me.

The uncertainty in Ashkelon settled and coalesced into a hard gem of reluctant decision. The connection between Gideon and Ashkelon broke, and he felt Gemelte retreat suddenly to avoid detection.

Darkmail gauntlets clenched as Ashkelon grated, "Fine."

SKALD SIGHED. "Ach, vould you stop that huffing and puffing? You vil blow down forest vith your spite!"

Anya Helsdottyr scowled and glared at him. The two of them led their horses by the reins, giving the beasts a much needed break as they guided the column of Estvik's refugees.

"He is a stupid fool."

Skald rolled his eye. "For sake of small-fang's dignity, should Skald pretend not to know vhich *he* ve refer to?"

Anya sucked in a breath, and the old Wolf raised a hand to ward off her anger. "Peace, venchling. As far as just-Gideon's stupidness, yes, Skald has noticed that you think this."

Anya turned her scowl straight ahead and trudged on, clearing a path through the snow for those behind her. She did not know that Skald grinned at the clouds of frustrated breath gusting from her mouth.

"So he is stupid. So vhat? This is not making him special among men."

Anya spat. The gobbet made a *piff* sound as it hit the snow, which just about summed up her opinion of the male race at the time.

She heard Skald sigh, and his steps lengthened to catch her.

Before he could draw abreast of her, Anya swiped angrily at her eyes, struggling to clear them before the Wolf saw the tears that threatened to fall.

A vain attempt, really. The wily veteran saw more keenly with one eye than most men did with two.

"Speak, small-fang. Tell old Skald vhat troubles girl-child."

Anya growled, trying to hide the tightness in her throat. "He *kills* him. He lets him *kill him.*"

Skald grimaced. "Ah."

The tears came now, and Anya felt shame burn her cheeks at her weakness. "I shouldn't even care. What is he to me?"

Skald remained silent, and Anya walked a few more steps before exhaling slowly. "Why do I care, Grandfather?"

Skald scratched at his beard thoughtfully. "Because boy is vhat you look for."

Anya whirled on him, but Skald held up his hand again. "I do not tease you, not now. Think. The boy fights vithout thought of self. Vhen danger strikes, his is first shield to cross Death's grey blade. He has saved dozens of lives, including princess of the Vulfen, and vhat has he asked in return?"

Anya chewed her lip and said nothing.

Skald pointed at her. "That is right. Nothing. Vulfen varriors vould demand small-fang's hand as payment for saving a fief of the jarl, and expect to receive such a boon. Not just-Gideon. Vhen he save story-teller from cannibal hordes, he demands no feast-tale to spread his glory. Instead, cruel master rams sword in his chest, and he begs to let him sacrifice more. Vhat man is like this?"

Glancing away, Anya muttered, "He's still stupid."

Skald chuckled and hugged her close with one great arm. "Aye, little she-Volf. He is. The best vones are. But think in this vay. The boy may be vithout sense, but he is also vithout self. A man without self is vithout fear."

Anya felt a smile tug her lips at that.

Skald saw it and grinned. "Ha, Skald sees your sneaky smile. So small-fang has little crush, eh?"

She squirmed in his grip, but to no avail. His arm held more strength than her entire body and she sagged against him. "You are a useless matchmaking old fool, Grandfather."

Skald chuckled. "If you ask nicely, I vill help you spy on him as he sleeps."

Anya's smile shone brightly this time and she squeezed him back.

Skald sighted a trio of figures cresting a rise next to the refugee column and grunted, "Ah, speaking of stupid, betrothed returns."

The dark one led them, his face set like iron and brooding. Gideon marched behind, his eyes alight with laughter.

Anya wondered at that. *How can a man be murdered by another and still laugh?*

More out of habit than anything else, she muttered, "He's not my betrothed."

"Apologies. Your prey, then."

She elbowed him, and Skald yelped and jumped away, rubbing his ribs.

He was about to call out a greeting to Gideon, but he caught sight of the girl following in Ashkelon's wake. Skald opened his mouth to ask, but Ashkelon snarled, "Do not speak. *Listen.*"

Skald's teeth clicked together at the force of the sorcerer's command. Ashkelon gestured toward the forest behind him. "A Venan warband massacred a village to the north of here. This is the only survivor. Do you care for such survivors?"

Anya answered for Skald, "Aye, some of the mothers and widows in Hammarfall run a shelter for the orphans of the war. They care for them there."

The child's dark eyes flicked back and forth between the adults discussing her, and she shifted closer to Ashkelon and wrapped her arms around him. Skald's bushy eyebrows shot to the top of his head, and Anya blinked in disarray.

Swaying slightly from the tightness of the girl's grip, Ashkelon closed his eyes, lifted them to the sky and sighed. "She is also somewhat attached. To me."

Both Wolves stared. Skald cleared his throat. "Uh...vhy?"

Ashkelon's eyes remained closed. "I saw her taken by the warband and I...rescued her."

The stare shifted to Gideon, who was not even trying to conceal his delight. "Absolutely true, every word of it. He slaughtered the entire raiding party to keep her safe. She hasn't been more than a sword's length away since."

Silence reigned for a few seconds as the Wolves digested this.

Ashkelon's breath hissed through his teeth with impatience. "Her name is Saima, and according to some ill-defined universal code I was not informed of, I am now responsible for her well-being. If you can overcome your incredulity, she requires warm food and clothing. Ensure that she receives them, or my displeasure will be severe."

Anya and Skald glanced at each other, and the old Wolf shrugged expansively. He stepped forward and knelt to the little girl's level. "Hello, tiny girl-cub. I am Skald, mightiest varrior in all of Northland. I have slain dragon and put him in a soup. You must help me eat it."

The girl eyed him suspiciously. The corner of Skald's mouth quirked slightly, and he gestured back at Anya. "Mighty Skald does not lie, as Princess Helsdottyr can tell you. I killed dragon vith vone sving of my mighty hammer!"

Anya smiled at the little girl and held out her hand. "It was a goose. Grandfather battled a goose. And he almost lost."

The little girl finally cracked a smile at that and moved forward to take Anya's hand. She glanced back at Ashkelon, who rolled his eyes and nodded permission for her to proceed.

As Anya and Skald led the girl away, Skald continued. "Do not listen to doubting voman, for story is more fun this vay. I, mighty Skald Dragon-smasher, say so. If it vas goose, it vas fearsome *fire-breathing* goose, vith red eyes and black iron feathers that no arrow can penetrate! I vooed him to sleep vith beautiful song and smote him vith magic hammer to retrieve golden eggs vhich...."

. . .

THREE HOURS and several goose-fighting tales later, Skald leaned back in his saddle and grinned. "Ach, there she is. The old mother volf herself."

He pulled out a carved horn and blew a long ululating blast into the valley. Gideon asked, "What was that for?"

Skald glanced at him. "So they know ve are coming. And do not shoot us for being ghosts vearing the faces of friends. Is problem here."

He gestured down into the valley opening up before them and said, "Behold, Hammarfall, lair of the Vulfen, the iron fangs on vhich break the demons of the North."

11

WEAPONS

Hammarfall lunged out of the hollow of the mountain. The peak and cliffs cradled the fortress, sheltering it from snowfall and the bite of the wind. Stone towers jutted like lupine fangs out of crenellated curtain walls dotted with dozens of murder holes. Torches flickered and marched slowly along the battlements, held aloft by prowling sentries, as great spear-throwers peered out at the killing field beyond the wall.

A patrol of mounted scouts turned at the sound of Skald's horn and galloped toward the caravan spilling out of the woods. Upon recognizing Skald, they lifted their weapons in salute, turned their horses toward the woods and rode for the end of the caravan, wary of predators seeking to cull stragglers.

A steady stream of people, wagons and animals flowed into the Jaws of the Wolf, the great iron gates of the citadel. Skald frowned at that sight. "Many flee the Demon Queen. Too many."

He pointed. "Look. Those are from Aldrik. That is miles avay from Estvik, and yet they arrive vhen ve do. The Venans strike every hearth."

Anya nodded, her brow creased with concern. "We cannot feed all of these people. And if they siege us...."

He exhaled slowly. "Aye, this is true. But ve do as ve must, and let the Almighty provide as He vil."

Anya glanced around. "Where are Feros and Fyrss? They should have been back by now."

Skald shrugged. "Still smarting from beating just-Gideon gave them. They vil turn up."

He gestured ahead. "Go now. Tell Gunther the number ve bring from Estvik, and that the jarl returns soon."

Anya nodded and urged her mount forward. Her hair whipped behind her as she galloped toward the Jaws, seeking the gatekeeper.

Skald turned to see Gideon standing nearby. The younger man's eyes tracked Anya's descent toward the gate, and despite his concerns, the old Wolf grinned to himself.

The young are all the same.

He decided to have some fun with the boy. "Magnificent, no?"

Gideon blinked out of his reverie and looked at Skald. "Uh, yes. Your fortress is very impressive."

Skald just smirked at him. "Eh, is just cold pile of rocks in forest. I vas referring to other thing."

Gideon flushed red and glanced away. Grinning broadly, Skald swept his arm toward Hammarfall. "So vhat do you think? You are good vith sword. But can sword of Gideon Hordebreaker defend this?"

At Gideon's inquisitive look, Skald shrugged. "I am talespinner. You need deed-name so legacy is remembered from all other Gideons. In Vulfen feasts, varriors are given deed-names by their comrades. Vhat is yours?"

Gideon fingered the hilt of his sword. "I don't know. I haven't thought about it."

"Hm. Then old Skald vil find you deed-name."

The boy continued to look uncomfortable, and Skald chuckled. "Relax, it vil be good vone, I svear. Skald is very good at giving memorable name. Is vhy they give me this job."

"I really am fine with just Gideon."

The veteran eyed him thoughtfully. "Of course. This is man you are."

Skald pointed at Gideon's blade. "Vould you like Vulfen sword? Ve have many forges and good steel."

Gideon smiled and shook his head. "No, thank you. This sword belonged to the man who took me in as a child. It has been in his family for generations."

Shrugging, Skald said, "Eh, do not take wrong vay, but it has broken many times. You cannot have sword that breaks in battle, not vhen you face vhat ve do."

Gideon pursed his lips. "It is my father's sword, Skald. I cannot cast it aside."

Skald grunted. "You honor his memory, and this is good. All fathers should be so lucky to have son like you to revere them in death. But more than honor, boy, fathers vish their sons to live. I am not just-Gideon's father, but I am sure he vould vant his son to bear sound blade in battle."

The old Wolf clicked at his mount and began to make his way down the slope toward the fortress, leaving Gideon to ponder his words.

AT THE SOUND of snow crunching underfoot, Ashkelon sighed. "Are you here to delight in my discomfort some more, apprentice?"

He turned to see Gideon standing with his sword bared in his fist. Ashkelon arched an eyebrow. "Valantian required the work of decades to gather the strength to face me. If you believe yourself ready to duel me after a few short months, I would counsel you to evaluate yourself a bit more harshly."

Gideon shook his head. "That is not what I am here for. I need to ask you a favor."

Ashkelon tilted his head, his expression inscrutable. "That is unusual. Ask."

Gideon's words came with difficulty. "I need you to make me a better sword."

The sorcerer remained silent, his cold eyes considering the young man. Gideon would not meet his gaze. "I love this sword, master, I do. I love what it represents, and what it means to me. But these people cannot be defended by a sword that keeps breaking. I have to—I need to—"

Ashkelon held up his hand. "Enough. I will do this."

Gently, Ashkelon took the sword from his apprentice, and Gideon's shoulders slumped, half in relief, half in dismay.

The sorcerer studied the blade, turning it over in his black gauntlets. After a moment, he spoke. "Once I begin, the blade will be irrevocably altered. It will no longer resemble your father's sword. Is that a sacrifice you are willing to make?"

Gideon nodded, resolve warring with sadness in his countenance. "There is nothing I will not sacrifice, master."

The sorcerer eyed him thoughtfully. "We will see."

Ashkelon turned to leave, but Gideon stopped him. "Another request?"

The sorcerer regarded him. "Being?"

"I really don't want it...to scream."

Ashkelon smiled without humor and turned to walk away. "I understand."

As Ashkelon descended to the Wolves' fortress, Gideon sensed something familiar, and sighed. "You always wait until he is gone."

I apologize for the inconvenience to you, but I prefer my liberty to the Soul Cage.

Chuckling ruefully, Gideon lowered himself to the ground and muttered, "Well, I guess that's not your fault."

The revenant considered him for a moment, and said, *You have commissioned the Dark One to forge your sword.*

Gideon closed his eyes and nodded, "Yes."

You wish a sword for a hero to be crafted by the murderous champion of the Everlasting Dark?

He squeezed the bridge of his nose, trying to hold off a headache. "I know."

Gemelte sat silently, content to wait for further explanation.

Gideon sighed. "You are from his world, aren't you? A scholar?"

Yes.

"Tell me, then. Who understands destruction more than Ashkelon?"

Gemelte sighed. *This is not a virtue, Gideon.*

Gideon opened his eyes and speared Gemelte with his gaze. "Ashkelon destroyed both good *and* evil on your world. I just need to destroy the evil on mine."

The shade remained quiet for a moment. At length, he spoke. *I do not fault you in your commitment, Gideon. But be careful that in your pursuit to banish the Darkness, you are not consumed by it in turn.*

"I'll be careful."

Gemelte laughed bitterly and looked off into the distance. *My brother also thought as you did. It did not save him. Even the act of facing the Eternal Dark takes the best of men and changes them beyond recognition.*

Gideon shook his head. "And I have seen God's light bring them back. I do not lose faith when evil happens; it is to be expected. I fight so that the light can work."

The ghost took in a sharp breath. *Ahhh...*

Confused, Gideon asked, "What is it?"

You actually believe you can...save him? You think you can save Ashkelon?

Gideon looked away and did not answer.

The ghost rocked back in its seat, its visage shimmering oddly for a moment, flickering in and out. *My. That is unexpected. Who knew you were so...ambitious?*

Gideon glared at Gemelte. "No one is beyond redemption."

The ghost laughed, a throaty chuckle that echoed weirdly in the cold air. Its appearance settled back into that of the old man, but Gideon noted the fluidity of the guise.

I can see why he likes you. Ashkelon always respected absolute certainty, even after he annihilated it.

"I do not need your mockery, ghost. Go haunt someone else."

Inclining his head in deference, Gemelte rose to his feet. *I am sorry, Gideon. I meant no disrespect. I respect the nobility of your intentions. I do. But some men are just lost.*

The scholar paused. *Is this why you stay with him? Through the agony and the murders, you stay with him...because you think he can be saved?*

Gideon rose to his feet and looked down toward the fortress, where the crowds parted to avoid touching the malignant shadow knifing through their midst.

"No one is beyond redemption," he repeated.

GREAT ROARS of laughter rose from the gate as Ashkelon swept towards it. Peasants took one look at his dark armor and scattered from his path, clearing a corridor through the stink of humanity. So near the gate, Wolves bearing the leashes of hounds moved among the crowd, checking the newcomers with sharp glances while their dogs snuffled for the scent of taint.

The Wolves saw his approach, took note of his menacing aspect and surreptitiously nudged their animals in his direction. Their grips tightened on the hafts of their weapons as their keen eyes sought any sign from their beasts that Ashkelon served demonic powers.

Ashkelon did not wash as ordinary men did. He blended his knowledge of science and the arcane arts to strip dirt, blood and oil from his pale skin without the need for soap or water. As a result, he emitted almost no scent at all.

The dogs appeared confused by his lack of odor, but did not bristle as they would have against a Hell-worshipper. Their eyes still sharp with suspicion, the Wolves did not halt Ashkelon's progress.

The sight that met his eyes at the gate made Ashkelon's lip curl.

Skald leaned against the great stone of the wall joining the gate, clearly mid-saga as he gestured broadly to a fat warrior seated on a barrel by the gate. The barrel groaned under the man's weight as he leaned back, his cheeks bright red as he roared his mirth, a horn of ale sloshing in his fist.

Anya stood by, arms crossed, patiently waiting for Skald to finish. Her eyes caught sight of Ashkelon and her visage darkened.

As Ashkelon neared, the obese man wiped his mouth with his forearm and wheezed, "He did what?"

Skald brushed tears of his own from his eye. "I svear to you, Gunther, it vas sight to behold. He knocked Jarl Heimdall to the ground vith vone blow and then dared him to get up again."

Gunther clutched his belly as another fit of laughter struck him, and he nearly fell from his barrel.

The gatemaster saw him, and all jocularity fled from his eyes. He reached down next to him, lifted a huge axe and laid the weapon across his lap. "Ho there, stranger. Declare yourself and your business, and perhaps you will be allowed entrance."

Skald put a hand on the gatemaster's shoulder to hold him in place on his barrel. "Not this vone, Gunther. He has countenance of the jarl. Also, I am not thinking you can stop him."

Gunther sniffed at that. The man would have stood as tall as Skald, but his gut protruded above his leather belt. A bushy auburn beard cascaded down his chest, and Ashkelon felt mild disgust at the sight of crumbs and gristle entangled in its curls.

The gatekeeper pounded his chest and said, "I am Gunther, gatemaster of Hammarfall, Skald. All guests enter on my troth, and I will not admit a viper to my jarl's lair."

His patience frayed, Ashkelon snapped, "Are you finished?"

A fire lit in Gunther's eyes and Skald tightened his grip on the man's shoulder, keeping him down. "*What?*" Gunther roared.

Ashkelon's eyes burned blue-white as he snarled, "I am the emissary of entropy everlasting, and you an obese manufacturer of manure. I left the wrought gates of the noblest cities of Avalon shattered and the holy Zantyne keepers strewn in my wake, their life's blood spattered across their domain. So I will not submit myself for inspection to a drunk who can barely see straight at mid-afternoon, much less endure his tiresome posturing."

Gunther's eyes flicked back from Ashkelon to Skald. "Is he serious, Skald?"

Skald screwed up his face ruefully. "As heart attack. Vhich he can also do."

Gunther combed his beard with his thick fingers and eyed Ashkelon suspiciously. "He has countenance of jarl?"

Skald nodded.

Gunther cast his gaze toward the sky. "Well, I am not jarl..."

"Thank the Almighty," Skald interjected.

"So you may enter. But if you cause trouble, you will have me to contend with. It will not be first heart attack I have lived through."

Ashkelon arched his eyebrow. "That, I believe," he said dryly.

ONCE THEY WERE within the city, Anya walked alongside the dark-armored visitor, more to keep an eye on him than anything.

Ashkelon walked along the central roadway that cut through Hammarfall, swiftly evaluating the defenses of the fortress. The walls stood high and thick, bearing the scars of centuries with stoic might. Great spear-throwers swiveled at regular intervals on oiled track-ways, manned by teams of serfs who constantly scanned the forests outside the city.

Inside the walls, the city of Hammarfall sprawled under the mountain, most of it on Ashkelon's left as he walked in the gate. The main road speared from the gate straight to the mountain, where a stairway stretched to the mouth of a door carved into the side of the mountain. The rune of a wolf's head gleamed above the dark doorway, and Ashkelon's gaze lingered upon it before turning to the city itself.

On either side of the road, stone homes with thatched roofs butted up against one another, almost jostling for attention. The air was thick with the aroma of burning wood, cooking meat and animal sweat. The city crowded with people, refugees from more towns than Estvik.

The land of the Wolves was under siege in its entirety.

A familiar sensation, like a scent and a gasp mixed together, breathed on the wind, and Ashkelon halted in his tracks.

"What is it?" Anya asked.

The sorcerer said nothing for a moment, his head tilted to one side, his eyes like chips of ice in his black hood. At length, he said, "Some one is dying near here."

Anya blinked and answered, "Yes. Yes, Brida. Her blood has been poisoned for months. She is not expected to live out the night."

Ashkelon nodded. "May I see her?"

Unable to keep the suspicion from coloring her tone, Anya asked, "Why, Dark One?"

Without the slightest hint of sarcasm, Ashkelon answered, "To pay my respects."

"No."

At the low growl, Ashkelon and Anya turned to see Skald emerge from the shadows of a nearby alley. His eye gleamed storm-gray, and there was steel in his voice.

Ashkelon looked at him and cocked his head. "No?" he repeated.

Skald did not budge. "Brida is fine voman, a helper of vidows and feeder of orphans. She vil pass to Heaven's halls surrounded by those she loves. She has no need of murderer's respects."

Ashkelon arched an eyebrow. "Perhaps I can prevent her passing."

Skald's grey eye narrowed and one hand reached behind his head to grasp the haft of his warhammer. "Perhaps, fatechanger, but answer still stands. You vil not enter her hall. No vile necromancer shall defile the body of vone such as Brida, this I svear."

Ashkelon exhaled slowly. "You would let her die rather than allow me to heal her?"

"If Brida vere dying of thirst, should I bring her vater from poisoned vell? I say no. I have seen so-called healing, and I do not trust your generous heart. You vil not go near her."

Ashkelon locked his gaze with the steely veteran, and nodded slightly. "Very well. I will not enter her hall. But I will remain outside it."

Skald squinted. "Vhy vould you do this?"

"Because I wish to."

Glancing at Anya, Skald shrugged. "Ach, do as you vish, then. All who vant to freeze alone on road may do so. But do not think that your shivering vil grant you passage to Brida's bedside. I vil be there to be sure."

Ashkelon's eyes flashed with amusement and he seated himself on a cut log. His fingers steepled before his face and he looked at Skald with wry challenge. "Is here acceptable?"

Skald growled, "So long as you remain there, I do not care."

Footsteps sounded around the corner, and they turned to see Gideon approaching them. His jade eyes took in the scene.

"Is this a bad time?" he asked.

Ashkelon indicated Gideon with a jerk of his head. "And my apprentice? Does he have leave to enter? Or is there an invitation he should procure...?"

Skald sighed. "Yes. The boy may go in. This is not nobleman's tavern in capital city. Only evil necromancers and child-slayers may not enter."

The corner of Ashkelon's mouth turned up. "So you think I am a child-slayer?"

"It is assumption I vould vager much upon."

Clearly amused, Ashkelon turned to Gideon and said, "Well, apprentice, you will attend this death, then, as it is highly privileged. Ensure, however, that you do not kill a child or raise one from the dead. These activities will deny you access to this exclusive event."

Lacking anything else to say, Gideon answered, "Uh, noted, master."

"Excellent. Now, off with all of you. Night is falling, and you would not want poor good Brida to meet her end without you."

Skald narrowed his eye at Ashkelon. "I do not like you."

Ashkelon looked at him as if he had not heard him correctly. "You do not...*like* me?"

The Wolf veteran glared at him in silence, and a smile slowly tugged at the corners of Ashkelon's mouth. "Very well, then, story-teller," he said. "You have given me a great deal to think about. I shall sit here quietly and consider the many choices that have led me to this fate, lest I fall tragically further in your esteem."

His dark laughter mocked them as they stepped into Brida's hall.

. . .

THE THREE OF them sat around Brida's bed on wooden stools, listening to her labored breathing, sipping hot tea and tending to a fire to ward off the chill of the night.

Skald sat the closest, holding Brida's hand gently in his own massive fist. He murmured quietly to her, quoting songs and poems to ease her spirit. Gideon found his gravelly voice soothing.

Seated in the corner, Anya struggled to stay awake. Her eyes continued to hang heavy of their own accord and she constantly shifted position, but the night was late and the day's journey had tired her.

Gideon saw her head dip and her shoulders slump as the jarl's daughter succumbed to the inevitable.

"She never can stay avake," Skald said, a smile creasing his eye as he looked at Anya. "In so many vays, she is still little girl."

He glanced at Gideon, who sat with his hands folded in his lap. "Vhat? You do not tire?"

Gideon grinned ruefully and stretched languorously. "I've been living with Ashkelon for months now. How much do you think I sleep?"

Skald conceded the point and turned back to Brida. "Ach, Brida. I remember vhen you vere bright-eyed girl of sixteen vinters. You did not deserve this."

Brida's gray hair still held the touch of auburn, like the ghost of autumn clinging through winter. Her skin was sallow, her eyes recessed and her frame wasted. The disease had stolen much from her.

Gently sweeping a strand of hair from her face, Skald spoke, his voice quiet in the gloom of the chamber. "She vas vone of best vomen I knew. Alvays ready to help those around her. Never vas her door closed to a traveler, and her table vas crowded with hungry mouths."

He looked at Gideon. "Ve called her Brida *Baresark* behind her back."

Gideon furrowed his brow. *"Baresark?* A berserker?

Skald grinned through the tears forming in his eye. "Aye, lad, Brida *Baresark.* The *baresark* takes a vow, you see, vearing no armor and drinking til he feels no pain on eve of battle. Vhen he hits enemy line, enemy must break and run or die, because the *baresark* cannot be stopped."

Gideon smiled. "And how was Brida like a *baresark?"*

Skald scratched at his beard. "Because vhenever Brida glare at you and say she pray for you, no matter how strong you think yourself, you break. She has been heard pacing in this hall, bellowing at the Almighty to save some lost varrior's soul. I have seen jarls break in less than fortnight vhen that voman bend her knee to pray, veeping and promising to repent their pride if only she vould stop."

Skald looked back at her, affection in his eyes. "She vas fearless, just-Gideon, a shieldmaiden of the Vulfen. Vhen she see the face of the Almighty, she vil recognize Him as oldest friend, and He vil rise and call her name as that of honored champion before the varriors in His hall. Vhat more is there, I ask you?"

Gideon shook his head. "Hearing you talk, I wish I had known her."

Skald sighed. "Ach, you vould have liked her. And she vould have liked you. Not that that makes you special, of course, she liked everyvone..."

Just as Gideon chuckled, Brida inhaled sharply and arched on her bed. Skald gripped her hand and whispered, "Be brave, Brida. You see Him soon."

Her breath caught in her chest and Gideon winced, waiting for the inevitable.

The temperature of the air dropped suddenly, so far that Gideon could see his breath crystallize before his face. The fire guttered and died, plunging the room into a near-complete darkness. The two of them sat frozen, trying to understand what was happening, when they heard Ashkelon's voice hiss from the darkness.

"Back."

Floorboards creaked as the forbidding sorcerer moved forward toward the dying woman, his eyes burning sapphires set in black. Skald half-rose to his feet, growling, "I thought I told you..."

Ashkelon's sword rasped out of its sheath, filling the room with shrieks and cutting Skald off mid-sentence. Gideon's spine froze at the appalling clamor, and he rose from his seat, unsure of what to do.

Ashkelon's searing gaze focused on something else, however. He thrust out a hand curled into a claw, as if trying to repel or *hold* something past Skald. Ignoring the dumbfounded old warrior, Ashkelon's eyes locked onto a point just above Brida.

Gideon hesitated. Now that he looked, he thought he could see something looming over the dying woman, staring back at Ashkelon.

Shadow seethed around Ashkelon's outstretched gauntlet like liquid smoke, and his voice snarled at the apparition.

"Because I *will* it."

Lit in the darkness by the twin fires of his eyes, Ashkelon's face showed cold hate, disgust and disdain. The air vibrated, like a cord pulled taut and plucked by a child. The sorcerer tilted his head, hearing something lost to either Skald or Gideon.

He answered it. "Lawful or not, I claim this woman's life as my own. You will withdraw."

The air hummed once more, and Ashkelon narrowed his eyes to slits of cyan. "Screech all you will, outcast, but do not lay another claw on her."

Skald and Gideon stared, not sure just who Ashkelon was speaking to. With a growl, Ashkelon wrenched his clawed hand to the right. An instant later, something hit the wall with enough force to rattle the hall, and the air vibrated so strongly, it made Gideon's teeth itch.

Anya, startled awake by the sounds, gasped as Ashkelon stalked toward the wall, one darkmail gauntlet held out as though he gripped a throat, the other holding Acherlith low at his side. Gideon drew his own blade and asked, "Ashkelon?"

The sorcerer ignored him. All of his attention focused on that bare stretch of wall, where something like the suggestion of smoke writhed beneath his hold as a black flame kindled in Ashkelon's empty hand. Breath hissed out of his clenched teeth as he rasped, "I. Hate. You."

The boards groaned as they bent inward under Ashkelon's glare, and the fire in his palm seethed hotter. Ashkelon was not finished. "You and your kind—you think you own us, that we are subjects in a realm created for you. You think man your plaything in an eternal vendetta, powerless in your pathetic drama. *I* am here to show you differently."

Before their astonished eyes, scratches formed on the wood, gouges raked by invisible fingernails or claws. The air thrummed again, and Ashkelon bared his teeth. "Tonight, you remember that you were created to *serve* man, not be feared by him. Tonight, your masters requires tribute of you."

The shrieks of Acherlith vied with the thrumming of the air. Ashkelon raised his other hand, and the flame within darkened further, black folding impossibly within itself to unknown depths of shadow.

More ravines formed on the wall, deeper gouges ripped from the wood in panic, and even the planks of the floorboards groaned.

Ashkelon rasped, "You know what this is."

He held up the black flame consuming itself in his hand. "Abyssal fire, pulled from the Chasm of the Lost itself. The only element capable of judging your kind."

With a long, smooth draw, Ashkelon pulled the blade of his sword through the flame in his palm. The edge of the screaming sword smoked in the heat, and Ashkelon leveled the blade just short of the wall. The not-smoke drew back, flinching back from the sword screaming beneath its throat.

"This is your choice, tallyman. I require essence. I would prefer it granted willingly, but I will take it nonetheless. Offer your hand, or I will take your skull instead."

Splinters exploded from the wall and the air fairly seized like a maniac with unseen forces. Gideon, Skald and Anya drew closer to each other, their spirits quailing before a horror they did not understand. Ashkelon seemed unfazed. "Spare me, reaper. Is it not better to live maimed and diminished than burn entire in the Everlasting Dark?"

After a few tense seconds, the air thrummed quietly, like the chord of a bass instrument plucked once. Ashkelon inclined his head. "Wisely chosen."

He hacked down with his superheated sword at the wall. The air exploded with unseen agony and a hand-shaped portion of the wood buckled, as if something had gripped it so hard it had broken through.

Something thumped against the ground as Ashkelon relaxed his clawed hand and the black flame died. The air shivered one last time as *something* tore its way out of the hall, blasting the occupants with unnatural wind. At its passage, the fire in the hearth guttered back into life and warmth returned to the chill air.

Ashkelon remained standing before the abused wall, head bowed over his screaming sword.

Skald was the first to break the silence. "Vhat in name of Hammarhand's hairy—?"

Ashkelon sheathed his blade and answered without facing Skald, "We have lived too long at the mercy of the exiles who roam the unseen. Man was not meant for such servitude. It is good to remind them of what we can be. That one will flee and tell the others."

Anya put her hands on her hips. "You expect us to believe...that that was—?"

She did not finish the question, and Ashkelon glared at her in irritation for the lack of discipline. "One of them, yes."

They stared at him, unsure of what to say. Skald muttered, "This is...troubling."

Ashkelon sighed and stepped past him. "I will leave you to come to terms with it on your own. My task is yet incomplete."

The sorcerer knelt at Brida's bedside, laid a black gauntlet on her brow and closed his eyes. Immediately, her breathing calmed, and her eyes opened. She looked up into Ashkelon's face and smiled.

"Ah, you must be Death. You are more handsome than I thought."

Ashkelon opened his eyes and shook his head slightly. "The

distinction must be made between Death and its keeper. It answers to me, not the other way around."

He laid Gideon's iron blade across her chest and folded her hands over the weapon. Brow knit in confusion, Brida looked from it to Ashkelon without understanding.

Ashkelon stepped back from her and the blade. "Now, old one, if you please. *Pray*."

"Vil someone explain to addled old man vhat in Halgar's hairy *hafferscheim* just happened!"

The three of them stood outside Brida's hall, ushered outside by Ashkelon and the door closed in their faces. Gideon shrugged. "Ashkelon...interfered."

Skald glared at him incredulously. "He interfered? How does vone interfere vith *Death*? Vhat kind of man is this that such forces bow to his vill? Can he even die? And that is other qvestion. Can *she* die?"

Anya rubbed her eyes. "I do not know, Grandfather. But Brida is alive, and we can at least be thankful for that."

Skald scoffed. "Thankful? I vil be thankful vhen the man who can maim the Death-bringer is out of Hammarfall."

The door to Brida's hall opened with a creak, and Ashkelon stepped out, Gideon's blade sheathed at his side once more. Skald stomped toward him. "Is she dead now, or did you only maim her, too?"

Ashkelon met the warsage's fury with ice in his eyes. "The woman is well. I have cleansed her blood, and the service I requested is fulfilled. Now, if you will excuse me, I have a sword to forge, and you a siege to break."

Skald squinted at him. "Vhat?"

Shouts barked from the walls, and horns blew in alarm as men rushed to the stairs, weapons in hand. Skald bellowed at one of them as he dashed past, pulling on a leather jerkin. "Ranald! Vhat happens?"

The Wolf called Ranald shouted back as he struggled to clasp the armor on the run, "Children of Mammon, Greymane! They are here!"

"Already?" Anya asked incredulously. "They were days away."

Skald growled low in his throat. "Whoresons must have marched through night vithout stopping for rest. To the vall, Vulfenkind! Ve show them vhat happens vhen they come for the volf in its lair!"

Skald strode toward the wall stairs, drawing his warhammer and roaring battle sermons to the serfs and Wolves rushing to war.

Anya made to follow him, then hesitated. She turned back to Gideon. "Are you coming?"

Gideon stepped forward almost without thought, but Ashkelon stopped him with a hand. "He is not."

Anya blinked at the blunt declaration, and Gideon looked askance at Ashkelon. "Master..."

The signal fires lit, bathing the lair of the Wolves in golden light and illuminating the killing fields outside the walls. The glow of their flames reflected from Ashkelon's pale skin, rendering him almost hellish.

"You and I have a sword to forge."

THE INQUISITOR and the Slaughterlord stood on a hill, overlooking the snarling mobs of cannibals and mutants working in the forest below. They watched in silence as great catapults were erected under the supervision of siege engineers.

Abram's lip curled. The siege engineers were captives, no doubt; taken from some of the Whore's other raids and coerced into contributing their valuable skills. His suspicions were validated when one crew finished setting up their trebuchet and a single rotten apple was thrown to the engineer in charge. With jerking movements, like a starving bird, the man snatched the apple out of the air and began wolfing it down. His comrades stared at him sullenly, hunger vying with insanity in their eyes.

Abram sighed and glanced at the titan next to him. Ursus stood like a column of basalt, still as the stone, his huge greatsword sheathed on his back. At times like these, it was impossible to imagine the depthless violence the man was capable of, the hate that could transform him from motionless statue to a whirlwind of oblivion.

"They hunger."

Ursus' voice rumbled next to him, and Abram could have sworn he felt the bass of the giant's voice shake the ground beneath his feet. He nodded. "The Way of Mammon. He is the Faminefather and the Gluttonlord, giving with one hand and taking with the other. I imagine their enforced fast pleases their dread master."

The titan's eyes swept across the Wolves' keep. It was a formidable fortress, sheltered under the mountain and buttressed by sheer cliffs on both sides. Stone walls three times Ursus' height loomed over the Venans, and fires burned from the eyes of graven wolves set into the towers overlooking the iron-wrought gate. Barrels of arrows dotted the walls, lending the defensive archers almost unlimited ammunition in the event of attack. Spear-throwers turned to aim their eight-foot shafts toward the horde, ready to unleash murder on the greater beasts in the Mammonite assembly.

Ursus' ears, keen to a superhuman level, could hear the defiance waking in the city. Warriors, trained and well-fed, rushed toward the walls, roaring orders to one another and preparing the implements of death to be visited on the cannibal hordes besieging them.

Amongst the Venan mobs, lesser masters of Mammon swayed, shrieking aphorisms and proverbs of the Hungry Lord. They bestowed bread at random around them, with slaves gibbering and clawing after the offerings as though they came from the hand of the Exile himself.

Abram kept his eyes on Ursus, watching him intently. He had never met a man with a better grasp of death than the chief of the Tor Kayn. He spoke quietly. "So...can they win?"

Ursus grunted, and Abram felt his heart shiver at the sound. "Barely. If they starve them."

Abram acknowledged Ursus' contempt with a nod. The man was the very definition of *blunt instrument*. Ursus and his pack of savages would never even consider waiting that long to kill something. He considered it something of a miracle that Ursus and his coterie of Brides had not charged already.

"Are you going to join them?"

Ursus flared his nostrils at the inquisitor's question and answered, "Demonhunters. Warriors. Would be good fight. "

Abram heard the need under the killer's words. Ursus lusted for this fight, to match his strength against the finest of humanity's warriors. But he would do nothing unless Carcharoth willed it. That was the strength of his loyalty. His *honor*.

Abram gestured toward the city. "You have the leave of the Hand to kill as you will. Slay their champions. Add their skulls to your trophies, and bellow your victory to Mammon's sickly dregs. Let them see the might of a servant of Carcharoth, and the impotence of their feeble god."

Abram crossed his arms again. "I will evangelize among the Venans. The hordes of Mammon will be ready to turn when they see your power."

Ursus growled in acknowledgement, the sound chuffing from his iron helm. They stood for a few moments more, watching the siege weapons being built, when Ursus spoke again. He gave voice to the question that had been gnawing at Abram through the hours of their vigil.

"Where is she?"

Abram sighed again and surveyed the keening wretches beneath him, once again failing to find the architect of this endeavor. "I don't know."

THE DOOR of the smithy clanged shut behind them, and Ashkelon turned to cut Gideon off with a gesture.

"Let me guess. You want to know why you are in here, and not out there."

Wrong-footed, Gideon let out his breath in a frustrated exhalation. "You train me to fight, and then you do not let me fight."

Ashkelon snapped at him, "I train you to think. You have no

weapon, and the worshippers of the demon just arrived. They will not strike the wall for some time, possibly hours. You have sufficient time to forge your weapon."

Of course, Gideon could not argue the point. He cleared his throat. "I, ah, apologize, Master. I was...excited."

Something registered in his mind. "Wait. You want *me* to forge my sword?"

Ashkelon turned from him and walked toward an anvil set centrally in the smithy. The fires of the forge were dead, extinguished. With careful movements, Ashkelon laid out the Halcyon family blade on the anvil. Still not answering his apprentice, he removed something from his cloak.

Gideon squinted. "What is that?"

Ashkelon held it out. "That is Death's hand."

It was ghostly white, with purple showing under the black finger-nail-claws. Gideon swallowed. "You—you took it from that thing?"

Ashkelon smiled slightly. "No, it gave it. An important distinction, given what we are doing here."

He whispered a few words and the hand ignited, burning brightly before dissolving to ash and falling on the sword beneath.

"And what is it we are doing?" Gideon asked.

Ashkelon turned to face him and crossed his arms. "We are going to forge a symbol."

"A symbol?"

Ashkelon nodded and began pacing the room. "The universe is rife with symbols, apprentice. These symbols are representative of an invisible realm, acting as reflections of the spiritual world. In my contemplations of the universe, I have often wondered at the sheer proliferation of such symbols. The sun, for instance, is almost universally worshipped as a god amongst idolatrous cultures, and understandably so, as it gives light and warmth to all life. The wind, with no discernible origin or destination, still moves through the world, driving the world's life-giving rain cycles like breath through a body. It is almost as if a higher power wishes us to see such things and follow them like bread crumbs to His presence."

Gideon's eyebrows rose to the top of his head. "I...would agree with that."

Ashkelon glared at him. "Calm yourself, apprentice. I have never denied the existence of your God, just the depth of His involvement in your affairs."

Gideon clamped his mouth shut. Ashkelon went on. "So now we come to you, a hero in need of a hero's blade. A symbol. You have asked me to forge you such a weapon, and I am regrettably unable to do so."

Gideon opened his mouth, but Ashkelon held up his hand. "Not unwilling, apprentice. Unable. We are not simply shaping metal into a killing edge, as could any craftsman hungry for coin. No, we make a *soul*, a spirit to inhabit your weapon and connect you to the invisible realm beyond."

The sorcerer gestured toward the sword waiting on the anvil. "What is a sword, student? What is its purpose?"

Gideon considered the question for a moment. "To kill?" he asked.

Ashkelon held up a finger. "Specifically, to kill *men*. No other weapon forged by man is so singular in its purpose. Swords do not hunt prey, chop wood or cut vegetables. They are designed to cut the threads of men. In many legends, even, it is thought that after men fell from the Light into Darkness, exiled angels offered them the secrets of sword-making in return for their daughters, so they might breed agents into our reality."

Gideon blinked. "Is that true?"

Ashkelon waved the question aside. "Perhaps, but it is unsubstantiated, meaningless trivia, something doddered fools love to argue about in dusty libraries. The point is that you have asked for a sword, and you should know the symbolism of such a thing."

He gestured toward the ashes on the anvil. "Death's hand, freely given. It is representative of the authority to end human life. It is neither good nor evil of itself, Gideon, as any instrument of power."

Ashkelon pointed toward the sword. "This blade, however, grants you *moral* authority. A sword imbued with generations of unswerving, unselfish service to the cause of justice. It is the legacy of your adopted family. A sword with the Halcyon spirit will demand the highest standard of righteousness from the warrior who wields it. I also had a holy woman pray over it, to pass the blessing of your God into it and connect it with the supernatural."

Ashkelon looked at Gideon, his eyes sharp in the gloom of the forge. "When you blend Death and Justice, apprentice, you forge a new element: Judgment. This blade will yearn to pass judgment on the evil and the good. It will hunger for the relief of the oppressed, as it will for the necks of the oppressor. It is a solemn calling, and not one to which I am bound."

Gideon narrowed his eyes thoughtfully. "What do you mean?"

Ashkelon smiled faintly. "I am a murderer, Gideon. I have taken the lives of thousands without regard as to whether they were righteous or deserving of their fate. I cannot touch your blade in the forging process, else it would be tainted by my sins."

Gideon let out his breath slowly. "I am not a swordsmith."

Ashkelon seated himself on a stool in the smithy. "There are many things you are not. Fortunately, you are not required to be a craftsman. Simply take the hammer and strike the blade. I will shape it from here as you strike, without polluting the blade with my soul."

Gideon picked up the hammer and stood over the anvil. He looked at Ashkelon. "Isn't there supposed to be fire?"

Ashkelon nodded. "If this were an ordinary sword, yes, but we create its spirit as well as its edge. You must imbue this weapon with your own fire. When you strike the blade, remember why you fight as you do. Usually, such spiritual energy is lost in the creative process. I will entrap the power you produce, and redirect it into the blade."

Gideon stared at him.

Ashkelon sighed. "Just hit the sword with the hammer, and remember why you need the sword."

He bit his lip and turned back to the weapon on the anvil.

It did not look like much. It looked like ashes scattered on a cheap broken sword, actually.

Here goes.

Gideon lifted the hammer and struck.

. . .

MEN THRONGED the walls of Hammarfall, carrying weapons and arrows. Anya ducked a pallet of spears and moved to Skald, who leaned on his warhammer, glaring into the dim light of dawn. He turned at her approach and smiled. "Smallfang. Vhere is handsome beau?"

Anya ignored his jibe and answered, "In Heimlich's forge with his leash-holder. They're forging a sword."

Skald squinted into the town beneath them. He could hear tinny hammer blows, but no smoke rose from Heimlich's smithy. "Are you sure they know how?"

Anya glared into the darkness, not at anything in particular. "It does not matter. We do not need him."

Skald chuckled, "Ach, but ve vant him, and *that* matters."

Anya turned her glare on him, but before she could berate him for his teasing, her father pushed through the men working on the wall. Jarl Heimdall Fangthane opened his arms and his daughter embraced him quickly. She looked up at him. "When did you get back? I did not hear you return."

Heimdall squeezed her close. "Aye, it was a close thing. We saw the Venans spreading as they advanced and knew they would siege the hold. We drove our horses til the poor beasts foamed, and made it back just before the wretches could close their grip."

He swept the fortifications with his gaze, grief tinging his voice. "So this is all that could make it? Pah! Estvik was not the only place to feel the Venans' knives. These damnable cultists have infested our lands like a dog with fleas. There are reports that they are taking survivors away in chains, Almighty only knows where."

His eyes dark with sorrow, the jarl glanced about. "Where is young Hammerhand and his master?"

Anya pulled away and shrugged defiantly. "Why do you ask me? I am not their minder."

Jarl Fangthane eyed her warily, and directed his words toward

Skald. "Old one, if you can manage it without biting my head off, tell me where our guests are."

Skald jerked his head toward the sounds of hammer strikes. "Heimlich's. Forging a sword, apparently."

The jarl squinted at the little building and its cold chimneys. "Are you sure they know how?"

Without thinking, Anya retorted, "He knows what he is doing!"

Heat rose in her cheeks as the two men regarded her. Anya broke eye contact and muttered, "I need to see to the fire squads."

She stomped away, feeling the eyes of the men of the wall track her all the way down the stairs.

Heimdall glanced at Skald and indicated his daughter with a jerk of his head. "Greymane. Should I be concerned about this?"

Skald shrugged. "Who can say, my jarl? But I vould be more concerned about fate of all Vulfenkind than boy trying to beat sense into cold blade."

SWEAT DRIPPED from Gideon's brow onto the anvil as he hammered the sword. Nothing happened, and he hit it again.

Nothing.

He swung the hammer again, and this time he struck the blade wrong and cracked it down the center. Exploding with frustration, he threw the hammer aside with a clang.

"This is *stupid!*"

Ashkelon's voice overrode his panting. "If you continue like this, I agree with you."

Gideon gripped the edges of the anvil and tried to corral the anger rising within him. "If you have any suggestions, they would be appreciated. Like starting a fire in the furnace, perhaps."

Ashkelon rose to his feet. "The problem is not the fire in the furnace, it is that you do not understand the fire within you."

Gideon pounded the anvil with his fist. "What does that even *mean?*"

Ashkelon narrowed his eyes. "It is ironic that you require me to explain this to you, since I excised sentiment from my consideration centuries ago. You need...*to feel.*"

Gideon looked at him incredulously. "What?"

Ashkelon regarded him coldly for a moment before speaking. When he did, acrid irritation soured his tone. "I accept that every creature deals with trauma in its own way, but this is unspeakably dense, even for you. Do you remember why you fight?"

Gideon blinked, confused by the direction the questioning was taking. "To...to save people?"

"'To save people'?" Ashkelon mocked. "Really? You have died on my blade a dozen times or more, and returned begging for me to accept you as my student again, and it is to 'save people'?"

Gideon shook his head, trying to think. "I don't..."

Ashkelon's voice knifed through his awareness. "Have you actually forgotten her?"

Blinking in surprise as the question, Gideon shrank as Ashkelon stalked behind him. "What? Who?"

Ashkelon's words dripped with poison. "By the Dark, you have. Which is it? Do you suppress her memory so you can sleep at night? Or do you ignore her when she arises in your dreams to accuse you?"

Gideon's voice wavered. "Ashkelon, what are you..."

Ashkelon stopped across the anvil from him and snarled at him. "Her, Gideon, *her*! The woman you failed! The woman you mistake for your mother! The woman you let *die* because you were too powerless to save her when evil came."

Gideon recoiled. "What...there was nothing I could do! *What could I do?*"

Ashkelon sneered. "How long did it take her, apprentice, before she finally expired? A week? A month? How long after the broken corpse of the child you also failed passed from her womb, and her spirit died within her?"

Gideon's breath came in heaving gasps. "Ashkelon...," he warned.

The sorcerer ignored him, leaning over the anvil, teeth bared. "*Failed*, Gideon. You *failed* her, you *failed* her child, just as you fail every day since, trying to wipe away the unspeakable stain on your soul with pointless heroics just so you can finally banish the face of the helpless pregnant woman who died because *you were not enough!*"

The hammer was in Gideon's hand before he became aware of it. Roaring, he whipped it toward the side of Ashkelon's head. Ashkelon met it with his vambrace and hammered his forearm down, catching the haft of the tool and slamming it onto the blade between them.

The air split with the impact, and with a roar, the furnaces exploded into life around them. Gouts of fire lunged from their mouths, superheating the air in the smithy. The Halcyon blade on the anvil glowed a burnished gold, and the sound of the strike shook the air with the tone of a great bell.

Gideon stared at the glowing blade, hearing a slight keening from the sword, almost a...seeking.

His sweat-drenched hair hung over his eyes, and he was glad, because it masked the falling of his tears. His hands fell to the anvil, holding him up as his mother's face swam before his eyes.

Ashkelon's voice, no longer vicious but relentless still, reached him through his grief. "It is not just your sword that was broken, apprentice. For too long, you have tried to hide a shattered spirit. No more. No. More."

Vision blurred, Gideon looked up at Ashkelon. His master offered him the hammer he had cast away and rasped, "Now do as I did. Take your brokenness, forge it into a weapon, and *never* fail again."

Taking in a ragged breath, Gideon nodded. He grasped the handle of the hammer, and looked back at the sword. His tears dropped from his face onto the blade, but the tears did not simply splash where they fell. Where they met Death's ashes, pools of azure light flared brilliantly before fading into the metal of the sword.

The image of his mother arose again in his mind's eye, and this time, Gideon did not look away.

"Never again," he whispered, and raised the hammer.

. . .

AT THE SOUND of a muffled explosion, the Wolves looked up from their preparations. All of them saw the smoke billowing from Heimlich's forge and heard the steady ringing of a hammer on an anvil.

Skald looked around and remarked, "Looks like boy discovered fire."

The Wolves chuckled as the flames billowing from the forge, just for a moment, banished the gloom of Hammarfall.

12

PREPARATION

T he problem was that no one took the time to understand her. Small minds called her deluded. Perverted. *Lost.*

They did not understand the glory of the revelations she had been given. The generous magnanimity of the Being who in the midst of His bitter exile saw her pain and exalted her.

Now she stood in this hallowed place, far to the north of the battle she had orchestrated. She had no need to be present for the downfall of her enemies. That was not what she had been sent to accomplish.

Her bloatguard stood in motionless vigil around the perimeter of the birthing chamber as she paced back and forth, muttering these truths to herself. Slime oozed from the joints of their armor and slopped onto the blessed stone.

Ja'a did not think them repulsive, though. She ran dirty, chewed talons across the breastplate of the nearest of her guards, a mother's caress to a favored child.

"We are all misunderstood, I think," Ja'a whispered, her eyes wet with polluted tears.

Her gaze crept across the room and rested on her two favorites. Feros and Fyrss stood clad in dirty rags, shivering in mute obedience. The blessed toxins in their bodies caused their skin to take on a green tinge even as their eyes yellowed. Their saliva drooled from their mouths, hissing faintly as thick droplets struck the ground.

Feros swayed back and forth, eyes rolled back into his head, and Ja'a smiled to see it. He would turn soon, a willing vessel for Mammon's gifts.

His brother, on the other hand, still looked upon her with broken hate. He had no strength of character to sustain his resistance to her affection. He merely despised his own weakness and saw her as the instrument of his downfall.

The Consort frowned. "Men," she muttered crossly.

As her acolytes moved about the chamber, mumbling the many incantations required to placate the Great Beast, Ja'a turned her thoughts to the host she had abandoned at the Wolves' keep. Her lip curled at the thought of the preening Jahennan acolyte, desperate for something new to worship, and the blood-maddened titan, following blindly he with the most strength.

Fools. *They* were lost. Not her.

They called her Whore. The Mad Queen. The Little Lost Girl.

Words hissed through her ragged lips. "I'm not lost. He *found* me. I was lost when you cast me out! Should I have stayed lost, just so you'd be happy?"

The spiders around her twitched at her venom, hungry to obey her whims. The bloatguard shifted in their rusted armor, sensitive to her moods. The sight of them calmed her. Whatever little men may preach, He had given her servants, mighty and numerous.

Now she would give Him one in return.

Ja'a turned to the chrysalis in front of her. The translucent pod reached to the ceiling of the cavern, twenty feet in height. Beneath the chitin, enormous legs uncurled, straining against the confines of its life-giving prison. Waiting for the offering to complete its birth into this world.

She smiled, poisoned saltwater forming in her eyes as emotion swelled within her. They called her lost, but He called her Beloved.

He understood her, he *listened*, so she would give Him the world.

· · ·

A BLADE FLASHED for his neck and Ashkelon slipped inside the strike, his forearm hammering into a sensitive nerve point on his attacker's arm. As the man's arm deadened, Ashkelon took a short step and punched his elbow into the thug's diaphragm. He completed his turn, slicing with hooked fingers to tear out his attacker's throat.

More enemies approached, and Ashkelon spun toward them, hands reaching in claws of dark iron, seeing—

—the tiny dark-haired girl standing there, watching him.

Saima. It required effort to recall her name.

The sorcerer's breath came strong but steady, his lungs working like a bellows. His nostrils flared with the force of his respiration, and aggression radiated from his dark frame.

Saima did not seem to notice, and for the first time since Ashkelon had met her, she spoke.

"What are you doing?"

Ashkelon exhaled slowly, banished the phantom soldiers from his mind, and dropped his hands. "I am...practicing."

Saima continued to stare at him. "Practicing what?"

Ashkelon felt awkward, speaking to a child. There was something about the size differential, as well as the sheer mutability of the potential before him. Anything he might say or do might be integrated or imitated by the tiny creature observing him.

He elected to keep his responses short.

"Killing."

The little girl looked around and remarked, "There's no one here, though."

"I am imagining them."

"Oh," she answered. Then, "Are you winning?"

Ashkelon considered her for a moment, and resumed his stance. "I always win."

He lashed out with a high crescent kick, impractical in most battles but cathartic in practice. As his imaginary opponent reeled from the force of the impact, Ashkelon kicked in the back of his knee, gripped him by the throat and dropped to a knee to slam his skull into the ground.

Ashkelon growled as he watched the life bleed from his victim's eyes, projecting his hate into the death of his enemy.

A childish growl to his left broke his concentration, and Ashkelon glanced over to see Saima on one knee, her palm thrust onto the ground in imitation of him.

Ashkelon narrowed his eyes.

"What are you doing?"

She looked at him, all innocent intensity. "Practicing."

Ashkelon straightened slowly and looked down on her. "Are there no children for you to...recreate with?"

Saima rose to her feet, then performed the same technique, throwing a kick then repeating the palm strike to the ground. Ashkelon frowned, unable to resist analyzing her form. "Your kick should reach the chin of your enemy, not his waist, and you should be on the other knee."

She hurriedly switched sides. "Like this?"

Ashkelon nodded curtly. "My question stands. Why are you not with the other children?"

Saima swept her raven hair out of her eyes. "They're all hiding, and I don't want to hide anymore. I want to win, and you *always* win."

Ashkelon looked down at her. "There are others who can teach you how to k—win. They are more suited to dealing with children."

Saima planted her tiny hands on her hips. "I want to be with my angel."

Ashkelon froze. Of all excuses he had been expecting, that was not among them. "What...did you call me?" he asked.

She did not hesitate. "An angel."

Ashkelon shook his head slowly. "You are terribly mistaken, little one. I am no angel."

Saima cocked her head. "You have to be. When I was in trouble, I asked God to send an angel to save me, like in the stories, and then you came. So you are the angel."

His fists clenched. "Then I am not a *good* angel."

A roar swelled from beyond the wall, thousands of voices raised in praise of lust and slaughter. Giants brayed, spiders screeched and mutants bellowed the names of their false god as they worked themselves into a frenzy. The hatred of the deceived for their brother man shook the air itself, and Saima shrank closer to Ashkelon at the savage tumult. Her tiny arms wrapped around his waist, and Ashkelon ground his teeth at the unwanted contact.

In a small voice, Saima said, "I don't think we need a good one."

To take Ja'a's army would have been impossible for any other man. To subsume command of an entire horde dedicated to one of the Three would have required months of politics, bribes and assassinations.

Ursus, however, was not any other man.

Japheth the Unconsumed, proxy of the Consort, shrieked his blasphemous creed before the thousands of Mammon. Worms continuously writhed through his flesh, chewing and devouring, yet the man still lived. He was counted as blessed among the Venan clans, an avatar of the Faminefather's favor and a symbol of his undying hunger.

"The false Wolves cannot kill the faithful sons, for the great lord watches over his children with a hungry eye! We shall take these walls, and drink the blood of the heathens within! We shall infest! We shall consume! We shall feast!"

As Japheth ranted and chanted the tiresome hymns of their god, whipping the Mammonite horde into a lathered frenzy, the Slaughterlord of Carcharoth stalked up to him from the midst of the army. In his wake prowled the savage Brides of Ursus, their faces striped with ragged slashes of black paint. They fanned out to divide the oblivious Japheth from his moaning monsters, serrated blades held low and ready.

Japheth continued swaying and frothing for the glory of Mammon until Ursus gripped the avatar by his head. The giant's hand wrapped around the prophet's skull and lifted him up for his followers to see. The horde stuttered to silence as the last Tor Kayn grasped Japheth's gyrating legs, and stretched the man over his head.

Ursus took in a deep breath and bellowed, "If Mammon be god, let god save him!"

The army hesitated, glancing at one another in uncertainty. These things did not go this way. They worshipped and they killed, or they died. Bereft of any leadership besides the muffled screams, which they could not make out anyways, they stood, shifting from foot to foot and waiting for an answer to present itself.

Ursus waited for a handful of moments, the silence from the heavens stretching on, then shrugged. "Nothing."

With the sound of wet cloth ripping, the titan tore Japheth in half.

In the shocked stillness that followed, Ursus bellowed, "Your 'god' did not save him. Why do you think he will save you?"

Rearing his arm back, Ursus hurled the maggot-ridden torso into the horde. "He will not! You no longer kill for careless exile! Now, you kill for Carcharoth, Lord of Unbroken!"

This blasphemy proved too much. One of the lunatics tried to lunge forward, a shrill denial bursting from his lips. Still bearing Japheth's flopping legs in his other hand, Ursus sidearmed the limbs at him, and the force of the impact flipped the would-be dissenter backwards like a rag doll.

Before he could rise, one of Ursus's maidens fell upon him, teeth bared. After a few seconds of screams and stabbing, she rose, face and chest bathed in dark blood, and all resistance died away.

Ursus paced in front of the army. He stopped in front of a starved-looking wretch, who began to shake uncontrollably at the Slaughter-lord's regard. Ursus lowered his voice, but all heard him regardless. "You. Do you hunger?"

The creature stared up at Ursus, quaking as he met the bloody gaze of the Tor Kayn chief. Finally, he nodded hesitantly.

Ursus sneered at him and shouted for the horde to hear, "*Answer!*"

An acolyte of Mammon could only answer in one way. The Venan raised a tremulous voice and screamed his devotion. "Y-yes, master!"

Ursus nodded and spread his arms. "Then follow me."

He turned his back to the horde and stabbed a finger toward the Wolves' lair. "No gods here today. Mammon has not left his throne of thirst to watch you die. Kill for yourself, not him. Not to sate his endless hunger, but yours."

Cannibals nodded in a frenzy, mouths watering.

Ursus drew his enormous greatsword, and the slab of black iron angled toward the fortress. "I am Ursus, and I say there is new law! If you have strength to take, take. Let nothing stand in your way! No men, no wall, and *no gods!*"

The Brides threw back their heads and shrieked, *"No gods!"*

The Venans roared back, *"No gods!"*

It became a chant, swelling and echoing through the valley. Giants brayed, their minds too stunted to understand the message but adding to the volume.

Ursus roared with them, but his eyes picked out the dark inquisitor watching the happenings. Surrounded by screaming fanatics, Abram inclined his head in respect.

Ursus grunted in derision. The ex-Jahennan had doubted him. No more. Now this army had alloyed itself to his will, the will of Ursus, and they would tear the stone walls of the demonhunters down to the naked earth.

Then Ursus might find someone worthy to kill.

EVEN AS THE Carcarathine champion slew the Consort's lieutenant, Jarl Heimdall Fangthane planted his fists on the rough wood of the table and leaned forward.

"My loyal Wolves," he growled.

Fifty warriors growled in return. Anya narrowed her eyes, feeling the kill-urge rise in her soul. Beside her, Skald gripped the haft of his warhammer, his nostrils flaring with every breath.

The lord of Wolves met the eyes of each one as he spoke, his own bright like the ice on a glacial sea. "We are the last."

The Wolves received this in silence. They awaited the word of their liege lord.

His voice low, Heimdall said, "For many passes around the sun, we have denied our nature. When we would have charged, we have fallen back. When we would have spent our lives as freely as an inheritor's coin, we have hoarded every Wolf like a sun-starved miser so we could live. So we could rise again."

The Wolves thumped the butts of their weapons against the floor once. The jarl spoke truth.

Heimdall pounded the table gently with his fist, his voice husky with emotion. "No more."

Anya drew in a shaky breath. *At last.*

The jarl stalked before them. "They wish us to fight? We will fight. They think to back us into a corner in our own keep and lead us out on leashes? I think they have forgotten!"

Weapons pounded the floor again.

His voice rose to a shout. "They have forgotten the Vulfenkind! They think us like the untested swords and soft men of Samothrace!"

Growls mixed with dark laughter.

Jarl Fangthane snarled, "Remind them, brothers. Gather your serfs, man your appointed places, and remind these demon-cursed dregs that the Vulfen stalk the night still!"

Once again, weapons thudded into the floorboards, and fifty champions mounted the walls of their home with howls of defiance, pride and death.

As his warriors took up their axes and orders barked across the walls, Heimdall felt a dark despair threaten to overtake him.

Anya stepped to his side and squeezed his hand. He did not look at her, but she could see the tears threatening to spill out as he watched his beloved Wolves fearless in the face of their doom.

"They are...magnificent," Heimdall rasped. "Every one of them."

Anya rested her head on his shoulder. "Yes, Papa."

He wrapped an arm around her and hugged her, hard. "You will stay with the innocents, daughter. They will need your bow at the end."

She looked at him wryly. "As if there were anything that could keep me from your side, Papa."

Heimdall smiled and squeezed her again. "I say, do *not* go there, and you go. I say *go*, and you declare that you will stay. I have raised a stubborn and willful daughter."

She smiled in return, but still did not move. Heimdall chuckled and shrugged. "Ach, fine. I will find someone who can obey the last command of their jarl."

"I'll do it."

Heimdall raised an eyebrow and turned to see the tall figure of Gideon approaching from the direction of the forge. His sword hung sheathed across his back. From this distance, Heimdall thought the grip of the blade appeared different, but could not be sure.

The jarl squinted at him and asked, "You?"

Gideon nodded, halting next to the door and crossing his arms.

Heimdall planted a hand on his hip. "Boy, no Wolf takes that post unless I threaten to break his skull. I was going to find some wounded gray father to do it. There is no glory in it, no sagas of the one left behind to nursemaid the women and children while his brothers fight on the wall."

Anya spoke up, challenge sharp in her tone. "And only those who fear battle want to be left out of it."

Gideon narrowed his eyes and lifted his chin. The jarl saw the signs of affront and spoke swiftly, "Peace, daughter. Our guest is a man with a man's pride, rightly earned by his reputation. No Wolf here would speak of Gideon Boarcrusher's sword as untrue and think to be heard by his brothers."

He turned back to Gideon. "Yet the question remains. Young men do not risk being forgotten in the sagas. Why do you?"

Gideon's eyes remained steady. "You have fifty warriors and their serfs to hold the wall against thousands. The Venans will get in, and they will come for the weakest among you. I would rather fight for innocents than a wall."

Heimdall shrugged slightly. "As you will. Daughter, take him to the Doom."

Anya pursed her lips, but obeyed. Gideon turned to follow her, but felt a hand grip his bicep. "And boy? I do not care how many Venans you kill, how many spiders you crush or if you banish the bloody Whore herself."

The jarl leaned in close, and his voice dropped to a lethal snarl. "When you are alone, and romance threatens to invade your soul, and you think that this may be your last night this side of Hel, remember my words: whatever you do to my daughter, *I will do to you.*"

Anya whirled, her cheeks burning furiously. *"Papa!"*

"That goes for you, too, wenchling! Keep your lips and romantic womanly notions to yourself!"

"Pah! As if I would ever kiss any man! I would be too afraid of catching his stupidity!"

Gideon touched his fist to his chest. "I swear, jarl, I will protect your daughter's honor as my own."

Stomping furiously in her fur-lined boots, Anya shouted, "Who needs it?"

Heimdall looked into the young warrior's eyes, searching. He found nothing but grim iron. He nodded slowly. "Go, then. Before she leaves you behind."

Gideon nodded and ducked out into the cold, following his daughter's furious pace.

ANOTHER ROAR WASHED over the battlements, and the pair quickened their steps. Gideon jogged just behind Anya, dodging serfs carrying shafts for the spear-throwers or water to put out the inevitable fires. The square just outside the jarl's hall teemed with humanity, and they were forced to push their way through.

Anya's hair danced behind her, only loosely secured by a leather thong. Despite his promise to her father, Gideon found his throat dry and his head fuzzy.

This woman is beautiful.

Her voice snapped him out of his reverie, and Gideon blinked a few times to clear his head. "I'm sorry, what did you say?"

ANYA GLARED at him and pointed to her left down the lane. "The King's Doom is this way. The innocents are in the hall in the mountain. Sit in the doorway and keep any stragglers from reaching them."

Gideon nodded. "Understood. Thank you."

She nodded brusquely, then glanced back toward the wall, where her father prowled atop the stone curtain.

When she looked back, Gideon already jogged toward the Doom, his sword swaying on his back. Strangely annoyed, Anya called after him, "What? No romantic notions to cause my father to spit you upon his spear?"

Gideon hesitated and looked, just as she had, toward the wall. That look spoke a great deal to her. Anya swallowed, her throat suddenly thick.

He turned back to her, and for an instant, she felt the fierce intensity of his eyes as he gazed at her. For that brief moment, as monsters roared in the background and men shouted in response, Gideon Halcyon *looked* at Anya Helsdottyr. She felt self-conscious and vulnerable, but she did not turn away. For the first time in her life, she welcomed a man's regard.

At last, with effort, Gideon tore his eyes away and shook his head to clear it.

"You are not mine."

Disappointment tinged Anya's soul. "You must pursue to make it yours. This is why it is called pursuit," she offered weakly.

Gideon sighed. "It is not that. I have no permission to pursue you, and your father is very clear on his wishes."

Anya's eyebrows rose. She could not think of a single man that would wait for her father's permission to *marry* her, much less begin a pursuit.

"You know why he called you Boarcrusher?"

Gideon shook his head. "No."

Anya smiled. "Boarcrusher was the Wolf who trained my father to fight. Papa says the man feared nothing and would fight to his last breath to save the smallest child. He also punched like a gate-breaker."

Gideon smiled back. "So, he likes me?"

Anya nodded. "He likes you."

His smile widened to a grin. "Let's keep it that way. I will, uh, talk to him. After. About you."

Heat flooded her cheeks. Nodding again, feeling like a fool, Anya answered, "Good."

The moment shattered as a burning stone smashed into the street a dozen yards away, bringing them back to cold reality. Earth and stone sprayed from the impact site, and they looked up to see ten more arcing through the air like comets.

The pair burst into movement, dashing for the cover of a nearby hall. As the flaming projectiles burst around them, scattering rock and mortar, Gideon said, "We need to go."

Anya nodded and said, "Stay alive, Gideon. When my father gets ahold of you, you will think this easy."

Gideon grinned again. "Looking forward to it."

ASHKELON STOOD in the shadow of the gateway to the final redoubt. The Wolves showed a streak of fatalism in calling it the King's Doom. It was nothing more than a cave set behind a carved doorway, with an open platform before it above a stone stair.

Behind him, hundreds of humans huddled and crouched, comforting one another and praying to their silent god. As a matter of interest, he noted that men and women were equally represented, as opposed to the majority female contingent he had been expecting, and these were all too old, too hurt, too pregnant or too young to bear blades. Wolves appeared to care little whether a man or woman bore the axe. A few elderly men and stripling boys sat closest to the door, more of a concession to their masculinity than a last gasp of defense.

He watched as beneath him, Gideon reached out and squeezed the Wolf princess's hand. Ashkelon's pale face tightened into a scowl.

Beside him, his young shadow stirred. "Is that your student?"

Ashkelon growled. "When he chooses to listen, yes."

Saima crossed her arms. "Why don't you train me like you do him?"

Arching an eyebrow, Ashkelon answered, "Because for all his failings, he is a warrior physically and mentally suited for the rigors of combat, whereas you are more suited to become a victim."

She glared at him. "But I would *listen.*"

Ashkelon spared her a glance. Her dark eyes bored into his, defiance alight within them.

She vies for my favor. By the Dark, she is jealous *of me.*

Ashkelon pondered this as he silently held her gaze. At length, he said, "You are too dissimilar."

"But you are my teacher, too!"

"And yet you are different than he," Ashkelon snapped. "A teacher is not to be the same to all of his students. He is the guide on their paths, providing necessary instruction for their success, not adhering to some pitiful notion of fairness."

He gestured toward Gideon as the oblivious young man jogged toward the gateway. "That is a hero born, child. There are lines he will not cross, nor suffer to be crossed. He would spend his blood to the last drop to save a dying leper if the wretch but asked him."

Saima's eyes followed Gideon as he mounted the steps. Ashkelon continued his lecture. "He is entirely predictable, a fixed point in morality, a bastion that evil must assail to reach its prey. Therefore I temper him with death, the ultimate price should he fail. He bears on his body and in his soul the lurid scars of his failures, and they drive him to strength beyond that of ordinary men."

He looked at her. "Does that describe you?"

After a moment's hesitation, she shook her head.

Ashkelon dipped his head toward her, satisfied with her honesty. "Of course not. You are different. You are much as I was, a piece of flotsam cast in the terrible wake of uncaring forces. If you wish to achieve survival, you must be infinitely flexible in your ethical code, which is something a hero cannot do."

He looked back to Gideon, watching as the young man seated himself on the steps before the door. "So you will be silent, you will observe, and you will learn."

Ashkelon crossed his arms and beheld the wall once more. "As I did."

So...you will sit out the battle?

Gideon reached down, grasped a handful of dirt and began to rub it into his hands. The texture of the earth roughened his skin, increasing the traction of his grip.

The escaped revenant Gemelte sat on the stone railing of the stairs that led to the Last Hall. Down the cobblestone roadway, men shouted at one another as they shored up the gate against breachers. His strange eyes watched Gideon, awaiting an answer.

At last, Gideon replied, "The battle is here, ghost. So I will be, too."

Gemelte's eyebrow arched, and the spectre glanced toward the wall. *Is this some sort of dramatic statement that the souls of innocents are the true battleground?*

The roar beyond the wall swelled. From inside the hall, women peered out fearfully at the clamor, their eyes fixing on the foreign warrior who had volunteered to stay away from the walls. Their heads shook and their tongues wagged at his cowardly actions.

Gideon closed his eyes and took deep breaths to stretch his lungs and prepare for the fight ahead.

"The Wolves don't need me on the wall. They don't even *want* me on the wall. I don't know their tactics, and I would get in the way."

Reaching back, Gideon tapped the hilt of his newly-forged blade a few times. "But I do know how to stand in a door with a sword."

Ursus, as was his right as commander, stepped from the protection of the tree line first. He walked alone, his greatsword slung on his back, as siege weapons set back in the tree line continued to hurl their fiery payloads to crash against the walls in bright flowers of flame. His breath sucked into his flared nostrils, and blasted out from his mouth. His eyes, sharp as any hunter's, could pick out the Wolf defenders on their high walls of stone.

He walked, unafraid, up to the first marker, and stopped.

Too many thought Ursus a braindead murderer, forever lost to the fog of murder that dampened the thoughts of so many other barbarians. They thought him enthralled to the spray of hot blood, the sound of weak bone snapping, the corpse-smell of a man's ruptured body.

They were not far wrong. Ursus did indeed appreciate these things.

But the Slaughterlord had been entrusted by his master for this mission to the Spiderlands because Ursus possessed something most other butchers lacked: discipline. Ursus held tight the reins of his bloodlust, and his mind, the mind of a chieftain of the Tor Kayn, remained.

So it was that a synthesis of discipline and murder approached the first marker line, and did not cross it.

The first engagements of any siege were between ranged weaponry batteries. Catapults would fling solid boulders, buckets of shot pellets or burning casks of pitch. Bowmen would loose flights of darts, crossbowmen their armor-piercing volleys, and ballistae their great beast-killers.

Each missile weapon had specific ranges, both a maximum range and an effective range. Competent commanders, on the eve of a siege, measured the ground outside their walls and laid markers for their ranged batteries. Those markers were often stones, as in this case, painted white on the side facing the fortress, but appearing as bare rock to the besiegers.

Ursus stood just behind the first marker. It should have been invisible to him, just another stone among the thousands littering the floor of the valley. But Ursus had picked out the weapons on the fortress, appraised their ranges, and found their corresponding stones on the killing ground outside the fortress.

He bent down and lifted the marker stone from the earth, palming it in one meaty hand. His eyes never left the wall as he raised it for all in the Wolf lair to see, then crushed it to crumbling shards with a single spasm of his fist.

· · ·

JARL FANGTHANE'S eyebrows climbed to the top of his forehead as the giant in the horned helm smashed the trebuchet marker stone to dust. The size of the warlord staggered him; he had seemed merely large until compared against the size of things around him.

The serfs murmured among themselves; Heimdall could hear the worry in their voices.

A gesture must be made.

A boisterous laugh erupted from the Wolf king's mouth, ringing out over the valley. His serfs started at the sudden sound, and even his warriors glanced at him warily. Heimdall flung his arms wide, flipping his wolfskin cloak over his shoulders, and stepped up onto the parapet, clearly visible to both armies. He stamped on the stone of the wall and bellowed, projecting as much arrogance as he could at the mammoth warrior in the distance.

"Pah! That is a good trick, but come try this one on for size!"

Skald laughed with him and shouted, "I am thinking he does not have stones for it, my jarl!"

Jarl Fangthane roared with mirth at Skald's response, and chuckles broke out amongst the gangs of serfs. The Wolves sent up torrents of laughter, roaring mockery at their enemy. Gauntleted fists and weapon hilts pounded against the unyielding stone of the Vulfen fortress, as the defenders of Hammarfall gave voice to their defiance.

URSUS GRINNED.

Good. They feared nothing, as should be.

He gestured behind him, and a moment later, one of his Brides arrived at his side, keen to hear his command.

"Kill them all," he said.

13

THE WALL

The woods filled with the sounds of snarling, slavering and heavy breathing as the Venan army emerged from the treeline. Yellowed eyes stared hungrily as toxic saliva dropped from the ragged lips of Mammon's devoted. The earth trembled as twenty giants, mind-shackled by Hell's sorcery, dragged the trunks of mighty iron-wood trees behind them.

One hundred spiders, the last of the Consort's brood, skittered alongside the army. On their armored backs, two Venans each clung, quivering with worship at the proximity to their god's avatars. These, the Jahennan Abram took for his own, whispering commands into their ears that set the Venans giggling helplessly.

The brood turned aside from the wall and vanished into the woods, scuttling for the mountain itself at fiendish speed.

The horde shambled forward, the cannibals shivering with the cold and adrenaline.

The Wolves on the wall remained still. Not an arrow was fired, not a shout answered the snarls rising from the field outside the wall. They could have been statues, monuments raised to the memory of fallen heroes, not men of flesh and blood.

With a sudden intake of air, Ursus Skull-taker roared, his voice an explosive catalyst on a silent field. The lurching shamble transformed into a screaming flood of diseased flesh as the Venans charged the walls of Hammarfall.

THE DISEASED TIDE reached the third marker.

The honor of calling the first volley fell to Skald Greymane, keeper of the death-songs. Any fool could gauge when the enemy approached missile range; the markers were not difficult to use.

But to break an enemy's will, one needed a sense of drama.

Skald narrowed his eye at the onrushing hordes, measuring their speed, their cohesion, their spirit.

"Arrow," he growled, and the serfs of Skald fitted shafts to the strings of their bows. Skald had no need to shout the order; the serfs of the other Wolves matched the actions of Skald's squad. Besides, the serfs were not warriors; shouting at twitchy men holding bows made little sense. A faint clattering sounded along the wall as arrows clacked against bows.

The Mammonites continued to charge, thundering past the fourth marker and into fire-at-will range. The giants led, twenty feet tall, brandishing gate-breakers and bearing giant ladders on their backs. The hordes funneled behind these, like streams through ditches.

"Draw."

Wood and sinew creaked as hundreds of bows pulled to full extension. They could not remain so long; if Skald left them there, bows would begin to snap from the stress and the serfs would tire.

But discipline held, and all Hammarfall awaited the Howl.

One of the Mammonites glanced up and made eye contact with Skald, and the old Wolf grinned.

Skald inhaled sharply, threw his head back and unleashed a blood-chilling war-cry into the sky.

A deluge of shafts scissored through the air. Each serf crew followed the action of the crew beside it.

Skald's new friend jerked backward, knocked off of his feet and pierced through by the devastating volley. All around the fourth marker, demon worshippers screamed and collapsed, reaped in a terrible harvest.

Skald punched his warhammer into the sky and howled again.

The spear-thrower crews, already sighted in on their targets by Vulfen siege masters, tripped the release levers. Six-foot-long shrieker bolts loosed from their cradles, tiny holes in the shafts causing the bolts to scream as they took flight.

The giants closest to the gate bellowed in pain as the spear-throwers hit their marks. One giant whipped around completely from the force of one shaft before another punched through the back of his skull and pitched him to the earth, crushing four Venans beneath his bulk. Five of the creatures reeled from direct hits. Three of them did not rise.

The crews were already reloading.

Keeper Greymane howled one final time and slammed his hammer onto the stone parapet before him.

On the grounds behind the wall, another battalion of archer serfs sighted on targeting marks set into the battlements and loosed. Flights of flaming darts arced over the battlements, clearing entire planes of the killing ground behind the fourth marker.

Trebuchets launched with creaks and snaps, and canisters filled in pitch and set alight tumbled through the air like comets, slamming into the ground at the fifth marker and exploding into flame. Patches of the horde burned like dry twigs, flailing about in agony.

Hundreds died. Ruptured bodies carpeted the ground outside the walls of Hammarfall, burned, pierced and broken. The first volley alone would feed the scavengers for days.

Such losses shattered armies. The fighting spirit of hardened veterans snapped like brittle sticks in the face of such overwhelming firepower.

The servants of Mammon slowed only to eat their own.

· · ·

JARL HEIMDALL LOOKED over the battlefield and rubbed his jaw. As fearsome as Greymane's volley had been, the Venan horde continued to swarm toward the keep. It would be close, this one.

All along the walls, the Wolf Lord could hear his warriors encouraging their serfs.

"You have a shot, take it. Don't wait for commands from me. And, boy, for heaven's sake, take a breath!"

"You didn't miss, lad; he'll bleed out on his own. You have limited shafts, and each one has a different scum-infested home out there."

"All together now! Send these bilge-drinking bug-fondlers back to their hidey-holes!"

Flights of arrows winged out from the ramparts at regular intervals, cutting down shrieking swathes of cultists like wheat before the scythe. A giant lowed mournfully as old Ragnar's spear-thrower team pinned it to the ground with a shaft through the thigh.

"Aye, good shot, Ragnar! Not bad for your dim eyes!"

"You might hit something, too, if you pulled your head out of your—"

Heimdall leaned over the rampart. "You watch your mouth, Ragnar! My little girl's up here!"

Not about to be cowed in the heat of battle, Ragnar roared back, "My jarl, if she wants to act like a man, she can bloody well listen to me talk like one!"

Anya loosed an arrow that took a Venan off of his diseased horse and shouted, "Oh, are there *men* up here? I thought I was at a nattering old wives quilting bee!"

Heimlich's voice rose above the laughter. "All right, boys, give'em the needle!"

A spear shaft leapt out of its cradle and took a giant full in the chest, toppling it backwards with a crash. Amidst the cheers, Heimlich jumped on top of the wall and shook his fist at his fallen target. "Take that, demon turds! When you reach Hel's halls, you tell them how Heimlich threads the needle!"

In answer, poisoned darts hissed by his head, and the Wolf jerked back reflexively. Losing his footing, the Wolf yelled as he fell backwards off of the rampart.

The Wolves laughed as they killed. It was good, Heimdall thought. Their spirits are high.

They would need that.

HUNDREDS OF MEN died before Ursus's eyes, but the Slaughterlord felt nothing as he watched. These men had been nothing before Ursus had sent them to die at the Wolves' wall, and their sacrifices conferred no additional value upon them. They died as they were meant to.

Even at this distance, over the screams of the dying and the explosions of canister shells, Ursus could hear the laughter of champions as they slaughtered their lessers. It made saliva rush into his mouth, awakening the old hunger that had once driven him to bend his knee to a false god.

He stretched his neck and growled, reveling in the sensation.

His Brides stood arrayed about him, as close as they dared, and they watched the battle unfolding as hungrily as he. Broken from the chains of gods and men every one, his Brides. They came to him beaten and violated, and in turn, he alloyed them into howling blades of their own vengeance on the world of men.

Ursus gestured. "Signal."

One of his Brides, Tora, a savage killer with a mohawk dyed white and stiffened with bear grease, nodded curtly and stalked away to find a horn.

The Slaughterlord watched her go, admiring her form as she obeyed. It was not out of some primal urge that he watched her; lust dug its claws into Ursus only rarely. Instead, as he watched Tora sink her blade into a herald's back and tear the horn from his side, Ursus gazed upon her strength.

Her figure, once layered with fat and fit for nothing but the beatings she received, resembled now the body of a lean predator. Her movements, before hesitant, clumsy and shaking, now glided with grace and confidence as she pulled the blade from the corpse and lifted the horn to her lips.

Her chest swelled as Tora took her breath, and Ursus clenched his fist appreciatively at her lack of fear. Before she had become Tora, she would have feared to call attention to herself. Now she would blow a horn to command giants.

Strength. Ursus demanded it, nurtured it, and when the time was right, used it.

ANOTHER VOLLEY OF SPEARS LOOSED, and the decade of giants still standing staggered backward, arms raised to ward off the deadly shafts. The Mammonite cults huddled about their feet, the ladders and rams of the giants their only route into the walls of Hammarfall.

Heimdall shouted, "Give it to them again! Kill them and we end this!"

The spear-thrower crews worked feverishly, dropping spears into their launch cradles and winding the tension cables back for further casts. Their Wolf overseers roared encouragement, each desperate to mark the most kills amongst the hulking mutants and take the place of honor in the battle song.

A horn sounded in the distance, low and braying, and Heimdall's ears pricked. Roars sounded from the tree line to the left of the fortress, and the jarl turned to see another column of giants burst from cover. These creatures did not lumber scattered and divided like their brothers, but loped forward in a disciplined lock-step that ate the ground between them and Hammarfall. The sound of their charge shook the air, and Heimdall could hear them snarl in cadence.

The monsters bore iron-headed rams, two giants to a ram, and mighty siege ladders. The two giants in the front also carried thick shields draped in hide to protect their fellows behind them.

Ragnar's crew, late to fire in the last volley, sighted the charging column and wheeled about to target them. The spear leapt from the cradle and shrieked across the killspace in the blink of an eye.

The giant in front lifted his shield high and turned his shoulder into the massive bolt. With a wrench, the shield bearer battered the projectile with his shield, swiping the shaft out of the air with a *clang*. Aggressive roars rose from his comrades, and they thundered toward the wall even faster.

The jarl gritted his teeth. The enemy would mount the wall for sure, now.

"Wolves!" he shouted. "Axes out!"

Serfs and Wolves alike loosed their final shafts and immediately shifted to the next stage of Hammarfall's defense. Half of the serfs defending the wall laid aside their bows and picked up axes, spears and shields lying at their feet. The other half slung their bows and sprinted for the towers on either side of the curtain wall.

On the ground, the archers dashed to stack their bows and stand by piles of stone and timber. The catapult crews continued to fire unabated, launching their incendiary payloads as directed by Wolves on the wall.

The jarl caught Anya glancing at him, trying to hide her worry. He nodded at her. "We will be fine, daughter," he lied. "We will hold."

GASPS SOUNDED behind Gideon as the first siege ladder, a behemoth of iron and wood, slammed against the parapet of the curtain wall. Heavy metal hooks slammed down, anchoring the ladder to the wall and preventing the serf crews that rushed toward it from dislodging it.

Gideon felt the weight of the sword on his back. The scabbard felt...warm.

Having seen the weapon, he had a feeling he knew why.

They mount the walls, and yet you remain.

He exhaled in irritation. "Yes."

Gemelte glanced back at Ashkelon standing in the doorway. *He has killed you for withdrawing from combat before. Why will he not execute you for cowardice now?*

Gideon grunted derisively. "I thought you understood Ashkelon."

That would be quite the claim.

The sound of metal slamming into stone rang across the fortress like the strikes of a blacksmith's hammer. The rams were working to breach the walls now.

Gideon cracked his neck and rotated his wrists. "Fine. Since you will not leave me to focus, I'll tell you why I'm here."

He pointed with his sword at the walls. "What do you think the Venans are here for?"

The revenant spread his ethereal hands. *Tell me.*

"They are not an army. They have no discipline. The only reason they are even here in the numbers they are is because the consort of their god commanded them to."

Gideon gritted his teeth. "No, those cannibals are out there for one reason, and that's to eat the people behind me. Do you really think that once the Venans get through the wall, they will turn to help their brothers?"

Gemelte remained silent.

"Of course they won't," Gideon hissed. "They will run through the streets, searching for the most tender flesh they can find. The women. The children. Babies in their cradles."

Gideon tapped his chest. "I will not let that happen. I will kill them all first."

Gemelte smiled at that. *Your teaching shows, soldier. Another man would have said that he would die first.*

Gideon held his gaze evenly. "My master has no equal when it comes to killing, and he is a very good teacher."

After a moment, Gemelte inclined his head. *Conceded.*

Gideon nodded shortly and started to turn away, but Gemelte's words halted him.

In the legends of the Fall, after Darkness entered the world, the Almighty placed a sentinel at the gate of the first Garden. The angelic watchman wielded a supernatural sword, a blade that burned with righteous zeal to keep the way of innocence against those who might defile it.

Gideon chuckled, amused, and turned back to face the wall. "There are only a few small differences between me and the Guardian of Eden."

And yet your sword burns.

THEY DID NOT CHARGE the gate. Most defenses on the wall could swivel to fire on the ground before the gatehouse. The death toll to take it would be astronomical. Instead, the Venans sent their giants at the wall itself.

Poisoned arrows sliced through the air by the defenders' heads, and the wall shuddered under their feet. Scant yards beneath them, roaring giants heaved the trunks of ironwood trees into the wall, grinding deeper holes into the stubborn bones of the fortress with every strike. Ladders crashed against the wall and their heavy hooks grasped the parapets like the fingers of a drowning man.

The tide surged against Hammarfall, the mass of starving wretches funneling toward the dozen ladders that offered access to fresh meat.

The first ragged Venan to scale the wall leapt from the ladder and brandished his rusted blade, screeching in joyous anticipation. He maintained his position on the wall for a single second before an immense warhammer thudded into the cultist's ribcage and hurled the screaming man from the top of the wall.

Skald's lip twisted in contempt and he bellowed down at the besieging army, "Is this all you bring? How is mighty Skald supposed to forge immortal legend vith foes like this?"

More cultists vaulted the wall, spilling over the parapets in a tsunami of diseased flesh and dirty iron. They crashed against well-made shields and sharp spears wielded by the scions of daemon-hunters, and died in droves. Dark praise and maniacal laughter were met with boisterous shouts and defiant song as the Wolves defended their lair with ringing blades.

Skald fought alone on the battlements, eschewing the shield wall of his serfs. He sidestepped a dagger encrusted with filth and punched the cannibal in the side of the head. The force of the strike cracked his attacker's skull against unyielding stone, and the once-man sagged as death took him to a deserved Hel.

All around him, Venans met their ends, spitted on spears, riven by axes, pierced by darts or cast from the walls. Discipline on the wall held, and the Venans dragged only a pittance of the serfs down and none of the Wolves. Fueled only by diabolical faith, the emaciated Mammonites could not overcome healthy warriors defending their homes.

Skald swept another cretin from the top of the wall and dared to hope that they might win this.

"THE VENANS ARE on the walls, lord."

Ursus could see this for himself. He asked a question, while knowing the answer already.

"And?"

Tora sneered. "They are being slaughtered."

Ursus nodded. "Expected. Where is the Jahennan?"

Skylar, his First, her head shaved save for a scarlet braid falling to her ankles, answered, "He nears the summit, lord."

Ursus reached back and gripped the haft of his blackened greatsword, drawing the mammoth blade with exaggerated slowness. Without a word, the Slaughterlord of Carcharoth began to stride toward the embattled walls of Hammarfall, all ten of his Brides falling in behind him.

Incendiary canisters burst across the killing zone of the Wolves' fortress, igniting Venans into howling torches. A lucky shot roared overhead and slammed into a catapult crew struggling to reload their machine, spilling liquid fire over the precious weapon. Screams sounded behind the Slaughterlord as the crew thrashed on the burning ground.

Volley after volley of shafts arced down like driving rain, a dozen or more sparking from his breastplate, but Ursus paid them no heed. He was the king-killer, the breaker of champions. No mere shaft or catapult shot would end his legend.

In the midst of death and ruin, Ursus moved inexorably toward his target.

· · ·

OVERCOME by the heat of battle, Jarl Fangthane no longer shouted orders. He snarled them.

"Have Skaelon whip his dogs and put some fire in their bellies! If those barriers are not up by the time those circus freaks break through, the defense is lost."

Wolves nodded and raced back to their serf-gangs to relay their lord's commands. On his left, Anya twisted and loosed a shaft into a cannibal leaping toward him in his blind spot. Heimdall grunted his thanks, buried the smile of his axe blade in the chest of a Venan berserker and roared, "Aksel! The cauldrons! Now!"

The Wolf they called the Twisted barked at his serfs, and the gang lifted their cast-iron burdens and made their way toward where the wall shuddered from repeated blows. Wizened old Aksel cleared their path himself, shoving serfs and Wolves aside with shouted curses and hacking down any invader unfortunate enough to cross his path.

The archers raining arrows down onto the breachers quickly retreated at the sight of Aksel and his pots.

The giants did not, roaring strained trumpeting cries like mammoths and hammering at the breach with relentless force. The abused stones cracked and shattered under their savage blows, widening the breach further and bringing the slavering mutants closer to breaching the wall.

Moments later, Aksel had his men where he wanted them, and the Twisted looked to his jarl for the signal. Heimdall punched his axe into the air, and Aksel shouted, "Push!"

Their shoulders cushioned by heavy cloth pads, the serfs hurled themselves into the sides of the cauldrons, tipping the mighty pots over. Bubbling tar poured from the vats, drenching the devil-worshippers beneath. Their aggressive roars changed to panicked lowing as several of the blackened giants staggered back, dropping their rams and desperately clawing at their faces to scrape the super-heated pitch from their skin.

Heimdall bellowed, "Skaelon!"

On the ground behind the wall, amidst sweating serfs stripped to their breeches, the Wolf called Skaelon heaved another log into place and shouted back, "Working on it!"

Heimdall gritted his teeth and nodded back. It would have to do.

Already, surviving titans shoved their moaning brothers aside, lifted their rams and smashed at the wall. Archer-serfs leapt to their positions and loosed shafts into the giants' necks and shoulders, but each arrow only stung the creatures like gnats, failing to truly penetrate their hardened skin.

In return, the giants waiting to breach swung their clubs at the top of the wall, crushing parapets and forcing the archers back. One lucky swing caught four men before they could withdraw and shattered every bone in their bodies. The cauldrons themselves tumbled from the rampart, metal clanging against the broken rock beneath.

The Venans capered and shrieked around the mutants, cheering madly at every stone that fell and urging the giants on.

It took only a few more strikes. The giants of the North knew how to crush stone like no other, and before their craft, the tortured wall relented. The giants slammed their rams into the stones, only to feel the iron-tipped logs burst through to the other side. The serfs shouted in alarm as rocky shrapnel exploded from the wall, scoring lines of red across bare flesh, and a cloud of chalky dust billowed into Hammarfall, obscuring vision.

Silence descended across the battlefield at the import of the event. Only tumbling stones broke the stillness caused by the breath held in every man's chest.

Then a swelling bray rose from beyond the wall as the cannibals howled their mania into the heavens, and the giants feverishly pounded on the hole, widening it enough to allow the passage of troops. They pulled at the sides of the breach with their hands, using brute strength to peel back the stony shell of Hammarfall to get at the sweet meat within.

Heimdall, unable to see through the dense cloud of dust, shouted, "Skaelon?"

After a moment, a familiar voice shouted hoarsely, "You nag like a wife, jarl."

A grin spread across the Wolf lord's face as the warriors around him chuckled, morphing from relief to ferocity.

"Now let them come," he snarled.

VENANS SHOVED PAST THE GIANTS, who as yet could not fit their bulk through the breach in the wall. They ran screaming into the cloud of dust, lifting rusted daggers, axes and mauls. Dozens of cannibalistic warriors squeezed through the rent in Hammarfall's stone, desperate to feast on the repast within.

They collided with a stubborn mass that loomed out of the dust. The Venans in front slammed into it and their fellows piled in behind them. Swiftly, those crushed against the mass began to shriek a different tune, as the weight of their brothers crushed them against the strange obstruction.

At last, the Venans ceased pushing forward, and as the dust began to clear, peered through the murky fog to see what held them back.

It was a wall.

Another one.

Built of pre-cut logs, rising just above where a man's hands could reach. Beyond that, the serfs who had built it waited, crouched on rooftops and in second-floor doorways, arrows on the string. Above them on the ramparts, the wall archers angled their weapons down into the entrapped Venans, bows creaking as they bent back.

Skaelon took in a mighty breath and cried, "Loose!"

In that first instant, dozens of bows snapped like the boughs of a forest in a storm. The air hissed in fury, the displacement creating a false breeze. Arrows fell on the Venans in such density that the shafts knocked against one another in flight and fell to the earth, wasted. It did not matter.

The Venans were blasted backward, some pierced by half a dozen darts or more. The cultists in the gap collapsed, choking the entry point and carpeting the ground with their corpses. Missed shafts *thock*ed into the logs and clattered off of the stone wall, masking the meaty tears of arrows piercing diseased flesh.

Heedless of the massacre within, the giants continued to pull at the stones of the wall, some bashing their rams against the ragged corners to shear off chunks. The screams diminished in the walls, but the dark praise never ceased.

Skaelon shook his head in frustration and called out, "My jarl! They come still!"

Heimdall drew his axe and called out, "Huscarls! To me!"

The bloodsworn guard of the Wolf Lord drew about him like a cloak, and Jarl Fangthane stepped forward to join his warriors at the breach.

A hand slammed into his chest, halting his steps, and Heimdall turned to glare at Skald. His wrath was wasted, however, because Skald was not looking at him.

He was looking where a half-naked painted woman heaved herself over the battlements and rolled onto the stone walkway. Froth dripped through her torn lips as she lifted herself to a crouch, hands held behind her with serrated daggers. Her head tilted to the side as she stared at the crew of a spear-thrower, and her lips parted in a drooling pant as the serfs charged her.

The four serfs lasted seven seconds against her. The woman shrieked, a horrible sound that pierced the clamor of the battle, and threw herself forward. One lithe leg kicked forward, driving into a serf's shield and knocking him back, before hooking gracefully back to slam her heel into a second's temple over his own shield.

Dark steel blurred, and hot red blood spurted from ripped throats and sprayed across the savage's face and chest. She lifted her head to welcome it, eyes stark and white in her tattooed face.

Skald pointed and growled, "That is not a Venan."

The siege master Ranald saw his men die, and he leapt down from his spear-thrower with a roar of fury. His aged limbs moved with a speed borrowed from many winters past, and he whipped his axe toward the murderess's waist with all the power of his withered frame.

Impossibly agile, the woman bent back, her spine curving to the breaking point before she flipped over to land on her feet. Ranald powered forward, his axe rising from his lateral cut to chop down into her chest. The murderess sidestepped and raked her dagger along the siege master's ribs, the serrated steel tearing into the old man's body and ripping out a welter of blood to spatter the wall.

Ranald merely grunted. With a short step, he powered his fist into the woman's face, snapping her head back and staggering her back a pace. His axe swept toward her neck, and the woman barely ducked the blade, blood streaming from her broken nose and lips. She launched forward from her crouch, and buried her dagger deep into the old Wolf's thigh.

Now Ranald bellowed in pain, and the feral woman twisted the blade and jerked it out, her mouth open to catch the hot spray from the Wolf's artery.

Heimdall surged forward, rushing toward the invader in a storm of furs, his huscarls a step behind him.

But ancient Ranald was not done yet. Even as the damnable woman exulted in his life's blood, he reached down and gripped the wench by her top knot and belt. With a heave, he lifted her above his head, shouting in effort and rage. She shrieked in return, burying both daggers into his shoulders, but her demise was written.

The siege master stepped forward and hurled the invader from top of the wall. He collapsed, clutching at the battlements so he could watch her split open on the broken ground outside the walls.

Heimdall reached his side in time to hear the old Wolf snarl, "Get off—my wall."

Sagging, the Wolf fell to the stones of his beloved fortress. His last words were uttered, as was proper, to Skald, keeper of the sagas.

"Don't you forget to put that in there, you bloody deaf pile of horse droppings."

Skald smiled tightly and gripped Ranald's fist as the life faded from his eyes. He looked at the Wolves around him and said quietly, "Let Hel hear you."

With a sharp intake of breath, Skald threw his head back and howled. As one, the jarl and huscarls joined the lament. Across the wall, Wolves took up the cry, and as a pack, they sent their fallen brother to the Almighty's halls on a tide of their grief.

The howl faded, and Skald rose to his feet. He met the eyes of those around him, and he said, "Do not let sadness still your axes today, brothers."

He pointed to several yards down the wall, where nine more panting barbarian women pulled themselves over the ramparts. The first, a shrieking savage with a white crest of hair, buried her dagger in the spine of a Venan blocking her path while her comrade decapitated another with one sweep of her giant sword.

"She has sisters."

Gunther the gate master belched loudly and commented, "Oof, sisters. Never get in the middle of that, believe you me."

The Wolves chuckled dangerously and edged forward, weapons rising in their fists.

They stopped dead when the maidens' master mounted the ramparts.

URSUS SKULL-TAKER, Slaughterlord of Carcharoth, last of the mythical Tor Kayn, stepped onto the stones of Hammarfall and felt them crack beneath him. He gripped his mammoth goreblade in one hand, the iron black and thirsty. His eyes gleamed red as he swept his gaze across the battlements, searching for a worthy foe as his Brides launched toward the shield wall before them.

He growled.

This was nothing new. Ursus growled in place of taking breath. Every utterance that fell from his scarred lips, the very few there were, burned with menace.

This time, however, he growled in disappointment. The slaves of the Wolves slaughtered the pathetic dregs of Mammon, to be sure, but his Brides sliced through them like a blade through wind. Shields and spears flew from the top of the wall, followed by the ruptured bodies of their wielders. The Brides screamed and cackled as they killed, rejoicing in the deaths of men.

Beyond them and their victims, for he could not call them warriors, Ursus sighted something.

There.

A warrior swathed in furs raced toward Ursus's Brides, axe in hand, his eyes alight with the wrath of a king attacked in his own hold. Warriors, true warriors, followed him, devoid of fear or doubt.

Before him, the Brides finished slaughtering the survivors of the shield wall and made for a second.

Ursus stepped forward, hefting his blade in both hands.

"Move."

His voice was so low, it sounded like boulders crashing against one another. The Brides immediately fell back, dancing lithely behind their lord as he advanced.

The second shield wall looked up from their shields and saw what was coming for them. Some of the shields dipped as shock registered at the size of the warrior coming for them.

Ursus could have lowered his shoulder and bulled his way through the wall. He could have ordered his Brides forward to tear it down, slitting the throats of men screaming for mercy.

But their king approached, and Ursus wanted him to see.

With a snarl torn from the depths of the Abyss, Ursus swung his sword at the shield wall. One blow, powered by Ursus's undying hatred for the weakness of men.

There was nothing they could do. That single blow hacked through every one of the eight men. Their armor. Their shields. Their swords. Nothing even slowed his dreadful blade as it sheared straight through the formation and wedged itself into the stone of the rampart beside them, spraying dust and stone chips from the impact. A lake of blood spilled from the ruptured corpses, running along the stones as if fleeing.

The Slaughterlord jerked his goreblade from the rampart and stalked forward to stand in the midst of the carnage he had wrought. With a thunderous clang, the point of his greatsword split the stones at his feet, both of his scarred hands resting on the pommel. He loomed in the obscurity of the dust, a titanic figure spattered with blood, surrounded by ruin, waiting.

The message was clear.

Build your walls. Flesh or stone, nothing stands before Ursus.

EIGHT MEN DEAD IN AN INSTANT.

Heimdall and his huscarls skidded to a stop, momentarily stunned into immobility by the sudden deaths of Ranald's remaining serfs. The enemy warlord stood twelve feet tall, the weapon before him taller than any Wolf present. Battered iron plates strained to contain the sheer mass of the figure, and every hateful breath blasted from his horned helm like a smith's bellows.

Barbarous women prowled behind their master, their flesh striped with black tiger-rakes and their hair wild. Every weapon they bore possessed metal teeth to saw through bone for the taking of trophies.

Jarl Heimdall Fangthane, master of the fortress of Hammarfall and lord of Wolves, stepped forward from his huscarls toward the gargantuan creature seething before him. It took all of his willpower to approach the monstrous warrior, but it would not be said that Wolves lacked courage.

"You," the Wolf lord growled, angling his axe toward the warlord. "Name yourself, so I know what to carve onto my axe handle."

The titan stood motionless for a moment, before uttering one grinding word.

"Ursus."

Heimdall straightened and slammed the haft of his axe against his chest. "I am Heimdall Fangthane, jarl of the Wolves. Prepare to meet the Almighty and be judged for your sins."

The creature named Ursus considered him for a moment, then gestured around them.

"Listen."

The battle continued to crash. Archers continued to fire their volleys into the Venan horde assaulting the walls, serfs fought with cannibals on the ramparts and Skaelon fought to hold the second wall against the cultists flooding through the breach. Screams and roars mingled in the frigid air, tainted with the scent of smoke and iron.

Heimdall snarled, "I hear heroes fighting for their home against godless swine."

He turned back to Ursus. "What do you hear?"

The warlord's red eyes flickered within his helm. "No god."

The jarl hesitated, wrong footed. "What?"

"Your god—not here. Just you, and weak men."

Heimdall narrowed his eyes. "What do you want?"

Ursus pulled his blade from the stone and rested the mammoth blade on his shoulder. It scraped against the dull iron of his shoulder guard. His hellish gaze never wavered.

"Give a man, and we fight together. If he win, we serve. If I win, you serve."

The jarl chuckled. "Or how about we just kill all of you and call the battle won?"

Ursus did not react to the Wolf Lord's dismissal. He merely raised his sword and pointed the blade toward the heart of the keep, the King's Doom.

"Come," the giant rumbled, "and see."

ABRAM HELD A VERY dim view of personal combat. There were servants of Gehenna who delighted in the fractious chaos of melee fighting, glorying in their prowess as hot blood splashed across their bare chests. These servants lived brief, violent lives; barely even flickers in the span of eternity.

Not so Abram. Abram and his legacy would live through the eons.

So it was that while Ursus drove the mass of cultists against the walls of the fortress, Abram waited. The inquisitor watched with unblinking gaze as hundreds of Mammon's servants perished, reaped by the Wolves' fearsome defenses. He waited for the moment to present itself, that delicate fulcrum upon which the entire battle rested and could tip the scales either way.

Behind him, hanging from steely thread attached to their unholy idols, swayed two hundred Venan murderers. These were the most patient of Ja'a's servants that Abram could find; those able to endure the sight of the spilt blood and rent flesh beneath in order to reach a greater prize. Still, though, they murmured, their empty bellies aching with the hunger of their ritual fasting.

Above them, claws anchored securely to the stone while their burdens dangled beneath them, one hundred spiders crept along the underside of the peak overlooking Hammarfall. The Wolves, so confident in their fastness delved from the hollow mountain, never bothered to look up.

Though a vassal of Carcharoth and a firm believer in his revolutionary doctrine, Abram still cleaved to the teachings of Aganyn from his youth. There would be no breaking the Wolves from without their walls; the warriors were too strong, too well-trained and too galvanized by the sight of an ancient enemy.

They had, however, exposed a soft underbelly in the disposition of their non-combatants.

Abram held up a hand, his eyes knifing through the chaos beneath to find the event he sought.

There.

The lord of the Wolves raced along the battlements, his retainers close behind, furs flying and blades out. There was almost panic in their mad dash, and as Abram continued to watch, he could see why.

There was no mistaking the hulking figure of Ursus, even from this height. Abram shook his head slowly, marveling as the gargantuan warrior swept an entire shield wall from the parapets with a single cleave of his blade.

And still the Wolf Lord defied him. Abram grunted in respect at his audacity as the man bellowed challenges inaudible from this height. To face a creature like Ursus and charge without the boons of madness...

No matter. The time had come.

Abram chopped his hand down, and the Venans issued a demented chittering to their mounts. The creatures responded, venomous drool dripping from their churning mandibles, and as one, the infiltrator force lowered on a hundred threads into the courtyard the Wolves called the King's Doom.

The Venans began to shriek in praise, frothy spittle spilling from their lips. Their cries echoed from the hollow mountain, transformed by the structure's acoustics into a choir of Hell's denizens.

WITH HIS CLEAR EYES, Heimdall followed the angle of the blade the monster held, and his heart froze within his chest. From the mountain peak of Hammarfall, a brood of monstrous spiders bearing cackling cannibals descended upon the keep, clustered about the hall housing the innocents.

Not only the jarl looked to see the demonic infiltrators. Cries of woe rose from the serfs as they beheld the creatures dropping toward their families. Weapons dropped, concentration broke, and the Venan hordes surged against them, reaping a dreadful tally in dead men and women.

At the second wall, Skaelon roared desperately, "Back to it, lads! If they break through here, it won't matter anyway!"

Pained horror writ on every man's face, they slammed themselves back against the cultist tide. Already, Jarl Fangthane could hear the names of wives, children and mothers being called out, warnings broken by weeping screamed toward the Doom.

Heimdall felt his heart break at the sound. His people, those who depended on him, were trapped. None of the Wolves could afford to break contact with the Venan tide, as the walls only just held as it was. There was no egress for the innocents within the Doom.

Despair, long held at bay over the years of attrition and loss, took hold in Heimdall's soul, and he fell. His knees slammed into the rock of his keep, and his back bowed with the weight of his failure.

Ursus looked down on him, the stink of death emanating from the titanic warrior. His voice rumbled like the thunder of a distant storm. "Your keep is lost, king. Your women, children, your young and old: they belong to Mammon now. All that remains is a good death."

His heavy blade scraped along the stones. "Come now, King of

Wolves. Fight. Fight as greatest warrior of this place against me. I will give you good death."

Heimdall met the hellish warrior's red gaze, and saw his end there. The end of all Wolves, of centuries of faithful service. Something in his heart rebelled against the thought, and anger kindled in his eyes again. He gripped his axe, spat to one side and raised to one knee.

"Fine, then, demon-slave. Give it your best—"

He was cut off when a woman stepped in front of him, hands planted on her hips, bow slung on her back.

Anya Helsdottyr looked up at Ursus, her chin jutted out in defiance, and hawked a glob of spit at his feet.

"Pah!"

"No!"

Heimdall surged to his feet and gripped Anya's shoulder, trying to haul her back. She swept his hand from her shoulder and stood her ground.

The Slaughterlord looked down at the splat of spit on the ground, then at her.

Anya glared at him, fury hot in her gaze. "You think this is the end? You think killing our king will end the Wolves? You know nothing of Wolves!"

Ursus loomed over her, his breath gusting like a desert wind. In the face of a force of destruction, Anya remained fearless.

"In your ignorance, you assume two things. First, that my father is our greatest warrior."

Even as his walls burned around him, Heimdall had enough pride in him that his eyebrows shot to his hairline.

Before he could splutter a denial, Anya crossed her arms and tossed her chin toward the Doom. "And also, that my love will allow any of your rabble to even set foot across that threshold."

Now Heimdall did not hesitate. "*Your what?*"

Two hundred Venans, backed by one hundred spiders, stood packed in the wide courtyard of the King's Doom, panting and drooling.

Abram, inquisitor of Gehenna and loyal servant of Carcharoth, stood at their head, savoring the pain to come. Before them, a stone staircase tapered to a single gateway, leading to the most precious possessions of the Wolves: their loved ones.

Within that gateway stood a single warrior, arms crossed, face impassive, blade sheathed on his back.

Abram sighed and spoke to those behind him. "Wait here. I will sacrifice this one to the gods, and then you may feast."

The Mammonites hungered, but even they understood sacrifice. They would wait.

Abram drew his rapier and uncoiled his painlash, allowing the poisoned and barbed strands to drag on the stone of the stairs as he ascended. The wide brim of his hat concealed his eyes, only the scars on the lower half of his face visible to the motionless warrior before him. It often had an intimidating effect on the fools unfortunate enough to face a Jahennan inquisitor.

As he reached the top stair, Abram lifted his chin, letting the soon-to-be-dead man gaze into his lifeless eyes.

Involuntarily, Abram recoiled, staggering backward and raising his sword as if to ward the warrior away.

"You...," he gasped.

Ashkelon, face draped in shadow and eyes aglow with icy light, inclined his head slightly, as though trying to place Abram's face.

"You recognize me. Curious. Survivors are rare."

Abram's breath came fast and hard, and he stabbed a finger at the wraith from his past. "You...you are the one who burned my master."

Ashkelon raised a manicured eyebrow, ignoring the army behind Abram entirely. "I burn many masters. You will have to provide some context."

"Aganyn!" Abram snarled. "The lord inquisitor of the Pain God! Only recipient of prophecy in a hundred years!"

Ashkelon cut him off. "Thank you. I could have done without the string of meaningless titles. How is he? You refer to him as though he still lives."

Abram narrowed his eyes. "He is...blessed, now. After you left us to die in that wasteland, I found him. He was a charred corpse, gasping for every breath, but his hate sustained him until I could get him to the Three. Now, he is more powerful than ever, and he will lead us to destroy all gods and take the heavens and the earth for ourselves."

The dark sorcerer shook his head, his pale eyes alight with amusement. "You are mistaken. The temperature of the flame I buried within that man's chest would have incinerated his organs in seconds, so he certainly did not survive. I don't know who it was you think you rescued, but it is certainly not the warlock."

Abram sneered. "As if you would know. You will not fare so well this time. I have a few more servants with me than when last we met."

Ashkelon yawned. He lifted a hand to cover his mouth in a half-hearted attempt of decorum, but the pure boredom radiating from his eyes staggered the inquisitor. Abram stared at him. "What—do you hear me? Do you see what stands behind me? These wretches will tear the flesh from your bones, and then the spiders will *drink* you."

Ashkelon nodded wearily and waved his hand in a small circle. "Yes, yes, of course, and my soul will be damned for all eternity while the demons of Hell cackle around me. Why is it that the threats always end this way? From both Light and Dark, strangely enough."

Abram opened his mouth, but Ashkelon continued speaking. "No, I've had enough of your words, slave. Just tell me the name of this master who miraculously survived the star I put in his chest. They always change their names after a supposed apotheosis."

Pride straightened Abram's spine, and he looked the insolent sorcerer in his icy blue eyes. "His name is Carcharoth, mage. And you will remember it, for I will make you scream it once a second for every day of life I leave you as I offer your pain to the God of Agony."

Ashkelon spread his arms. "Anything to end this conversation."

Abram snarled and cracked his painlash on the stone stairs. The horde of Venans and spiders edged forward, sensing the beginning of the promised feast. Abram heard the hungry snarling behind him, the hellish hissing of the monsters granted to him, and he angled his blade toward the mouth of the hall.

He spat three words, and his skin prickled at the weight of history they bore.

"Make them *suffer.*"

The horde surged forward, cannibals shoving past one another to be the first to the screaming repast within the hall. Spiders chittered and lunged forward, mandibles drooling acidic vomit. A tide of voracious monsters crested the top of the steps and dashed to the doorway.

The dark figure made no move to draw his sword. Instead, just before the cannibals and monsters flooded through, Ashkelon stepped to the side and rasped three words of his own to a figure standing behind him.

"You heard him."

THE WULFEN FORTRESS OF HAMMERFALL

14

DOOM OF KINGS

Ashkelon told him to wait for his "introduction", so Gideon waited.

Behind him, fearful mutters and muffled sobs rose from women clutching their children to their chests. The air reeked of fear's bitter taint.

Before him, Ashkelon mocked a legion of the children of Hell, driving them into a frenzy. He set the stage for his apprentice's debut, a baptism of blood and ichor sure to cement his legend in the sagas of the Wolves.

Gideon could not care less about that. But that left a question burning in his mind.

What do I want?

He closed his eyes and felt the world still. Sound faded to a bass rumble, and words ceased to have meaning.

He gripped the haft of his sword. The handle, at least, felt like that of Armand Halcyon's. He sighed, letting the solid familiarity of the handle reassure him.

The question remained. *What do I want?*

Gideon opened his eyes, and his mother stood before him. Talia stood with one hand on her hip, a playful look in her eyes as she looked down at him.

A touch of a sad smile tugged at Gideon's lips at the memory of her. She was beautiful, hale and healthy again. Her golden hair danced around her in a light summer breeze, and her smile lit up the darkness of the room.

He was a child again. He was always a child in these echoes of memory.

Lady Halcyon smiled at him and knelt to his level. "Is that a sword, little one?"

Gideon chuckled softly, remembering his earnest answer. "Yes, ma'am!"

The light played about her head, washing everything around him in warm tones. It was impossible to separate her from sunshine.

Talia looked him in the eye. "If you must have a sword, Gideon, you must always use it to protect others. Be a *hero*. Can you promise me that?"

Gideon opened his eyes and sound rushed back. Roars and shrieks flooded his senses again, and the first of the Venan cultists crested the steps and swept through the doorway. Ashkelon stepped aside, leaving them free entry, not to the terrified innocents, but to the single warrior awaiting them.

In the black, a blade ignited with a hiss, and a grieving son whispered, "Yes, ma'am."

THE FIRST RANKS of Venans had no idea what hit them.

Gideon Halcyon struck the horde like a meteor, the battle cry sounding from his lips ringing through the courtyard. His first stroke swept through no fewer than five Venans with a single backhand. His sword flashed brightly as it cleaved through flesh and bone like smoke. An aftershock of power blasted the corpses back, flinging bodies flailing into the air with a crackling bang.

The sword born of Death and Justice gleamed like a bolt of azure lightning, silver shining from its single killing edge. Its blade hummed with power barely encased in the metal, and the tones of a great church bell rang in the wake of its thunderous strikes.

The second rank of cultists stutter-stepped at the sight, pulled back, tried to turn, but the ignorant horde behind them rammed them closer.

Gideon slashed again, and another line of Venans fell back in pieces, the carved edges of their flesh sizzling like cooked pork. When his blade sliced through them, he felt the resistance of hacking through a sunbeam. The sword shimmered with heat and light, and by instinct, the oncoming cultists squinted or turned away from the blaze.

Gideon had a heartbeat to appreciate the advantage his weapon gave him. His soul marveled at the power and beauty of the sword, its weight and heft perfect as it whipped around his body. Above all, the light the blade gave off lit everything around him in warm rays of sunshine.

Tal. Your name will be Tal, like her.

The sword keened slightly, almost as if it acknowledged his dedication. Then his training took hold of his movement, and Gideon began to kill.

He killed more than he ever thought possible. The blade scribed arcs of brilliant silver and gold around him as it slew the corrupt. In a handful of seconds, he scoured the doorway of invaders, and Gideon turned his shoulder into the press from the door.

Each time he felt a lessening of resistance, he lunged forward another step and killed more of them. The Venan's bodies barely provided resistance for the sword's edge, and any weapons that managed to interpose themselves between their bearers and the glowing blade exploded into fragments upon impact.

Worse still, for the Venans, was Gideon's tutelage. Gideon had been trained to kill by Ashkelon, the Onyx Mage, the man who forced Death to kneel. His savage teachings took hold of Gideon's mind, his body, and the blade in his hands began to whip around him, faster, more efficient in the lives it reaped per motion expended. Throats opened like second mouths, limbs flopped to the stones and arteries gouted bright around the terrible warrior.

It began to rain blood on the steps of Doom.

ANYA WATCHED in amazement as the tide of Venans broke like surf upon rocks in the door of the Doom. Gideon brandished a sword seemingly plucked from legend. Nothing could withstand the gleaming blade; even shadows fled from it. In the years to come, she swore that she could hear it roaring defiance of the Dark in her soul.

The Venan infiltrators surged forwards in a panic, seeking to drag the warrior down with sheer weight of numbers. Gideon vanished from sight beneath a wave of diseased flesh, and Anya sucked in a little gasp.

Then she saw him, expertly rolling around the crush of the horde and hacking into its flank. The Venans staggered, off-balance, lost as to where their target had disappeared to, and Gideon swept his sword around, wading into the press as he lopped heads and limbs with inhuman precision. Weapons exploded into fragments and men pitched backward, bleeding rivers of scorched blood onto the stones of the Doom.

Gideon's blade never stopped moving. Every invader felt its attention and none were forgotten, as the blade sheared through legs and arms, dropping potential attackers all around. Wounded Venans shrieked on the bloody steps, clawing at the steps to drag themselves away before the fiery sword found them again.

Anya's breath caught in her throat as she saw Ashkelon standing in the doorway, the sole shadow not banished by the light of the sword. His arms crossed, his visage cold ivory, the warlock seemed a revenant from Sheol, bearing silent witness to the deluge of souls rising from the piles of the dead.

The Jahennan inquisitor stumbled away from the relentless onslaught, shoving Venans between him and the seemingly unstoppable warrior. His eyes were wide, his breathing bordering on hyperventilation at Gideon's implacable advance.

The last Venan in the first wave died with Gideon's blade scorching the back of his throat. Gideon lifted his gaze to see the remaining horde charging forward, and Anya's heart chilled when she saw his eyes. A cold hate burned there, fearless, devoid of horror at the slaughter he wreaked, calculating how best to repeat the devastation.

Faced with hundreds of Venans and monstrous creatures, Gideon was taking a breath to *assess* his enemy.

Well-protected in the horde, the inquisitor turned and shouted toward the wall, "Ursus! Kill him! Kill him now!"

Anya glanced at the titanic warrior. The warlord called Ursus did not move at the inquisitor's desperate call; instead, his eyes drank in Gideon's every step and cut. His breathing had quickened, the growls from his chest coming faster as Gideon stalked forward to slaughter the Venan army single-handed.

He is as rapt as we are, Anya realized.

"Ursus!" the inquisitor screamed.

THE SLAUGHTERLORD REMAINED in his place. He paid no heed to the Wolves within striking distance, to the woman who had defied him, or even to the pathetic squallings of Carcharoth's herald. He saw nothing but the warrior who plunged alone into an army of mutants and monsters, who *alone* drove them back and burst them asunder with the strength of his arm.

His great frame, formerly invulnerable to the cold of the frozen North, shivered.

GIDEON THRUST his blade into a Venan's neck and twisted. Crossing his foot behind him, Gideon spun, whipping Tal around and killing everything within the blade's deadly arc. The survivors staggered backward, tripping down the stairs, and Gideon advanced, driving the corrupted back with the holy light blazing from his sword.

Faintly, above the roaring of the sword in his mind, Gideon heard voices. The serfs, embattled with the hordes on the walls, cheered. Hope returned to their eyes and with it, strength to their limbs. They hurled themselves with renewed vigor into the Mammonite invaders, spears and axes flashing on the ground and the wall. Gideon's own purpose steeled even further, and he launched forward into a flurry of slashes that took him halfway down the stairs.

The Jahennan shouted syllables that made the Hell-worshipper's throat bleed, and cracked his whip. With a hiss like volcanic steam, the spiders scuttled forward, acidic saliva dripping from feverishly working mandibles.

"*HYVA!*" Skald shouted, pounding the butt of his hammer onto the stone of the wall. "*Hyva selva!*"

All along the wall and around the breach, the Wolves and their serfs pushed against the Venan horde, their swords and spears biting eagerly now. Skald felt his poet's spirit soar as the Wolves tore into their prey, inspired by the figure striking from the hall to protect their wives and daughters.

But they could not fight and watch Gideon at the same time. The weight of saga took hold of Skald's soul, and he roared over the battlements, "Fight on, brothers, and I vil tell you the tale of Gideon Doomhold!"

The Wolves shouted as one and the air shivered with their voices. "*Hyva* Doomhold!"

A hundred spiders lurched into the fight, limbs like lances punching into the turf and stone of their homes. The nightmarish creatures surrounded Gideon, clattering along the ground or sideways on the rock of the King's Doom courtyard. They screeched in demonic rage, and Skald felt a grin break across his face like a sunrise as Gideon strode forward, face set like stone, lifting a sword that shone ever brighter as his enemies grew ever more numerous.

By the Almighty, the saga tells itself.

Gideon struck, thunder cracked, and chitin and inhuman screams erupted across the Doom.

Skald pounded his hammer again and fairly roared, "He holds, brothers! Almighty be vith him for a fool, he holds! Lift your veapons and be counted, ye Vulfen, for the stories valk among us this day!"

HE KNEW EXACTLY what they were going to do and where they would be.

Gideon wrenched his blade out of a spider's spasming corpse and danced to the side as a thicket of limbs punched into the ground where he had been standing. The body of the monster prevented attack from that side for at least another second, and he whirled, Tal singing through the air to interpose between him and the spear-like legs seeking his heart. As soon as the sword locked with the creature's limbs, it flashed like a newborn star. The weapon melted through the armored exoskeleton and seared straight through the spider's limbs to bury itself deep into the creature's thorax.

Even as he killed, Gideon began to understand the weapon he had been gifted. Tal *wanted*. It wanted to destroy evil. It channeled that savage desire into Gideon, and burned away his fear and exhaustion to drive him on further.

The blade itself defied imagination. The Venans, it cut like silk; the spiders, more corrupt and born of hellish incantation, it ignited on contact. As men praised the name of the Almighty for deliverance, it gleamed with ever greater power and shunted it into Gideon's frame.

Riding on instinct, Gideon performed an experiment. He stepped forward into a creature's lunge and whipped his arm to the side, hurling the sword like a beam of light into a spider creeping along the face of the wall of the Doom to get at the children in the hall. The sword stuck the giant arachnid like an insect on a schoolchild's board, and it screamed horribly at Tal as the weapon boiled its insides to steam.

Gideon cannoned his fist into the spider in front of him. Where before his strike would have scuffed chitin and chipped mandibles, now the power of the sword flowed through him. The beast's face shattered into shards of carapace, and it reeled backward with a keening wail. Gideon struck again and again, ichor spattering his face as he advanced and beat the monster to a drooling husk with nothing more than his hands.

The spiders hesitated. Even their singular minds struggled to process the sight of it. Humans could not *do that*, not to them.

Again, not knowing what would happen but expecting it anyway, Gideon held out his sword-hand. With a hum and the sound of steel scraping against stone, Tal jerked out of the wall and the spider it impaled, soared through the air and slapped into Gideon's waiting palm.

The only sound in the battlefield was the giant corpse of the spider sliding off of the building and squishing as it struck the ground.

ABRAM SWORE, viciously, slowly. He had thought two hundred cultists and a century of spiders to be overkill on an ungodly scale, but the rate that warrior was chewing through them was *unthinkable*.

"Ursus!" the Jahennan shrieked. "Now, you stupid whoreson!"

The Carcarathine champion still did not move, watching intently. The spiders made another charge, and the golden-haired warrior met them with that infernal blade of his. Every time Abram laid eyes on the thing, it drowned out his thoughts and filled it with the sound of an enormous bell being rung, vibrating in his mind to the point of insanity. By the Thirsting Throne, the blade attacked him in his *mind* just for the sin of looking on it.

Severed limbs clattered across the stones like loose bamboo stalks, and a crushed thorax smashed down next to him, eliciting another curse from the inquisitor and forcing him back a few steps.

He lifted his voice again, and this time, terror made him hold nothing back. "Are you a coward, Tor Kayn? Is that it? Do you fear to face him?"

"LET ME KILL HIM," Tora hissed. "He insults you."

Ursus grunted dismissively and shook his head, though he marked the note of fear in her voice. He focused on the ragged warrior who slaughtered Mammon's servants with peerless ease. He fought like a young god, every defense an attack, every attack generating two or three more, never moving backward, always forward.

There was a sacred terror taking hold of the Venans. Ursus could feel it, like the charged air before a lightning strike. Their gods were dying by the brood before their very eyes, hacked apart by a magic sword or smashed to death with inhuman force. The avatar of Judgment walked among their false gods, and they found themselves reaped like corn before the sickle.

It was time to end this, if they were to salvage anything from this raid.

As he lifted his black blade to kill another hero, Ursus felt something like a dim shade of regret. He liked this one.

SKALD NOTICED that the creature Ursus did not have a chance to take so much as a step. As if he could sense the purpose welling up inside the Carcarathine warlord, Gideon ripped his blade out of a dying spider to point it directly at him.

His voice, punctuated only by heaving breaths, rang out across Hammarfall, clear and strong. "You!"

The Slaughterlord hesitated.

Gideon reversed his grip and without taking his eyes off of Ursus, slammed the shining blade down through the chitin of the monster beneath him, eliciting a death scream and a stream of ichor. Unblinking even as the creature's blood spattered his face, Gideon twisted, jerked the blade free and stalked forward.

Toward Ursus.

THE FIRST CLUE Anya had that something was amiss was when the Brides of Ursus stepped away from their master. Hurriedly, almost frantically, the group of savage women backpedaled away from the Slaughterlord, a couple of them tripping on the loose stones.

If they're *afraid...*

That was when Anya heard the second clue.

A low rumble emitted from the titan's chest, like an eruption building power. Ursus's frame began to shake, his shoulders rocking back.

Anya and the Wolves followed the Brides' example and backed away as Ursus began to laugh.

THE FEW SURVIVORS of the Venan force fled from Gideon as he stalked forward. Before him, the titan stepped from the wall of Hammarfall. The ground split at the impact and a cloud of dust exploded around the champion.

A Wolf named Torvald disengaged from the melee at the inner wall and lunged toward him, bellowing a war cry as he lifted his axe.

The warlord backhanded him with the flat of his gargantuan sword. Torvald's neck crunched like chicken bones, and his body flew like a marionette with its strings cut. It smashed into the wall of Hammarfall twenty feet up and flopped boneless to the ground.

More Wolves, undeterred by their comrade's fate, perhaps inspired by it, began to surround the unnatural warrior in their lair.

Gideon began to run.

"No!" Heimdall shouted. "Stand back! Let the boy take him!"

The Wolflord had never seen a man kill like Ursus. Torvald had died with no more effort than an old woman wiping a plate. Far too many of the pack would die to bring the enemy's champion down, and there was still a battle to wage.

He had also never seen a man kill like Gideon.

Next to him, Skald whispered, "By the Almighty, he runs to him."

Skald spoke true; Gideon streaked down the thoroughfare toward Ursus, blade almost molten in his grip. No declaration of his name, no recitation for the sagas, no curses called out on his enemy. Gideon hurtled toward his enemy like a thunderbolt riding wings of flame.

Ursus himself strode forward to meet him, gaze gleaming hellishly under his horned helm. He lifted his monstrous black sword over his head as Gideon closed to scant yards of him, still running.

The blow would not only kill Gideon, but carve a ravine into the foundation of Hammarfall.

Gideon reached the Carcarathine monster. A blackened blur of unholy steel rushed down toward him with a howl, and Gideon's newly-forged sword lifted to meet it. The jarl winced at the sight to come.

An instant later, Heimdall's mouth dropped open.

Ursus's massive goreblade did not kill Gideon. It did not split his skull, crack his bone cage and spill his guts onto the ground. It did not carve a ravine into the foundation of Hammarfall.

When that black blade hit the fiery sword, Gideon grunted.

That was all.

He stood firm under Ursus's shuddering sword, legs braced wide, veins popping out in his neck as he pushed back against the Slaughterlord's weapon. Somehow, the black sword remained suspended above his head, straining to reach out and kill him, but just held back by the clean silver edge of Gideon's sword.

Still exerting tremendous force to bring his blade down, yet clearly heard by every man present, Ursus muttered. "Huh."

ONLY ONE MAN dared to break the sanctity of the silence that followed.

"*Hyva!*" Skald screamed.

The noise that followed was cacophony. The Wolves and serfs pumped their weapons in the air and roared in release, the relief of Gideon's survival pumping the shock of adrenaline into their systems. Anya joined them, shouting savagely into the sky.

Beside her, her father, Jarl Fangthane, gripped her wrist and raised it up, howling like a young wolf. She looked into his eyes, and saw that it was gone. The weight, the hopelessness, the despair, the guilt: all of it.

Gideon Doomhold, the Boarcrusher, the apprentice of Death, banished it all when he met the blade of the Slaughterlord and held him fast.

ABRAM BLINKED and shook his head to clear it. He blinked again.

That warrior should have exploded like an overripe tomato under Ursus's strength. Abram had seen minotaurs torn in half, golems of stone and metal split open, armor shredded like fine silk. Even if the warrior's magic sword somehow held true against Ursus's overhand strike, the man's arms should have splintered like dry kindling from the sheer force alone.

Instead, somehow, that unreal soldier bent under Ursus's might, but did not break. The fortress exploded in the Wolves' celebration, and Abram became very, very aware that he was very, very alone in the rear of the enemy's lair.

THE SOUNDS of celebration did not seem to faze Ursus. In the seconds they remained locked, Gideon felt the titan shift his angle of force three times, testing Gideon's unexpected strength. Gideon gritted his teeth, feeling Tal pour power into his arms, his back, his legs, trying to resist the awesome power of the titan. Despite the power of the fiery blade, his arms began to quiver ever so slightly.

Ursus cocked his head and regarded the blade that held his at bay for a moment, then shifted his eyes back to Gideon. When he spoke, the Carcarathine's voice bordered on tectonic. "You are...god-warrior?"

Gideon glared at him through sweat-drenched hair and poured strength he did not have into pushing back. "Sure."

Ursus's shoulders bunched slowly towards him, and Gideon blew out his breath slowly as the ungodly pressure actually *increased*, strain crossing his face as the edge of Tal began to creep back toward his face.

His tone conversational despite the overwhelming force he exerted, Ursus said, "Gods fail."

The fiery blade inched back toward Gideon's face, and he grimaced at the knives of lactic acid biting into his muscles. His strength was giving out. He could not hold this.

Ursus's voice was bereft of strain, giving no indication he was overpowering a superhuman sword as he pressed his goreblade inexorably toward Gideon's skull. "Soon now."

Gideon narrowed his eyes.

In a flash, he stepped to the side. Ursus over-balanced at the sudden loss of resistance and stumbled a step forward. With a roar, Gideon thundered a right hook into Ursus's jaw.

It was like punching granite, but it snapped the titan's head to the side. The Slaughterlord wrenched his head back around after the blow, too seasoned a killer to leave his throat exposed for long.

His hellish gaze locked with Gideon's blazing green eyes.

"How's that for weakness?" Gideon snarled.

For a half-second, Ursus did not move. He simply looked at him, the greasy hair hanging on his back from under his helm waving slightly in the chill breeze. Blood trickled from his cut lip, but he made no effort to wipe it away.

At last, he spoke. One word only.

"Good."

Before the young man could blink, he backhanded Gideon through a house ten yards away.

SEVERAL EXCLAMATIONS SOUNDED across the wall as the Carcarathine mountain slapped the Wolves' champion through the battlefield to crash into a distant hovel. Wolves winced and some involuntary curses slipped unwary lips. From atop the wall, an archer woman's sharp cry, quickly stifled, knifed through the cold air.

Abram raised his eyebrows. The warrior was good, that was for sure. If his reflexes had been any slower, if he had not managed to jerk back and take the blow on his shoulder, the blonde hero would have had his rib-cage crushed like rotten kindling.

As it was, the warrior cartwheeled through the air, flopping end over end like a rag doll and smashing into a cheap house. Pottery shattered within, dust billowed out of the doorway and a chicken actually sailed out with a comical *ba-GAWK*.

Abram stepped over to the titan, and Ursus spared the inquisitor a glance. Abram inclined himself toward Carcharoth's thug in a sarcastic bow. "See what happens when you apply yourself?"

The Tor Kayn's crimson eyes ignited with hate, but he did not punish Abram for his disrespect. Carcharoth suffered no infighting in his ranks.

Abram waved a hand insouciantly about the fortress. "Now let's finish this and bring the master his prize."

Pottery slid across pottery and shattered on stone. Abram turned at the sound, and before his dumbfounded eyes, the warrior appeared in the doorway of the shattered home.

Pain creased his face and he rotated his shoulder to work the kinks out, but the battered champion's eyes still seethed with the same fire blazing from his blade. He spat a wad of chalky phlegm on the ground and shouted, "Was that it? You looked bigger up on the wall."

Dimly, Abram realized he gaped. He had seen death wishes in his time; for pity's sake, most of his peers ached to sacrifice their bodies and souls on the altar of a mad god's whims.

But by the Three, this madman had taken a hit from Ursus the Slaughterlord, survived it and was now *taunting* him. There was no precedent for this behavior. It did not *happen*.

Ursus did not break his crimson gaze from the warrior as he rumbled, "He is mine."

Abram blinked away his disbelief and snapped, "As you will. Send your Brides to the hall so we can finish this. The World Eater awaits us, and we cannot afford further delays."

Ursus grunted in agreement and raised a mammoth arm. He

splayed his fingers wide, then clenched them in a fist and punched toward the entrance of the Doom.

Without a sound, all seven of his surviving Brides dropped from the wall and padded toward their prey, as their master bore down on his.

After a second's consideration, Abram called out, "And the gate, Ursus!"

GIDEON'S CHEST burned with every breath, and he did not want to think about whatever was grinding in his torso, but he still stood upright and still held a sword. God could handle the rest.

And He was going to have to, because Gideon was starting to get a healthy respect for the other warrior.

As the feral warrior-women scattered in the city, the colossus walked the few yards to the gate of the city. A massive beam of hardwood cut from the Ironback Mountains hung suspended across the gate in mighty wrought settings, winched into place by great chains. A ram would take many minutes to break that barrier.

No ram would survive the torrent of boiling oil, arrows and spear shafts from the towers on either side of the gate. It was a killbox, a trap set by Wolves to slaughter would-be gatebreakers.

Unfortunately, those defenses only worked against enemies outside the gate.

With a roar, Ursus chopped his sword deep into the beam, cleaving it halfway with a single blow. The gate bent outward from the blow and dust exploded from the seams. Wolves in the towers screamed for the oil and spear-throwers to be turned, but there was no way to position them in time.

Ignoring the panic above, Ursus pulled his blade free of the tortured wood with a twisting jerk and put his back into a second blow. The beam shattered and the iron settings snapped off of their mounts. The titan turned back to face Gideon as the gate groaned open behind him, and the army of starved demon-worshippers, denied the walls for so long, rushed it.

Wolves and serfs rushed down stairs to plug the gap, plunging into the demented cultists with swords and curses, and Gideon could hear Heimdall bellowing orders among them.

Ursus ignored them. He had bloodshot eyes only for Gideon.

Gideon could feel the earth tremble beneath him as Ursus walked toward him, that dark iron sword gripped in one huge hand. The man was a tower of scarred hide, muscle and bone, almost created for ending life in close combat. It was not even accurate to call him a killer. The term implied that Ursus took the time to kill men one at a time, rather than just massacring them en masse.

Shaking off the spiderweb of agony gripping his torso, Gideon walked to meet him.

Months of dueling Ashkelon had taught Gideon how to assess reach and distance. The awareness of balance and position rose to the forefront of Gideon's instincts, an unconscious constant appraisal of combat which updated on a second-by-second basis in Gideon's mind.

Which is why he grimaced as soon as he knew he had reached Ursus's striking range. He was still over a yard from his.

The titan moved from a plodding tread to raging bull in the blink of an eye. Gideon threw himself to one side as Ursus lunged with shocking speed for his size, his sword lashing out to crush Gideon. Gideon felt his bones shake as he blocked the thunderous impact, the power in Tal not only lending him strength but keeping his skeleton knit together under the awesome force smashing into him.

No words passed between the two fighters. Ursus slang his sword around in a blurred crosswise cut that would have torn a tree in half. Again, Gideon blocked the blow, the impact ringing like a blacksmith's anvil, grimacing at the savage force rattling his teeth.

I cannot keep doing this.

The hit knocked him reeling. Gideon hurled his sword skyward just in time to parry Ursus's goreblade and drive it into the earth.

Attack him. Do something!

He ducked another earth-shattering backhand and lashed out with his sword, scoring a charred line across Ursus's shoulder.

The giant did not even wince. Again, he brought his blackened sword crashing down against Gideon's smoldering blade, spraying sparks in the young man's face.

Gideon parried the hit, deflecting the dark goreblade into the earth, and powered his fist into the side of Ursus's skull.

It did nothing. The giant did not even blink in his horned helm.

Instead, he reared up like a volcano rising from the sea, hurling Gideon yards away with a sweep of his arm. Gideon hit the ground and rolled, finding his feet in time to see the gargantuan warrior striding towards him, relentless, fixated.

Gideon began to back away.

WHILE GIDEON DUELED the warlord of Hell's forces, Ashkelon watched the killers approach.

Seven savage women with tattoos writhing across their tortured flesh and barbarous haircuts prowled towards the entrance to the aptly-named Doom. They did not see into the deep shadows on their right where Ashkelon stood, arms folded across darkmail, a shadow lost within shadows.

Ashkelon did not move to intercept the murderesses. Again, he did see them. He just did not care. He was more interested in his student's bout with the enemy champion.

Next to him, the girl Saima stirred.

"Will you not help them?"

She meant the crowds of peasants cowering in the hall, filling it with the repulsive stink of their fear.

Ashkelon answered without breaking his gaze from Gideon. "They are not my concern."

The girl remained quiet for a moment, which Ashkelon vastly preferred. Then, inevitably, she spoke again.

"Am I your concern?"

Ashkelon's brow furrowed slightly. It was a surprisingly difficult question to answer.

"I...suppose," he allowed, after a moment.

She nodded once, as if that confirmed something for her. Before Ashkelon could even think to stop her, the girl scooted out of the protective shadow Ashkelon had conjured and ran toward the Brides.

SKYLAR HELD her knives low as she led her sisters toward the crying weaklings. Her blades were fangs of jagged obsidian, a material she found pleasing to drag through the hot flesh of her victims. The thought of heart's blood spraying into her mouth dizzied her for a moment, and so she almost ran into the little girl who appeared from nowhere and stopped in front of her.

Next to her, Tora edged forward, hissing, "Young blood. Fresh blood."

Skylar slammed the presumptuous whore back with a brutal forearm strike to the woman's chest. "First blood is mine, Tora! I am the alpha!" she growled.

Behind her, one of her jealous rivals, she could not say who, muttered, "If you have to say it...."

Skylar twisted to face them, spit flying as she snarled, "I am the favorite, then! I have been with him the longest. I have survived the most beddings. I am First!"

They glowered at her, but did not try to move past her again. Satisfied, Skylar turned back to the little girl, already salivating at the thought of young blood wetting her lips.

She then made the worst mistake she could make.

With a savage backhand, Skylar slapped the little girl to the ground. The child fell with a pitiful squeak, and she began to wail from the shock and pain.

Skylar grinned and lifted her knife. Fear added so much to the taste of blood.

Crunch.

Crunch.

Crunch.

Skylar's brow furrowed at the sounds of a measured stride crushing loose gravel. She turned toward the oncoming sounds, and bared her teeth at the sight of a man clad in black mail stalking toward her.

Lank white hair fluttered in the breeze as his cold gaze fell upon her. His eyes blazed like icy suns, and wisps of ethereal energy bled from the edges, dissolving with faint hisses into the air. His fists were clenched in what Skylar knew to be overwhelming rage.

Sorcerer.

She saw him in this shape for only an instant.

The man blitzed forward, too fast to be seen. He struck like a raptor seizing a rabbit, smashing Skylar back with a kick and catching hold of the little girl in his arms. His form *split*, one a winged creature bearing the girl away to the safety of the doorway, the other a nightmare standing between the Brides and their prey.

ASHKELON SET Saima down and examined her face.

"Thank you," the little girl sniffled, her voice shuddering.

"Be still," he commanded, prodding at the delicate bones of her face.

At last, he sat back on his haunches and said, "Your face will bruise , but nothing is broken."

"You," he barked at the closest woman. It so happened to be the woman he had saved previously, Brida. "Apply cold compresses to her face and hold back the swelling. Make her comfortable until I return."

Brida nodded sharply and took the girl up in her arms. "It will be done, Deathbringer. Come along, child."

Ashkelon let out his breath and snapped back to the form he left in the courtyard.

Never, not in the all the ages of his existence, had Ashkelon felt the towering rage that exploded through his body when the barbarous woman had struck Saima. His words hissed between his teeth as he pointed at the offender.

"That...was a mistake."

In an instant, he was on her. Her knives clattered to the stones of the courtyard, and she scrabbled at the gauntlet squeezing her throat in a vise. It did her no good.

Ashkelon backhanded her. It was the exact technique she had used to hit Saima. The strike likely broke several bones in the side of her face, and she sagged in his grip.

Ashkelon did not release her.

Instead, he slapped her again. And again. Repeated open-hand strikes blurred with unnatural speed, snapping the woman's head back and forth, too fast for her companions to intervene.

Only when her breath stopped wheezing through her shattered mouth did Ashkelon release her. Her body tumbled to the courtyard's floor, and he turned to see the remaining Brides staring at him with horror.

In perfect hypocrisy, one of them stabbed a finger at him and accused, "What kind of man are you?"

Ashkelon reached behind his back and drew Acherlith, filling the courtyard with unearthly howls. Against the backdrop of ethereal screaming, with dark wings sprouting from his shoulders and blood dripping from his gauntlets, he hissed, "I'm an *angel*."

OF THEM ALL, Skald had seen the most winters. His beard had silvered in wars most of the Wolves living considered legends. He had fought demons, champions and the ancient drakes when they stirred from their subterranean lairs. His mighty warhammer had crushed the skulls of cyclopean giants and conjured golems.

Never had he seen a duel like that of Gideon and the Slaughterlord.

The hellish warlord bled from a dozen wounds and showed no sign of slowing. Ursus laid earth-shattering blows with his dark greatsword down onto Gideon with metronomic regularity, striking sheets of sparks from the young man's shining blade. His size did not slow him, not like the giants who hammered the walls with dull roars. The champion never stopped, every movement hurling another skull-jarring impact into Gideon. Every time Gideon fell back or dodged, the monster followed a second behind. Every time Gideon passed within reach of that dread blade, Ursus hit him again.

Skald had no idea how the young man even still lived.

Somehow, no matter how many hammer blows the titan rained upon him, Gideon had an answer. Desperate deflections saw the black goreblade shear through stone houses instead of Gideon's flesh and bone. Strikes that could cleave hundred-year-old hardwoods met last-second blocks that blazed like newborn stars.

Gideon was on the back foot, though. No matter where he retreated, the Carcarathine pursued, the dark sword never ceasing its assault. They smashed through buildings in their combat, Ursus pulverizing the edifices in explosions of rock and timber while Gideon staggered back, desperate to keep his footing among the debris fouling his steps.

Anya loosed arrows only rarely now, unable to look away as Gideon took crushing hits from the Carcarathine chieftain straight onto his fiery sword, which only flashed in brighter wrath with every blow.

Skald laid a worn hand on Anya's shoulder, which she immediately pressed to her cheek like a lifeline. He squeezed. "Do not vorry so, small-fang," he assured her. "I have seen battles like this a hundred times. Boy vil be fine."

She glanced at him. "Really?" she asked.

Skald looked back to the battle, where Ursus caught Gideon with a full cross-body blow when the boy did not have his feet planted to receive it. Gideon disappeared as if snatched by banshees, smashing through a nearby house and digging a furrow in Agatha's freshly-tilled garden plot.

Skald did not quite manage to keep the wince from his face as he answered, "Of course really, little vone. A hundred times. I svear it."

THE LAST OF Ursus's Brides slipped from Ashkelon's black gauntlets and fell to the stones at his boots, eyes wide and filled with the blood of her ruptured veins. Even as he had strangled her, he had poured a thousand lives' worth of terror into her mind.

Idly, he wondered which fear had killed her first.

With a sigh, Ashkelon dusted his gauntlets and cast his gaze about him. The bodies of the chieftain's chosen littered the courtyard, sprawled atop Gideon's own tally of slaughter. And of course, behind him, the sniveling wretches who had now been saved twice through no merit of their own.

No doubt they would try to thank him.

These fools condemned me for the color of my armor. Now, after killing seven women in a fit of temper, I am their savior.

I hate this species.

Pressing his lips into a thin line, he turned his attention to the wider battle. So far, the demon-worshippers appeared to be contained on the wall and by the gate, save for the champion his student dueled.

Ashkelon glanced about as he murmured, "Where *is* my student?"

His answer came swiftly as Gideon hurtled from a nearby street and crashed into a stone structure, the broken plates of his armor scraping sparks on the stone beneath him.

Ashkelon looked down at him, one eyebrow rising.

"How are things?" he asked.

The boy gasped for breath, blood flecking his lips. Panic threatened to flood his eyes as he groped about him, struggling to simply stand to his feet. His remarkable sword still burned in his grip, but the light seemed to gutter within the blade, like a candle in a strong breeze.

Ashkelon's eyes flashed for an instant, and Gideon's flesh faded to transparency before his gaze. Within the throbbing mass of organs laid bare to his sight, blood dripped from numerous hemorrhages, pooling in the recesses of his body. Black liquid seeped into the boy's lungs, one of which seemed dangerously close to collapse. Over two dozen hairline fractures spiraled through his skeleton, mostly in his arms, shoulders and rib cage.

Ashkelon's lips set into a thin line at the inescapable conclusion.

Supernatural sword or not, Ursus was killing him.

"Get up," he rasped.

Gideon's wild eyes roved for a moment before they focused on him.

"I said, *get up.*"

Obeying instinctively, Gideon lurched to his feet, but immediately fell to one knee. His hand quested for something to stay him, finally gripping a support beam and steadying his swaying. His breath sawed in and out of his lungs as he gasped, "I can't. He's too strong."

Ashkelon glared at him with contempt. "And so you think yourself excused?"

Gideon squinted at him. "What?"

With a growl, Ashkelon reached down, gripped Gideon under the arm and slammed him against the wall. His other hand wrenched Gideon's wrist, bringing his dying sword before his eyes.

"Look."

Gideon's head lolled about and his eyes rolled back as he struggled to obey. Ashkelon let a touch of power into his words as he barked, "I said, *look!*"

This time, Gideon focused. His jade green eyes locked onto the supernatural blade at Ashkelon's command.

"Do you really think you forged that sword?" the sorcerer hissed.

Gideon stammered, "I...I don't—"

Ashkelon pushed the blade away and gripped Gideon's jaw in his chainmail gauntlet. "Be silent; this babbling is pathetic. I will tell you the answer. It is 'no'. None of the power in that blade proceeds from you."

Gideon's eyes flicked from the sword to Ashkelon. The sorcerer shook his head sharply, irritated that he even had to explain. "No, I had nothing to do with it, either. No sword forged by my hand would bleed light."

Masonry shattered nearby, and the titan Gideon dueled rounded the corner. His massive shoulder scraped against the house, breaking the stone facing to rubble. His ferocious gaze found Gideon and he stomped forward, his greatsword rising.

Ashkelon's sigh was almost a growl. The sorcerer turned and

glared impatiently at Carcaroth's champion. "We're busy," he snarled, and thrust a hand toward the giant warrior.

A wave of force ripped Ursus off of his feet and threw him back down the street from where he emerged. A house crumpled in an explosion of stone as the creature's enormous body pulverized it on impact.

Another sigh, and Ashkelon turned back to Gideon as if a colossal lord of murder had not been there seconds ago. "There. Do you see?"

Gideon laughed helplessly. "Sure. Absolutely, master. I will keep that in mind."

Ashkelon slapped him.

Strangely enough, Gideon could not remember being slapped by Ashkelon. Stabbed, yes. Burned, lanced, drained, and drowned, yes. Of all the things inflicted upon him by Ashkelon's dark hand, he had never been slapped.

His face burned from the impact of Ashkelon's gauntlet, and he sat down sharply in surprise.

Ashkelon bent closer to him, his voice lowered to a hiss. "I will flense you like a goat set upon by river predators if you ever disrespect me again. Am I understood?"

Gideon blinked away the sting of the slap. He said, "Yes, master."

"Good. Get up."

Gideon obeyed. He rotated his shoulder, wincing at the pain that produced, and said, "What am I doing wrong?"

Ashkelon stepped back and locked Gideon's gaze with his own. "You credit me with power while ignoring your own."

Gideon furrowed his brow. It was hard to think, which was probably due to the numerous buildings he had been blasted through. "I don't understand," he said at last.

The sorcerer chuckled darkly and he lifted his gaze toward the sky. "The irony of this situation does not escape me, You can be sure."

He looked back at Gideon, a sardonic tilt to his head. "God, student. Is the source of your strength," he waved his hand in a little circle, "...God?"

Gideon put his hands on his hips and breathed quietly, thinking. After a few seconds, he answered, "Yes."

Ashkelon's gaze became a little more mocking. "Are you sure?"

Gideon hesitated again. "Yes."

Ashkelon spread his hands. "Then why are you losing?"

Gideon did not receive a chance to respond. Ashkelon went on, his words cold and biting. "Is He not all-powerful? Is He not named the Almighty? How then does a mere man of flesh and blood, giant or no, still stand against a warrior empowered by God?"

Gideon did not answer. His eyes, steady now, did not so much as twitch from Ashkelon's own.

The sound of boots crushing stone echoed up the alley. The Slaughterlord would be upon them in moments, but neither man cared.

Ashkelon gestured toward Gideon's sword, glowing faintly in his hand. "If your God truly gave you the power in that blade, then you would not simply hold this mortal creature at bay. You would not merely *survive*. You would overcome. You would crush fearsome champions like beetles beneath your boot."

He stabbed a finger at Gideon's face. "It is what I hate about you and all your self-righteous kind. You are *stupid*. You claim that over-whelming power lies within reach of your fingertips, and yet you whine and wheeze about how life presents you with such trials. You gasp and pray for strength while a sword that breathes fire dangles in your grip, *gifted* to you by your omnipotent Creator. You sicken me with such purposeful weakness."

Ashkelon's eyes ignited with sapphire flame and shadows clawed up his face to form his death mask. "The knowledge I possess, I ripped from the minds of dying mages over *centuries*. Acherlith was my prize for murdering the Guardian City. In my wake, boy, are the charnel houses I made of the bastions of men and angels as I plundered their secrets. Entire religions had the time to form in the wake of my quest for the power you dismiss so lightly. Everything you had given to you, I tore from the unwilling powerful."

Ashkelon reached for Acherlith on his back as he turned toward the alley where he had cast Ursus. "No god cared enough to give me anything, not to survive, and certainly not to conquer. Think on that, as the Darkness exerts itself to save you once more, because the weapon you were given by an almighty deity is somehow not enough. When I return, perhaps you can explain to me just why it is that you call yourselves *believers.*"

A hand gripped his wrist, preventing him from drawing his accursed sword, and Ashkelon twisted, ready to deliver a viperous rebuke.

His student's voice was quiet. "You're right."

Ashkelon stilled, words dying on his lips.

Gideon refused to meet Ashkelon's gaze. "I am failing, and it is because my faith is weak. I don't know what I have been given, and so it's hard to be grateful. I've never done anything like all this," he gestured to the battle around them, "and for some reason I think that God did not give me enough."

He looked into Ashkelon's eyes. "That's why I'm stupid, isn't it? I have more monsters to kill than this one, and I fail to believe at the first."

Ashkelon crossed his arms. His voice did not accuse, but stated as fact. "And how real could God be if His own sons do not trust Him?"

Gideon nodded and hefted his sword. In the distance, rock crumbled and shattered as a monstrous devil ripped itself from ruins to come again.

"Again?" Ashkelon asked.

Gideon nodded and wiped blood from his mouth with his forearm. "Again."

Without a backward glance, Gideon marched down the alley, sword blazing in his grip.

Ashkelon looked after his apprentice, lost in thought. Something scratched on the stones behind him, and the girl-child came to stand beside him, taking hold of his chainmail cloak.

Saima looked up at the brooding sorcerer. "Will he win?"

Ashkelon looked down at her, specifically at the hand holding his cloak, and very pointedly stepped away from the child, pulling the garment from her grasp.

The situation rectified, he glanced toward the alley down which Gideon had disappeared.

At last, he answered, "I am not sure. This is my first time, as well."

YOU SICKEN ME.

Ashkelon's hateful words sizzled in Gideon's mind and settled into an bitter ache in his heart.

The truth of them burned.

Why are you called believers?

Before him, the Slaughterlord lifted himself from the ruin of a house and stalked toward him. Gideon could hear vases and furniture rattle in the homes around them at his thunderous tread.

Is He not called the Almighty?

Twin coals smoldered in the recesses of Ursus's horned helm. His greatsword, black with the blood of thousands, lifted for another bone-cracking blow. The first of many the titan would unleash on him.

You would overcome.

Gideon leapt off the ground, kicked off of a stone planter, and launched himself toward the giant, his weapon wound up behind him. His blazing sword swept toward Ursus's chest without finesse or subtlety in a downward strike. The champion swung at the same time, his great cleaver of a weapon interposing between himself and the oncoming blow.

IT TOOK a second for Ursus to realize what happened next.

The impact of their swords cracked and rang with the cataclysmic force of lightning striking a church bell. A violent explosion of light detonated in the alleyway, drawing fleeing shadows along the homes of the Wolves. The smell of ozone, iron and incense filled his nostrils.

Ursus had time to notice all of this before he finally stopped flying through the air and cratered the cobblestone street with his back, cracks spiderwebbing beneath him. Rock chips blasted away from his body as his weight pulverized the compacted stones.

He blinked for a few seconds, then craned his neck from where he lay to find his enemy.

The god-man stood *yards* away, chest heaving, eyes still burning. His sword gleamed in his hand, a veritable wildfire roiling beneath the skin of the blade.

He slowly rolled to his feet, planting his sword in the ground for support. His grip slipped and he almost fell again.

This fact alone stirred the embers of worry in Ursus's heart. He could not remember the last time he had been unsteady. He could not remember the last time a man had leveled him with a single blow. He could not remember when *anything* had.

He stood to his feet and hefted his greatsword before him. His uneasiness grew as he beheld the single notch in the blackened blade.

That had never happened before.

Ursus allowed his gaze to fall back to the god-man. "Different," he rumbled, rolling his shoulders.

The sword in the god-man's hand blazed brighter, hurting Ursus's eyes when he looked upon it, and the only man ever to strike Ursus from his feet strode forward, saying, "Yes. It is."

The warrior picked up speed, the light from his sword intensifying to a soul-scorching glare. Ursus lifted his notched blade to guard against the blow to come, and just before the god-man hit him again, he winced.

"SOMETHING IS DIFFERENT," Skald murmured to Anya. His head twitched back and forth, like a bird tracking an insect, his eye narrowed and roving.

Around them on the wall and beneath them at the gate, Wolves and serfs beat back the tide of diseased and demonic. Anya sighted down a fresh shaft and loosed into a spider that had managed to gain the wall. The shaft sank to the fletching in a cluster of the creature's eyes, and it toppled, shrieking, to the ground within the walls, where a crowd of serfs with spears and timber axes hacked it to death.

As she reached for another shaft, her eyes flicked back to the last place she had seen Gideon disappear. "What do you mean?" she asked.

Skald moved to a ladder nearby and kicked a Venan warrior in the chest. The impact of his boot cracked the skeletal famine-warrior's ribs and sent him screaming to die in the mob of his brethren thirty feet below. Skald barely noticed, too caught up in his observance.

"Boy is not breaking our houses any more."

That was true. The sounds of shattered stone and shrieking iron had risen above the grunts and shouts of the battle, and the clouds of powdery dust had yet to settle as the duel tracked through Hammarfall.

Anya shot another Mammonite as he scrabbled to clear the secondary wall. The man arched his back in agony, then pitched back to the earth where opportunistic carrion-eaters, unable to attain the wall themselves, set onto him.

Her next arrow was a mercy.

"Grandfather?"

At her tone, Skald glanced sharply at her. "Yes, small-fang?"

She bit her lip as she tracked another Venan with her bow. Skald noted that she took far too long to make the shot, and her target disappeared in a melee. She lowered her bow with a muttered oath and swiped at her hair to clear it from her eyes, blinking quickly.

"Boy is fine, little she-volf," he said, grunting as he gripped a cannibal from behind by the head and pelvis, and hurled him bodily from the wall. The Venan's scream trailed off as he fell, then cut off abruptly.

Anya's hair fell back into her eye, and she blew at it out of the corner of her mouth. "He's going to get killed."

"He has died before. You vorry too much for wrong person," Skald grunted, smashing the top of a siege ladder with his hammer into a cloud of kindling. A hand black with infection clawed at the stone for purchase, and Skald smashed the appendage with the head of his hammer.

Anya snapped her bow up and skewered a Venan archer before she could loose a filth-smeared shaft at Skald. The woman clutched at the arrow protruding from her chest and pitched backward off the wall.

Skald grinned and wiped his forehead clear of sweat and blood with his arm. "See? And old Skald think small-fang no longer cares."

She mock-glared at him. "Next time, I will let her shoot you, and maybe the lectures will stop."

An explosion of light erupted from the streets of Hammarfall, tinting the dark houses golden for an instant. The smell of burnt metal washed over them, and the ringing echo of some ferocious impact vibrated through the cold air. For a breath, the fighting paused, men hesitating at this new development.

Skald did not even turn to look as he gestured toward the sound. "See? The boy is fine. I tell you this, but you don't listen."

A few seconds later, a second impact sounded, and something huge careened into view on the main roadway, throwing up a cloud of pulverized stone and shrapnel as it plowed into the street and rolled to a stop.

It was the demon champion, Ursus. Audible moans of disbelief rose from the Venan forces at the sight of their leader, bleeding, groggy, scraping at the dirt with his forearms as he struggled to rise.

Excitement flushed hot through Anya and pinked her cheeks as Gideon stepped into view, and a great roar swelled from the throats of the defenders of Hammarfall at the sight of him. His armor was dirty and torn, blood trickled from his lip, but his jade eyes glinted like fiery emeralds in the light of his sword.

He looked like every hero Anya had imagined from the stories, and she involuntarily tucked her hair behind her ears and adjusted her armor, hating herself the whole time.

It's happened. I'm one of those brainless swooning women.

Gideon swiped at his bleeding lip with a broken vambrace and marched toward Ursus, his jaw clenched, his blade held ready behind him.

Anya shook her head. *No. Those women never had a man like this.*

Watching her, Skald chuckled helplessly at her for an instant, then leaned over the wall and roared, "Boy, if your saga gets any longer, Skald vil charge you double!"

ABRAM HAD NEVER SEEN Ursus reel—from *anything.*

Throne's sake, he had seen a bloatguard bury an axe in the warlord's side, and Ursus had shrugged it off like a backslap between comrades.

Now, however, the goliath struggled to rise. Ursus planted his goreblade in the earth to steady himself, like an old man leaning on a cane. He managed to stand, but staggered back a step, holding out an arm as if looking for balance. Blood trickled from a nostril, and the giant sniffed it back in.

Ursus shook his head to clear it, flinging blood and sweat in a salty rain from his steaming skin. His blood-red eyes focused once more on the warrior striding towards him, burning blade in hand. Incredibly, a grin tracked its unfamiliar way across the giant's ravaged face, and a second wind expanded his lungs.

Ursus hefted his immense greatsword in one hand, clenched his other in a fist and roared. The sheer power of the sound shook the air and deafened Abram and everyone else even remotely close. Abram had heard dragons vent their rage with less volume than Ursus projected at the battered fighter advancing on him.

The madman was *enjoying* this fight.

SKALD WATCHED as Gideon turned his shoulder into the wave of sound. He could see the boy's armor shivering from this distance as the sound shook his bones. He saw Gideon clench his teeth to keep them from rattling in his gums.

And he saw Gideon start to run.

The brazen blade lifted as Gideon took it in both hands, pulling it behind him as he charged toward the dark champion. Ursus charged at almost the same instant, still bellowing the depths of his rage, raising his black blade high to crush Gideon into the ground.

The earth churned beneath their feet as they rushed toward one another, hate twisting—

"—their faces into death smiles of bloodstained teeth and gore-flecked cheeks."

Skald realized he was speaking out loud and grinned at himself.

"Ach, he makes an old Volf feel young again. I need to write this down before I forget it."

GIDEON AND URSUS smashed into one another full tilt. This time, however, they did not lock blades.

Gideon caught the full force of Ursus's great sword and turned it aside to carve into the blasted earth. His sword whipped back to slice the giant's neck, but Ursus ducked and the burning blade seared nothing but air. Ursus's shoulder crushed into Gideon, but the warrior danced aside, turning it into the most glancing of blows even as he cut back, straight into the Slaughterlord's raised guard.

The blades leapt from each other and crashed together again, Gideon's darting like a tongue of fire against an unyielding pillar. The combatants did not step back from each other, even as sparks showered from their blades' contacts and sizzled on their skin. Every time Ursus bore down on Gideon, he escaped the strength of the blow. Every time Gideon thrust for Ursus's throat, heart, arteries, the Slaughterlord turned the weapon aside with his goreblade.

A god-man and a giant whipped around each other in a bladed whirlwind, smashing blow after blow into one another's defenses without thought for safety. Walls of wind blasted from the impacts as the enchanted blades fought one another in their masters' hands, the force of Light warring against the power of murder.

From the corner of his eye, in the flashes of sight between blows, Gideon saw Ashkelon watching, twin sapphires burning in a shadow as he regarded his student's stalemate.

His failure, he realized.

You would overcome.

A terrible rage exploded in Gideon's heart as Ursus swung his great sword again. Gideon screamed and powered his blade into it.

URSUS HAD BEEN Slaughterlord for decades. He had seen countless champions fall, either to his goreblade or those of his followers. He had seen swords break in their bearers' hands, had seen the instant of shock and the inability to process what had happened.

It had never happened to him.

Ursus's greatsword had been with him since he killed his father to take it. As the gigantic butcher lay on the earth, pouring his life's blood into the ever-hungry embrace of Mammon, Anak declared his son a lord of slaughter and placed Ursus's hand on the hilt of the goreblade. It was his sign that he should rule the Tor Kayn, and any other weak enough to be broken by its weight.

The sword had drunk the blood of thousands, its iron hardening beneath the countless curses of living within demon lands. It had never so much as chipped in all its centuries of constant use.

Gideon hit it so hard, the sword disintegrated in Ursus's hands.

Black shrapnel peppered Ursus's face and chest. Blood cascaded down his face and into his eyes from a hundred cuts. A five-foot-long section of blade spun off and chopped through the logs of a nearby longhouse.

Ursus did not freeze, as so many others had. His mind did not blank in shock and realization. Instead, at that instant, that eternity, he stared at the shattered hilt in his hand and knew defeat.

GIDEON DID NOT STOP, even when the giant did. He had been killed too many times believing he had gained the upper hand to ever hesitate again.

Even as Ursus's eyes flushed with tears for the first day in an age, Gideon rocketed his right fist into the giant's jaw. He knew immediately that it was the hardest punch he had ever thrown. The bones within his gauntlet cracked as they smashed into Ursus's skull, penetrating and lifting with all the force Gideon could tear from his body.

The Slaughterlord, wrong-footed from the destruction of his sword, twisted half around from the impact, his eyes dazing for a precious second.

Gideon twisted in a full circle and dragged the silver edge of Tal through Ursus's left hamstring. It was like sawing through a gnarled oak, such was the thickness of the monster's leg, but Gideon put his back behind the cut and *pulled*. The blade bit deep, severing taut bunches of muscle fibers and rasping against the titan's femur before exploding from his leg in a welter of black blood.

WHEN GIDEON TORE his sword from their champion, the Mammonites moaned as one. Weapons sagged in their grips, and their mouths hung open, not in fevered hunger, but disbelieving shock.

They forgot the Wolves they faced. In the two seconds before the Venans remembered themselves, the Wolves and their serfs massacred every invader on the walls and most of those who had made it through the gate. Axes chopped, swords cut and spears pierced through diseased flesh. It immediately shifted from battle to butchery as the Venans lost their will to fight and turned to stream into the forest.

The siege of Hammarfall was lost to them now.

URSUS GRUNTED in agony and staggered, his warrior instincts lunging him forward and twisting him back to face his opponent. His leg would clearly not support him, and the titan collapsed to one knee. The blood of the Slaughterlord smoked from Gideon's blade as he brought it to his cheek to deliver the final blow.

He caught sight of the broken look in Ursus's crimson eyes just before he drove the blade home.

ABRAM WATCHED in disbelief as Ursus fell, blood pouring from the rent carved in his massive thigh. The soldier did not stop; like silk swirling around a dancer, he twisted and cocked his glowing blade back by his ear for the killing thrust.

At the last second, though, he did not drive the lethal edge through the champion's throat. Instead, he tilted the blade away and rammed his elbow into Ursus's temple. The sword flashed with golden light, and a miniature thunder clap sounded in the courtyard.

Slowly, bonelessly, the Slaughterlord crumpled to his face in the cold earth of Hammarfall.

Shock gripped the inquisitor's heart and clenched it tight.

This was not supposed to happen.

Behind him, women and children emerged from their hiding place, stepping over dozens of ruined corpses of Venans and monsters. The legs of enormous spiders stabbed toward the sky, while others lay on their backs, legs curled around them in their dying throes.

Abram looked from site of ruin to site of ruin, his breath coming faster, his mind racing to fix this.

This is not possible.

The warrior with the divine sword looked down on Ursus's motionless bulk for a moment, then raised his eyes to meet Abram's.

Twin emeralds flashed with sudden recognition, and he stalked forward, blade shifting to his left hand, his right clenching to a fist.

No, no, no.

Abram drew his rapier and uncoiled his painlash. His hands trembled like a hunted rabbit, and he glanced around desperately for a way, any way, out.

His former prey blocked his egress, dozens of men and women emerging from the Doom to cut off his retreat. He stood alone amidst the bodies of his failed decapitation blow, in the back of a fortress his army now abandoned in torrents.

Just before the golden warrior ripped his weapons from his hands, cocked his right fist back and broke his nose with a sickeningly familiar snap, Abram conceded that he may have made a tactical error.

"YOU WOULD OVERCOME."

15

THREAT

As serfs moved about, clearing bodies and stripping weapons and armor in the age-old aftermath of battle, Skald squinted at Gideon with his one eye, rubbed his chin, and spat on the ground.

Then, pointedly, he peered at Gideon again, as if trying to work out a puzzle.

"You knocked him out?"

Gideon rubbed the bridge of his nose. "For the third time, yes."

Skald shifted his feet and spread his hands, as if trying to explain something to a child. "Vell, I am vaiting for reasonable answer. Vhat exactly is plan for vhen titan vakes up? He vas somevhat of a problem before, or is Skald's memory finally leaving him for greener pastures?"

Gideon said, "Ursus is not going anywhere. He's chained in the Doom."

Skald threw his hands up in the air. "Vith boat chains and anchors, yes! The largest and strongest ve can find. And Heimlich is still not sure if they vil hold that monster if he decides to get up!"

Gideon sighed. "If he's a problem, I'll put him down again."

Skald raised his bushy grey eyebrows. "Oh, as simple as that? Well, vhat do ve have to vorry about, then? You barely survived the last time, and wrecked half of our houses in process. Again, I ask you. Vhat is plan? Vhy did you not kill him in first place?"

Gideon hesitated, flashing back to the instant Ursus's blade broke in the giant's hand, and the look in the man's eye.

At last, he shrugged, trying to find words. "He was defeated already. When his sword snapped, he was done."

He patted his breastplate to make his point. "There was no need to kill a broken man."

Skald ran a hand through his thick mane and scratched the back of his neck. After a pause, he said, "You know the jarl vil have him killed, yes? Too many of the Vulfen died at this beast's sword for any other outcome. You have not saved him."

Gideon nodded. "I know. I have no issue with justice."

Skald pursed his lips and nodded. "So long as you know."

They stood together in silence for a while, watching the survivors of the attack work. Men worked in teams to load the diseased bodies of the Venans onto wagons, carting them off to burn piles set without the walls. A Wolf walked among the bodies yet to be collected, jabbing each in the neck with a sharp spear.

"Why stab the bodies if you're going to burn them?" Gideon asked, for lack of anything else to say.

Skald shrugged. "Safety. The fire exorcises any spirits vithin, purifies the disease in the flesh, kills the maggots. Yet burned bodies may rise again, if ve are not complete."

Gideon glanced at Skald, a question in his eyes. Skald returned his stare unflinchingly. "You have not fought the creatures of Sheol yet, just-Gideon. Ve have learned things, and ve are careful now."

Conceding the point, Gideon glanced over at the Doom, where Wolves stood guard over the entrance with weapons in their hands. "And what is it you will do with the captives?"

Skald heaved a great sigh. "Vell, it has been long time since ve have prisoner. Venans usually fight to death or flee, but these two are strange to us. I am sure Jarl Fangthane vil deal vith them in his visdom."

At the mention of the Wolf chieftain, Gideon searched the interior of Hammarfall and swiftly found the man, seated with Anya by the shattered gate. For once, it did not seem like they were in conflict.

"Anya?"

She looked up from her work to see her father approaching her. Black blood flecked his face and chest, and he had yet to wash it out of his beard. He stood a distance from her, not entering her space, holding his helm in his hands awkwardly.

As if seeking permission.

She smiled at him. "Is it this conversation already, Papa?"

The awkwardness dissipated like smoke, and Heimdall grinned sheepishly, coming to sit next to her. "I am that transparent, am I?"

Pinching her forefinger and thumb together, Anya said, "A little bit."

They sat together in silence, both sets of eyes locked onto the same young man as he spoke with Skald. Anya's eyes trailed across his armor, taking in the sheer ruin wrought on his armor. In places, cracks spider-webbed across the plates attached to his ringmail. In others, it crumpled inwards, giving way before terrifying blows. Some pieces of plate were missing entirely.

A sigh from her father, and a shaking of his head. "A miracle the boy lives."

She glanced at him, and was surprised to see him considering Gideon thoughtfully. Heimdall continued. "It has been too long since we had such a miracle."

Anya reached over and squeezed his hand. "You have been a long time without hope, Papa. We all have."

His throat tightened and his voice grew hoarse as he said, "It had almost had me, daughter. First your mother, and then these twenty years of losses. To decide which villages we could save from the Hell-worshippers, and which to leave to their fates. I thought the Almighty abandoned us. That even God felt nothing but scorn for my failures, and turned His back on me."

His voice fell to a whisper. "I thought I would be the last Wolflord."

Anya did not know what to say. She had never heard her father speak this way.

At last, Heimdall growled, clearing his throat. "But then you had to go and find a hero, didn't you?"

She had to smile at that. "Yes, Father."

He nudged her with his shoulder. "That's what I get for marrying your mother. You are like her in many ways."

The jarl jerked his chin to indicate Gideon. "She would have liked him, too."

Anya felt tears sting her eyes at the thought. "I hope so."

Heimdall chuckled. "Pah. No hope about it. If a warrior had come to our hall when I was young with such fire bound in his blade and eyes, you might never have existed. She would not have looked twice at me, nor thought once about doing so."

Anya laughed quietly, and they sat together in silence for a few more minutes, enjoying each other's company.

Anya felt her father put his arm around her. "We have had a rough time, you and I," he said quietly. "I needed your mother more than I knew to help with such a strong daughter. I fear I have failed more than I have succeeded."

She laid her head on his shoulder and returned his hug. "No, Papa. You did fine."

Heimdall grunted. "I yell too much. I do that when I don't know what to say."

Anya answered, the furs of her papa's cloak soft under her cheek. "Me, too."

They looked out at Gideon together, and Anya heard her father give a quiet sigh of surrender. "He has no idea what he is getting into, does he?"

Anya grinned. "No."

Heimdall's lips parted in a smile. "Poor lad."

THE FIRST THING Abram noticed when they dragged him into the longhouse was how big each Wolf was.

Each man stood at least six feet tall, their massive frames wrapped in the lean muscle of lifelong predators. Generations of breeding only the strongest broadened their shoulders and elevated them above ordinary men. Even the one-eyed graybeard, bent by age, towered over ordinary men.

With an entire council of them standing around him, Abram understood the defeat a little better. It would have taken ten Venans to kill a single one of the Wolves, much less the chieftain sitting in judgment of him.

Eight puffing warriors dragged Ursus into the lodge, as well. They had needed mules to drag the warlord from their pathetic stone cells in the mountain. Enormous chains still wrapped around Ursus's arms and legs, but he made no attempt to break them. He kneeled before the jarl's throne, the fire in his crimson eyes naught but embers.

"You."

The Wolflord's voice rumbled like distant thunder on the mountains.

He gestured with one hand. "You will tell us what we ask, or you will die. The Ferryman is in Hammarfall, collecting lost souls, and he charges less if we deliver in bulk."

Growling laughter echoed around the throne room from the warriors standing at the walls.

Abram rested on his haunches, ignoring the spikes of pain in his thighs, and smiled.

"Do you think to scare me with *torture*, lord of dogs? I was schooled by the best of Gehenna's thornmasters. I have reached depths of pain of which you cannot even conceive."

The Wolflord grinned over at the scarred graybeard to his left. He indicated Abram with a jerk of his chin. "Did you hear that, Skald? He thinks we will torture him."

Skald shook his head soulfully. "How barbarous, my jarl."

"Uncivilized," put in the young woman to the lord's right.

Heimdall nodded sagely. "Indeed."

Skald spread his hands. "Also, ve do have reputation to consider among socialites of Samothrace. Vhy, Princess Helsdottyr might lose her seat at opera if ve tortured prisoners!"

The woman flashed her teeth at Abram. It was not a smile.

The jarl leaned forward in his throne, his voice low and cool. "No, little lord of beggars, we will not torture you. You will tell us what we ask because you are a good person, and because you do not want to be *six* good persons."

Heimdall's tone turned glacial. "I, with my own hands, will tie you between four horses and hang you over a fire. Then I will stand over you as the children you tried to murder whip the horses to run, and I pour molten silver into your blasphemous mouth. There you will remain until the animals have pulled your limbs off, the fire has burned you in half, and the silver pours out of the back of your boiling skull."

Abram snarled, "Save your words. The lovers of the Almighty do not do such things. Your weakness is famed throughout the courts of the Three."

Heimdall furrowed his brow and leaned back. "I forget, grandfather. Do we not do that?"

Skald shook his head. "Never, my jarl. Ve have alvays vanted to, though."

"Always time for a new tradition," Anya offered.

None of them had taken their eyes off of the prisoner. Their eyes held none of the humor of their words.

Abram spat at their feet. "*Please.* I will not be cowed by the pathetic posturing of those who breathe only because they were themselves saved."

He looked to the door, where the golden-haired soldier and the dark sorcerer stood. "The only reason the servants of Mammon are not defecating the flesh of your children in this hall right now is because of *him.*"

Growls echoed around the room, and warriors moved forward, the leather of their axes creaking as their grips tightened.

Abram did not care. "It was over, you mongrels! Ursus would have killed this tiny lord like a fishwife swatting a gnat. Your women and children would have been fallen upon in the streets and ripped apart before your eyes, if your hero had not fallen out of the sky with a weapon crafted by angels!"

At that, the sorcerer sighed and rubbed the bridge of his nose, irritation creasing his forehead.

Abram went on. "Your pathetic tribe teetered on annihilation. You were nothing but embers to be ground out under the boots of your betters! So do not think I will grovel and weep before the beneficiaries of fate in this pathetic farce of a trial!"

Heimdall held up a hand, and the Wolves ceased prowling forward. He seemed unmoved by Abram's outburst. "Yet you kneel, and we do not. The Almighty granted us salvation, and raised up the man we needed in our darkest hour."

His eyes narrowed. "Where was your god in your hour of need, I wonder?"

Abram straightened, pride stiffening his spine. "We serve no gods, Wolf. We have broken those chains."

Skald raised an eyebrow. "Is that so? You are Jahennan by dress and speech. These others are Mammonite; this ve know of old. Gehenna and Mammon are no longer gods to you?"

Abram laughed, starting as a breathy convulsion with his head thrown back. His laugh gained volume and grated on the ears of every Wolf present. When he could speak, Abram wiped the spittle from his mouth with his shoulder and attempted to rise to his feet. Wolves slammed their hands onto his shoulders and kept him on his knees.

"My master was right. You truly have no idea with whom you contend. We are of the New Way."

Skald shrugged. "New Vay?"

"Sounds new," Heimdall offered.

Abram rolled his shoulders back and stood as tall as a man could while on his knees. "The prize is nothing less than the kingdom of Men. No longer will we spend our sweat and our blood for the enrichment of embittered exiles who pretend to possess all power and yet demand our worship. *They need us.* Our prayers now go to no one but ourselves, for who can be gods but us?"

Abram lowered his voice to a sibilant hiss. "Godhood is for those who seize it."

"HE SOUNDS LIKE YOU."

Gideon and Ashkelon stayed in the recesses of the chamber, slipping in and out of sight as the torches flickered. Both of them rested in the shadows, arms folded, watching silently. Gideon noted with mild concern his tendency to imitate his master's habits.

Ashkelon glanced at him. "So I sound like a convert spewing slogans to you?"

Gideon grunted in amusement. "I would like to meet the preacher that tried to convert you."

The corner of Ashkelon's mouth turned up. "Actually, there was one, long ago."

Gideon raised an eyebrow. "You're joking."

Ashkelon looked back to the kneeling Jahennan. "I am not. It was one of the bravest things I had ever seen."

"What happened?"

Ashkelon shrugged. "At the time, Acherlith was held in a vault in the City of the Guardians. They were a monastic warrior sect, authorized by the Scion to pursue forbidden relics and seal them from being used by Avalon's various internecine conflicts. I approached the city and stood outside the gate."

Wind gusted through the chamber, driving the torchlight into a flickering frenzy. The light play across Ashkelon's features was disturbing.

"They ordered that I leave. I answered that if they did not give me the blade of the Dark, I would make their vigil eternal."

Gideon sighed. All of Ashkelon's stories were like this. "And they refused."

"They did."

"And you killed them all."

"I did."

Gideon stretched his shoulder muscles and winced at the pain.

"And you bound their souls to the burning city as eternal guardians, this time only of their failure."

Ashkelon smirked. "Almost, student, but well-guessed. I encased them in stone, and left in place a spell that would rejuvenate their bodies without need of food or air."

Gideon sighed. "Why not just bind their ghosts to the city? Seems like you went to a lot of work."

Ashkelon shrugged. "The message was important to me then, and I was young. As to why I did not bind their souls, once a body has been destroyed, it is impossible to cage the soul on this plane. Believe me, I have tried."

Ignoring the horror implicit in that statement, Gideon furrowed his brow. "What about the souls in Acherlith?"

Ashkelon blinked for a second, then chuckled. "I am surprised that you are taken in by that bit of theater. The blade traps only the final screams of its victims, not their souls. The effect evokes the thought of billions of trapped revenants, and is often misunderstood, to my benefit."

Gideon licked his lips and chose his next words very carefully.

"You are telling me that there is no possible way that one of those screams could…get out? Or try to communicate with someone?"

Ashkelon narrowed his eyes thoughtfully. "That would be highly unlikely; as I have said, there are no souls to be found in Acherlith, only echoes."

His gaze intensified. "Why do you ask?"

Gideon pushed any memories of the revenant Gemelte to the back of his mind and answered, "No reason, master. My mind must be conjuring things."

Ashkelon eased back, but his gaze remained fixed on Gideon. "Perhaps."

They remained that way for a few moments, watching the interrogation before them.

At length, Ashkelon murmured, "Spirits can lie."

Gideon glanced at him. "What?"

"Spirits," Ashkelon replied. "You should not trust them, for they have as much reason as the living to deceive. Entire religions have sprung from an errant spirit spreading so-called revelations. If you should encounter such a revenant, be sure to test its allegations for truth, lest you be led astray."

Gideon bowed slightly. "Yes, master."

After a moment, more to redirect Ashkelon's attention than anything, Gideon asked, "And the preacher?"

Ashkelon smiled, his eyes growing distant. "I will never forget that old man, walking over the shattered marble of the Gate of the Worthy. Not an insecure step did he take, not a second of hesitation at the hundreds of moaning statues in the courtyard leading to the Vaults. He barely saw them, in fact. His staff clicked with regular monotony as he walked through the horrors I had wrought, searching for me."

Gideon raised an eyebrow. "What were you doing?"

Ashkelon reached back and tapped the hilt of Acherlith. "Looking for this. He found me at the entrance of the deepest Vault, destroying the automaton constructs guarding it."

Seeing the look on Gideon's face, Ashkelon clarified. "They were like golems, but built like clocks with great wheels powered by steam. Strong as minotaurs, but with no flesh to rend. They were relics in and of themselves, products of great scientific genius, and it saddened me greatly to destroy them."

His eyes unfocused again. "I stood at the last gate. I could hear the faint shrieks of Acheron, at that time the only scream in the blade, through the great bronze door. Yet behind me, this old man strode through the wreckage of priceless guardians without fear. My blood still beat hot from the battle, and lightning still trailed from between my clawed fingers. My gaze snapped to him."

Remembering, Ashkelon chuckled once. "He did not flinch back. That was the first surprise."

His voice altered in timbre as he considered. "It was, in fact, the first time in decades someone had met my eyes and not recoiled."

Gideon regarded him, intrigued despite himself. "What did he say to you?"

"He asked me what I wanted," Ashkelon answered quietly. "We

stood in the wreckage of the most famous vaults of forbidden weapons in the world, and he asked what I wanted."

"What did you say?" Gideon asked.

Ashkelon shook his head. "Nothing, at first. It was not a question I was prepared for. I needed a moment to provide an answer."

"At last, I told him that I did not care for any of the weapons or trinkets within the Vaults. I wanted to see if the vaunted Guardians of the city could hold me back."

Gideon thought about that for a minute. "You were there for the Guardians?"

As soon as he finished speaking, realization hit him. "You thought they could defeat you. Why would you want that?"

"Because none of the so-called champions, princes or prophets had managed it yet, "Ashkelon answered. "I wanted to see if anything in the Light was capable of defeating the Dark, so I chose one of the Light's most celebrated bastions to give them the chance."

Gideon blew out his breath slowly. "And they failed."

"Imagine my disappointment."

Again, Ashkelon tapped the hilt of Acherlith. "Still, I obtained this, so it was not a total waste of time."

Shaking his head, Gideon squinted at Ashkelon and said, "Wait. You *want* the Darkness to be defeated?"

Ashkelon turned to him. "As much as you do, and probably more. Does this surprise you?"

Gideon nodded and glanced at the kneeling Jahennan. He was still being interrogated by Heimdall. "Yes, master. That surprises me."

Ashkelon shrugged. "I do not wield the power of the Dark through choice, apprentice. It was what I was left with. When it came time to do battle with the Light, well, I found nothing in its ranks to respect. Every warrior I faced was poisoned by the Dark already, their souls painted differing shades of black. None were pure. None were righteous, not a single one of them."

"Except Valantian, right?" Gideon said.

Ashkelon hesitated before answering. "So I believed."

Gideon heard the weight behind that admission, and felt it was not the time to push it. He asked a different question instead. "And the preacher? Did you kill him, too?"

Ashkelon shrugged. "I let him live. He was no threat to me, and he made me question myself, which I found valuable."

He sighed. "I did him what honor I could, for his courage. I ensured he died of natural causes, before I launched the crusade that killed his world."

BY THE TIME Ashkelon concluded his story, the Jahennan had endured several rounds of questions.

"Again, to vhere have the Venans fled?"

The inquisitor Abram merely smirked.

Skald paced before the Wolflord's throne. He raised a finger and asked, "How many of their forces remain in Volflands?"

No answer.

"Vhere is the demon's concubine, the wretch called Ja'a?"

Abram's eyes darkened at the mention of her name, but he grinned nevertheless.

"Oh, I am sure you will know where she is very soon."

Heimdall pounded a fist on the armrest of his throne with decisive force. "Grandfather, the limit of my patience has been reached. If he will not speak the truth, he can scream it. Crush his foot."

Skald hefted his warhammer and stomped over to the kneeling prisoner. The two Wolves on either side of Abram clamped their hands onto his shoulders as he began to thrash.

Skald stepped behind the Jahennan, ignoring his threats and curses, and angled the head of his hammer down, ready to drive it onto the man's foot as though he were driving a fence post.

The tectonic growl froze his hammer in place.

"Whore..."

.   .   .

BOTH GIDEON and Abram were saved from further interrogation by a voice that grated like the stone slabs of a tomb. It resonated with such power that every man felt it in his chest like an avalanche.

Ursus lifted himself from his bowed posture to kneel erect, defying the hundreds of pounds of heavy chain wreathing his body. Wolves surged forward from the walls of the hall, brandishing axes, as the titan rose.

The Slaughterlord flexed his shoulders, and chains exploded from his body, hurling shattered links out into the lodge.

Yet he did not attack. He lifted a hand, palm open, out to his side. Chains and weights hung from that arm, but it did not shake. "Hold," he intoned.

Swiftly, Jarl Fangthane raised a clenched fist. "Hold, brothers."

The Wolves froze in mid-step, axes raised still. Their lord glared down from his throne at the kneeling giant. His jaw clenched around words he clearly despised. "We will hear what he says for now."

Heimdall leaned over to see around Ursus to Gideon. "You may want to get that pretty sword ready, Doomhold."

Gideon tugged on the blade, loosening it in its sheath. His body twinged even at that simple act, and in a moment of weakness, Gideon begged silently, *Please don't get up. Please.*

Tension hung thick in the hall as they awaited the Slaughterlord's words.

The chieftain's raw lips worked, as though he wished to speak, but he found the words difficult to chew. At last, Ursus bowed and rumbled, "I...serve."

The room stared.

It was the Jahennan next to Ursus who spoke for the room. "*What?*"

Ursus did not look at him. His bloodshot eyes remained locked on the floor. "I gave oath on the wall. If I lose, I serve."

Heimdall leaned back, eyebrows clawing for the crown of his head. "I was not expecting that to be a serious offer."

Abram snarled, "No one did, you simpleton! Your oath lies with Carcharoth!"

Ursus lifted his gaze to regard him, and Abram fell silent, struck dumb by the nameless dread the Slaughterlord's size and stench inspired. The titan smelled of carnage, of the ruin wrought of men's blood and bones, and the room could hear the metal of shackles groaning to contain the creature's wrists.

Ursus growled back, his every word forced into existence through the violence of his being. "My oath lies with the strong. Burned Lord defeated me; I serve. God-man defeated me; I serve."

The giant turned back to face the Wolflord squarely. His eyes came level with Heimdall's, even kneeling. "If he commands, I tell you of the Whore."

Gideon froze. Slowly, he became keenly aware that every eye in the room had turned to him.

Deadpan, Ashkelon said, "Congratulations. You own a Slaughterlord. Your decision to keep him alive is justified, if after the fact."

Under his breath, Gideon muttered, "Not. Helping."

Ashkelon glanced about the room. "Now that you command a warrior the equivalent of their filthy tribe, they seem to want you to say something."

He turned back to Gideon and backed one step away, but not without a final barb. "Commander."

Skald, grinning like a fool, leaned to see Gideon past Ursus and waggled his eyebrows. "Vell?"

Glaring at Ashkelon, Gideon stepped forward into the chamber. He walked forward, trying not to limp in front of these heroes, and came even with Ursus. It did not help that his head reached the kneeling champion's shoulder. He addressed Jarl Heimdall. "What do you want to know, lord?"

ABRAM WAS NOT KNOWN for his courage, his strength or his battle skill. He could, however, read a situation and turn it to his advantage. If Ursus confessed all he knew, Abram's life would be worth nothing. He would almost certainly die in the next few moments.

He spoke quickly, before the lord on the throne could draw a breath to answer the golden-haired warrior.

"Very well. *I* will tell you the Consort's plans."

He glared at the giant next to him. "If only to avoid suffering through this traitor's attempts at speech."

Heimdall eyed him with the look of a predator considering its next meal. "So tell, then. Spin this tale, and see if it saves your life."

Abram chuckled helplessly. "Your threats are worthless, little lord. Whether by you or the claws of the Venans, my life is already over. Nothing can change that now."

The Wolf on Abram's left powered his fist into Abram's jaw, splitting the inside of his cheek and spilling salty blood across his tongue. "Speak with respect, whelp," the warrior barked.

Jarl Fangthane held up a hand. "Peace, Anjover. Nothing he says can either harm me or spare his life. Let him speak."

Abram grinned through pink teeth at the Wolf. "You heard him, little one. I get to speak."

He turned back to the jarl, and glanced around the room, meeting the eyes of each Wolf there. "Ask yourselves this. Do any of you know where the Consort of Mammon is? Why she was not present at this battle, while her army broke itself against your walls?"

The one-eyed veteran shrugged. "Ve vere busy. You vould know better than us."

Abram chuckled. "You short-sighted idiots. She was not here because this battle was not the one that mattered."

Heimdall leaned forward in his throne. "It felt differently this side of the wall. Explain."

Abram picked his words carefully. "She is not here because she is in the Crown of Rachna."

The tension in the room thickened. Skald's one eye narrowed to a slit, while several intakes of breath sounded across the room. Gideon glanced around, surprised at the reaction.

"Vhy," Skald growled, "is she *there?*"

Abram grinned again, but this time, it was more of a feral baring of his teeth. "You know why, keeper of tales."

Skald leaned on his warhammer and regarded the kneeling prisoner before him, aware of the murmurs starting around him. "You speak to us of a myth, demon vorshipper. There is no reason to fear legends."

"I speak of a myth, do I?" Abram sneered. "Then tell me, how many of your people have gone missing in the last year?"

Skald glanced at Heimdall. Grim lines etched across the man's face, and he did not answer.

Abram's laugh hissed from his mouth. "It's a significant number, isn't it?"

His laughter built to echo in the hall. "You fools did not even know what Ja'a was doing, did you? She gave you exactly what you wanted here, *lord*, and you, blinded by your despair, looked no further while she fed your people to nightmares beneath the mountains."

Heimdall's knuckles cracked on the armrests of his throne. "And what is it I wanted?"

Abram's laughter died, and his voice deepened in mockery of Heimdall's growl. "A noble death in your own hearth."

He erupted in laughter again. Ignoring the cackling inquisitor, Gideon strode forward to Skald. "What is he talking about? What is the Crown of Rachna?"

Anya answered him, worry creasing her forehead. "It is a tale told to children by their mothers. If children misbehave, the monsters come and take them to the spider mountain in the north, where the spiders feed them to Rachna, the mother of the demons."

Gideon's eyes flicked to Skald. "Anything else?"

Skald sighed. He looked old. "There are myths from time before Samothracian historians began writing. In ancient days, vhen the demon exiles battled their mad brother Thanatos, Mammon used his magic and forbidden science to create Rachna, a creature as a great as a mountain and capable of overflowing the vorld with its starving children. The spiders from north are said to be those children."

Gideon pursed his lips. "What happened in the story?"

Skald squinted, trying to remember. "Vell, in the vone I remember, Rachna gave birth to mighty race of spiders, the size of horses. They overflowed the earth like great flood, eating everything in their path and surrounding Thanatos. The archangel fought the flood and

Rachna, smiting the great spider down. Before he could finish the creature, Thanatos vas dragged avay by his brothers, veakened by the battle. Over the ages, mountains grew over the monster, and the mages of old lay great vards in the stones, praying that the creature never rise again. For this, ve call those mountains the Crown of Rachna."

Gideon sighed. Now he felt old. "I would like to hear that these stories are not true now."

Heimdall leaned back in his throne. "In part, maybe. Rachna itself is certainly the child of overactive imaginations and story-weavers hungry for audiences. But the spiders do come from the mountains of the Crown. Their nests run for miles beneath those hills, and every attempt to burn them out has failed. Thus far, their numbers have been limited by the desolation of that land, but if she has found a way to increase the birth rate of these creatures…"

Gideon closed his eyes and cracked his neck slowly. "Ja'a is trying to bolster her forces. She kept us tied down here with chaff, while traveling north to awaken these monsters. Why? Why not lead this army here herself?"

Behind him, Ursus rumbled, "Gift."

Gideon, Skald and Anya turned to look at him. "What?"

Abram rolled his eyes and interrupted the giant. "Do not harm yourself with full sentences, traitor."

Abram turned back to the gathering and said, "Ja'a is the Consort of Mammon. She loves him more than anything in this world, and will do anything to please him. She means to awaken Rachna, whatever it is, and present both it and the spider race as a gift to her lord for his wars."

He met their eyes squarely. "She's been there for days, guiding the waking ritual in the nests while we fought here. You think there are hordes of monsters now? Wait until Ja'a revives the World Eater. You have seen *nothing*."

. . .

AFTER THE REVELATIONS of the Jahennan, the throne room stood empty. The warriors departed, taking with them the prisoners to return to their chains.

Heimdall sagged in his throne, expression bleak. His daughter and saga-spinner stood beside him, waiting to hear his thoughts. Gideon and the dark one remained close.

At last, the Wolflord spoke.

"It is strange, that the Almighty should have sent us salvation, only to see us destroyed despite it."

Skald grunted. "That is not how the Almighty vorks, my jarl."

Heimdall sighed. "I know, grandfather. And yet, despair threatens to flood my soul once more regardless."

His gaze fell across the carved frescoes on the ceilings, the frayed banners of victories won long past. "We did as we were bidden. We kept our oaths and hunted the demon. We remained in this barren land long past our ability to stem the tide, when we could have had warmer, richer dwellings, and now it seems we are discarded."

Anya put her hand on his shoulder. "If we faint in the day of adversity, our strength is small, Papa."

Skald nodded. "She quotes the holy writings rightly, my jarl. None other but the Vulfen could survive this long. No other leader but you could have held the Pack to its course in this bleak vinter. Ve have been given vhat ve need."

At that, Heimdall's eyes fell on the golden-haired warrior. "Speaking of which…"

Sensing the time for silence was over, Gideon stepped closer. His armor remained broken still, pieces hanging loose from his muscular frame. Streaks of blood and ichor striped his face and battle plate. His sword hung at his side, a faint glow burning in the metal if one looked close enough.

The jarl shook his head as an involuntary grin crossed his features. "First of all, young man, what would you have us call you? You have been with us a matter of days, and yet you have earned the names Champion-Slayer, Boarcrusher, Doomhold and now Titanbreaker. I fear you will have to pick one for old Greymane, lest he get confused in his tales."

Gideon dipped his head, uncomfortable. "Just Gideon is enough for me, jarl."

The grin faded to a smile, and the jarl shook his head yet again. "Remarkable. That, then, is how you shall be remembered in our sagas. Gideon the Just, sent in the Wolves' darkest hour with a fiery sword to drive back the night."

Gideon bowed again. "I just want to help any way I could, jarl."

Heimdall sighed once more. "I fear that time has ended, boy."

Straightening, Gideon asked, "Why is that? We can gather horses and launch an attack now. The Venans are still retreating. If we are fast enough, we can disrupt whatever it is that Ja'a is doing."

Heimdall glanced at Anya and pointed at Gideon. "Make him stop being so likable, daughter."

Anya smiled back. "I have yet to discover that trick, Papa."

The jarl looked back to Gideon. "Boy, look at yourself. Your armor is rags. You have fought with little pause for days, the last battle being a duel against the Devil's champion that shall be sung of for an age. You have yet to determine the extent of your wounds or even wash the remains of your enemies from your face. And now you wish to ride to the north into a spider-infested mountain to kill a fallen angel's lieutenant?"

"Whatever is needed," Gideon's voice hardened. "I will go."

Skald grinned. "I vould be careful with this vone, small-fang. He is trouble. He vas sitting safe in back of fortress, and trouble find him. How bad vill it be when he goes looking for it?"

Gideon straightened. "Regardless of how ready I am, the Consort must be stopped. It is not just your people that will die if I fail, jarl."

Heimdall laughed once, a harsh bark that echoed in the throne room. "Listen to him. The arrogance of youth, the confidence in his invincibility."

Skald raised an eyebrow and shrugged. "I vould agree, but it is not as if he has not earned it."

Heimdall conceded with a nod, but turned to Gideon. "A Wolf you are in spirit, if not birth. I appreciate your help, boy, but it is not possible to do this thing. The Spiderlands are in turmoil. We have not been able to ride in the north for years for fear of being dragged into their vile burrows, and that was before we lost half our strength in this war. I will not send warriors to be slaughtered so that we can see if our prisoners' fear-mongering is true."

Gideon's eyes gleamed with emerald anger. "So what will we do? Nothing?"

Heimdall shook his head. "No, boy. I would have you take my daughter far from this place, so that she lives."

Silence fell across the room. Even Skald seemed shocked by the jarl's words.

"Lord? You vould have us run?"

Fangthane's voice was iron. "There is nothing for us here anymore, grey father. Our strength is spent. The Consort will return, with or without her monsters of legend, and our last fortress is already breached. The time of the Wolf is over. It is time to leave."

His words held a death's knell in their import. Anya found herself speechless.

Skald did not.

The old Wolf strode across the room to stand before his liege. "You vould have us as oath breakers, then?"

Heimdall closed his eyes. "What do you want from me, old one? There is nothing left to give. We are spent."

Gideon cocked his head. "What oath is he talking about?"

Skald answered without looking at him. "Long ago, ve svore to the princes of Samothrace that ve vould hold the north against the demon lords. For three hundred vinters, ve have hunted the demonspawn through these lands."

His eye bored into Jarl Fangthane. "And as for your qvestion, I vant you to honor the oath. Do not let us die faithless."

Heimdall opened his eyes and glared at him. "That oath will have our people killed, Skald, and the Samothracians will never trouble themselves to know what happened to us."

Skald was unmoved. "And yet, it is still oath. No less binding because it is hard."

Heimdall held his advisor's steely gaze. His nostrils flared and his fists clenched, but Skald did not flinch back. Something went out of the lord at that point, and Heimdall nodded. "Aye. You are right, Skald."

The old Wolf sniffed. "I know. It is my job."

A tired smile tugged at Heimdall's lips. "Thank you, friend, for hearing and correcting an old king before his people could hear his cowardice."

This time, Skald smiled, and he clapped his lord on the shoulder. "Is also my job."

Boots scraped on stone. The two men turned to see Gideon moving toward the bearskin door. Skald narrowed his eye. "Pup? Vhere are you going?"

Gideon did not stop. "North. Somewhere in the mountains. I'll figure it out when I get there."

Heimdall stood from his throne. "Did you not hear what I said, boy? It is not possible to do. You will be dragged down miles before you even reach the Crown."

Gideon halted and turned back. His eyes shimmered in the light of the torches. "I was reminded recently that it is not the Almighty's will that we merely survive. It is His will instead that we overcome, and I was not given this weapon so I could run."

Heimdall glared at him. "I cannot command you, boy, but I can command these Wolves. You will go alone. I will not spend what is left of our strength in a futile gesture against a threat from myths."

Gideon shook his head. "I will not be alone. As my master so kindly reminded me," he inclined his head toward Ashkelon, "I have a Slaughterlord."

ASHKELON FOLLOWED his student out of the throne room and into the cold wind. His darkmail cloak flapped in the gusts, and the frost bit at his cheeks.

Amusement and mild curiosity colored his voice in equal measure. "So what is your plan, apprentice?"

Gideon did not turn to answer him, but spoke while he beckoned to a serf for a horse. "Ride north. Find the Consort. Kill her."

Ashkelon's tone was dry as dust. "If only such an opportunity had manifested itself earlier."

That drew a glare from Gideon. "Yes, master. You told me so. I know."

His irritation may as well have been a spring rain running off Ashkelon's cloak for all the effect it had. His eyes flickered coldly. "Then remember that in the future, when the life of your enemy is in your hands and you withhold their judgment."

Gideon exhaled a hissing breath between his teeth as the serf led a horse up to him. "This, then."

Ashkelon folded his hands behind his back, gathering his darkmail cloak behind him, and paced around his student. "Explain to me why you permitted the Slaughterlord to live."

Gideon tightened the saddle fittings on his horse and said, "He did not need to die."

Ashkelon waved his hand dismissively. "Mere hours ago, you were on the verge of weeping because you could not defeat him. Then, when his execution was nigh, you stayed your hand because 'he did not need to die'?"

Gideon's voice was firm as he answered, "That is correct, master."

Ashkelon narrowed his eyes. "I note an alarming predilection to sentimentality in your decision-making, my student. First, you neglect to engage the demon witch to stand with men once your enemies. Then you spare the champion of a cultist army you practically splintered yourself. Now you wish to ride into the north alone to confront unknown odds, and possibly a creature of mythic proportions, for a fading tribe of fatalistic warriors unwilling to save themselves."

"What is your point, master?" Gideon asked. He gripped the saddle, clearly ready to mount the horse.

Ashkelon put a hand to Gideon's shoulder. His black gauntlet did not crush his student's shoulder this time; it was no cruel grip to wrench the muscles on the bone. The touch was almost gentle, lacking the force he ordinarily used against Gideon.

More shaken by the gesture than anything else, Gideon hesitated.

Ashkelon's voice was low. "Your sentimentality will get you killed, student. It has the power to grip hearts and minds and cause them to follow you, but it will eventually destroy you."

Ashkelon looked around the fortress of Hammarfall, encompassing the ruined citadel with his glance. "It feels marvelous to be the hero of the weak, Gideon, but no man can save them all. There will always be the poor, the vulnerable, the needy. They will claw at you for salvation, and it will gnaw you apart inside to be so incapable of helping them."

This was similar to Ashkelon's prior teachings, but somehow, this moment was different. This was personal to Ashkelon.

"How do you know that?" Gideon asked at last.

The slightest wince creased the corners of Ashkelon's eyes. "This is how I destroyed Valantian."

At Gideon's stare, Ashkelon continued. "His advisors would not allow the Scion to be drawn into open combat. As the Guardian of Avalon, his death would have shattered the little unity the kingdoms possessed and plunged their populations in despair. So I struck at him through them to draw him out."

Gideon blew out his breath slowly. "What...did you do?"

Ashkelon looked past Gideon, his eyes unfocusing as he looked into the past. "Plagues. Famine. Disasters. I made him watch his people suffer before they died. I let him cup the black, dead earth of his world in his hands and see it blow away like ash in the wind. I let him hold the withered bodies of starving mothers while their young ones lay cold and grey in their cradles. The Darkness of Avalon tried for centuries to overthrow the Scion, Gideon. I broke him in less than a decade."

Ice gripped Gideon's heart as he struggled to fathom Ashkelon's words. "This...this *happened*? You did this?"

Ashkelon met his gaze evenly, though something dark raged

behind his eyes. "Learn from the horrors you have not yet had to witness, Gideon. Do not spend yourself for this temporary feeling of virtue. When Valantian finally faced me on the last day of Avalon, he was…not himself."

Gideon stared at him. "What was he?"

His master glanced away before answering. "Haunted. Broken. Bitter. Nothing like the hero I wished to face. I poisoned my own cup to have the opportunity to drink of it."

At last, Ashkelon withdrew his hand. "I would have better for you, that is all."

An uncomfortable silence stretched between them. Gideon opened his mouth to say something, anything, but a cry from the gate cut him off.

"Runner!"

THE WARRIOR that lurched toward Hammarfall had changed.

He could feel it in the creaking of his bones, the hollowing-out of his self to make way for another thing. Every breath he took rattled in lungs half-filled with oily mucus. Poisoned sweat trickled down his body, tracking around his distended belly before dripping to the earth.

Things swirled in his vision, dancing in the corners of his eyes. He could never see them, no matter how he focused. He tried to catch them as he plodded, grasping vainly at the giggling phantoms just beyond his reach.

Blessed, she had called him. The things he felt stirring in his belly, tickling his guts with their feathery legs, told him otherwise.

The wights would take him soon, he knew. He did not have much longer, and so, though every fiber of his being screamed at him to lie down and rest, he staggered on, driven by half-remembered snatches of duty.

The horse had died five miles back. The Venans had not been kind to the animal in its captivity, and the proud beast succumbed to its affliction, its great heart failing at last under the burden of bearing its master one last time.

Fyrss ate enough of it to take the edge off of his soul-consuming hunger, and forced his failing body to move toward Hammarfall. His home.

He could hear shouting, faint, at the edge of his perception. It was not the mockery of the wights, but the clean sound of Vulfen warriors.

He had made it.

The thought immediately loosened his muscles, and Fyrss collapsed to the ground outside the citadel.

"MAKE VAY!" Skald shouted at the press of Wolves crowding the gate. "Get out of vay before he taints you all!"

The throng backed away, conditioned to honor the elder warrior, and the venerable Wolf shouldered his way through the ruined gateway. His keen sight saw where Fyrss had fallen and he rushed forward to take a knee by the man.

His eye ranged over the warrior's form, drinking in every detail. So much had changed. Fingernails grown to claws, mucus leaking from nostrils, mouth and the corners of the eyes, his warrior frame wasted to a skeleton. He shuddered all over like a man gripped by fever, and his eyes thrashed behind his lids, caught in nightmares he could not wake from.

"Ach, lad," Skald whispered," Vhat have they done to you?"

"Make way for the jarl!"

The crowd again parted, and Heimdall and Anya burst from the gate. Skald punched his open hand toward them and bellowed, "Hold!"

Even kings obeyed the voice of the Greymanes, and Jarl Fangthane jerked to a halt, his daughter with him. "Is he taken, Grandfather?" Heimdall shouted, his arms spread to keep his people back from the curse outside the walls.

Skald did not answer, his hands moving across the fallen warrior, never straying far from his knife.

. . .

"WHAT IS HE DOING?"

Anya and Heimdall turned to see Gideon and his master in the crowd, watching Skald kneel over Fyrss.

She answered quietly, "He is the Watcher."

Heimdall saw that Gideon did not know what she meant and elaborated, "Skald is the Greymane of our pack, and performs the duties of the role. He sings of the Scriptures to our pups to teach them of virtue, witnesses the fallen and remembers their deeds for our memorial feasts, and serves as champion and advisor to the jarls."

"He also beats young Wolves within an inch of their lives," Anya put in drily.

Heimdall frowned at her. "Not enough in some cases."

The jarl gestured toward the veteran. "The greatest of a Greymane's duties, however, is to be pure. The ways of the enemy are insidious, and they can change a man if he is not vigilant, like worms writhing through earth. When one of us turns, or shows signs of the infection of the Hell-worshippers, Skald must be first to confront the taint, and to do so, he must himself be blameless, untouchable by temptation. Only a Greymane can be trusted to endure the moral threat of Hell."

Anya glanced at Gideon. "This is why he checked you after the dark one killed you."

Heimdall nodded grimly. "Our walls are strong, and our blades are sharp. But only the vigilance and sacrifice of the Greymanes keep us free from the spiritual darkness. He watches sleeplessly against corruption for his pack."

An irritated voice rose from behind the jarl. "And yet am not appreciated. Or paid."

Heimdall turned his eyes up to the heavens for a second, then shifted back toward Skald. "What is your judgment, under-appreciated one?"

The veteran beckoned them forward. "This vone is near death. If you are to hear his vords, you must come now."

. . .

FYRSS'S yellowed eyes rolled in his skull as he lay on the ground, and he shuddered and flinched from phantoms only he could see. When Heimdall knelt beside him and took his palsied hand, the young warrior relaxed with a sigh.

"My jarl."

His voice was harsh and phlegmy. His breath rattled in his lungs as though the Wolf's body forced air through a cloth to breathe. Old blood spread from his mouth down to his chest in a fan of gore.

Heimdall cared for none of these things. He did not flinch as he held Fyrss's hand, the corrupted oils of the man's skin sliming his palm. He looked into the man's poisoned eyes and answered, "My loyal warrior."

Fyrss closed his eyes at his jarl's words and nodded shortly. "Always, my jarl."

Heimdall squeezed his hand and leaned closer. "Speak your words, Fyrss. Then you may rest."

And Fyrss did.

"IT WOULD SEEM," Heimdall grumbled as he paced slowly before his throne, axe in hand, "that the right of it lies with Doomhold."

These were the first words Jarl Fangthane had spoken in an hour, the first since the burning of Fyrss's body. His Wolves lounged in the chamber, predators awaiting their alpha's command. The resignation in his voice elicited a smile from Skald. "Of course it does, my jarl. Vhen has it been other than this?"

Heimdall glared at him, then pointed his axe at Gideon. "Do not let this go to your head, boy. All men are wrong in their turn."

Gideon opened his mouth to answer, thought better of it, and settled for something between a nod and an awkward bow.

Heimdall sagged into his throne, then seemed to summon the strength to speak. "Wolves of Hammarfall, the war is not yet won."

Grumbles and scoffs rose around the room. Heimdall rode it out and said, "The witch Ja'a still lives. Using the few moments left to him, Fyrss has confirmed to me the words of that filthy Jahennan. She is trying to wake up something in the Crown of Rachna. He believed it would be a tide of monsters to drown the world."

Silence hung heavy in the room at the implications of that statement. Gideon was the first to break it. "A nest. Like the Jahennan said."

Heimdall inclined his head toward the young man. "An old one. When Mammon first forged these abominations, he made them to always lay their eggs. Yet to prevent them from overrunning the world on their own, they require sorcerers to actually energize and hatch them. The whore has been able to birth a few so far, but if this ritual is to awaken an entire brood laid for so many winters...."

He did not need to finish the sentence. Glances exchanged between warriors, with one thought shared between them.

Heimdall nodded, his face grim, and spoke their shared conclusion aloud. "Aye. This was a diversion, and by the hand of God, we barely survived it."

Anya interjected, "Did he say anything of Feros, Papa?"

Heimdall sighed and waved a hand. "Taken, in mind and body. He did not have the will of his brother."

Troubled exhalations echoed around the room as each Wolf reacted to the news. One, a red-faced giant of a warrior, shouted, "These are lies! Feros was one of our strongest! He would not fall to corruption!"

Some exclamations supported him. Skald's face hardened to stone, and he strode forward and slammed his hammer head into the stone of the floor. The metal rang like a blacksmith's hammer against the hewn stone. "You can shout as much as you like, Baldr Ironbreaker, but the Enemy is cunning beyond imagining. Feros ignored the old vays. He believed himself vithout need of the Scripture, that his axe arm alone could save him. Look on his fate, and let that be lesson to you all."

Baldr spread his hands and retorted, "These are fine words, Grandfather, but they will not break our enemies or save our children from such a fate. What actions do we take? Are they also in the Scriptures, or do you waste our time?"

The hall divided, some shouting in assent, others roaring at Baldr to hold his tongue. Men shoved one another and more than one blow was thrown at a brother. Heimdall clenched his jaw in anger for a moment before holding up his hands for quiet. Shouts of "The jarl speaks!" and "Shut your teeth!" accompanied by liberal slaps to the back of heads quieted the room down.

"We cannot fight so many," Heimdall declared. "No Wolf has walked the Crown of Rachna in a century. The demons there are old and numerous. If the Pack were to assault the mountain, the second we broke a strand of their webs, it would attract every creature from their burrows, and we would be destroyed."

Skald sighed and leaned on his hammer. "Yet ve cannot do nothing, my jarl, lest they drown us in demons."

Baldr stomped forward. "We cannot fight. We cannot stay. I say we leave."

Skald's glare should have seared the Wolf to ash where he stood. His voice dropped to a tectonic snarl that demons had flinched from. "You speak...of *cowardice.*"

He gestured at the Wolves around, his eye cold. "In these halls, among these men, these heroes who have buried brothers in the cold earth. In the presence of such courage, you dare suggest ve run?"

Baldr stood his ground, steel of his own hardening his tone. "I was one of those who buried brothers, old one. When the horn of war called, I howled in answer and stood on the wall. I was there when Ulfred and Oggi were slain by the giants, and I collected the weregild of their blood from their killers. After, I clawed their graves from the earth myself. I stand here with the cold dirt under my fingernails, and I say that it is not cowardice to be outmaneuvered, Greymane. We are lost. There is nothing more to be gained here, nor by spending our lives in the Crown. Let us take our families and ourselves and begone."

Baldr looked at the men around him and asked quietly, "What more can be asked of us?"

His words echoed in the chamber as every man and woman

present felt the truth of them. Anya looked to her father, hearing the echoes of his own despair in Baldr's words.

Heimdall shifted in his throne and stood to his feet. He walked forward slowly, a battle-king tired beyond his years, and laid a hand on Baldr's shoulder. The Wolf met his eyes without shame, a faint sheen glimmering in his eyes at the grief threatening to consume him.

The jarl spoke. "You are no coward, Baldr."

He held out his other hand and encompassed the room. "And his words are correct. If we remain, we will be destroyed."

Heimdall turned his gaze back to Baldr. "Yet our oath stands."

Baldr glanced away and scoffed. "Those old words to soft-skinned city-dwellers? What is such an oath to those who banish us?"

The Wolf king squeezed his shoulder and glanced at Skald, a feral light gleaming in his eyes. "An oath, still."

After a moment, Baldr dipped his head and stepped back reluctantly into the crowd of Wolves, leaving his master alone. Several of them clapped him on his shoulders to encourage him, even those who shouted against him. Wolves respected men who spoke their minds without fear.

Jarl Fangthane looked around the room, and his heart simultaneously swelled and broke with pride at their indomitable courage. "So, my loyal Wolves, we cannot attack, we cannot defend, and we will not break our oaths to run."

He smiled then, more a baring of his teeth than an expression of humor. "We are honored among the children of men, in that we may choose where we die. How many can say that?"

As the Wolves continued to deliberate within their throne room, the student slipped out with his master to spar.

"So," Gideon said. He hefted his sword and brought it up into a guard. "Do you still think I am being sentimental?"

Ashkelon regarded him with his cold eyes and saluted with his blade of conjured ice. "The necessity of the venture does not remove the tactical flaws in your execution of it. If you had gone alone, as you intended, you would have been slain, and no amount of good feelings or flaming swords would have saved you."

Gideon stepped forward, cutting towards Ashkelon's hip. "So it is hopeless to try?"

Ashkelon stepped aside, blocked the blade as it redirected toward his head and grunted. "Firstly, remember that these are not your people, and you have no responsibility to them beyond what you assign yourself. When they die, your legend will not be diminished, should you withdraw from this theatre, and you can start fresh in your next battleground."

They circled one another as they spoke, exchanging ringing blows without pause as they spoke. Gideon felt like a clumsy ox next to Ashkelon, who glided like a wraith almost contemptuous of the need for footing at all. He shook his head and answered, "Not happening."

"Of course not," Ashkelon snapped. "You are more concerned with sleeping well at night without their faces haunting your dreams than you are with banishing their demons in the first place! Remember that these people you profess to care for are only in this position because of your refusal to hear me in the first place. You insist, *still*, that the moral high ground you allegedly hold grants you special revelation concerning the battles you wage, and so you ignore my warnings."

His blows darted and slashed at Gideon, who struggled more and more to deflect them away. His words struck Gideon to his core, dropping his reaction time, and Ashkelon, in typical ruthless style, seized on his weakness.

The blade of ice smashed onto Gideon's wrist, loosening his grip, and the sorcerer ripped the sword out of Gideon's hands. Gideon tried to recover, launching a backhanded strike with his fist, but the mage's onyx vambraces blocked the blow and stabbed the blade of ice into Gideon's throat.

Gideon gasped in shock, but he did not feel the familiar cascade of hot blood flowing over his chest, the strength of his body draining away as his vision faded. Instead, he felt only a waspish sting in the hollow of his throat. The blade had penetrated enough to break the skin only.

Ashkelon withdrew his blade, a single drop of blood suspended on the tip. He pointed it at Gideon, letting him see the dot of red gracing the point of ice. "You lack precision. Your emotions blind you, and so you overcompensate."

Gideon put his hands on his hips and looked at the ground, his expression pensive. At length, he looked up to Ashkelon, light igniting in his eyes.

"I am so stupid."

"I must deny a rush of euphoria in hearing you acknowledge that."

Gideon glared at him. "How is that going for you?"

"Not well."

GIDEON SHOULDERED through the bearskin door and found the Wolves still deliberating. They stood in groups of two or three, speaking quietly to one another. A grim fatalism seemed to have taken hold of them.

Gideon took a deep breath and strode forward, his voice ringing out in the dark room. "Jarl Fangthane!"

The lord of the Wolves looked down at him, an eyebrow quirking upward at the interruption. Next to him, Skald chuckled. "Ah, just-Gideon, do not bother. Old Skald vil guess. You vish permission, *again*, to ride north alone and kill the vitch by yourself."

Gideon grinned broadly, his eyes gleaming. "Almost."

Skald lifted his one eye to heaven. "How do I alvays know? And about vich part am I wrong?"

Gideon did not stop grinning. "I don't need your permission."

In spite of the doom hanging over them, amused chuckles rose from the Wolves in the chamber. Skald ducked his head with a chuckle and conceded the point with a gesture. Gideon continued, addressing the room, "Your Greymane is right that I wish to ride north alone. He is wrong in that I wish to kill the witch alone."

Skald chuckled and spread his hands. "Ach, excuse old man his confusion. He forgets that young vones have all the answers."

Gideon ignored his lighthearted mockery. "Within the Crown of Rachna, Mammon's consort will be too strong for one man to kill. She will be surrounded by her most powerful creatures and able to call on the spiders within the mountain itself. So I need the Wolves of Hammarfall to stand with me."

Squaring his shoulders, Gideon continued. "I acknowledge, however, that they cannot *ride* with me."

Skald squinted at him, and looked back at his lord. As the Wolves in the chamber murmured, Heimdall furrowed his brow. "Speak plainly, Titanbane. What is your plan?"

And Gideon told them.

16

TOMB OF RACHNA

The ranger Findley did not want to go to the Spider Mountain, and he made it as obvious as he could, by repeating it again and again to everyone who would listen.

"I don't want to go. I hate spiders. I *hate* them. I don't think I can go. My poor mother, she would be worried sick. The stress of the past few days, and then me being gone and her worrying about me, it might push her over the edge. In good conscience, I can't go."

Skald weathered his excuses up to a certain point. Then the venerable warrior lost his patience. He clutched the hapless man by the ear and roared into it, "You vil take this great hero, vithout whom you vould be dead in your hut, to the Crown of Rachna, so that he may vonce again save vorthless hide! You are ranger! Go range!"

And that was that.

They spoke little on the ride north, Findley glancing furtively all around and murmuring prayers to himself. They rode through cloying mists that grew thicker the further they rode. Gideon could feel his skin beginning to burn from the mist's corrosive touch.

As the day began to darken into evening, the ranger pointed into the distance. "There, lord. That is the Crown."

Gideon shaded his eyes with his hand and peered toward the horizon. In the failing light, he saw the outline of a great mountain rising from the poisoned fog. Eight lesser ridges jutted out from all sides of the mountain, arched like segmented joints. Silhouetted, the mountain transformed into a monstrous tarantula, poised to leap onto its prey.

A shiver ran through Gideon's body unexpectedly, and he glanced at Findley to see if he had seen. With a wry grin, he pointed at the mountain and commented, "Well, that explains where the name came from."

The ranger did not smile in return. "Am I released, lord?"

Gideon glanced at him. The man was fingering his reins, practically wringing them. His eyes continuously darted into the mists around them. Feeling some compassion for the man, Gideon nodded and said, "Thank you for your guidance, Findley. Be safe on your journey home."

The man did not say another word, but wheeled his horse around and trotted back the way he had come. In under a minute, the mists had swallowed the man up and for the first time in some time, Gideon found himself alone.

His horse whickered beneath him, and Gideon patted the creature's neck. "I know. Easy, girl."

He sighed and gently urged the horse forward, his nostrils flaring at the scent of death on the breeze blowing from the Crown. "I smell it, too."

Gideon could not say how long he rode for. The mists had a way of disorienting his senses, and the sunlight faded quickly, leaving him in a grey world of crumbling soil, creaking tree limbs and the soft footfalls of his mount. The branches of black oaks, bare of leaves, snaked through the mist, like claws reaching for him as he rode beneath them.

Something soft, almost weightless, brushed against Gideon's ear, and he turned to see a cloak of gossamer threads hanging from the tree above him. It clung to his shoulder with sticky tenacity, and when he tried to brush it off, it wound itself about his hands.

Realization struck him, and he looked ahead to see similar curtains hanging from the trees before him. Some had black bodies trapped within them, and Gideon could only identify them by the stray claws or wings protruding from the webs that draped from the dead forest's branches.

The ground itself was not free from the corruption within the trees. The webbing lay so thick on the ground, the way ahead resembled a new-fallen carpet of snow.

So you seek the lair, young knight.

Gideon closed his eyes and sighed. "The plan was to be alone, phantom."

To his right, the ghostly figure of Gemelte Asirius resolved from the mists. The revenant shrugged, its eyes alight with amusement. *I also had plans, while I was alive. How fortune twists our expectations.*

"Quit pacing, small-fang."

Skald shook his head as Anya whirled for another vehement march across the stone floor, her bow and quiver clacking across her back. "Ve have lost enough of Hammarfall vithout you vearing it down further."

The old Wolf sat on a stone bench, no cushion to coddle his age. One hand lay on the hilt of his warhammer, the other tugged at his salt-and-pepper beard. Other Wolves scattered around the throne room, talking in hushed tones, weapons clenched tight in their fists. The dark one sat cross-legged on the floor, forearms resting on his knees, back straight, eyes closed. His screaming sword hung in blessed silence in its back scabbard. The man could have been asleep, for all anyone knew.

With visible effort, Anya held herself in place and settled for a glare at Skald. "He should be there by now."

Skald shrugged. "He had a long vay to go. And that poor Findley did not vant to take him, so that might slow things."

Anya clenched her fists. "I hate waiting."

Skald chuckled. "You are not old enough yet to appreciate the value of patience. Vhen you are young and strong, you can vear yourself out running after every rabbit. But vhen the old volf's bones ache from years of rabbits, you learn to vait for the elk to bare its throat."

Anya blew her breath out slowly. "Is that what we are doing? I thought we sent a good man to die."

Skald pressed his lips together and sighed. "Small-fang, he vas going. Ve did not send him. It is miracle he thought to include us at all."

A voice interrupted them. "Excellent observation."

They turned to see Gideon's dark master. His eyes had not opened, though his head tilted toward them.

Anya's lip curled. "You have nothing to say I wish to hear, murderer."

A slight smile touched Ashkelon's pale lips. "For a culture that worships its heroes, you show surprising ignorance when you meet one."

Anya glared daggers at him, but the sorcerer showed no signs of caring. Which, of course, incensed her further.

Skald gestured with a broad sweep of his hand. "Speak, dark vone. I vould hear your thoughts on this."

Anya whirled on him. "Are you serious?"

The veteran held up a hand, his face stern. "Peace, small-fang. I have listened to demons try to justify themselves before my hammer broke them apart. I know how to separate truth from falsehood. Besides, it is not like ve have other things to do."

Skald turned back to Ashkelon. "So, tell us of this young man. Tell us vhat the Dark sees vhen Gideon Doomhold bares his sword."

"IF YOU'RE COMING, BE SILENT."

Gideon clicked his tongue and urged his horse forward into the mists. His eyes scoured the ground before him, clicking back and forth. He tugged on the reins often, forcing the animal to sidestep certain patches of webbing.

I cannot be heard or seen by others, young man. I am your ghost alone.

"Speaking of that," Gideon said, straightening in his saddle and cracking his neck, "Ashkelon seems to believe you cannot exist."

Gemelte raised an eyebrow. *And you believe everything he says?*

Gideon kept his gaze flickering through the dead forest, marking the shadows around him. "He has yet to lie to me, and in this case, I believe him. I do not believe you are who you say you are."

So, then. Who do you believe I am?

Gideon shrugged, swaying easily in his saddle. "A ghost? Possibly, though Ashkelon says it is not possible. I find it much more likely that you are an enemy of his."

They continued to walk together, Gideon directing his mount past dangerous areas and Gemelte passing through them without effect.

The wraith considered Gideon for a moment. *For the sake of exploring this fascinating theory, if I am not who I say I am, why would I concern myself with you?*

A stick snapped off to the right, and Gideon twisted to peer into the mists. He saw nothing but the smoky tendrils of fog creeping along the ground. "You probably see an advantage in the association. Ashkelon has never taken an apprentice before, and you might see an opportunity to strike at him through me, somehow."

Gemelte nodded. *A plausible hypothesis. You are wise to be suspicious. After all, spirits do lie.*

Gideon held up his hand and snapped it shut, the tips of his fingers touching the tip of his thumb in the universal signal for "shut up". He pulled on his reins, and his horse obediently sidestepped a patch on the ground.

The revenant ignored his gesture, of course, watching him with interest.

What is this that you are doing?

"Spiders use two kinds of thread when they form their webs. Everyone knows the sticky threads. They grab onto anything that touches them and wrap it until it can no longer move, and the spider comes in its own time to take its prey."

Snares.

Gideon nodded. "Exactly. It is not the sticky threads that are the problem, though. It's the alarm threads."

Explain.

His horse whinnied nervously, and Gideon patted its neck, trying to soothe it. The animal was becoming more agitated. He would have to abandon it soon.

He continued speaking, hoping that his voice would calm the creature. "I grew up on a farm. As a child, I would watch spiders build their webs in the rafters. Every web has many sticky threads, yes, but then there are the threads that are there solely to alert the spider that his trap has been sprung. If I trip one of these threads here, I'll probably be joining you as a whatever-you-are soon."

Gemelte considered him.

You assume that these creatures are the same as those you grew up with, and form your approach strategy accordingly?

Gideon shrugged. "If I'm wrong, I'm not any more likely to die."

The phantom grinned and looked off into the distance. *Ashkelon used to say the same thing. You remind me of him, when he was younger.*

Still peering into the mists, Gideon did not allow his expression to change, but he thought to himself, *And you supposedly did not know him then.*

Ashkelon opened his eyes, his irises a piercing blue that always shocked Anya when she saw them, and regarded Skald with an unblinking, measured stare.

"On the world of my birth, at the time of my birth, the Light held sway. The great battles had been fought eons past, for the champions of Avalon subjugated or destroyed the mighty evils of the world. Darkness retreated, falling into the cracks of the world, and the people of Avalon grew accustomed to the Light."

Ashkelon shifted to stare forward, his gaze distant. "In only a century or two, after the last of the champions died out, the people of Avalon forgot the price of blood that had been paid to vanquish terror. They became obsessed with wealth, pleasure, comfort and petty politics."

"They forgot how to fear, *what* to fear, and their ignorance weakened them. By the time I rose, the mightiest heroes of Avalon were pathetic imitations aping the legends of old. Having known nothing but Light, they could not correctly assess the threat of the Dark, and so did nothing but make excuses as the world grayed around them."

Skald leaned forward, his eye glinting in the firelight, and said, "Then you showed them the error of their vays."

Ashkelon reached back and tapped the hilt of his cursed blade, his gauntlet clinking against the black steel. "Acherlith bears their testament, to remind me of what happens when heroes fail to be torches in the Light as well as the Dark."

Skald shrugged. "And vhat does this tale have to do vith Gideon?"

The sorcerer tilted his head to look at Skald. "As I arrived on this world, I saw the same pestilent infection that had afflicted Avalon, just more brazen. Soldiers of Hell marching freely, and the people helpless before them, without defenders. Disappointment threatened to consume me, and I began to believe that mankind was truly lost, merely the final flickers of a candle's flame before it drowns in its own wax. But then one resisted."

A slight smile twisted Ashkelon's lip. "An orphan stole his patron's cheap sword, and stood in the doorway of a wretched hovel to defend a dead man's wife from a horde of slavers and a warlock. He believed in the stories of old, and shaped himself to fit their example. Through his simple faith, he inspired me to believe that perhaps, humanity had something of worth left in it, something to strive for beyond feeding the hungers of decaying gods."

Ashkelon fixed both of them with his icy stare, his eyes hooded beneath his pale locks. "What does the Dark see when Gideon unsheathes his sword? I see, for the first time, something that is not false. It is for his unfailing devotion to righteousness that I breathe life back into his blood after he rightly dies for his failures. It is for his unswerving commitment to purity that I still sit in this foul-smelling cave with a group of warriors that must pretend to be animals to summon the courage to fight."

Anya bristled, but Skald ignored the slight, leaning forward with the gleam of fascination in his eye. "I have qvestion."

Ashkelon acceded with a nod. "Ask."

Skald rested his hands on the head of his warhammer. "Do you seek to correct the sins of your past by training this boy to kill you?"

For a long moment, Ashkelon regarded him quietly. His hair hung lank over his eyes, but he did not bother to brush it away. At last, he said, "I committed those sins on the premise that something of Light would be there to stop me, and I would at last see questions answered that the Dark cannot speak to. Instead, I stood alone on the pinnacle of my masterpiece, and breathed the ash of immolated innocence. Their shrieks echoed on the mourning wind, and yet I stood, waiting. Waiting for that Being that claims to make all things and keep them to show Himself at last, and bring me to my knees for my transgressions against His law."

"Did He come?" Anya asked.

The hint of a bitter sneer touched Ashkelon's pale features. "He could not be bothered. I stood in a sea composed of the defiled bodies of His creations, a blood-offering a Hell-worshipper could only dream of making, and yet I stood *alone.*"

He took a deep breath, and his last words rasped out of his throat like a saw juddering through hardwood pine. "If there is nothing in this universe to mete out judgment for sin, then there is no reason to live in it. Gideon is the last hope for life worth living, the final test of existence, and if he fails, then I will not hesitate to kill him, you, and the rest of humanity. I will save the cosmos the burden of waiting for entropy take its course, and I will enact final mercy on our entire ruined race."

AT LAST, Gideon and his companion drew near to the base of the mountain. Fog drifted like smoke through the webs dangling in the mouths of caves set in the rock. The stench of the air rankled, a mix of sulfur, decaying flesh and old blood. Faint scritching chittered from the caves, mixed with the moaning of the wind.

Gideon's iron boots clanged against the hardened earth. The sound drew a sharp look from Gemelte.

Did you not reprimand me for noise discipline?

Gideon bent down, removed his gauntlets carefully and scraped up a handful of dirt. With slow, deliberate motions, he ground the earth into his palms, breathing in its scent. The death in the soil rankled his nose, and Tal's spirit flared in response.

He replaced his gauntlets and looked up to the Crown. His gaze flicked from point to point on the mountain, searching the caves.

Gideon drew Tal, the blade glowing dully in his hand. His shield, he carried at the ready as he took his first step onto the slopes of the Crown.

With that first step, he smashed his sword against his shield, filling the silence of the dead air with the sound of a pure bell tolling in the distance.

Clang.

Gemelte stared at him.

What are you doing? The creatures will hear you.

Nine steps later.

Clang.

ASHKELON SMILED.

"However, I have great hope for Gideon. The Everlasting Dark thrives on disappointment, despair, and fear. Yet every time he dies, he returns hardened. Each time I cut his thread, I find it restrung with steel. He endures terror, failure, suffering and death, and he has not succumbed to the comfort of compromise."

He glanced at Skald and Anya this time.

"I am eager to see what he becomes, after I have killed him a few more times."

. . .

CLANG.

Every ten steps, Gideon smashed the flat of his blade against his shield. His unblinking gaze focused on the mountain.

The revenant hovered before him, hands held up to stop him, consternation wreathing its features.

You will bring this mountain of horrors down upon you. Do you wish to join the dead so soon?

"I know what I'm doing," Gideon growled. As he marched past a cluster of webbing on the ground, he let his blade fall. The keen edge found a strand wound tightly on the ground, and with a twang, Gideon snapped it with a vicious flick of his wrist.

It cracked like distant thunder, and Gideon punctuated the sound with another *clang* of his sword against his shield.

A screech answered it, joined by another, and another, til the mountain itself echoed with monstrous signals of alarm.

Gemelte's ghost fell to an abrupt seat on a stone and stared at Gideon in something approaching horror. *You would force me to watch you die.*

Gideon's eyes never left the Crown. From caves and burrows in the mountainside, legs sprouted like foul weeds and wriggled frantically in the air, dragging thoraxes and abdomens from the poisoned earth. The mountain grew a second skin, which crawled and flowed in a deluge of flicking legs and jerking leaps. It sounded like scuttling gravel pouring toward him.

Gideon ignored them, his gaze flickering across the surface of the mountain, counting, assessing.

"There," Gideon muttered, and dashed forward, his boots kicking up chunks of dead earth behind him. His sword and shield pumped at his sides as he propelled himself toward his goal, leaving the ghost of Gemelte behind. Spiders swarmed down the mountainside toward the sprinting figure, hissing shrieks issuing from their dripping mandibles.

There was, however, only one cave with no spiders crawling from it, and Gideon arrowed straight for it.

· · ·

ASHKELON CLOSED HIS EYES, as if hearing music playing just for him, and Skald murmured, "And so you excuse your sins, believing yourself absolved by the boy's actions."

"Spare me, tale weaver," Ashkelon said. "You can't see what I can, or hear the symphony formed from my actions. The Dark itself begins to know Gideon's name, written on the corpses of its champions. They remember what such warriors have wrought on them in the past. I have set the arc of his path blazing into the heavens, and given him the skillset to survive the attention. The creatures of Darkness see the glory of his ascendance, and his Light strikes nothing but terror in their hearts."

Ashkelon opened his eyes and fixed them straight ahead. "He is the fiend to them, and it takes a monster to create another monster."

His head twitched to the side. "It is time. Ready yourselves."

GIDEON WAS fifty yards from the cave entrance when the first spider reached him. A creature the size of a horse lunged from his left side, legs spearing toward him with an explosive hiss. Gideon twisted and parried the first legs with his shield, severing the following set with Tal's burning edge.

Thirty yards.

The earth in front of him exploded. A spider sprang from the hole, trying to bodily crush Gideon into the ground, a shriek of rage blanking Gideon's senses. Gideon slammed his shield into its underbelly and lifted it, carrying it over his head, while his sword pierced its thorax and slid through its body like scissors through paper. Feculent vapors filled the air as its intestines slopped behind Gideon like half-melted butter.

Twenty yards.

Gideon deflected an attack from his right side, crushed another creature's mandibles with his shield, kicked off a grasping claw on his ankle and slammed his knee into a spider's face.

Fifteen yards.

They were swarming him too fast now. His pace slowed.

Gideon drove his blade around him in a series of desperate flurries that trailed flame in their wake. Chitinous legs stabbed at him or tried to envelop him in their grasp, trying to drag the soldier down. Gideon swept his blade in front of him in a blazing arc and managed one more step.

Fourteen yards.

Now, Ashkelon.

The spawn of Rachna slammed back, crowding toward him, sticky saliva dripping from their mouths. They sensed the end was near.

NOW, Ashkelon!

Gideon kicked a creature back and stomped on its head, detonating its skull beneath his iron boot. Another spider the size of a dog launched from above and landed full on Gideon, driving him back a step into the swarm behind him. Its claws dug into Gideon's flesh, and he punched the thing away, leaving blooming trails of blood on his face.

Taking a deep breath just before the brood struck again, Gideon screamed to the uncaring heavens, "Ashkelooooon!"

IN THE HALL of the Wolves, Ashkelon drew Acherlith. With a single cut, he tore a dark rent in the air before him, like a shadow without a body to cast it. Ashkelon took hold of one side of the tear and ripped it back, peeling back reality to form a doorway.

The Wolves stared with wide eyes, some making warding signs against the sorcery before them.

Ashkelon stabbed a finger to his side without looking.

"Loose him."

IN THE BOWELS of the Tomb of Rachna, Ja'a looked up from her work. The endless caravans of her children still scuttled toward the pool, dumping their moaning cargoes into the vast sulfurous lake beneath the mountain while her acolytes droned on and on in mind-numbing chants.

She could hear her guardians screaming, dying at the foot of the mountain. Someone was trying to get in.

Ja'a was attuned to everything in the Great Tomb. Every form of life here was beholden to her, save the mighty one she sought to wake. If she concentrated, no mean feat for her shattered psyche, she could see a man with a burning blade through a thousand eyes.

One man. She chuckled madly and whispered in sing-song, "One more body for the grist, one more grist for the mill."

Nearby, her latest work stirred in its amber chrysalis, the poison in its blood burning like fire in its veins. Too many limbs pressed against the translucent membranes holding it in, seeking escape from its transformative prison.

She laid a hand against the sticky surface and whispered, "Soon, lovely one. He will come so soon, and then you can feed. I promise."

Her voice soothed the nightmare within, and it eased back into the murky broth of its rebirth.

Her personal brood of Mammon's children spread out, placing themselves above, beneath and around the entrance to the great lake. Her loyal bloatguard hefted their brutal weapons and shambled over to block ingress with their beautiful bodies.

A dreamy smile crept across the Consort's face. It was so close now. Soon, she could bring a mighty offering to her lord. Soon, as he murmured to her his pleasure, she would be enveloped in his warm embrace.

She would be loved. Accepted. Wanted. Fulfi...

Ja'a screamed.

The sudden shriek startled her wards and guardians, and they twisted to see what was the matter. The creature within the chrysalis thrashed violently at her cry.

The Consort fell to her knees, clutching her stomach and kicking around wildly. Her screams tore from her as she felt the puncture wounds being stabbed through her kingdom, *her domain*. It lasted a few terrible seconds as a witch spear thrust through the heart of the Spiderlands, then the invisible blade withdrew, leaving a hole gaping in her realm.

Serk, captain of her bloatguard, lurched next to her. "Lady?" he inquired fretfully.

Shuddering, Ja'a rested a hand on Serk's mucus-crusted vambrace and stood to her feet on shaky legs. Her breath came in gasp and sobs. "What was that?" she cried. "Who did that?"

Serk did not have time to answer before a tyrannic roar blasted through the cave. The bloatguard immediately turned back to the cave mouth, and Ja'a knew why.

They remembered that roar.

JUST BEFORE THE guardians of the mountain swarmed Gideon, he saw the air open like a dark mouth. Warm, humid air gusted from the slit of shadow, then it tore open like a curtain being thrown back. The spiders around Gideon stepped over and on one another, trying to maneuver their bulks to face the new incursion.

One, and only one, warrior emerged from the tunnel Ashkelon had burrowed through reality. The creatures shrank back as an immense shadow stinking of blood and sweat stepped through the onyx portal and looked down on them with bloodlust gleaming in his crimson eyes, a black greatsword in his fist.

Ursus, Slaughterlord of the Tor Kayn, roared with enough fury to shake the mountain, and smashed his fist down on the nearest spider. The front half of the creature crumpled like tin, cracks crazing the exoskeleton, and its insides exploded out of the rear of its body, spattering its brood-mates nearby.

A shrieking spider leapt at the intruder, mandibles seeking Ursus's throat. Ursus blocked it with his forearm, crushed its head with a ferocious punch, ripped its legs off and punted the corpse a hundred yards away. Without slowing, Ursus raked the severed legs in a wide sweep, tearing away three quarters of the spiders assaulting Gideon and sending them tumbling end over end.

Suddenly freed, Gideon lashed out with his blade and cut open two spiders in front of him, spilling their slime onto the ground. He stabbed a third, igniting it with a flashing hiss, then smashed away the last with his shield. Ursus stomped on it with earth-shaking force, and casually scraped his foot along the ground to get the spider's guts off of his foot.

Gideon gasped for breath and managed to say, "I am very grateful I didn't kill you."

"God-man," Ursus rumbled in return.

Gideon glanced at him, his chest heaving, adrenaline charging his body. "Ashkelon reforged your sword, huh?"

The goliath lifted the blade and nodded. He looked strangely awkward at the admission.

Gideon grinned. "He's had a lot of practice lately."

He gestured at the spiders struggling to right themselves from Ursus's attack. "Can you hold them here while I'm in there?"

Ursus grunted in assent. "I kill here. You kill there."

Gideon had to smile. "And a plan, it is."

He turned to enter the cave, but not before saying, "Stay alive, Ursus. I am curious to see what kind of god-man you would make."

Ursus watched his new master disappear into the darkness of the cave, lit only by the orange light of his glowing sword.

His words troubled Ursus, though Ursus could not say why.

Then the first of the spiders touched his leg, and coherent thought dissolved into red smoke and black rage once again.

Gideon jogged through the tunnel, slowing only to make certain of his steps on the mossy stone and prevent a twisted ankle. As he surmised, no spiders lunged from the lichen-covered walls to drag him down. They all held back where they could protect the Consort as she enacted her vile ritual.

By the light of his sword, Gideon could see that the stone around him glistened. The rock was strangely wet, but not with water. It was something more like a transparent mucus oozing down the wall. The stone was also glossy in and of itself.

Gideon shuddered. "What have these things done to this place?" he muttered.

Behind him, the sounds of screaming and cracking chitin rang from the rock around him. Gideon shook his head half in admiration, half in dread. He had seen Ursus fight twice now, and the sounds were the same. Lots of screaming and breaking.

Ahead of him, the darkness lightened into a greenish-yellow gloom. By the low light of the cave and the glow of his blade, Gideon could see figures barring his path. Vaguely man-shaped masses stood before him, wielding great cleavers or spiked clubs.

He could not see any spiders, but he could hear them, the wet churning of their mandibles, the oozing of their drool dropping to the stone floor.

There were nearly thirty of the bloated mutants, standing about twenty paces from the entrance of the tunnel into the cavern. Not an impossible fight, but not necessary, either.

Behind the silent bloatguard, he saw the Consort pacing, the limbs growing from her back dragging on the ground like a wedding train. She swayed back and forth, muttering in low tones to herself, some-times laying a hand on what looked like a giant cocoon that reached up to the cavern's high ceiling.

The dull yellow light emitted from the great lake of rank liquid, casting sick illumination onto the walls. Heavy spores drifted through the air, and the cavern smelled of sulfur and vomit.

Gideon was close enough now to hear the Consort's ravings.

"It's enough, yes, it is, enough. Just one soul, need one soul, a strong soul, a beacon soul, a waking soul and…hello."

This last had been directed at him. The Consort had halted her pacing entirely, and her yellow eyes, like fireflies in the gloom, had fixed on him. Her head cocked almost parallel with the floor, like a bird.

"Ooh. *You* have a strong soul."

Gideon stepped into the cavern, Tal's light growing ever brighter to combat the oppressive unlight. Even in their heavy helms, the bloatguard shielded their eyes or turned away from the unforgiving gleam of Gideon's weapon.

Gideon kept his voice even. "Your army is destroyed, witch. Your plan has failed. The Wolves still live."

Ja'a giggled like a little girl. *That* was disconcerting.

"The Wolves still live? Well, I suppose some of them do. My followers did a very good job of keeping those nasty Wolves bottled up in their cave, I think, while my children did some...," her voice dropped to an inhuman growl, "foraging."

Gideon narrowed his eyes. "What do you mean?"

The Consort spread her hands, encompassing the whole space. "After so long trapped in the stone, the World Eater is very hungry, you know. For it to wake up, it needs its energy. So I drove the Wolves into their cave and helped myself to their people."

She wrapped her arms around the massive cocoon near her and purred, "We are very grateful, aren't we, my sweet?"

Nausea twisted Gideon's guts. "This is where the population has vanished. You killed them here."

Ja'a shrugged. "Fed them. Dropped them into the bowels. Rachna has served Mammon in famine for long enough; now it is time to worship in feasting. All I need is one more soul, a mighty soul, and the World Eater will awake."

The chrysalis growled. She soothed it, saying, "Not yet, dear one. You are not ready just yet."

Gideon leveled his sword at her. "Nor will it be ever. You die here."

Ja'a snarled at him then, her temper shifting from soothing to monster in a flash. "Shut up, shut up, *shut up!*" she screamed. "You're going to wake the baby!"

Unfazed, Gideon answered, "Your madness will no longer poison this world, Whore of Mammon."

A growling chuckle left the Consort's throat. "Really? You're alone, little man. Your gate is gone, and that traitor you summoned through it will soon be consumed by the mountain's children, and then both of you together will feed the eternal hunger of Rachna."

Gideon cocked his head and looked at her calmly. "Why do you assume my master can only open one gate?"

Ja'a reeled back as if punched in the gut, as a black blade screaming with disembodied horror skewered the air behind Gideon and slowly dragged down to the floor.

When the gash in reality ripped back, it manifested as a shadow hanging in the air. Darkness bled from the edges, dissipating like smoke as the gloom struggled to overcome its effect.

Again, a warrior emerged from the gate. His enemies saw him only as a darker shadow in the blackness. He did not erupt in bloodlust, as had Ursus. He did not roar in fury at his enemies or smash them in battlelust. On the contrary, he sheathed his blade as he walked.

Ashkelon drew even with his student, wrinkled his nose at the smell, and said to the gathered enemies, "Prepare yourselves. This is going to be unnecessarily loud."

Behind him, the gate erupted with fifty howling Wolves.

"*HYVA!*" Skald screamed, his eye wild, his warhammer held high above his head. At his side and just in front, as was his place as alpha, charged Heimdall Fangthane, the lord of Wolves. His great axe chopped into corrupted metal and flesh, and its keen edge split the first bloatguard like rotten fruit. Skald's hammer struck next, slamming another victim back and collapsing its ribs on its left side.

Arrows hissed through the air as Anya Helsdottyr snapped her bowstring back again and again, hurling darts into eye slits and armor joints. Before her, a tide of Wolves surged into the chamber, crushing against the bloatguard with howls of rage.

In the first seconds, the bloatguard gave ground, stumbling and overwhelmed by the sudden ferocity of the Wolf assault. Slowly, however, their unnatural resilience began to tell.

Skald's victim rose back to its feet, coughing up bloody phlegm, and swung its great cleaver into the mass of Wolves. Karden Stagbiter hurtled backwards, blood spilling from the canyon that nearly severed his body. Wolves found that it took four, five, sometimes seven or eight blows to put one of the servants of Mammon down, and even then, it was not a sure thing.

And then there were the spiders.

Olaf Axegrinder saw a shadow descend on him from above. He had only time to yell as one of the beasts slammed into him from above, trailing an elastic strand of webbing. Like a trap, the spider's legs enveloped the Wolf and the strand snapped taut, jerking the spider and its screaming prey up into the dark recesses of the ceiling, where soon even more horrible sounds assaulted their ears.

"Ware the sky!" Skald roared, and those Wolves not engaged on the front with the bloatguard turned their swords and axes high. The next spiders that sprang from above found no such easy prey, but fell upon upraised blades and in turn were fallen upon by the vengeful Wolves.

"Daughter!" Heimdall bellowed. "If you must be here, then make yourself useful!"

Anya ignored the jibe and shouted, "Heard, my jarl!"

Immediately, her arrows hissed up into the ceiling and spiders began to fall, their exoskeletons cracking on the stone floor.

Heimdall grinned. "That's my girl!"

He heaved another blow into the mutated man in front of him and managed to stagger it back a step. They had been fighting scant seconds, and already his arms burned from the effort it took to kill these things. Another Wolf toppled backwards, skull crushed by a bloatguard's mace.

"Boy!" the jarl thundered. "Whatever you're doing, do it now!"

GIDEON SAW INGVALD DIE. His body twitched forward, his soul longed to hurl himself into the shield wall and kill the verminous creature responsible for the man's death.

But he restrained. He glanced at Ashkelon, cool and impassive in the face of the chaos before them, and Ashkelon met his gaze evenly, unblinking. The cyan of his irises gleamed harshly in the gloom.

Well, apprentice? Do you have the discipline to hold to your own plan? Or shall we learn this lesson all over again? I am sure the Wolves have plenty more innocents who can die while you make up your mind.

Gideon let out a deep breath. "I can learn," he said.

Truly, a day of miracles.

Turning away from his master, Gideon focused on his target. The Wolves were here, sacrificing themselves in Gideon's gambit, for this one purpose.

The death of the Whore.

She hissed and spat behind her elite guard, her eyes weeping viscous yellow fluid as she clutched at the great chrysalis behind her. She had not expected such an assault, not in the heart of her sanctum.

Her eyes fixed on him, and Gideon charged.

He angled his impact at a point between two of the bloatguard. His teeth jolted as he hit, and Gideon exploded through the cultists' line, spilling over the two he struck. Tal flashed brightly as he lashed out, and the bloatguard collapsed on the ground, smoke seeping from the seams of their corroded iron.

A third Mammonite warrior lumbered forward, a great maul gripped in its hands. It raised its spiked mace high and brought it down with a gurgling bray. Gideon sidestepped the creature and lanced it through the gut, levering his blade around and eviscerating the bloatguard entirely.

It felt to its knees, trying to hold itself together, and Gideon hacked off its head with a precise execution blow before turning to face the true threat.

Ja'a swayed before him, her back to the throbbing chrysalis, her sulfurous eyes burning in the murky haze. The structure behind her pulsed rhythmically, like an enormous organ pumping blood into the mountain itself.

"How...how dare you! How *dare you!*" Ja'a shriek-sobbed, leveling a talon at him. "I just want to give him something wonderful! Why do you want to stop that? Why can't you just let me love him?"

Gideon rested his sword on the top of his shield, the point level with her throat. "This isn't love, demon. This is sickness."

He stepped forward, his body in balance, his spirit calm, nothing over-extended. "I am here to cure that sickness."

A guttural growl welled up from the Consort's throat, and she whipped around and slashed her finger claws down the chrysalis. Something within growled, a leonine snarl, and the dull shadow vanished in a frenzy of whipping limbs and blurred outlines. Gideon could see the faint shapes of segmented legs arching, stretching and reaching above.

"I know, precious, I know," Ja'a panted. "But he won't go away, and he's going to ruin my gift, so you have to come out *now*."

She tore at the chrysalis with her nails, and dark fluid gushed from the rents to spill on the ground with wet slaps. The thing growled again, the chamber echoing with its growing anger. The lake bubbled furiously, spitting acid into the air.

"*Hyva!*"

Gideon heard the battlecry behind him, and he shifted just enough to see Skald out of the corner of his eye bring his warhammer down on a bloatguard's skull and smash it down into its collarbone. Skald shouldered through the gap, dragging two other Wolves behind him before the hole closed.

Gideon did not take his eyes off of the draining chrysalis in front of him as Skald drew near him. The old Wolf smelled of sweat, dog and blood. The demon skulls and fetishes hung on his armor clinked and clacked together as he moved.

Gideon indicated the creature the Consort sought to free. "Is that the World Eater?"

Skald shrugged. "Is imprisoned beneath mountain. Is huge beyond belief. Is likely."

The one-eyed veteran shifted to take his warhammer in a two-handed grip. "But I am thinking I know exactly vhat this is."

He glanced sharply at Gideon, and his voice brooked no dissent. "You vil let me handle this vone, Titanbane."

Skald turned back as the rip in the chrysalis extended to the ceiling and the creature within stepped out. "This is matter for pack."

· · ·

THE MONSTER that emerged from Ja'a's chrysalis stood nine feet tall. The same yellow that burned in his mistress's eyes tinged his glistening skin. Cables of muscle wrapped around his body, hard as chitin. Twin mandibles sprouted around his mouth, further augmenting his inhumanity. Thirst burned in his blood, and hunger blazed hot in his bowels.

Feros arched his back to feel the strength of his ascended form, and eight segmented spears as long as he was tall unfurled behind him with the sound of cracking eggshells.

He opened his eyes and looked down on the puny men before him. The combat at the front of the cave stopped, as both Wolves and bloatguard looked upon the mighty prince Ja'a had wrought for her master. In particular, his eyes focused on the warrior with the burning sword, and they gleamed with recognition.

The Consort of Mammon wrapped her arms around his waist and ran her clawed hand down the hardened muscle of his leg. "Good morning, beautiful one," she cooed. "Did you have good dreams?"

His answer was a low, thrumming growl.

She swept behind him and snarled, "Kill them, blessed one, and give me their bodies for Mammon's feast."

Feros roared in acknowledgement and stepped forward, his bladed limbs angling towards the golden-haired warrior before him.

BEFORE GIDEON COULD MOVE, Skald stepped in front of him and barked, "That is far enough, vhelp!"

The authority in his voice made even the giant hesitate.

Skald sneered. "That is right, you know my voice, don't you, Feros? You know the voice of old Skald, who vatch over you from cub to man! You think I vould not recognize you? Pah! Now look at you."

He gestured with his warhammer. "Corrupted to core. How it breaks heart of old keeper to see vone of the Vulfen fallen so. To be creature of a madvoman, to jump at the snap of her fingers."

Feros snarled and lashed out with one limb. Skald batted it away with the haft of his hammer and stabbed a finger at the corrupted Wolf. "Oh, ho, is close to mark, I think. I know how you fall like this."

His words fell to a growl. "You are *veak*."

Feros screamed and lunged. Skald deflected two of the strikes, but the third speared his shoulder and threw him backwards. The other two Wolves surged forward, wordless shouts bellowing from their lungs.

Gideon made to engage, but Skald snarled at him, "Stay back, pup! Ve vill sanction our own!"

The first Wolf never got close. Feros impaled poor Saulog with a single limb, jerked him closer and tore into him in a flurry of stabbing limbs. With a twist, he hurled the body into the boiling froth behind him.

Garmon gave a great cry of grief and put his back into an axe blow that thudded into the meat of Feros's thigh to hitch there. The monstrous Wolf-spider grimaced, baring yellowed fangs, and kicked the Wolf hard, blasting the hapless warrior to rebound from the cave wall before he fell into the lake to dissolve and drown.

Feros turned back for Skald.

Blood gushed from the old Wolf's shoulder, but his teeth were clenched in a rigid snarl as he rose to meet the witch's spawn. "You never listened to stories. You mocked old Skald behind his back vhen he teach of the Almighty and His vays. You thought you knew better, and in arrogance you spurned the visdom of the old fathers. You plotted and schemed, never seeing the vorm of envy hollowing you out. Vhen the Whore took you, there vas no strength in you."

Feros's breath steamed the air before him, and he stepped slowly, menacingly, toward the wounded warrior.

Skald spat at him, standing straight, proud and defiant. "Vell, here is last story for you. Vone last story, and you never have to hear story from old Skald anymore. It is tale of young pup named Feros...."

Feros leapt forward, spider legs raised to tear Skald to pieces. Across the chamber, Anya screamed in denial as the horrifying spider-creature bore down on the bleeding old man.

. . .

GIDEON BLINKED. He did not know Skald could move that fast. The one-eyed Wolf lunged forward and to the side just before the tips of Fero's weapon-limbs could slam into his chest, and thundered his warhammer up under Feros's chin. The mutated Wolf's head snapped back from the heavy blow, fangs spraying from his ruined jaw.

Skald roared, "...who over-reached himself and left head open!"

The veteran stepped across and hammered his weapon into Feros's knee, pulping the joint with the force of the blow. He ducked a reprisal swipe of Feros's claws, his grey mane flying behind him, and splintered the other knee with another bone-cracking strike.

Feros collapsed onto his face, shrieking through broken teeth at the agony of his ruined knees hitting the unforgiving floor. He looked up at Skald, brackish tears leaking from his shattered face, the realization of death hitting him as hard as Skald's hammer.

A plea for mercy formed on Feros's lips, but all he could manage were snuffling moans.

Sorrow twisted Skald's features, but regret did not stay his hand. He hefted his warhammer onto his shoulder, and brought it down in one sharp, economic movement.

"*Nooooooo!*" the Consort shrieked. She collapsed to her knees, burying her face in her hands. "My baby! My gift!"

Ignoring the witch's cries, Skald stood over the broken body, shoulders slumped, watching the spider-limbs twitch in their last throes. At last, he muttered with a hitch in his voice, "I vish you had listened to stories, boy."

WHILE SKALD FOUGHT the demonically-corrupted Feros, Heimdall and his Wolves pushed the bloatguard into a tight knot, backs against the wall. Only five of the Consort's elite guard still stood, brandishing broken weapons at twenty of the invaders. The broken shells of spiders littered the ground behind them.

Anya's quiver hung slack and empty on her back. The jarl panted next to her, blinking through the blood that streamed down his face from a cut on his brow and feeling the sharp pain of a broken rib with every breath. The rest of his warriors were in little better shape.

Heimdall wiped his forearm across his brow, but only succeeded in mixing dirty sweat with the blood and stinging his own eyes. He grinned at the Wolf next to him, Sigvald. "A good fight, eh?"

Sigvald grinned back, wincing. "I would settle for an easy fight sometime. I am old."

Heimdall chuckled hoarsely and turned away, shouting, "Keep them penned, brothers. I do not want them getting away."

He saw his Greymane leave the young man with the witch, his shoulders stooped as if from a great weight.

Skald met him with a slight bow, and Heimdall clapped him on the shoulder. "Good work, keeper. And not bad, for a man of your age."

For once, Skald did not grumble at the slight. Tears tracked down his craggy cheeks, and his head remained bowed. "It vas my place, jarl. I failed him, so I put him down."

Wisely, Heimdall did not argue. He squeezed Skald's unhurt shoulder and said, "You are a good man, Skald."

With visible effort, Skald forced a measure of humor into his voice. "Ach, I am hurt man. Vhere is that svine she-volf that is never vhere she is told? Small-fang? Get over here and sew up old man before he bleeds to death in vile place."

As Skald limped toward Anya, grousing the whole way, Heimdall turned to Gideon. He jerked his head toward the weeping witch on the ground. "Finish her, so we can get out of here. This place stinks."

THE WOMAN LAY IN A HEAP, sobbing on the strange ground near the edge of the sulfur lake, her spidery limbs splayed about her. She cried into her elbow like a maid spurned by her lover. It sickened Gideon to see such behavior aped by such a horror.

Ja'a lifted her head as Gideon approached, her face blotchy from her tears. "Why would you kill him?" she whispered plaintively. "He was only a baby."

She gestured helplessly around her. "And now I don't have a strong soul to give my master what he wants, and he's going to be so disappointed in me. Nothing is working out!"

Gideon hesitated. "What? What do you mean?"

Ja'a pounded her fist into the wet stone. "My Wolf-spider! He was *supposed* to take the Slaughterlord and give him to the lake, but you killed him and now the World Eater can't wake up, because there's no soul strong en—"

The brimstone of the lake hissed behind her, and she sat up suddenly, swiping at her eyes with her forearm.

"That's it. It's all been a test, hasn't it? The final test of my love for him."

She stumbled to her feet and looked into Gideon's eyes, smiling girlishly through her tears. It chilled him to his core to see such ghoulish madness. "He...*needs* me. Me! I am the catalyst for his great work. I am the soul that my lord Mammon requires. I see it now!"

Strength filled the Consort's voice and she stepped back to the edge of the lake, the acids lapping at her feet. Ja'a spread her arms out wide, gazed above her at something only she could see, and whispered, "I will always love you. So much."

She fell back into the hissing sulfur and Ja'a, Consort of Mammon, was lost in a rush of fumes as the lake began to consume her.

At the entrance to the chamber, the bloatguard keened a low moan, their weapons sagging. One bull-rushed the circle of Wolves, managing with berserk fury to break its way out of the ring, only to run into a terrible shadow as it emerged from the tunnel. The bloatguard had an instant to see death coming before Ursus backhanded him and crushed him like an egg against the tunnel wall.

As the Wolves hacked down the last of the Mammonites, Ashkelon stepped up next to Gideon, looking down at the bubbling surface of the lake where Ja'a had vanished. He spoke.

"So, *again*, you have failed to kill her."

Gideon glanced at him, his brow furrowed in concentration. "She killed herself. That is almost the same thing."

Ashkelon shrugged. "Is it?"

His question seemed idle, which meant it was not.

Gideon sighed and looked around at the cavern. "No, she was behaving as though this was not finished yet. She thought she was accomplishing something at the end. Something is wrong here."

He looked at Ashkelon. "She said she needed a soul, a strong soul, to finish Mammon's great work. So the question is, if transforming Feros into the World Eater was not the great work, then what is?"

Ashkelon crossed his arms and waited, silent. Gideon felt his heart drop into his stomach. "Feros was not the World Eater."

Ashkelon shook his head. He gestured toward the sulfur before them. "Think it through."

Gideon turned back to the lake. "The Consort was dumping human captives into this lake. She said she was feeding it to awaken something."

His words came faster, more excited, as realization took hold. "She wept because we killed her chance for a strong soul. She grew Feros for this purpose, to feed Ursus to this lake."

Ashkelon crossed his arms. "So why would a lake need a strong soul?"

Gideon closed his eyes, feeling weary. "It doesn't."

Ashkelon raised an eyebrow, waiting. "Because?"

"Because it's not a lake."

The hissing suddenly died down, the light faded to a barely visible glow, and silence descended across the chamber.

It was then that they heard a distant wet sound, like a boot squishing slowly into muck.

SKALD COCKED HIS HEAD. "Vhat is that?" he asked.

They all stopped to listen. The sound did not stop, but went on and on, coming closer with each second. The Wolves glanced around, muttering amongst themselves.

Anya squinted and pointed into the dimness. "What are those?"

The walls were sprouting slimy bulbs the color of diseased pearl. Everywhere, the disgusting orbs blossomed, growing with unnatural speed. The ugly white bulbs started at the far end of the lake but spread toward them, covering the walls, reaching the ceiling, crawling along the floor.

Toward them.

DULL CRACKS of thunder sounded in the distance. They were not thunder.

"Oh, no," Gideon whispered, as he tracked his gaze across the chamber, taking in the blossoming globes, the thick mucus covering the walls that were not stone and never had been. "I am so stupid."

He looked at Ashkelon. "It's true, isn't it? The story is *true*."

Ashkelon gave him half a smile as the chamber juddered around them, and gestured back toward the flickering gateway. "Would you like to run now?"

17

KILLING GROUND

They ran. All of them.

Ashkelon's portal opened back into the throne room, dumping fetid air into the chamber. Wolves staggered through the billowing blackness of the sorcerous gate, dragging the bodies of their fallen comrades behind them. The looming mass of Ursus emerged behind them, carrying the limp bodies of no fewer than six warriors on his shoulders.

Anya burst through, almost tripping from the force with which she had been hurled. She caught herself and sprang back, but the figure of her father materialized before her, his broad shoulders barring her path. He shoved her back.

"No!" Anya shouted. "Gideon is still there! I need to cover him!"

Heimdall snapped at her, "Did you see what was hatching in there? How many? Trust me, a few broken arrows will not do the boy any good."

He swept the room with his gaze and barked, "I want every man, woman and child in this city in the Doom of Kings in twenty minutes. Grab as much food as you can: medicine, blankets, *everything.*"

Every man in the room waited for his next words. The jarl took a breath and ground out, "We are sealing the Doom. By the grace of the Almighty, what is coming will overlook us."

His voice dropped. "We'll figure out how to dig out later."

With a clap of thunder, the gate collapsed behind him.

THAT'S NOT NATURAL.

Gideon's mind raged at him to stop, to consider what was happening around him. The Tomb of Rachna shook around him, threatening to pitch him from his feet. The translucent orbs--

- eggs -

--twitched and throbbed around him with awful squeals. He could see legs flickering inside, thoraxes and abdomens bubbling and swelling at an obscene rate of growth.

Gideon and Ashkelon sprinted toward the gateway at the tunnel. Heimdall had just vanished into the blackness after throwing his daughter through the portal. Only Skald remained, his hammer in his fist, windmilling his other arm and shouting, "Now is not time to be stopping. Run!"

Gideon's pulse thundered in his ears as the chamber groaned around him. His shield clattered to the ground, but he kept a tight grip on Tal as he pumped his arms, willing more speed from his body. Beside him, Ashkelon dashed, his white hair flying behind him, the same half-smile on his face.

I've never seen him run before.

Behind them, Gideon heard the first of the Children of Rachna hatch. Thickets of legs burst from wet sacs, spilling heavy bodies onto the floor. Spiders exploded from the sulfurous lake, the acid running harmlessly from their armored frames. Screams of release filled the birthing chamber, as the freshly-born plague lifted their voices in blasphemous supplication.

They're worshipping something.

The master and the apprentice reached the gate. Skald grabbed hold of Gideon, and together they plunged into the billowing darkness.

Ashkelon's gate did not return them to Hammarfall, as expected. Instead, it spat them out onto a mesa of dead earth near the waking mountain, where the ground immediately rocked beneath them and cast them to their hands and knees. Waves of sound deafened them, pummeling the sense from their minds.

The dark mage stepped through the gate serenely, seeming to ride the bucking of the ground with a dancer's grace. His cyan eyes gleamed with a touch of amusement as Gideon struggled to find his footing.

As Gideon and Skald rose to their feet, Gideon caught his first glimpse of the transformation of the Crown of Rachna. Plumes of dirt and rock reached into the sky, forming columns miles high. Oceans of soil erupted from the ground, torn up and hurled like tidal waves. Even at this distance, dirt sprayed against their faces from the sheer force of the terrible birth on display.

The sound. By the Almighty, the *sound*. Explosions cracked one after the other in an unceasing cascade of sonic assault. The sound of millions of boulders and thousands of tons of rock slamming into one another in cataclysmic savagery thundered in Gideon's chest, more felt than heard. Skald's legs gave out entirely, unmanned as he was.

Not bothering to speak amidst the cacophony, Ashkelon held out a hand and pointed.

Struggling to maintain his footing as the ground quaked beneath him, Gideon saw the leg lift from the roiling torrent of destruction, and slam a claw down into the ruined earth.

Now Gideon's mind did shut down. It refused to acknowledge as real the scale of the thing.

That...that's not possible.

The leg looked like it had risen from one of the spurs of the mountain, breaking free and causing several dozen avalanches.

That made it nearly half a mile long.

The *leg*.

Skald knew he could not be heard, but prayers spilled from his lips anyway. There was no other reaction that could be had.

Seven more titanic appendages tore from the ancient stone bindings levied upon them and planted themselves on the ground. Vast rivers of soil and stone tumbled away, revealing pitted black chitin worn by unthinkable epochs. Mighty runes gleamed like azure lightning, etched upon the carapace by an unfathomable hand.

The octet of unreal limbs strained at these magical bindings, flexed, then lifted.

This explosion made the previous explosions sound like carnival firecrackers. The Crown of Rachna, inviolate for centuries, shattered into a billion fragments of shrapnel, billowing into the atmosphere like a newborn cloud. A shockwave of fortress-breaking force blasted from the ruined prison, scouring and obliterating everything in its path.

Something vast rose from the onslaught of destruction, and the world cracked beneath its weight.

Gideon saw its head, festooned with eyes the size of palaces. Its maw yawned open, mandibles like towers spreading wide.

After taking its first breath of free air after millennia of captivity, the World Eater, Rachna the Undying, raised its voice in blasphemous triumph and screamed at the poisoned sky.

The power of its cry tore the top yard of topsoil off of the ground like a carpet being ripped off of a floor. In the fraction of a second before the wall of sound hit Gideon and flensed him apart, he saw Ashkelon clench his fist, and the world vanished into darkness.

IN ONE OF the gate towers of Hammarfall, Anya slapped a woven lid onto a basket of smoked herring and handed it to a hollow-eyed serf. "There. That's the last of it. Put it with the others."

The serf hefted the basket with a curt nod and hurried to the stone stairs. Beneath Anya, men and women rushed about in the city, carrying everything they could find into the Doom of Kings to answer their jarl's command.

Heimdall had not spoken of what they had seen, and his warriors followed his example. The serfs bustled about, obeying their liege lord on faith alone. Jarl Fangthane spared his people the staggering truth of the death to come.

Where is Gideon?

He had not come through the gate before it closed, or Skald. Anya could not care less about the dark master, but she was sure he had something to do with it.

Trying to clear her mind of speculation on Gideon and Skald's fate, Anya reached for a stack of blankets. She stopped suddenly when the wind changed. It gusted into her face, sweeping her hair back. The sound of twigs snapping in the distance by the hundreds reached her ears.

She glanced outside, curious.

Her eyes widened as she saw the trees of the forest snapping in half as a wall of dust careened toward the city. Thinking faster than she ever had in her life, Anya whirled around and shouted with all of her might, *"Ware the sky!"*

Ingrained into their upbringing was the warning against raiders' arrows. Brigands might strike at any time, and every Wolf child was trained to drop to the earth immediately upon that command.

As one, the people of Hammarfall collapsed to their stomachs, and Anya's call saved hundreds.

The great wind slammed into the walls of Hammarfall and broke over it. Small children were carried bodily into the air, snatched back by attentive adults nearby. The warriors spread their arms across as many of the elderly and frail as possible, anchoring them to the ground with their weight.

Within the gate tower, Anya was spared the worst of the gale, but the men on the walls were blown off like straw in a hurricane. They soared, screaming, smashing into the edifices of Hammarfall or the unforgiving side of the mountain.

The blast of wind lasted only a few seconds, then died down to nothing.

Cautiously, the people of Hammarfall rose to their feet. Several shouts rang out, inquiries, cries for help, some sobbing at this new horror.

It all died down when they heard the distant scream.

In the courtyard, a tear opened ten feet up in the air and dumped three men into the midst of the killing ground before the Doom of the Kings of Hammarfall.

Ashkelon landed lightly as a cat, poised and controlled. Gideon landed heavier, turning his ungainly tumble into a roll that put him on his feet.

Skald crashed into a cart of foodstuffs, spilling root vegetables and beans over the slate floor of the Doom. His surprised curses rang out over the city, all the louder for the sudden silence.

Rachna's birth cry still sounded in the distance. Even here, miles away from the desolate Crown, Mammon's greatest creation could be heard, roaring its intent to devour all things.

Gideon looked around, his mind racing with almost panic. His eyes raced over the battlements of Hammarfall, assessing, rejecting, re-assessing. Every evaluation told him the same thing: there was no stopping the apocalypse to come.

He turned to Ashkelon, but his master was already moving down the stairs of the Doom. The serfs instinctively made way for the Onyx Mage, shrinking back from the darkness that exuded from his soul.

Gideon rushed after him. "What do we do?"

Ashkelon barked a harsh laugh, but did not break his stride. "Do? We leave, of course. This land is finished. It belongs to that thing now."

Gideon blinked. "Wait. We're giving up? We're *leaving?*"

The sorcerer stopped suddenly, and Gideon barely managed to keep from crashing into him. His master turned to consider him with a look of mild surprise. "It is not giving up, apprentice. You *lost.*"

Ashkelon's voice was almost compassionate as he elaborated. "You failed to kill the Consort, *again*, I might add, and as a result, her ultimate goal has been achieved. A creature of doom devised by demons to eradicate all human life has been unleashed on this world. You could throw a hundred enchanted blades at it; it will not feel them.

You could have all the courage and brotherhood in the world, and you would still die. Your only hope to stop something called 'World Eater' was to prevent its awakening in the first place."

He turned back to the gate and strode away, heedless of the serfs in his path. Ashkelon called over his shoulder, "I am not angered by your failure, apprentice. Some lessons truly must be learned the hard way. I trust the decimation of these peasants will linger in your memory and inspire you to future successes."

Ashkelon lifted a black gauntlet and beckoned without looking at Gideon. "Come. You have learned what you will in this place. It is time to continue your training elsewhere while the creature is feasting here, in the hopes that you may destroy it in the future."

"No."

GIDEON'S MASTER HALTED. All Gideon could see of him was his bleached white hair, the merciless black of his darkmail.

Ashkelon did not turn to face him. Instead, slowly, with perfect enunciation, he growled, "What?"

Gideon stood with his feet spread, burning blade in his fist. His jaw was set, his eyes afire with anger.

The young man spoke just as slowly, ensuring his master heard every word clearly. "I said, no. I am not leaving."

Now Ashkelon pivoted to eye his student with the sharp ice of his glare. "I did not leave room for refusal, *student*. Come, before my patience thins, my mercy evaporates and I force you to watch the fiend drink every man, woman and child in this backwater dry in the hope that you *learn your lessons.*"

Anger surged in Gideon with such force that his pulse pounded. His breath hissed between his grinding teeth, and his blade ignited with a dull sizzle.

Careful, young knight.

Gemelte's voice broke on Gideon's rage like surf upon rocks. *Consider what you say.*

Gideon ignored the phantom as he met Ashkelon's cold eyes.

Under the weight of that unholy stare, Gideon clenched his jaw and prayed for strength. "I'm not going anywhere."

Ashkelon grunted. "Is this some resurgence of heroic hormones I am unaware of?"

Gideon shook his head. "I can't leave them, Ashkelon. It is against everything I am."

Shaking his head slightly, Ashkelon replied, "Then you are a fool. Did you not see the creature that even now stalks this world? The angels themselves struggled to bind Mammon's creation. These vermin will be reaped like corn before the sickle."

Ashkelon turned from Gideon, gazing out of the gate to the south. "It will take eight hours of hard riding to escape the Spiderlands. Were it not for the fact that there are thousands of people here to occupy the Eater of Worlds, we would not make such an escape. Give thanks to your God for such a window."

Gideon spread his hands wide. "Then when am I to be a hero? When does that magically happen? When will you snap your fingers and proclaim me ready to be the world's light so that you can sate your own morbid desire for vindication?"

Ashkelon snapped his arm out, his finger pointing unerringly at Gideon as he retorted, "It will happen when I see that you are ready. Since you seem eager to sacrifice yourself for any and every misbegotten cretin that crosses our path, I have much work to do yet."

"I said no, Ashkelon. I will not sacrifice these good people to save my own skin."

Ashkelon stared at him for a tense moment, then did the last thing Gideon expected. He laughed, the sound cold and hard, his gaze never breaking from Gideon. "You think these people good? That they are worth sacrificing your life for?"

An armored fist snaked out and grabbed the nape of a shouting man's tunic. Without looking at him, Ashkelon hauled the man around to face Gideon and stabbed a finger in the serf's face. "Just last night, this man lied to his wife that it was his turn to stand watch so he could play dice and rut with his neighbor's wife. Would you die for *him?*"

Ashkelon hurled the man aside. Still glaring at Gideon, Ashkelon gestured toward a crying woman who stumbled past. "Or her? Who has been selling her body or stealing from every man, woman and child for any pathetic piece of silver that she can scavenge so she can satisfy her addiction to the lotus root? Is *she* worth your life?

Encompassing the village with his arm, Ashkelon shouted, "You would cast aside your life and the possibility of saving countless *thousands* of these miscreants as opposed to this handful, out of a sense of guilt and compassion when you see a bit of fear, blood and soil on their faces? Scant hours ago, you would have condemned their vices with the same passion with which you now defend them!"

Gideon gritted his teeth. "They are people, Ashkelon. *Lives.*"

Ashkelon blew his breath out in contempt. "Yes, Gideon, they are. Delicious lives that will buy time for you to escape, survive to continue your training and return to avenge them."

Gideon shook his head in angry wonder. "You truly feel nothing for these people, do you? Your heart is really as scorched and dark as you appear."

Ashkelon turned away. "Count yourself lucky that it is so. I have learned the value of sacrifice. There is no room in this world for mercy, compassion or kindness. Your enemies will laugh in your face as you quote your platitudes."

"Like you?"

Turning on his heel, Ashkelon whirled to face Gideon. "Do you really think that these people are so different from the Venans? Look at them. They *despise* each other. They despise you and the goodness they see in you. They suckle off of each other's misery like ticks at a vein, and their only solace comes from the phrase, 'I am not as bad as he'. Let me guess: a fair maiden fell into your arms and begged you to save her and her family while blinking limpid wet eyes? Or an old man declared you a paragon of virtue, a throwback to older days and values?"

Gideon said nothing.

Ashkelon snorted. "Did you ever stop to think about who those people really are? I have seen their kind, borne witness to their sins. I have passed among them as a shadow, studying the disease that infects all of humanity. I saw a lover talk her betrothed into lying about his age to go to war to save her family and home, and when he returned, it was only to discover that she wanted him out of the way to wed his rich coward of a friend who feigned sickness to shirk his duty."

The sorcerer stood so close to Gideon now, the cold light from his eyes seared Gideon's cheeks as he hissed, "Or perhaps a man you learned to call father, who espoused the higher virtues of duty, loyalty and discipline, who manipulated and groomed you as a child only to sell you as a slave for a high price to a prince with a sadistic taste for young boys, who, after he grew tired of making sport, sent you to the mines to die, forgotten and alone."

"The sentiments you feel now merely make you vulnerable to what these people are. I have destroyed empires, scorched continents and slain hundreds of self-proclaimed champions of virtue because they all held at their root, at their heart, the same rancid cancer as the warlocks they decry. They will say whatever they have to, they will do whatever they need to, to ensnare you and make you believe that you *should* sacrifice yourself for them, that it is *right* to stand in their place, so that they can continue their unending rape of humanity in the name of *honor*!"

Ashkelon was almost panting at the end of his tirade. His breath sucked between his teeth as he stood nose to nose with his apprentice, his unblinking stare daring him to say something, anything, to disprove him.

Gideon did not disappoint him. The young man did not take a step back when Death looked him in the eye. He did not flinch from the searing cold of his master's accusing gaze. He did not even hesitate. Instead, his green eyes flaring with captured fire, Gideon clenched his jaw and punched a finger into Ashkelon's breastplate.

"You...are *such* a hypocrite."

Silence fell at his words. The serfs and Wolves around them held their breath, disbelieving their ears. Even old Skald hung his head and whispered, "Oh, lad."

Gemelte flashed into Gideon's line of sight, just behind Ashkelon. He was on his feet, shaking his head wildly.

Gideon ignored them all. His eyes stayed locked on Ashkelon's, matching the dark lord's rage with his own. "You think yourself above humanity, that somehow your suffering has separated you from us stinking cattle and given you secret insight."

The soldier sneered and tapped his chest. "Yet you constantly sermonize about the need for heroes of the Light. You've searched for *years* to find one worthy of respect, and when you failed, you tried to make one of your own. Do you know what that tells me?"

"No, apprentice," Ashkelon rasped dangerously. "Tell me."

Gideon pushed his finger into Ashkelon, staggering him back a step. He advanced so that he loomed over the sorcerer. "You want a hero as much as we do. You, the world-ending psychopath lost to the Everlasting Dark, want to be saved as much as any common sinner here."

Gideon, no! Stop!

Gemelte's projections failed to hold Gideon back in the slightest. He shoved Ashkelon again, harder this time. "You scorn these people for their sins, but you know in your empty soul that you are as lost as they are. Your entire life, you have felt nothing but hatred and spite, and it has hollowed you out, leaving you a charred husk devoid of anything resembling humanity."

Gideon gestured behind him, toward the coming devastation. "You could save them all, couldn't you? The World Eater cannot pose much challenge to *you*, can it?"

Ashkelon sneered, "You do not want my intervention here, apprentice."

Gideon laughed sarcastically, "Of course not. Why would I?"

He shoved again, but Ashkelon slapped the arm away with a low snarl. "Stop that."

Gideon ignored him, too. "*You* are the failure. You murdered your entire race in the name of some twisted moral high ground, and it has left you confused and broken, you vile, despicable, murderous coward."

Gideon!

Ashkelon's eyes flared white hot even as his face darkened. "Careful, student," he hissed.

Gideon spat on the ground next to Ashkelon. "And now you're going to leave them. You will judge these people for their sins, and leave them to the fate the demons have set for them. These helpless, powerless people will die in their caves because you, the only one with any power at all to save them, will leave them."

Gideon ground out his next words through gritted teeth, stabbing every word into Ashkelon's chest with his finger. "Just like *he*…"

Stab.

"Left."

Stab.

"*You.*"

With a crack like thunder, darkness blazed like a beacon from Ashkelon, in defiance of natural laws. It tore through the unwilling audience, freezing their hearts in their chests and filling their minds with unadulterated horrors. The essence of nightmare itself seized on the Wolves with eager claws, and sank its fangs deep into their souls.

For his part, Gideon could not move. He suffered in an invisible grip of pure force that crushed him like a vise, and he could only stand paralyzed in the sorcerer's might, helpless against his master's wrath.

And suffer he did.

As though someone had torn open a floodgate in Ashkelon's soul, waves of hate, rage, despair and pain poured into Gideon's mind like a river down a channel. The depth of the guilt, the shocking *anguish*, stole his breath away and seized his heart in an ironclad fist. Ashkelon held nothing back, allowing centuries of rancid hate to pour from him and overwhelm Gideon in its entirety.

The warrior wanted to stop it. If he could have moved, he would have begged for it to stop.

Gideon could barely hear Gemelte over the howling black wind tearing from Ashkelon's soul. The ghost fell to a seat on the stone stairs, his face slack with horror. *Oh, Gideon…what have you done?*

Ashkelon carefully took hold of Gideon's finger in his chest and pushed it away, all the while keeping his eyes locked with Gideon's. His next words were not gentle, exactly, but rather something malevolent aping gentleness. It was the whisper of a tender lover, undergirded by the guttural growl of a devil.

"You want them saved?"

The night filled with ghastly shrieks as Ashkelon drew Acherlith from its sheath.

"Very well. *Saved,* they shall be."

ASHKELON DRAGGED his paralyzed student outside of the city by his foot and threw him sprawling on his hands and knees into the desolate plain before Hammarfall.

Before the birth of Rachna, a great forest had covered the land, but the World' Eater's cry had scoured the land clean of life both plant and animals. Only broken trunks and stumps now dotted the ravaged landscape.

Ashkelon's breaths came in ragged snarls. Gideon felt himself snatched by an invisible hand and forced to his feet to face the north.

Gideon tried to turn his head away, but Ashkelon hissed, "Oh, no, apprentice. You *earned* this."

Darkness slithered along his forehead like a serpent, wrenching his head around and ensuring he had an excellent view of the broken forest. Gideon strained against the magical bonds, but they held him tightly.

Ashkelon turned from him to face the north. "Try to close your eyes, and I swear to you, I will ram something under your eyelids, as well."

That made him stop struggling.

As Gideon watched, the horizon moved.

SKALD GREYMANE STEPPED from the protection of the walls of Hammarfall. As the dark stranger dragged Gideon through the streets toward the oncoming apocalypse, Heimdall ordered his people to hide within the Doom. No one save the Greymane gainsaid him. Even Anya Helsdottyr stepped within the stone gateway, weapons in hand. Ursus sealed the doorway by piling rocks, sealing them within.

Alone of his people, Skald disobeyed. It was his duty to witness the great events of the Vulfen and tell the stories. No jarl could prevent him. No jarl had the authority to do so.

Skald would witness, and he would tell.

He limped through the broken ground, trampled by the thousands of Venans that had besieged the city a day before. From outside the walls, he could see the battering the great walls of Hammarfall had taken, as dozens of tree trunks and the bodies of the fallen slammed into the stone after the shockwave of the World's Eater's release.

Above, thunder rumbled, and his sharp ears picked out the sound of distant rain. By the feel of the wind, he could tell it would be here soon.

Before him, Gideon knelt on all fours, his sword hanging on his back. His head remained locked forward, forced to behold his master.

The Dark One walked into the devastation of the forest, away from Hammarfall and his student, head bowed, hand clenched around the hilt of his screaming sword. His white hair hung lank and heavy down his back and the sides of his face.

Beyond him, the world's end.

Skald's breath caught in his throat.

The ancient Wolf had seen many battles in his time, epic clashes of men, beasts and demons that saw thousands dead in minutes. He had witnessed great keeps stormed by titanic armies, with great holes punched through their ranks by arcane sorcery and ingenious mechanisms.

Never had he seen anything like the Children of Rachna.

The skin of the world itself crawled. If every grain of sand sprouted eight legs and crept from its place, it might have rivaled the size of the swarm racing toward Hammarfall. It sounded like the thunder of a cavalry charge's hooves, but mixed with the sticky *tic-tic-tic* of segmented legs picking along a ceiling beam.

Nor did they come from the ground alone.

Lightning slashed through the sky in the distance, and the flashes revealed only part of the mind-shattering silhouette of Rachna. The avatar of the God of Hunger gobbled up the horizon with each illuminating flash, its legs stretching as far as Skald could see. The air around it was filled with thousands, perhaps millions, of white sacs, gently floating through the air on the wind like flakes of snow.

Beneath each delicate sail, a spider the size of a mountain lion dangled, limbs limp and spindly, blown toward the lands of men by the will of its enormous parent.

The sky itself hung heavy with Rachna's spawn. The ground teemed with it. With every moment, the World Eater took another step toward Hammarfall, eating up miles of territory. The earth shook as its weight sank into it.

Into this madness, this cataclysm unimaginable by human minds, Skald watched Ashkelon, the son of darkness, walk.

THE LAND DIED beneath his tread. The earth greyed and blackened, spreading like a shadow around Ashkelon as he stalked forward. Countless screams rode upon the wind like a hymn of death sung by Acherlith's voice, and the blade bled oily smoke into the land with every step.

Gideon could hear Ashkelon intoning a strange litany as he walked. His voice projected by sorcerous intent into Gideon's mind.

Athernon. Velas. Torian. Bartathus. Atrathius. Orthos. Pallas. Gildar.

The rain began as a gentle pattering around him, plucking at the dying ground with invisible fingers. It slowly intensified to a deluge, drenching Ashkelon entirely. Beneath the mess of his soaked white hair, eyes like newborn stars began to burn.

Thousands of spiders pounded toward him, mandibles frothing in terrible fervor. A hundred yards separated them from the lone sorcerer.

Eltrar. Quinan. Zebulon. Hayth. Magdalen. Nicalor. Bah'rat.

Skald squinted. Something was moving in the widening circle of blackened earth.

"Vhat is that?"

Gideon closed his eyes as he finally understood the long nights of listening to Ashkelon mutter beneath his breath. Watching the sorcerer stare at his screaming sword, searching it for something.

They are names.

Gideon flicked his gaze over to where Gemelte knelt on the ground, staring after the Onyxian in the distance.

The words he speaks. They are names.

"Names? What names?"

Gemelte looked tired. Parts of his skin flickered between the craggy skin of an old man, and the smoothness of youth. As if he no longer wanted to put the effort to the illusion.

At the Battle of the Great Pyramid, two million and eight hundred thousand soldiers of the kingdoms of Avalon gathered together to fight the Everlasting Dark.

Shadowy hands reached up from the ground and pulled dark figures bleeding smoke to their feet. Screams emerged from their gaping mouths, echoing the siren shriek of Acherlith, and they fell in behind Ashkelon as he advanced toward the legions of Hell.

Eskelion. Vertor. Talion. Istraylar. Paras. Myla. Heredor. Galas.

Gemelte shook his head in wonder. *And he remembers all of them.*

Skald's mouth fell open as an immense army of wraiths rose from the dying ground of Hammarfall. They started to run, flowing across the broken earth with inhuman speed.

Gemelte glanced at Gideon.

Do you still believe there are no souls in Acherlith?

THE FIRST SPIDER TO die was a mammoth creature of ochre and tan, streaked with black stripes. Its legs stretched out ten feet, and it devoured the ground as it dashed forward, leaping with a screech at its black-clad victim.

Ashkelon held up his sword, pointed it at the creature, and time froze.

Every spider in the horde hung suspended in mid-stride, legs extended, mouths sobbing with poisonous drool.

The fingers of Ashkelon's left gauntlet sparked. It was visible from the Doom of Hammarfall, a sudden flash in the darkness. It tracked across Ashkelon's forearm, coruscated across the mage's darkmail and lit his teeth with contrails of blue-white energy. Pebbles and bones lifted from the earth around him in a ten-yard-wide circle as gravity itself was defeated by the mage's power. The blackness on the ground spread even further as power built within him.

With a growl that built to a shout, Ashkelon thrust his hand into the air and cast a bolt of lightning into the storm-tossed sky like a mighty whip. With a snarl, he ripped it back down, and it descended with a thousand vengeful sisters. The world exploded.

Gideon found himself free to move just before the sheets of light struck. Even ducking away, eyes closed and shielded by his hands, the light of the blast nearly blinded him. He heard Skald curse just before the bow shock of the sound of a thousand claps of thunder blasted all hearing from his ears.

The entire leading edge of the Children of Rachna vanished in blue-white light. Spiders exploded as crooked arcs of savage energy blew them apart in grisly chunks of chitin and slime. The demons died in their thousands, completely obliterated by obscene power. Shrapnel whickered through the air and sliced into the following ranks, spilling hundreds more onto their faces, bleeding white ichor from a million wounds.

Congratulations, Gideon. You are about to witness the Onyxian kill everything for the second time.

Gideon grimaced in the face of the winds tearing at his frame, and shouted back, "That's a good thing right now!"

Gemelte shook his head. *You've never seen everything killed before. It is never a good thing.*

While the Children of Rachna reeled, the dead of Avalon struck, screaming like banshees.

Like the flickering shadows of raptors, they struck through the carcasses of the first victims. The wounded ranks of spiders had time enough to see a million shrieking shadows leap toward them. Geysers of yellow fluid jetted up from the impact, creating a fountain of demonic gore a mile long.

Nor were the soldiers of the Dark confined to the ground. Thousands of them launched from the ground with inhuman strength, springing into the air to drag down the floating spiders. The creatures shrieked and stabbed with their legs, but the shadows continued to tear into them, mauling them as they plummeted to crack open on the unforgiving ground.

Somehow, through the driving rain, the spots in his vision, the chaos of the destruction Ashkelon had unleashed, Gideon found his master.

His sword no longer screamed as it looped around Ashkelon's body in lethal arcs. Its occupants now fought alongside their dread lord, still casting their final cries to any who would listen.

A howl still filled Gideon's thoughts, however. An interminable cry of rage and despair bellowed in his mind, and Gideon knew the voice.

The last scream of the void blade belonged to its master. It dragged on and on, fading, building, fading again, but never ending. On the surface, it was the roar of a dark champion, steeped in hate and exultant in power. It fell now from Ashkelon's lips as the sorcerer hacked back and forth, a dread lord surrounded by an army of howling shadows.

But Gideon could hear the second cry, buried deep beneath the first. It was the muffled panic of a little boy, alone, forgotten in a cage, desperately sobbing because he was afraid of the Dark.

Gideon's lips moved soundlessly. *I am so sorry.*

The blood-drenched nightmare hesitated for an instant, then pure malice filled Gideon's mind, blanking out the sounds of the massacre before him.

Not as sorry as they are. All of them.

THE HORDE of spiders had no answer to the mass of shadows clawing at them. Their limbs scythed vainly through empty air, clutching at flitting shadows that darted back to punch through their armor. Spiders were dragged down by the dozen and cracked open like cloves of garlic, their screeches drowned out by the constant screaming of the dead.

The Children of Rachna melted away, streaming back to the shadow cast by their monstrous god.

Ashkelon stood at the front of his army, only visible among shadows through the shocking white of his hair against a field of roiling blackness. He did not pursue the broken mob of demons.

You need to stop him, Gideon.

Gideon turned to look at Gemelte. "He's destroying them. Why would I want to stop him?"

Look at the ground, you fool.

As instructed, Gideon glanced toward the earth. The blackness still spread throughout the soil, darkening and deadening it. It radiated out from Ashkelon, like he served as the epicenter for a shockwave.

The blackness seeped toward them, scant feet from the trio. Skald stepped forward, took a knee and scooped a handful of the black earth up. Almost immediately, he wrenched his hand back as if burned and backed away.

"The ground…it feels like Death."

Sword, Gideon.

The creeping death reached for Gideon, and obeying the revenant's command, Gideon stabbed the blade of Tal into the ground just before the edge of the shadow. The silver edge flared brightly, and the shadow recoiled. It flowed around the trio, repelled by the sword's light, and continued its creeping advance.

Toward Hammarfall.

Gideon sucked in a breath. "Spirit? What happens if that reaches the city?"

Skald pivoted to look at him curiously at the question, but did not interrupt.

With a deep sigh, Gemelte answered. *Ashkelon does not cast magic as most casters do. He wrenches power from the universe with his sheer force of will and shapes it with his pain, his hatred. It has a lasting effect on the world.*

The revenant met Gideon's gaze. *The last time I saw Ashkelon expend this much energy, he fought an army of millions. I estimate half of them dropped and died due to this plague of shadow draining them of their essence.*

Gideon's eyes widened, and his heart began to thunder in his chest. "You're saying that if he keeps fighting the World Eater...?"

Gemelte nodded, his eyes closing wearily. *The darkness will spread and drain everyone in the city. You will have saved no one.*

In the distance, Gideon saw his master turn, his eyes shining like sapphires and crackling with lightning. Coils of energy sizzled around his gauntlets, snapping around the hilt of Acherlith. Beyond him, the titanic vastness of the demon loomed into the sky.

Dread flushed through Gideon's soul. "If Ashkelon kills the World Eater, everyone dies. If he holds back, everyone dies."

Gemelte hung his head. *I tried to warn you. Ashkelon is no savior. He never has been.*

THE CARPET of monsters fled back to the shadow of their parent, and Rachna itself now closed with the diminutive being that threatened its progeny. Ashkelon stabbed his blade into the desiccated ground, and as suddenly as they had appeared, the army of shadows dissolved, pouring back into the blade in a torrent of shrieks, leaving Ashkelon alone in a sea of broken shells and jutting limbs.

He extended a hand, and with a crack, the earth rose beneath Ashkelon, lifting him from the wreckage on a platform of stone and elevating him to a point below the World Eater's face.

Rachna loomed over him, a creature capable of killing cities by itself, overrunning empires. The World Eater blocked out the sky, its legs stretching farther than Gideon's eyes could take in.

Its children gathered by its feet, regrouping, reforming, reenergizing.

Ashkelon looked down on them, then lifted his searing gaze to

Rachna's eye clusters, a sneer on his face, lightning dancing between his fingers.

Is that all?

Rachna roared at the tiny black thorn before it, and Gideon and Skald recoiled from the volume of the horrifying screech. Ashkelon's hair and robe blew back from the force of the cry, but he stood firm in the face of the creature's wrath.

From this distance, waterfalls seemed to flow from Rachna's megalithic carapace. They fell from its sides, along its legs, from its eyes like tears. Like a dread flood, thousands of newborn spiders joined the brood already on the ground. The swarm swelled and blossomed, til it appeared that no spiders had died at all.

The World Eater roared once more, and its children screamed with it.

A chuckle resonated in Gideon's thoughts.

Come, then. Yours are not the only children I have murdered.

THE SPIDER HORDES flowed toward the dark sorcerer, shrieking their unthinking hate. Ashkelon hated them right back.

Through his link to the mage, Gideon could feel bursts of emotion, like sun flares, every time Ashkelon struck. It was though Ashkelon drew on an endless well of anger, forever refilled from the injustice of the world around him, and manifested that rage in gouts of flame, blasts of lightning, blades of ice and other elemental assaults.

Looking behind him, Gideon saw that the dead ground now reached the gates of Hammarfall. Only a few hundred yards separated the life-sucking aura from the innocents of Hammarfall.

What do I do?

Before him, Ashkelon hurled twin fireballs onto his right flank, and hundreds of charging spiders plunged screaming into a new lake of fire. Lightning slashed down from the sky and annihilated a clutch of demons crawling up the ridge the sorcerer stood upon. Hail and sleet pounded the rocks, making them too slippery to climb, pitching opportunistic spiders back into their companions to shatter into freezing shards.

Fully a quarter of the newborn swarm lay dead at Ashkelon's feet in moments, and the Spider Lord had had enough.

Rachna lunged forward, a mountain of chitin and mouth crashing toward the tiny sorcerer on his little plateau. A demonic cliff accelerated forward, its maw opening wide to swallow the killer before it.

Ashkelon did not flinch back. Instead, he lifted a hand and beckoned behind him.

From the clouds beyond Hammarfall, an immense bolt of lightning was born. It ignited with a flash as a sky-borne river of energy, twisting toward the ground but never striking, winding like a snake. Ashkelon stiffened his hand to a claw and twisted, and the sizzling shaft obeyed.

Like a boxer's uppercut looping under an opponent's chin, the flickering stream of energy arced up under Rachna's mouth and detonated like a shipful of black powder. The blast wave crushed every one of its spawn for five hundred yards, and the force of the impact actually lifted it from its two forelegs. The impact halted its lunge in its tracks and the World Eater's mandibles slammed shut with a crash.

The surviving horde shrieked as one as their god staggered from the blow.

That's the problem with you creations of the exiles.

Ashkelon's voice growled through Gideon's mind. *You share your masters' hubris in that you think you own us.*

He reached up to the sky and clutched something Gideon could not see.

You falsely assume that sin relegates us to your dominion, that as the mightiest of the Fallen races of men and angels, you have free rein to exercise your will in this darkened world.

Ashkelon clenched his dark gauntlet into a cruel fist and pulled back, as Gideon heard his heart snarl, *You are mistaken.*

A dull roar filled the sky, one Gideon had heard before, and he looked toward the horizon, knowing what he would see.

· · ·

THE CACOPHONY BEGGARED BELIEF.

Anya and her father stood in the doorway of the Doom, holding onto the stone as they watched the monstrous battle outside. Ursus's pile had collapsed almost immediately with the shaking of the earth. Her mouth hung open as a mighty bolt of lightning slashed through the sky and blasted the colossal beast like a backhanded slap across the face. The rain pelted down around them, smacking the stone of the courtyard with fat droplets.

She noticed something. As the lightning faded and the thunder roared, she saw the rock of the outer wall turn black.

"Papa?"

Heimdall looked at her. "Aye?"

She pointed at a strange darkness oozing across the threshold of the gate. It crept toward them, surging forward with every flash of lightning.

"What is that?"

The roar of a comet slashing through the sky drowned out his answer, and the darkness leapt forward, swallowing everything up to the courtyard of the Doom.

GIDEON SAW Rachna actually lift its body to look up, just before the molten void-rock smashed into its thorax like a slap from the hand of God.

The meteor impact buckled its legs and crushed it to the ground. Every one of its children died, smashed by Rachna's fall, scorched to a crisp by the hellish heat or pulped by the force of the strike, their bodies hurled away in waves of burning chitin.

Gideon's mouth dropped open at the sight of the mythical demon kneeling before his master. Ashkelon spread his arms wide and looked down onto the keening World Eater, struggling to find its feet.

The World Eater roared again, but the sound lacked its fury from before. Gideon saw hundreds of thousands of pale bulbs sprout across its carapace as Rachna began to grow another brood, desperate to replenish its children.

Ashkelon cocked his head, his eyes wild and aflame with sapphire heat. *There should, I believe, be a great gulf fixed between thee and me.*

Gemelte gripped Gideon's shoulder. *You need to stop this. Now!*

And as Ashkelon tore open a doorway to Hell, Gemelte showed him why.

"BACK!" Heimdall shouted. "All of you, back away from the door!"

The survivors of Hammarfall pushed and stumbled their way back into the Doom, pressing against the stone of the far wall. Cries of distress rose from the rear as those nearest the wall found themselves crushed against it.

The shadow slithered inside, spilling across the threshold of the Doom with terrible inevitability. From this distance, it felt cold, and nameless dread fell upon every man and woman within.

A serf named Telin could take no more.

"We have to get out!"

"No!" Heimdall roared, but it was too late.

With a burst of terror-fueled courage, Telin dashed toward the door of the Doom. As soon as the sole of his foot touched the blackness invading the cave, he stumbled and fell onto his face. Gasping, he rolled over onto his stomach and looked back toward his jarl.

Black tendrils reached up from the floor like the fronds of seaweed, clutching at his face and body. Telin could only make a slow wheeze as his skin paled to deathly white, and he crumbled to ash, pulled into the darkness without a trace.

FOR HUNDREDS of yards on either side of the prostrate monster, the earth split open with a cracking groan. The ground fell away before Rachna's feet with a roar as the skin of the world peeled back from Ashkelon, leaving the dark sorcerer standing alone on his precipice of stone over a canyon lit by deep infernos. Blasts of heat gusted from the pit as towers of steam rose to the rain-slashed sky, released from underground reservoirs falling into the superheated blood of Sinai.

The World Eater backpedaled. Its claws dug into the earth, desperately propelling it backwards as the chasm opened before it. Avalanches of topsoil and rock tumbled into the darkness, driven by the creature's flailing limbs.

Gideon was already running. Somehow, his feet found purchase on the bucking earth and propelled him forward as he left Skald gaping behind him. The last sight of the Doom, of Anya and her people shrinking back from the malevolent darkness, put wings on his feet, and he sprinted toward the dark lord before him.

The pit ceased opening, a terrifying mouth yawning beneath the Spider Lord's feet. Rachna itself perched on the very edge, on the verge of tumbling into the maw of the abyss. The titanic demon reared back, all eight of its legs thrusting to push itself away from the edge.

Oh, no, not so easily, Ashkelon hissed, and he thrust his clawed hands forward.

Ropy tendrils of inky blackness exploded out from the chasm walls, reaching toward Rachna's limbs. The spider reeled, its eye clusters wide at the sight, but the tentacles, each one thick as a river, snaked around the demon's appendages and tightened like the coils of a monstrous anaconda.

From Gideon's perspective, the tentacles of an ebony kraken reached up from the bowels of the earth and grappled the great spider before it.

The World Eater screeched, shaking the sky with its cry, and heaved, first back, then to either side, but the shadow tendrils held it fast.

Gideon reached Ashkelon. The mage held his hands before him, palms out, fingers curled to rakes.

"Master!" Gideon yelled. "Ashkelon!"

Ashkelon turned, his hair hanging lank over his eyes. His black half-mask distended across his face as he snarled, *"What?"*

Gideon thrust his finger toward Hammarfall. "You need to stop! You're going to kill them!"

Ashkelon's gaze fell upon the black ground, and his eyes creased for an instant as through their bond, Gideon felt old pain at the sight of so much dead earth.

Across the canyon, Rachna shrieked, deafening both of them. Ashkelon gritted his teeth at the sound, and turned back to his victim.

It's too late, apprentice. No one is listening, and there is no salvation. Not for any of us.

Ashkelon tightened his claws to fists and pulled them toward him, eyes lighting to beacons of cyan energy.

All that remains to us is darkness.

The tendrils tightened, and slowly, inevitably, dragged Rachna to the pit.

The World Eater spasmed. The mountain screamed and hurled itself backward, its legs digging furrows hundreds of yards long. Its screams echoed the cries in Gideon's mind as the darkness crept forward again within the Doom, and without realizing it, Gideon drew his sword.

Ashkelon heard the rasp of the blade leaving its sheath, and he turned slightly, the skin around his eyes tightening as beneath his mask, he smiled at the sound. As Tal ignited in his fist, hungry to plunge into the dark lord's back, Gideon felt relief bloom in Ashkelon's soul as he braced for the blade's touch.

The distraction proved fatal. Rachna hauled back with a concerted push of its legs, and the tendrils holding Rachna's limbs snapped taut with the sound of ship's timbers straining. Ashkelon pitched forward, jerked off his feet by the monster's gambit. The sorcerer skidded along the stone of his platform, pulled by the backpedaling monster like a man tied to a bucking stallion.

Ashkelon found his feet. Before the dark lord pitched off the edge of the precipice, Ashkelon slammed his boots into the stone, halting his forward motion, and hauled back on the black tendrils with gritted teeth.

Gideon felt his master reach for more power, pulling it from wherever he could, and in his mind's eye, he saw the blackness in the Doom reach up toward Anya with questing tendrils.

In that split second, his decision was made.

. . .

HER FATHER'S palm pushed against her chest as he dug his feet into the stone, trying to press Anya further back with his fearsome strength, but there was nowhere else to go. The Wolves were packed against one another as tightly as they could against the back wall. Screams and sobs sounded behind them, and a hundred pushes from the crowd inched Anya closer to the death before her.

Strangely, she felt peaceful. She just hoped it would not hurt too much, and that she would not embarrass herself as she passed to the Almighty's halls.

The black fronds swayed in front of her, then froze. After a second, it puffed away like ash.

With it, the dread fell away, and warmth returned to the shivering crowd in the Doom.

Anya glanced at her father.

"Now what has happened?"

"WHAT...ARE YOU DOING?"

Ashkelon's body quivered against the strain of holding Rachna in place. Yet even with the incredible effort, he needed to ask that question.

No blade pierced his darkmail and sliced his organs open. His lungs continued to pull air into them, his heart forced blood through his veins, and his throat remained uncut.

Instead, Gideon stabbed the blade into the earth behind Ashkelon.

The act cut his connection to his power. Like a bucket of water on a campfire, Ashkelon's source of magic snuffed out. He could not pull it from the earth any longer as the sword repelled his touch.

Ashkelon had perhaps a handful of seconds of reserved power before the World Eater overcame him.

Gideon stepped around him and sank to one knee in front of him.

"*What are you doing?*"

"Take me," Gideon said.

Ashkelon wanted to sneer. He wanted to say that there was no way the life force of one man could sustain the level of power needed to drag the World Eater into the mouth of Hell. He wanted to say that Gideon had just killed them all with his intervention.

But he found that the words died on his lips.

Above Gideon's kneeling form, Ashkelon's eyes met the burning golden gaze of the Man shrouded in sackcloth.

GIDEON CRIED out as Ashkelon reached through their bond and *pulled*.

Life flowed out of Gideon in a torrent, a channel of soul energy that should have drained him to the dregs in an instant. He felt the equivalent of a dozen Gideons die, a hundred.

Yet the flow continued, and Gideon was not consumed.

The same could not be said for the demon.

RACHNA ROARED and fell forward with the impact of an earthquake, its feet digging for purchase in the loose earth already torn up.

Skald watched as Ashkelon stepped back to one side, his left hand forward, gripping black strands of shadow linked to the great tendrils. He cast his right hand behind him with a snarl, and brilliant lightning arced from his palm into the sky.

A pillar of blinding light speared from the storm-wracked heavens and pierced the World Eater just behind its head. In a flash, the interior of the demon's body was illuminated entirely. Skald could see hundreds of thousands of its children growing, hatching, reaching with spindly legs for freedom, just before bursting into flame as the blast coursed through the titan's body.

One eye cluster exploded entirely, spewing torrents of slime into the chasm. Rachna screamed and staggered, almost tumbling headlong into the chasm from that hit alone.

Ashkelon jerked back with his left hand, pulling the creature a few dozen yards closer.

Rachna pushed with its legs, straightening the miles-long limbs to extend its body away from the flame-filled chasm.

The Onyx Mage pointed at the creature and psychically snarled a single phrase at the beast, heard by everyone with a mind to hear.

Death to the false.

ASHKELON KEPT his finger pointed directly into the shrouded Man's face, and hit the World Eater again. Another titanic bolt of lightning, like the finger of God, arced through miles of stormy sky and exploded against its body, shoving it forward.

Again.

Again.

Crackling spears of lightning crashed into the World Eater every second now, lighting its insides with white fire, eating charred ravines into its body. He called swirling cyclones of black cloud and wind to descend from the heavens and impact on Rachna's carapace with thunderous detonations. The howling winds tore at Rachna's ravaged hide, stripping entire acres of chitinous armor from its back and leaving raw, burning flesh behind.

The screams of the demon lord changed as Ashkelon skinned it alive. Agony and rage gave way to plaintiveness and desperation.

And yet Ashkelon continued to strike it, eyes locked with that golden gaze.

Witness this display, and know that I come for you.

The Man inclined his head. ***You are welcome.***

The creature dug its forelegs in, fighting the sorcerer's inexorable grip and pulling Ashkelon's attention back to it. Ashkelon's hatred, however, was inexhaustible, and he projected all of it at the titan struggling to escape him.

Ashkelon lifted his left hand, holding the trails of the dark chains wrapped around the World Eater's legs.

Kneel.

Ashkelon clenched his left fist, and the shadowy coils around Rachna's limbs squeezed with unimaginable pressure. With explosive cracks that echoed across the ravaged Spiderlands, the chitin of Rachna's legs shattered inward like porcelain. With a keening moan, the World Eater buckled, its crushed legs unable to support its weight.

Ashkelon lifted his chin, looking coldly down on the lowing creature across the chasm, his hatred like ice in his veins. *You were never meant to rule. You. Serve.*

Hauling back with his hand as though he led a slave on a chain, Ashkelon dragged it through the torn earth to the very edge of the abyss, lightning slashing it every step of the way. Its face ground through yards of topsoil, plowing a great furrow through the land. Beneath the creature, miles down, lakes of fire bubbled and hissed. The reek of brimstone rose from the pit. Rachna screamed again.

When you reach the Bottomless Pit, when at last your soul is torn from this pathetic husk and you kneel in chains before the Gate Keepers with the rest of your mutinous kin, you will tell them it was a son of Man who did this to you. Ashkelon, the last of the Avala, a man, *broke you to your knees.*

Not when you had glutted yourself and lay stupefied from your supper of souls.

No.

In your moment of ascension, I gutted you. At the pinnacle of your triumph, I shattered your strength.

Tell this to all the other would-be gods. Tell this to all those who would sit upon thrones and demand fealty from the races of Men, that you could not stop me. Tell them that you lacked the strength, and therefore the authority, to find me wanting.

I offer you now as a sacrifice to all the spirits of Light and Darkness. Let them look upon you, a lord of their kind, and know fear that a man has wrought your ruin. Tell them to come for me, if they would save themselves.

Ashkelon lifted his left hand high, like an executioner's axe. He cocked his head, eyes still ablaze with the icy heat of a glacier's heart, and glared at the Man of the golden eyes.

Go. Go now into all the world—

Ashkelon clenched his fist.

--and tell them.

The chasm wall supporting Rachna's crippled mass collapsed into the abyss. With an earth-shaking wail, the demon lord slid into the chasm before Ashkelon's dark gaze, and the world swallowed up the World Eater.

GIDEON DID NOT SEE the Spider Lord die.

As a matter of fact, the only evidence he had that the monstrous creature was dead echoed in his ringing ears. The screams had approached something truly awful, as columns of foul steam and pus-colored smoke ejected from the pit.

Yards away, Ashkelon stood on the edge of the precipice, bathed in the sulfurous gases and glaring down into the hellish abyss. His void blade still stood erect by its master, the screams of the host contained within audible again as the demon's death-cries faded away.

Though nothing of the creature could be heard now, lightning still lanced down into the pit. The flashes of energy played across Ashkelon's face, illuminating his gritted teeth and lank hair. His expression did not change, a rictus of bitter hate.

Gideon did not know how much time passed. Every time Ashkelon struck the chasm, Gideon could hear the small grunt, like an exhausted snarl, the sorcerer made with each strike.

His master no longer pulled energy from Gideon's soul; that terrible draining ceased when the World Eater fell into the chasm. Through the fraying threads of his bond with Ashkelon, he could feel the dull flashes of bitterness sparking each strike.

It is so much effort to hate so much, Gideon thought.

Tal now rested in his sheath. He stood with Skald, watching Ashkelon continue to mutilate the corpse of Rachna.

"Why?" he heard himself ask quietly.

Skald sighed. "This vone is different, just-Gideon. For us, ve see the Spider God and vish to see it destroyed. I think for him, he saw the god, and that vas enough."

Gideon blinked at that.

Skald gestured. "He needs rest, boy. Go to him."

. . .

GIDEON PICKED his way through the shattered landscape toward his master. Discarded spider carcasses littered the ground, legs pulled up tight over broken carapaces. Wisps of smoke still rose from cracks in their blasted corpses as rain pattered on the broken chitin.

Blade after blade of lightning sizzled through the air to fall into the World Eater's grave. Now that he drew close, he could see the slight sway in Ashkelon's stance.

Gideon's boot scraped on loose gravel, and Ashkelon twitched slightly in his direction, his soaked hair dripping water. With a final grunt, another blade of skyfire seared into the abyss, and all was quiet.

Ashkelon's eyes closed for a second, and without warning, he swayed forward. Gideon dashed forward to catch his master by the shoulder before he fell in, and steadied him. Ashkelon sagged against him, his eyes struggling to focus, utterly drained by the battle. Gideon had never seen him look so weak.

With the enemy lying broken in the newborn chasm, the rage in Ashkelon's soul felt muted, his hatred reduced to embers, yet always present. All Gideon could feel now was an overwhelming exhaustion, and the aching desire to give in.

To finally be done.

Yet even in his weakness, Ashkelon reached out with quivering fingers and wrapped them around the hilt of Acherlith, dragging the cursed blade from the ground with a grunt of effort and sheathing it in its home on his back.

Gideon draped Ashkelon's arm across his shoulders, wincing at the bite of the darkmail in his neck and the lactic acid burning in his strained muscles. His own body felt exhausted from the draining he had suffered to save Hammarfall.

"So...you did not take your chance."

Gideon grunted. "There's no challenge in stabbing an old man in the back."

Ashkelon laughed quietly. "You may live to regret that, apprentice."

Gideon smiled and shrugged. "Probably."

They staggered together toward the walls of Hammarfall. The city stood defiantly in the face of the apocalyptic landscape a mile outside the walls. The few banners remaining flapped with every breath of bitter wind, lit by distant flames.

"The city still stands," Ashkelon said. "That should please you."

He nodded. "It does. The Lord has been good to us."

After a few steps of silence, Ashkelon asked, "Your deity...does He have golden eyes?"

Gideon hesitated. "I am not sure. I have never seen Him."

"Hm. Please find out."

They trudged along through the field of slain monsters. The walls of Hammarfall grew closer, pitted and stained from the catastrophe.

At length, Gideon broke the silence. "Why do you ask, master?"

Ashkelon sighed. "You asked me yesterday about spirits. While I do not believe that useless half-answer you supplied me, after today, I believe you have nothing to fear from the fallen. There is something greater with you."

Gideon shook his head. "I am only what I have been given. I am grateful for it all, the good and the bad."

Ashkelon exhaled slowly. "You miss my point. I do not care about what strength of heart you may possess; such ideals are the fodder of cheap tale weavers to hear coin ring in their cups. The drawing of the power I required to slay the demon should have killed you many times over, and it did not."

Gideon grinned. "Disappointed?"

"Intrigued. I saw great power in you, Gideon, and it does not originate from you. If it was your God, then today, I believe you pleased Him."

Skald met them by the gate. Rain ran through the crevices of his aged face, dripping like tears from his gray beard. The skulls and totems adorning his armor rattled quietly as he moved toward them, steadying his gait with the haft of his warhammer.

Behind him, the survivors of Hammarfall ventured from the King's Doom, looking with wonder on the devastated world within and without their walls. Gideon saw Anya push through the masses, searching for him. A quick grin of relief flashed across her face as she saw him still standing.

Gideon and Ashkelon halted before the warrior, who stood blocking the entrance to the gate. Skald laid the head of his warhammer on the ground and placed both hands atop the pommel.

"Hail, sorcerer," he said. "It seems the Vulfen owe you gratitude. You shall always be remembered in the stories as a savior of Hammarfall."

Ashkelon stopped dead in his tracks, pulling Gideon to a halt with him. "That is a mistake. I should not be remembered as such."

Skald spread his hands. "I do not veave the tales, dark one. I merely tell them as they happened."

Ashkelon considered him for a moment, then straightened, pushing away from Gideon's steadying hand to stand tall and dark before Skald. "I will now tell you a story of my people, Greymane. It is more a verse of warning, really, and perhaps from it you will learn of our wisdom."

Skald inclined his head, his eye keen as a blade. "I will witness it."

Ashkelon's eyes, in turn, were lifeless as he quoted, "Beware the stranger who saves you, and he with the power to lift your curse. Beware the dark ones, my child, for the man who slew the devil..."

Acherlith moved in a blur of blackened steel. It carved through Skald's shoulder guard and collarbone, sliced through his heart, and tore his left lung in two before ripping out of his pelvis with a shriek.

"...was worse," Ashkelon finished, flicking Skald's blood from his blade.

THE MIGHTY WOLF crumpled without a sound before the shadow that had slain him. Time seemed to freeze as Anya screamed from the stairs of the Doom and dashed toward Skald's fallen body. Heimdall Fangthane roared in fury and began to charge, his axe swinging high to take vengeance for the blood of Skald Greymane.

Gideon himself could not move. The murder had been ferociously fast, a flash of black carving a bloody ravine down Skald's torso.

Ashkelon, however, had not finished.

His left hand hardened to a claw. With a jerk, Skald's body lifted from the ground to hang before Ashkelon. The Wolf's head lolled to the side, consciousness and blood draining from him like wine from a punctured sack.

"Let us see, then, how the story changes now, shall we?"

His lip curling, Ashkelon clenched his claw into a fist, violet threads snapped around the warrior, and Skald began to scream.

EPILOGUE
EXILE

A gain, Gideon stood in a doorway, sword unsheathed, tip planted in the ground before him.

Rain sluiced off of his battered armor, dripping from the ends of his hair. Polluted by the death of so many poisonous creatures, the water irritated Gideon's skin, raising rashes on his cheeks. Chill sank icy fangs into his bones, and he clenched his teeth to keep them from chattering.

Before him, the Wolves prowled.

Jarl Fangthane held his axe in his hand, fury radiating from him like the heat from the torch he carried. A score of warriors stood with him, menace bleeding from each one.

"I'll not say it again, boy. *Move.*"

Heimdall's tone was glacial. Aggression dripped from his words like the burning rain falling from the wounded sky.

Gideon shook his head. "My master is resting. I'll not have him disturbed."

"I'm not going to disturb him," Heimdall growled. "I'm going to give him final peace."

"This is not worthy, jarl."

"Worthy?" Heimdall hissed. "*Worthy?* That bastard in there has destroyed us more completely than the foul servants of Mammon ever could! Our home is *gone*. His 'salvation' has poisoned the earth so nothing will grow. Game will never return to the few sticks of forest that still stand. It is a miracle of God that Hammarfall itself has not collapsed!"

Gideon remained where he was. "As it would have, had the World Eater not been stopped. By Ashkelon."

Refusing to be deflected, Heimdall spat, "And then there's Skald."

Gideon sighed and shook his head. "Skald did not cross the threshold of Death, jarl. You know this. Ashkelon raised him back as he has me, countless times. As he rescued Brida Baresark."

Frustration and despair entered Heimdall's voice. "But now I have no Greymane to test him for truth, do I? We are Wolves, Gideon. We will not bask in the defeat of Mammon by accepting the gift of Sheol. I cannot suffer a wight to walk among us, no matter whose face he wears. Skald, whether it be him or not, will be exiled from our people, which makes him as good as murdered to *me*, and I will have my blood price for my land, my people and my friend. Get out of the way."

Gideon kept his voice quiet, but firm. "No, jarl. I will not."

Heimdall gritted his teeth and stepped closer. "Get *out*...of the way," he repeated, injecting threat into every syllable.

With a rasp of steel on stone, Gideon lifted his sword to angle the tip at Heimdall's face. Gasps and murmurs of disbelief rose from the warriors and serfs gathered around. Anya hugged her arms around herself as the two men faced off in the doorway.

Heimdall looked from the sword to Gideon. "You would defend him? You, whom he has slain a dozen times?"

"You could have challenged him at any moment for any number of crimes prior to this moment," Gideon said firmly. "You cannot stain your honor by murdering him in his bed after he has saved your people, and I will not stain mine by allowing you to do so."

"Are you touched in the head, boy?" Heimdall exploded. "Did you not see what he is capable of? There is no dishonor in slaying a dragon while it sleeps to preserve one's family. This is the only chance we have to end this madman. Stand aside, and let me expunge this wickedness from the world."

The tip of Gideon's sword did not waver. Gideon did not blink. "If you step any closer, jarl, I will stop you. And thanks to the instruction of the 'madman' in there, you know that it will take far more than you have to get through me."

Heimdall flared his nostrils and took a deep breath. The fire of berserker rage chilled to ice in his eyes, and he stepped back, lowering his axe.

"Very well, Doomkeeper. You have made your decision."

Gideon pressed his lips together in a thin line. "I have, jarl."

Heimdall raised his voice so that the gathered crowd could hear him. "My hospitality to these strangers is ended. If any man offers them anything, whether it be food, water or a kind word, he will be cast from the Pack to die in the wilderness."

Anya stepped forward. "Papa…," she started.

Heimdall spoke without turning to her. "You are hereby forbidden from speaking with Gideon Doomkeeper. That is my command."

Tears gathered in Anya's eyes and she stammered, "But Papa…"

Her father whirled on her, the chilled rage flaring again. "You will *not* disobey me!" he snarled. His voice cracked in the courtyard like thunder. "Now get in the hall before I have you dragged there in chains."

Flinching back from her father's ire, Anya cast a look at Gideon. Pain creased Gideon's brow as he met her eyes, but he did not move from the doorway.

After a long moment, Anya broke eye contact, swiped at her eyes and moved away, vanishing into the lodge at her father's command.

Heimdall stabbed a finger at Gideon. "You leave at first light, with all the monsters you brought here. You are banished from the lands of Wolves. If you return, nothing short of the Almighty's intervention will save you."

Tears stinging his eyes, Gideon dipped his chin in acknowledgement. "Understood."

Heimdall turned away, and a slight catch entered his voice. "And take your wight with you. There is no place for him here."

The jarl stomped away, clearing his throat gruffly.

Gideon stood in the rain, alone at last. His body hurt. His pride hurt. His heart hurt.

Off in the distance, he saw the shadow of Gemelte standing, watching. The old man cocked his head at him, and a question whispered into Gideon's mind.

Is it worth it?

With a sigh, he planted the tip of his sword in the stone again. There Gideon stayed, standing square in the doorway, guarding a prince of the lost.

SCREAMS SOUNDED from the depths as Abram crossed the threshold of the Temple of the Architects. Worship did go on, as it ever did.

It had taken weeks. Bribes. Murders. Blackmail. But the inquisitor had done it.

His escape from the Wolves had been a simple task. With everyone's attention on the oncoming creature of Mammon, Abram had slipped his shackles and made a run for it. He crept south and then east, moving through the mainland of Samothrace by night or hiding beneath blankets in stinking wagons. Finally, after the humiliation of hiding like a mouse throughout the lands of the enemy, Abram stood tall and proud, waved into the seat of the Architects' power by pairs of fearsome guardians.

Clouds that were more industrial fumes than natural formations lazed across the yellow sky. Lightning forked across, and Abram winced at the thunder. Too much of that recently. The destruction of Rachna had been audible for miles.

The screams that heralded the inquisitor's arrival echoed from the Jahennan wing of the Temple, for the most part. That was not unusual. Gehenna did love so to be serenaded by the sounds of human pain.

What that signified was that Gehenna was physically present in the

Temple. And if Gehenna were here, then the other two members of the fallen trinity were likely to be here, as well.

However, Abram did not pass into the Tower of Agony to make obeisance to his former patron. Nor did he enter the Crypts of Sheol, or the Halls of Hunger. Instead, he marched past the three gateways to a small room set in the back of the Temple, apart yet central to the worship of the Three.

It was, fittingly enough, a new building, built as a recent attachment to the older, decadent Temple. It was small, spartan and almost unnoticed. There was no room for a gathering of the faithful to worship. It was a place of utility only, a room to fulfill a purpose. It was called the Chamber of the New Way, where the almost-heretics swore loyalty to the Chosen One of the Three.

Within that room rested a simple black throne.

Upon the throne, a man.

Abram hesitated before the door, gathered his thoughts, then strode in and fell to one knee. "Master, I return with tidings."

He did not look directly at the occupant of the throne. His master was...sensitive...about his appearance. Even so, he could smell the charred flesh, the weeping pus soaking the black rags swaddling the Chosen One's wounded body.

The man spoke, a gurgling rasp.

"Where is Ursus?"

Abram swallowed before answering. "Turned, lord. Sworn to the Wolves following his defeat."

His master remained silent a moment.

"And Ja'a?"

"She refused to join us, lord. She gave herself as sacrifice to wake the World Eater."

Rustling, as the man in black rags gestured. "And then, there is that. Where is Mammon's child?"

Abram hesitated a moment, unsure, now that he was in the moment, how to answer his lord. The Three were known to peel the messengers of bad tidings like fleshy fruit.

The Chosen One, however, might do that if he lied.

"Destroyed, lord."

A small intake of breath. Shock? Excitement?

"Destroyed, you say."

Abram, almost unmanned by his master's calm, began to babble. "My lord, I offer my most sincere apologies and..."

A rustle, as the man raised a hand to forestall his words.

"Abram. Look on me."

Wincing, Abram lifted his eyes to meet the golden ones of his master.

"Was it a man in black?"

Abram nodded cautiously. "Yes, lord. With white hair and eyes like the ice of the northern seas."

Charred flesh around his mouth cracked and oozed clear fluid as Carcharoth smiled and said, "That is exactly what I wanted to hear."

"It...it is, my lord?"

The Chosen One of the Three, his flame-ravaged flesh bandaged in black, leaned back in his throne and said, "It is time now. He has revealed himself. And he will come."

Abram wet his chapped lips with his tongue before daring to ask a final question. "He? Who, lord?"

The screams intensified in the distance from the Jahennan dungeons. Thunder rumbled as Carcharoth closed his eyes and murmured, "Aj-Gelun."

ALL WAS DARKNESS.

This was normal, especially when the Seeress came out of her trances. Very little remained of Avalon to give light anymore.

She sensed movement around her, and sighed quietly.

"No rest for the weary, Ekron?"

The silence did not mask his disapproval. "No more games. You have found the betrayer. Tell me where he is."

The Seeress rose languidly from her cross-legged stance and walked to a bowl of cold water set nearby. She splashed her face with the refreshing droplets, enjoying the heightened tension in the room as her visitor waited impatiently.

"You are both wrong and correct at the same time. I *have* found him."

"And?" Her guest prompted.

She shrugged. "That does not mean that I know where he is."

Ekron hissed quietly. "We have not felt a power discharge like that since Avalon died, and our prison was broken. Do you truly mean to tell me you cannot locate him from that level of release?"

She scoffed. "It is a long way away. It is like trying to pinpoint the origin of a shout when the shouter stands across the ocean. At a certain distance, it does not matter how loud it is."

She sensed growing anger, and with it, growing power. The air began to tinge red and the smell of ash grew strong in her nostrils.

Quickly, she spoke again. "But I do have a general direction. If he unleashes sorcery like that again, I can narrow it down. Tell the Ashen to be patient."

Somehow, her guest's sneer was audible. "Patience...we have been patient long enough, don't you think?"

The Seeress nodded, bitterness seeping into her expression. "There is a way. A soldier, someone he keeps close to him. He seems to be training him for something."

"And?"

"The soldier seemed to anger...him."

She stumbled over the last word.

A low laugh, sinister and mocking. "Him, him, him. You still cannot say his name, can you?"

Now the air crackled with frost. The Seeress had a temper of her own, and some things hurt too deeply, even after all of this time.

The other presence retreated somewhat, but remained close.

"Calm yourself, Gath. Keep on as you must, but beware. We expect results. Find Ashkelon."

She glared at him. "Oh, I will, Ekron."

She turned back and settled down into her stance, composing herself for the sending once more. She picked up her disguise, the robes of the old scholar lost to Ashkelon's vengeance, and settled it comfortably over her own skin.

Before she commenced her ritual, Gath focused on her target. That distant, expanding sphere of power expenditure, much like a supernova. She had not lied to Ekron; the shockwave of the blast itself blurred the exact location, and she needed more.

"I'm going to find you, my love," Gath whispered. "And when I do, you will stand before the Lady of the Dark, and explain *why* you betrayed us all."

THE END

KICKSTARTER EXCLUSIVE
SHORT STORIES

SON OF ANAK

The child was born, as were they all, among bared steel and gritted teeth. The first life he took was that of the slave woman who bore him, whose name he never learned.

When at last the sweat-drenched human fell back onto the bare stone table, life draining away and already forgotten, the conclave of the Tor Kayn clan considered whether to kill the child, as well.

Anak, Slaughterlord, chief of Mammon's titans, glared down at the tiny red creature which refused to cry. In his right hand, he gripped the hilt of his goreblade, ready to be first to slay his son, should he show weakness.

To his right, Arla Hornripper muttered, "It does not cry. Another failure."

Grunts of assent, like the sound of strained oxen, rose from the gathered giants at her words. There was no Tor Kayn more dedicated than Arla. She held them all, Anak included, to the highest ideal, and she would not hesitate to enact sanction herself, should Anak fail to.

The gathered clan began to shift away, their postures declaring they had other tasks to accomplish. Anak knew his people; they had seen enough to judge. Births among the Tor Kayn rarely succeeded, for the titans themselves could bear no children, and they found few slaves capable of bearing their seed to delivery.

They stayed only to see Anak keep the tribe pure. To prevent weakness from polluting the clan, they remained to ensure that the Slaughterlord killed his son.

The child, large for a normal infant and a death sentence to bear for a human woman, opened his eyes and met his father's impassive gaze without fear.

Anak felt the kill-urge from the clan, their impatience hot on his back like the rays of the desert sun. They thought the baby weak.

He would have agreed with them. He had cast his share of failed offspring to the beasts, grimly justified as the strong devoured the weak.

Now, however, he did not agree. The child was not weak; rather, it seemed calm. It gave him pause, even as the child closed its eyes sleepily and its lips opened, searching hungrily for a breast to give it suck. The sight mesmerized the old titan for an instant, before he shook it off.

Anak snorted. Sentiment could not be allowed in a Slaughterlord of the Tor Kayn. He lifted his goreblade for the strike, and the iron, blackened by centuries of bloodshed, scraped against the stone of the birthing altar.

His son's eyes snapped open, and he saw his father standing over him with a raised sword.

His red face screwed up. His tiny arms and legs kicked frantically, and from his mouth issued an ear-shattering yell of defiance and rage.

Anak lowered his sword and glanced at his clan brothers and sisters. Several of them blinked at the sheer force of the child's shrieks, and many looked to him with rough grins splitting their ugly faces. He met Arla's gaze and raised an eyebrow. She shrugged and turned away.

Not without a gleam of congratulation in her eye, however.

Sheathing the weapon on his back, Anak barked, "Nurse!"

An overweight slave bustled in and took the squalling child in her arms, already baring a breast to feed it. The child fought her touch, and she struggled to keep the child from flailing out of her arms onto the floor.

Anak realized that he smiled, as well, relief and vindication flooding his spirit. His son had been born, and by the Three, he was strong.

Arla halted at the doorway, moved to his side and shoved his shoulder. Her chin jutted forward as if daring him to strike her.

"What is his name, then? What is the name of the Slaughterlord's heir?"

Anak closed his eyes and breathed for a moment. He remembered the look of fury, bereft of terror at the sight of Anak's raised blade. He remembered the powerful bray that erupted from the boy's lungs, like a great black bear defending its cave.

He turned to the clan and spoke, his voice thunderous. "Call him...Ursus."

The slaves are permitted, encouraged, even, to bear their own children. The transient encampment of the Tor Kayn was always filled with brats of various hues and sizes, heirs to the legacy of servitude to the dark giants of the East.

But they are not friends.

Four children sprang from the shadows to wrap themselves around Ursus's legs, entangling his steps. Another hit him in the small of his back, trying to pitch him off his feet, while another ran toward him, hefting a club too big for her slight frame. Ursus grunted at the impact, hammering down with his fist onto the back of one of the children holding his right leg. The blow smashed the smaller child into the ground, but another two children tackled Ursus in his chest and knocked them all sprawling.

He was six winters old.

Ursus slammed onto his back and rolled, knowing that to stay on the ground amidst these dogs is to invite death. The slaves are not stupid. They know who Ursus is. They cannot challenge the son of

Anak individually, so they attack only in packs, employing strategies formulated by their enslaved parents.

This is at the behest of his father. He rewards the children who make Ursus bleed.

When standing, Ursus is a full foot and a half taller than the other children his age. On the ground, however, this advantage gives him nothing.

Ursus scissored his legs, scraping the children clinging desperately to his limbs off of each other. He rolled to his feet and backhanded another child away, breaking her jaw and spinning her to the ground. The pack surged forward once again, but this time, they could come from only one direction, and their advantage of surprise was lost. Defeat filled their eyes, and some turned to run.

Ursus roars and waded in.

"Hit the wagon."

Twelve winters have passed since his birth, and already, Ursus matched full-grown men for size. Today, he confronted his next lesson.

The wagon looked like an armored box, with sheets of plate nailed to the reinforced chassis. The wood itself was solid oak, rare in these blasted wastelands. Arla had told him that the princes and commanders of far-off Samothrace used these contraptions to hide themselves from the armies of the Hellscape. Bloodstains still spattered the frame, which told Ursus how well these wagons served.

Anak stood immovable a short distance away. His arms, criss-crossed with scars and bulging with muscle, crossed over his chest. He watched only, content to allow Arla to teach his son. Several others of the clan watched casually, sharpening weapons while they observed the education of their newest member.

Arla, his combat trainer, repeated her command.

"Hit the wagon. Knock it off its wheels."

She did not give a reason. She did not have to. This was the way of the Tor Kayn.

Ursus sucked in a deep breath, launched off of his left foot, and barreled toward his target. He lowered his shoulder and crunched into the side of the wagon with a loud bang, not flinching before the impact, as a coward would.

The wagon rocked from the impact, lifted from its wheels, but did not go over. Quiet laughter rippled around from the observers, and there were more than a few raised eyebrows.

"A good first hit!" one called out.

His shoulder is a mass of pain, yet he does not make a sound. He betrays no weakness.

Ursus glanced back, almost guiltily, to see his father looking at him. Anak's crimson gaze gleamed with amusement and more than a touch of pride.

Arla looked to Anak for permission, an eyebrow raised. He chucked his chin for her to continue and turned away, leaving Ursus to his teacher.

Arla grinned and pounded her fist into her palm. "Again," she growled.

Until this day, Ursus has only fought men.

He excelled at fighting crowds of slaves. He had done so every day since his fifth winter.

His skin did not fit him. His skeleton was too tall, and his muscles had yet to catch up with his lengthening frame.

The Tor Kayn mocked him whenever they could. "All bones, no meat. Only good for making broth!" they said.

The growth hurt. His bones ached every minute of every day, and every morning brought new pain. Spasms of rage twisted his behavior from something acceptable into something more bestial, and Arla punished him severely for the lapses.

He stood taller than his enemy, but it was no advantage to him.

Across the circle of turned earth, a beast snuffed out its breath in a cloud of hot steam. Its hooves dug into the ground, carving furrows into the churned earth. Two horns sprouted from its skull and curved toward Ursus, while it beat its bare chest with thick, almost-human hands.

Gantok, adolescent prince of the maksai warherds, arched its head back and roared into the sky. The minotaurs encircling the kill-ring bellowed back, led by their barbaric king, Bagral.

Behind Ursus stood only Anak and Arla. Neither appeared interested in the ritual.

Ursus lowered his shoulder and charged forward. By this time, he has hit the wagon every day, ten times a day. The wagon had yet to fall.

Today, the wagon struck back.

The maksai knocked Ursus off his feet, its horns scoring deeply along his ribs. Ursus was too tall. His center of gravity was too high. He did not have the weight or the mass to properly counter the dense, twisted muscle of the monstrous prince confronting him.

Ursus hit the ground with a thud, his hands clawing at the earth to pull him back to his feet. Hooves pounded towards him, and a great roar of victory rose into the air as Gantok's horns rammed into his side once more.

The last sight Ursus saw before consciousness smashed from his grip was of his father and Arla walking away.

He served.

With snorted laughter, the spiteful maks ai forced Ursus to perform slave's work for them. The heir of Anak hewed wood, carried stone, and drew water at the behest of even the least of the Herd. His flesh suffered the bites of their whips, and his neck was rubbed raw by the collar and leash with which they dragged him about. At times of council, when Bagral of the maksai received ambassadors, he kept Ursus chained to his throne, spitting and pissing on the Slaughterlord's heir in full view of the messengers of Mammon.

Ursus did not fight back at his treatment. He did not cry. His lessons rang true in his mind, inculcated by his merciless education.

The weak serve.

The lesson sank into his bones with each sunrise, when he awakened from his pitiful few hours of rest and felt the aches of a hundred bruises gained the day before. It burned into his heart with each lungful of stinking cinders he breathed as he stoked the beasts' dung fires.

The weak serve.

The maksai chortled at the Tor Kayn's silence. They jeered at his chains, jerked his leash to choke him, and trampled him with their hooves.

So Ursus learned to hate.

How long he served, Ursus did not know. He did not count the sunrises or sunsets to mark the time. To his knowledge, he would serve the Herd forever for his defeat.

One night, as he lay in the dung heap given to him for his bed, Ursus heard something.

There is no masking the sound of a Tor Kayn's approach. Ursus had often tried it, but even at his age, his weight shivered the ground when he walked, not to mention the countless tendons and muscles that cracked in his ankles and knees with every step.

So Ursus knew the sound of one of his kind when they attempted stealth. One of the great giveaways was the lack of sound anywhere else. The cicadas of the steppes no longer sang, the jackals no longer howled, and the birds ceased their song when the Tor Kayn drew near.

Ursus glanced at the sentinels. Those of the Herd assigned to keep watch over the encampment were usually those of low rank or on punishment duty. They did not keep a sharp watch; most of the time, they slept at their posts.

Blinded by the fires they kept to ward away the chill, they did not see the dark masses moving through the tall grass. Dulled by rotten liquor, their senses did not register the tremors in the ground with each approaching footfall.

Ursus gathered his feet under him, taking care not to allow his chain to scrape upon the ground and wake the guards. His eyes remained locked on the gargantuan shadow that emerged from the grasses, stalking toward the nearest sleeping guard.

The minotaur woke from its slumber with a hand gripping its

throat. Its eyes widened in shock at the terrible sensation of its hooves leaving the ground. It tried to take a breath, to scream, to warn; but the inexorable grip strangled all sound that could come out of its throat. Its windpipe cracked, and the creature's eyes rolled back in its head.

Anak cast the body aside, and it thudded to the ground in a tangle of limbs. With a casual motion of his arm, he hurled a spear the size of a beam into the second guard as the maksai turned to see its companion. The gigantic weapon punched into the sleeper's side, crushed its lungs, and threw it to vanish into the waving grass of the steppe.

Ursus knew his father. He would not enter the crude dwellings of the Herd and slay them as they slept. Such tactics reeked of cowardice.

Instead, Anak called them to war.

He took a deep breath and shattered the stillness of the night with a tyrannical roar that bellowed out over the lands of the Herd. With his summons, Anak invited the maksai to confront the death in their midst with blades in their fists.

Anak roared for twenty seconds, his massive lungs projecting his intent at his ancient rivals. Maksai stumbled from their tents, shaking exhaustion from eyes still dull with sleep.

They milled about, unsure of which way to go or what to do, until Bagral, chieftain of the maksai horde and father of Gantok, exited his tent. Bagral was enormous for one of his kind, a brute weighing half a ton of iron muscle and thick hide. He brayed and punched his followers, beating them until they cowered in submission before him.

Bagral took one look at the twelve-foot monster in his encampment, and the lesser Tor Kayn chained in the dung heap. His eyes gleamed with calculation, rare among his kind, and he grunted. "Stupid giant, to come alone."

He clapped Gantok on the shoulder and shoved him forward. "You. Go kill. Bring head."

Gantok snuffled in obedience and lumbered forward, dragging half of the Herd with him. He smashed his axes together and shook his horns, spraying a rain of sweat droplets from his neck. The air grew charged with the heavy musk of the creatures as they worked themselves into a lather, preparing for the charge.

Anak stood above his son, his great goreblade sheathed on his back, arms crossed across his chest.

Bagral hesitated for an instant, not believing the Slaughterlord had yet to attack.

Ursus could not believe Bagral could not feel the ground trembling.

From within the grasses, Shadrach Whalegutter threw his harpoon. The barbed shaft lanced straight through one of the minotaurs at Gantok's side and hurled him into one of the hide teepees. The Herd flinched and turned to face the attack. Those few of them with crossbows prepared lifted the weapons to fire blindly into the grass.

The clan struck them from behind.

The trembling in the ground turned to thunder as two titans exploded from the grass, battlecries shredding the eardrums of their victims. They were sheathed in iron plate, and they towered above the beasts they had come to cull.

Pison and Gihon, the Brothers, slammed into the Herd with bone-cracking force. Spines snapped like twigs, and war-brays turned to squeals of agony as maksai were blasted back to thrash to death amidst their brethren. Pison shattered a minotaur's skull, four inches of hardened bone, with a single devastating hook, while his brother lifted a six-hundred pound male off of its hooves and spiked it into the ground on its head, smashing the creature's vertebrae in its neck.

Ursus heard Arla roar. He could not see her, but her cry echoed the dragons of the elder days. The brays that answered her were higher in pitch and whined instead of raged. She was among the Herd's calves.

Bagral snapped his gaze back to meet Anak's steely glare. The Slaughterlord stood near Ursus, but made no move to break his chain. The screams of Bagral's calves rose in the background as Anak's eyes bored into Bagral's.

The skin around Bagral's eyes tightened, and in helpless fury, he gestured sharply toward Ursus.

"Take. Leave."

Anak raised his goreblade over his head and roared once again, a shattering saurian blast. Immediately, the Tor Kayn in view disengaged from their butchery. With visible lack of haste, they turned their backs on the Herd and stepped into the grasses once more. The darkness swallowed up their massive silhouettes as swiftly as they had emerged.

Ursus looked up to see his father also turn and stride away, the ground shaking beneath his footsteps. It almost seemed as if Ursus had been forgotten.

But Ursus knew his father. The message was clear.

Break your own chains.

Ursus had never broken chain before. It was why the maksai used it to restrain him. They mocked him for not being Tor Kayn, for lacking the strength of his kinsmen.

But Anak continued to walk away.

Ursus's mind worked as the maksai looked on. If his father left him to break his own chain, then that meant Anak thought him strong enough. If Anak thought him strong enough, then Ursus was.

In times to come, Ursus would learn a word for what caused him to lift his chain. It would describe the acceptance that calmed his spirit as he stretched the metal links across his chest and set them quivering with tension.

Faith.

As his chain snapped across his chest, there was one who could not bear to see Ursus free. Gantok, son of Bagral, howled in fury and barreled forward, horns lowered.

Snapping the chain from the collar on his neck, Ursus sidestepped the maksai's bulk and whipped his chain around the creature's throat. Gantok's eyes bulged as Ursus hauled back on the chain with a bellow, digging into the beast's neck. Gantok clutched at the chain frantically, but his brutish fingers could find no purchase on the chain. Ursus jerked and heaved, channeling months of shame into the catharsis of bellowing and unfettered violence.

When last they fought, Ursus had fallen. Now, however, Ursus had his hate, and it flooded his muscles with fiery strength.

Bagral lunged forward, but stopped short as five towering warriors emerged from the grassy plain, weapons held casually at the ready. Nine more remained within the shadows, enough killing power to wipe the Herd from the face of the earth.

The Tor Kayn stood watch over the heir of Anak as the Slaughter-lord forced Bagral to watch helplessly as Ursus throttled the life from his son.

Ursus kept his distance from the clan as they returned to their home. His shame nearly overwhelmed him, and he stayed away to prevent his taint from spreading to the warriors. It did not help that his father did not speak on the trip.

When at last they arrived at the encampment, Anak stepped into his hut without a word for his son. The other Tor Kayn equally departed for their own sleeping quarters. None washed off the blood of their prey.

Only Arla Hornripper remained with her charge. She looked down on him, her silver hair curling over her shoulder in a heavy braid.

Her words remained with Ursus for the rest of his life.

"We all fail the first fight."

Ursus glared at her, uncertainty warring with self-recrimination in his hard eyes. She glared back. "Get that look out of your eyes, before I cut it out. I do not speak these words for your comfort."

"Every one of us has served the maksai. In this way, we learn the penalty for weakness. We learn the hate and feel the madness. Every one of us has broken the chain from our necks."

Ursus nodded in understanding. "I am not special."

A smile touched her lips briefly. "Perhaps. None of us, not even Anak, strangled the heir of the Herd on our way out."

That act garnered the young Ursus a modicum of respect among the clan. Each titan remembered their servitude beneath the maksai lash, a shame each bore. To see the son of Anak rise from his shame and humiliate the Herd to their faces sparked grim pride in each warrior.

When Ursus had seen thirty winters, he had nearly grown to his full size. He stood as tall as his clan brothers and sisters now, and his mass already equaled theirs, though he had more to grow. His muscles were hard as the stone of the mountains, and the fire of rage remained forever stoked in his breast.

He no longer fought slaves. No ordinary human would have survived the contest, and the Tor Kayn were not frivolous with their servants' blood. Not only that, but such combats would have taught Ursus nothing, and fanned the flames of his youthful blood-madness.

Instead, Ursus crushed stone. He swung great hammers and split boulders down the middle, relishing the immense power of his body. He exulted, as only the young could, as trees exploded into clouds of splinters at his blows.

And he fought the clan.

Ursus learned the way of the spear from Shadrach, the axe from Arla, the great-bow from Laban. He grappled with the Brothers Pison and Gihon, and fended off the knuckle-claws of Gisela. He took wounds that might have killed a mortal, injuries that hardened into ropes of scars across his body.

He bested each of the Tor Kayn at least once.

All except Anak.

The Slaughterlord moved far too fast for a creature of his size, and when he struck, his target ceased to be. None of the other Tor Kayn even approached Anak's level of skill, and when the titan bore his goreblade, no one dared try him.

Except Ursus.

When Anak stepped into the circle with his son, he did not hold back. Ursus might last a few seconds against the whirling black greatsword, but he always crashed to the ground outside the circle, bleeding from a new ravine. Ursus studied his father's motions, learning how he generated so much power and speed. He observed the sublime efficiency of Anak's movements, how he burned less energy than the others and appeared to never run out of stamina.

On his own, in the safety of darkness when the clan rested, Ursus practiced to be like his father.

One day, Anak received a messenger. A mortal, nervous and sweating, stood before the Slaughterlord, the marks of Mammon apparent on his right hand and brow.

Ursus joined the others as they towered around the runner. Though not a full Tor Kayn yet, he was to participate in all clan rituals and gatherings to learn from the proceedings.

As Arla took her place beside Anak, the Slaughterlord gestured toward the messenger. "Speak."

The messenger did not offer a scroll, for the Tor Kayn did not bother to learn to read, and terrible things happened to messengers who implied the ignorance of the Tor Kayn by offering written instructions.

In a voice that only shuddered slightly in the presence of titans, the messenger said, "The Slaughterlord Anak and his clan are called to the Faminelord's Court at the forward temple in Bel Farak. The great and holy Father of Feasting wishes to know if the Tor Kayn's initiation ritual is complete, and if they are ready to rejoin the war against the impure."

As one, the Tor Kayn looked to Anak. Nothing externally had changed, but new energy had entered the hut. Ursus felt the same excitement thrill through his veins.

Bloodshed.

Anak steepled his hands before his face and rumbled, "Leave us. You shall have your answer."

The messenger bowed and gratefully backed out of the room.

Anak's eyes fixed onto Ursus, and the calculation in that crimson gaze made Ursus's blood run cold.

Without looking away, Anak asked, "Is he ready?"

Without hesitation, Pison and Gihon slammed their fists against their chests. Laban and Shadrach followed after a moment's consideration.

One by one, the others gave their assent. Raphela Shatterspine,

Gisela Fleshtearer, Dekel Bonegrinder, Jabal Skysinger, Zillah Wyrmhunter, Irad Skintaker, Mesh Horsegutter and Kali Deathsight: all raised the fist to their chest in approval.

Finally, Arla Hornripper stood alone without her fist to her chest. Anak glanced at her. "And you?"

She narrowed her eyes at Ursus, and, at length, said, "No. Not ready."

Zillah grunted in derision, "He has not destroyed enough wagons?"

"His training is finished," Arla snapped, "but he needs more time. He is young, and his blood is hotter than most with the madness. He does not yet control it."

Ursus glowered at her. His heart beat thunder in his chest. Without a unanimous accord among the clan, he would remain a child in their eyes.

Laban scoffed, "You are too careful. How can he learn to temper the rage if he never feels it?"

Arla whirled on him. "Would you risk losing him, as we lost Bys'sal? Would you have another of us chained in Hinnom?"

Anak's voice was level, admitting no bias. "Mammon calls us. If Ursus does not come, one must stay."

The clan looked to Arla, and her lip curled. No Tor Kayn could abide nursemaiding a child while the clan went to war, and Anak knew it. As the sole dissenter, there was only one logical choice for who would stay.

At last, Arla lifted her fist, but did not quite raise it to her chest. "On one condition."

Anak nodded. "Speak it."

Arla looked at Ursus. "He does not kill. He watches. He learns. He moves with us. But he will not shed blood. Not until he gains control of the madness. I will not lose another."

Some of the Tor Kayn scoffed, but Anak lifted a hand to still them. "Arla has spoken. Who knows better than she?"

Grunts of assent, some grudging.

Ursus burned to give voice to his rage, but it was not permitted him to speak in the council, only to listen. Dekel sported only one ear as a token of his failure as a youth, while Arla wore the other as a dried strip of leather on her belt.

Anak gestured. "Again. Vote, knowing the condition."

As one, the Tor Kayn raised fists to their chests.

At last, a smile crept across Anak's face, even as frustration blazed furious and hot within Ursus's heart. "Call the mortal. Tell him to tell Mammon that the Tor Kayn march to war."

The clan arrived at the temple of Bel Farak in the span of a month. Their slaves immediately set to erecting a forge before they built the encampment, for when the Three called upon the Tor Kayn, the armor and weapons of the clan swiftly required repair. The clan was not easy on equipment.

Dull booms sounded miles away, and Ursus knew he heard the reports of cannon, the contraptions of Men that hurled hot metal through masses of troops and felled the greatest monsters. These cannons were the only reason the Three had not yet overrun the battle lines of Bel Farak.

Lines of cultists, demons and beasts marched toward the distant battle line. Packs of wolves barked and howled, siege breaker monsters roared as their handlers jabbed them with goads, and formations of warriors shouted as they jogged in lockstep to the war.

Ursus and Arla accompanied Anak as he entered the temple. The Slaughterlord made no obeisance as he passed the icons and statues of Mammon, eliciting hisses of disgust from the others gathering there. One, an emaciated woman with sulfurous eyes and a train of spiders' legs, spat at them, but dared come no closer.

Anak ignored them all. He reached the great bronze doors of Mammon's sanctuary and passed inside without announcement, leaving Ursus and Arla without.

Arla crossed her arms over her chest, leaving the handles of her twin axes within easy reach. She wore a death mask over her face, a snarling demon's skull torn from the body of a magma-haunter. She seemed unconcerned by the warlords of Mammon all about them, glaring at them.

Ursus felt rage flare within his chest at their blatant disrespect for the Tor Kayn.

He sidled closer to Arla. "They hate us," he stated without preamble.

Arla nodded. "Yes."

"Why?"

Arla took a moment to respond, as she often did. Arla said nothing without thinking through it first.

"We serve, but we do not slave. We honor, but we do not worship." She looked at him. "And we never will."

Ursus considered her words and scanned the temple once more. All of them bore marks of allegiance to Mammon in one way or another. Some were as innocuous as tattoos, but others bore his gifts in their bodies. Bloated bellies, rail-thin skeletal horrors, distended jaws and more: each slave of Mammon had been altered or mutated to reflect their lord's gifts.

Behind them, the portal yawned open, and Anak emerged. He stalked past Arla and Ursus, again ignoring the throng of warlords in the temple. They made way, for none wished to dare the wrath of the Slaughterlord. There were old bloodstains on the vaulted ceiling that bore silent testament to such encounters.

Outside the temple, the Tor Kayn already assembled. Fourteen goliaths sheathed in thick iron stood still as stone in a knot of killing power, awaiting the word of their lord. Cannon fire echoed in the distance, the sounds of Samothrace's continuing defiance.

Arla asked first. "So, what do we kill first?"

The fortress of Uld-Galad had stood for a thousand years. Built by the ancient kings of Men to stem the demonic tide, the great bulwark sat upon a mesa overlooking one of the few passes through the Spine of Farak.

It had changed hands dozens of times in the generations-long conflict. With the advent of cannon, Samothrace had successfully held the fortress for fifty years, decimating assault wave after assault wave with devastating artillery. The open ground beneath the fortress was a hellscape of craters, shattered weapons and broken armor.

It was into this killing field, a half-mile stretch of broken ground and exposed visibility, that the Tor Kayn walked.

Ursus walked with his clan to the field itself, but he did not wear armor, as he would not charge with the clan. He bore no weapon other than a simple spear. Arla had handed him the weapon with a growl, saying, "Use it to defend yourself only. Do not let me see you kill."

Laban, keenest of all the Tor Kayn with his senses, cocked his head and muttered, "They see us. We should go."

Anak nodded. "Then we go."

As one, the Tor Kayn broke into a loping run. Anak thrust out his arm, fingers splayed, and the clan spread even further, leaving yards between each warrior.

The first cannons fired. Puffs of smoke rose from the distance, and the sounds of dragon's passage through the air overhead heralded the arrival of the ordnance. Flowers of earth and flame sprouted from the field beyond the sprinting clan, concussive booms rippling like thunder.

It fascinated Ursus. Such power, at such range. It was as though Samothrace could summon the fists of the gods and slam them into their enemies.

A second barrage followed, a blaze of fire and smoke from the distant wall, and the explosions erupted again, blasting chunks of rock out of the abused landscape.

Ursus narrowed his eyes. Those shots should have struck dead on, but between the firing of the cannons and the impact of the explosives, the Tor Kayn slowed to a jog. The shots fell far short of their targets.

And with that, he saw his father's genius. The weapons of the enemy were powerful, easily capable of killing a Tor Kayn in full armor, but they required calculation to place the rounds on their targets.

The siege engineers of Uld-Galad had had fifty years to range their weapons, but on their first volley, they had not counted on the sheer speed the Tor Kayn could summon. The first shots had passed well overhead, but after the second volley sounded, Anak signaled for the clan to slow, causing the placement of the rounds to throw up geysers of dirt in the battlefield instead of landing on target on the advancing warriors.

Anak thrust his goreblade forward, and this time, the Tor Kayn sprinted, zig-zagging as they ran. Ursus saw the panic begin in the pattern of fire from the defenders. Explosions rippled along the top of the wall as cannon crews desperately loaded and fired at will, trying to sight their guns on the small, fast-moving attackers.

Cannon fire blitzed above their heads, throwing dirt and rock into the air. Ursus's blood boiled with excitement at the thought of dodging such powerful blasts, and his vision sank into red for a moment.

However, Ursus tamped the rage down and forced it back. He would not prove Arla right. He would control himself, and one day, take his place at the front of the clan's assaults.

Eventually, the cannons, designed to decimate siege beasts and hordes of enemies, could not traverse low enough to hit the evasive elites approaching. Too late, archers mustered atop the battlements, but the mesa itself worked against them and fouled their angle of fire.

The Tor Kayn reached the base of the mesa and began to climb. Their fists and hands punched into the sunbaked stone of the mesa, hauling the warriors upward. They reached the base of the wall, and the archers, finally finding targets, loosed their shafts. Arrows fell like rain upon the giants, but their heavy armor stood proof against the deluge. Ursula saw Irad jerk an arrow from his thigh, and Zillah simply ignored the shafts embedded in her shoulders.

Arla shoulder-barged a door set into the wall, probably set so the Samothracians could sally out to recover wounded. The tiny gate smashed inward, and bells of alarm sounded within the keep.

Anak ducked through the doorway first, as was his right.

Uld-Galad was devoid of human life an hour later.

"Failure?"

The word hissed from Arla's lips. The clan gathered in the wreckage of the fortress, staring at the messenger of Mammon and the damning message he brought.

The man swallowed, but continued. "The fall of Uld-Galad was not the only objective of this assault. My lord Mammon also wished to procure the weapons within and repurpose them for his forces' use. Your failure to secure the cannon leaves him disappointed, and doubtful of the legendary reputation of the Tor Kayn."

"I am not listening to this," Raphela growled. The messenger let out a short squeak just before her hammer tore his head off of his shoulders.

Anak chuckled, and the rest of the Tor Kayn looked at him. "Lord?" Zillah queried.

"You are too sensitive, Shatterspine," Anak said. "The words of this wretch belong to our enemies, not Mammon."

He gestured around them, at the broken corpses and blood-painted stone. "Fifty seasons, they have striven to take Uld-Galad. Numbers have died that cannot be counted, and we, the Tor Kayn, have done so in one night without loss. These words mean nothing besides that we are feared by Mammon's slaves."

Jabal cocked his head. "And the cannons?"

Anak shrugged. "If I had such advantage over my enemies, I would destroy it as soon as they gained entry to the fortress. The cannons were destroyed when Arla gained us entry, and the gunnery commanders fled on horseback. All papers were burned. These knew their craft well."

"Not well enough," Irad commented, and that drew some chuckles from the others.

Ursus stepped forward, and the others quieted. The young were encouraged to question, and the clan considered it their responsibility to answer.

"Why do we allow these lies?" he asked, a smolder underlying his voice. "Why do we not fight these enemies who speak false?"

Anak leaned back. "A good question. Pison, you shall answer it."

Pison grinned and rolled his shoulders. "This is how the weak fight: with lies, whispers and falsehood."

His brother Gihon finished his thought. "This is not our way."

"Instead, we will be strong enough that their plots mean nothing," Laban said.

Gisela picked a chunk of flesh out of her knucklespines and said, "To follow them in their games is to lose sight of our purpose."

Anak pointed at Gisela and said, "And that...is weakness."

He looked at them all. "Our next assignment shall not be worth our effort. Those jealous of our strength cannot allow us to have such glory again so soon, and Mammon will heed their words to appease his other forces."

The Slaughterlord, as ever, was right.

Orders came to secure the area behind the new battleline set by the fall of Uld-Galad. A caravan, trying to flee the raiders of Hell's armies. Anak accepted the assignment without a word, and minutes later, the Tor Kayn departed.

In less than an hour of travel, they saw the caravan in the midst of the salt plains of Bel Farak, an expanse of white sand broken by spires of salt-encrusted rock. The heat came off the sand in shimmering waves around the milling mass of humans as they tried to mount a broken wheel.

The Tor Kayn stood on a spire a full mile away.

Anak considered the target. "Thoughts?"

Mesh Horsegutter scratched at his chin. "It is exposed. Far from the rocks. This is wyrm territory."

Arla shrugged. "According to the seers, they burrow to the north of here. This will not take long enough to attract their attention."

Anak nodded. "We go then."

Ursus lifted his spear, but Arla's hand slammed into his chest. "Not you. Stay. Watch."

Ursus opened his mouth to say something, to roar in exasperation, but Anak cut him off. Lowering his iron helmet over his head, Anak said, "No glory here, boy. This is not the fight to gain a beating from the Hornripper over. Wait until there is something worthy to kill."

Forcing back the red from his eyes, Ursus swallowed his fury and bowed. "I obey."

Arla shouldered past him. "Yes. You do."

Minutes later, Anak considered the corpses of the caravan before him.

Flames guttered in the ravaged hulks of the overturned wagons, burning something sweet and heavy in spice. The bodies of soldiers littered the naked earth, practically torn apart by the savagery of the clan's assault.

His gaze turned to these. Of those mostly intact, he could see they wore leather armor only, of the cheapest make. They bore spears in place of swords or shields. Each bore a slave's brand on his cheek.

It was this brand that concerned him.

"Too few," Arla muttered nearby. The titan crouched by the sundered bodies. "The boy could fight this and not feel a thing."

Anak grunted his assent. This was not right.

One did not send Mammon's slaughterers to such a pitiful prize as this, even in a jealous fit. Especially when the victims bore Mammon's own brand upon their cheeks.

He opened his mouth to disperse his warriors, and an earth-shattering roar stole his words.

Simultaneously, all fifteen Tor Kayn warriors snapped to see the source.

There, cutting them off from the safety of the ridge, writhed a sinuous monster of hateful legend. It roiled toward them, the sun flashing from its beryl-colored scales, as long as ten ships. Its mouth, a chasm of fangs and sulfurous breath, gaped open wide, the fury of Hell hissing from its maw.

Anak opened his mouth and bellowed, "Firewyrm!"

The blood of every titan present flushed cold in their veins, and they sprinted for the nearest rock formation, arms pumping furiously to clear the hideous mile of open space in which the firewyrm found them.

Running as fast as any of them, Anak cursed the seers of Mammon with the breath he could spare. Those damnable soothsayers should have known a firewyrm roamed this region. They should have warned the tribe of the danger, that they might have stayed closer to the mesas dotting the landscape for protection.

From the brands he saw on the bodies, he had a horrible feeling the seers had known exactly where the firewyrms hunted.

"Anak!"

He twisted to see Arla skidding to a halt, some yards behind. She looked back to the firewyrm.

No, not the firewyrm. Anak looked in time to see a young Tor Kayn launch himself from the ridge with his spear raised high and a ferocious war cry that rang across the barren wasteland.

Ursus.

The boy landed on the neck of the hellish creature and slammed his spear between the ridged scales into its undulating flesh. The firewyrm screamed in rage and turned from the clan, snapping furiously at the determined young titan clinging to his spear. Even from this distance, Anak could see him hauling on the spear, forcing it deeper into the monster's body, forcing it away from his family.

The screams of the wyrm and the roar of the Slaughterlord's heir vied for volume as the monster tore a hole into the earth and dragged them both down underground.

Arla glanced at Anak accusatorily and leveled her finger at him. "You said he could fight a worthy foe."

With another snarl, Anak wrenched himself around and launched himself toward the hole, goreblade gripped tight in his fist. The battle roars of the tribe rose behind him as the Tor Kayn joined their chief, fourteen giants thundering across the waste to slay a dragon. For a moment, a glimmer of pride touched Anak's soul at the sight of his son's fearlessness, even as he wondered how in the name of the Three they were going to kill this thing.

Ursus ducked as the firewyrm smashed a hole in the ground with its armored snout and dragged them into it. Rock and sand exploded past Ursus's head, and he dropped to his stomach as the lip of the crater flashed toward his head, gripping the titanic wyrm for all he was worth. The butt of his spear clipped the edge, and the impact snapped the staff, tearing it out of the firewyrm's hide and leaving the blade embedded.

Darkness swallowed him completely as the wyrm burrowed deeper. Ursus was forced to keep his head down and away from the direction of the wyrm's passage, lest the torrent of silt and pebbles fall down his throat and choke him. The cacophony of breaking rocks threatened to deafen him, and the noxious reek of the firewyrm's hide made his head swim.

With a cracking explosion, Ursus and his mount broke out into open space. A vaulted underground cavern met Ursus's eyes, lit dimly by a distant hole in the ceiling above. Ursus clenched his grip even more tightly, and it was fortunate that he did so. The wyrm wrenched to the side, trying to buck the giant off of its back. Ursus felt his body go weightless, but with a bellow of denial, he dug his fingers into the creature's flesh and rammed his feet under its armored plating.

Screeching, the wyrm slammed its body against the cavern wall and twisted, slithering against the stone face with all of its weight to scrape him off.

The fire in Ursus's blood ignited in hatred, threatening to deaden his mind. He yearned to keep his grip, tear the wyrm apart with his hands, but his mind shouted for him to release and not be torn to strips of bloody flesh.

He is too young. He cannot control it.

Ursus bellowed and leapt from the monster's back just before the rock tore him apart. He hit the cavern floor and rolled to his feet. The wyrm twitched its head toward him and lunged, mouth opening with ring upon ring of serrated teeth. Ursus dashed to the side, dodging the creature's mouth by a yard, and rammed his fist into its armored nose.

The wyrm reared back and slapped him with its snout. The only thing that kept Ursus from being instantly killed by several tons of wyrm weight behind the impact was the rocky pillar the firewyrm smashed against before hitting him.

Even so, Ursus flew fifty yards through the air and rebounded from the side of the cavern. Even though stars flashed behind his vision, Ursus pushed himself to his feet in time to see the firewyrm in front of him again, emerging from a tunnel, mouth gaping with a terrible fire within.

For a moment, Ursus's mind seized as he rolled to the side, clawing at the dome-like rocks to pull him out of the way of its flame breath. It could not do that. It was not possible for it to move that fast.

And he was correct.

From behind him, the firewyrm roared. The one in front of him answered.

Two of them.

Ursus slammed a palm down onto one of the stones to get a grip and tried to stand. But the surface of the rock broke beneath his palm, and his hand punched down into a thick, warm soup. A sulfurous smell blasted into his face, and he nearly retched from the reek.

Ursus withdrew his hand and saw a trail of yellow slime clinging to his fist.

"This one!"

Anak heard Laban's shout and thundered toward the hole the Tor Kayn had chosen. He and the others reached the lip of the crater and saw that it peered down into the cavern Ursus fought in. Chest heaving from the sprint, Anak squinted.

"Jabal?"

Jabal Skysinger was their hunter. He knew the beasts of the hellscapes far better than any other.

"Lord."

Anak pointed. "Why are there two mouthfires?"

Jabal looked down and winced.

Anak glanced at him sharply. "What?"

The Skysinger's eyes looked reticent. He did not want to give this information. "Two males, lord."

Anak's eyes widened. "Two?"

Jabal nodded. "There is something else."

Anak's growl bordered on fratricidal. "What. Is. It."

Jabal gestured helplessly. "The cavern. It's a nest. These males are fighting for breeding rights with a female."

Anak's heart dropped. "A female?"

"And...."

"And what?"

Jabal looked as though he would rather be anywhere else at that moment. "And your son just crushed an egg."

Ursus did not know any curses. None of the Tor Kayn swore around him; for a young Tor Kayn, control was everything, and swearing represented a lack of control.

When the cavern rocked around him from the earth-shattering impact of yet another firewyrm, Ursus wished he knew at least one, so that he could say it over and over again.

The two males backed away, their snouts lowering to the ground in deference to the newcomer.

She was huge.

The female and lady of this nest towered above the other two wyrms. Her body was as thick as a battleship, pitted and scarred from centuries of burrowing. Her mouth flaps gaped open like petals, revealing a veritable cavern in itself of razor-sharp fangs with a dull orange furnace smoldering behind.

She gave an odd snuffling sound, a series of several short pants as she waved her head about.

Like she was sniffing.

Then her eyeless head snapped toward Ursus, who still bore the noxious slime upon his hand.

The snouts of the other two wyrms followed suit, all focusing on the Tor Kayn who bore the death of their young on his hands.

Silence hung in the air for a moment. Ursus looked from wyrm to wyrm, then at the yolk on his hand.

Hit the wagon.

His lips twisting in a sneer, Ursus stomped on another egg, grinding it with his heel and splattering the ground and wall with unborn viscera.

The queen shrieked in outrage, and Ursus roared right back.

Barks of shocked laughter burst from several of the Tor Kayn as Ursus pulverized another of the wyrm queen's young.

Arla gritted her teeth. She was doing a lot of that today. "I said, he was too young. I said, leave him behind."

"If we had, we would be dead," Anak snarled. "Laban, Raphela, find a way down there."

They glanced at him.

"For what?" Raphela asked. "Your heir is doomed. Make another one."

Gisela shrugged. "He is too weak to fight the wyrms, lord. He will die bravely, as we all hope to."

A hundred yards down, Ursus dove aside as the queen lunged forward, rocks spraying from the floor as she slammed into the stone. Another of the males leapt forward, landing on the supine body of the queen to snap at Ursus. She snaked around and smashed her snout into the plates just behind the prow armor of the creature's snout, and the male cried out in pain.

Fury poured through Ursus's veins like channels of magma, but even in his haze of bloodlust, he saw the armored crest of the wyrm separate from the flesh for an instant.

A weakness.

The queen thrashed angrily under the weight of the male, spitting fire, and the smaller firewyrm struggled to withdraw, to heave its bulk away from her in obedience to her will.

He would never have a better chance. Ursus took two steps back, dashed forward and catapulted himself on top of the male. As his body impacted into it, Ursus wedged his hands under the armor plates of the neck opposite the side the queen attacked. It tried to rear up, but the queen struck it again, and it dropped again to shield its vulnerable neck joint, hissing furiously at the assault.

Timing his moment on the bucking monster, Ursus lunged forward. His shoulder slammed into the underside of the male's fanned prow plate, and with a shout, he thrust with his legs and lifted. With a wet tear, the plate tore free of its skull anchors, exposing glistening pink flesh beneath.

The male's scream deafened even its kin. Ursus grimaced and took a step forward, levering the plate up further. She had to strike soon.

The male's thrashing atop her enraged the queen beyond thought. The gigantic wyrm coiled back and struck, her own armored prow smashing into the hapless male's neck again. This time, however, Ursus thrust with his legs again in a mighty heave, hurling his shoulder into the armored crest.

Like a wagon.

The front half of the firewyrm's skull sheared off completely at the combined impact. Slime sprayed in every direction from the awful wound, and Ursus struggled to find his footing. He launched himself from the wyrm's back as it started to die. Its body convulsed explosively as the pent-up energy within its body began to whip it around.

Like a chain stretched to unthinkable tension and snapped, the wyrm's corpse lashed out. The other male was smashed against the cavern wall by its rival's death throes, even as it shrank back to avoid the hits. The headless body battered the queen beneath it, cracking her ancient armor with repeated impacts and beating her against the floor.

With a furious hiss, the queen managed to shuck the writhing corpse of her lover off of her and regain her balance. She reared back, sniffing once more to find her prey.

She found him, when one of her eggs exploded across her snout.

Breath, hot and furious, gusted from Anak's nostrils. "To fight two firewyrms and a queen with empty hands is not weakness."

Mesh, youngest of them to bear the mantle of Tor Kayn, could not refrain from speaking. "To die is."

They never saw Anak move. One second, he stood at the lip of the tunnel, arguing for his son's life. The next, Mesh lay on his back, the killing edge of the goreblade digging into his neck.

Ropes of spittle sprayed from Anak's mouth as he snarled, "You would have left him to die at birth, as well. Yet he has proven to be the strongest of us."

He glared at the Tor Kayn around him. "Below us, the wyrms circle a hero. I find them more honorable than those that would leave him to die."

The world rocked as the wyrms roared and crashed beneath them. The Tor Kayn struggled to keep their feet, and Anak snarled, "What was that?"

Jabal glanced down the crater and started to chuckle.

"What's so funny?" Arla glared at him.

"He's killed one," the hunter commented.

As one, the Tor Kayn turned to him.

"You jest," Gisela said.

Jabal shook his head. "Tore its skull off. Looks like the throes hurt the others."

They stared at him. Jabal looked back down. "And...now he is throwing eggs at the queen."

Arla gave a disbelieving chuckle. "By the gods that are not, he is your son."

"I," Anak breathed, "am done talking about this."

Ursus snatched up another egg and sidearmed it up at the towering colossus. It exploded across her neck, leaving yellow streaks across her broken armor. The creature inhaled deeply and lunged forward, vomiting a stream of molten chemical fire toward her tormentor.

Ursus leapt for the cover of a massive stalagmite, bellowing in pain as the top layer of his skin blackened from the heat. The air scorched his lungs even as he breathed it, and he was forced to close his eyes against the fire, lest the orbs be cooked in their sockets.

As though a dam had closed, the blast cut off, and Ursus staggered from his cover with blistered skin. Forcing his feet to pound the stone, he managed to dodge another lunge by the queen, but found his way barred by the second male.

Both wyrms circled him now, and there was nowhere else left for Ursus to run. His joints were locking up from the searing blast, and he found it nearly impossible to move.

The male lifted its head and shuddered in the grip of fury. The petals of its mouth opened, ready to gulp its prey down. Ursus growled and readied himself. If he were to be eaten, then he would tear it apart from the inside before the flames boiled his f—

died.

Something dark and sheathed in iron landed on top of the firewyrm and slammed a weapon into its back behind its skull. The firewyrm reared back in shock, and with a roar, the figure gripped the hilt and fell, dragging the blade vertically down the firewyrm's back, splitting it open like a torn seam. The monster fell backwards, and its foul organs slapped against the ground wetly before the bulk of the beast crushed them.

Anak, Slaughterlord of the Tor Kayn, hit the floor, jerked the gore-blade from the spasming firewyrm, and stabbed it at the queen wyrm with hatred in his eyes.

"Get away from my son, you wyrm whore," he rasped.

Ursus never saw anything like the battle again. The wyrm queen tried everything to kill the Slaughterlord. Anak endured torrents of fire to carve pieces of the monster away. He dodged the crushing weight of her body and rammed his goreblade up to the hilt in her spine, twisting and ripping to try to sever the great cord running down her back. The floor of the cavern sloshed with the wyrms' combined blood, lapping at Ursus's feet like a fetid tide.

Anak should have been a battle-king from the legends. Ursus watched in awe as his father battled the great wyrm queen in close combat in her own nest. Firelight gleamed from the Slaughterlord's armor as he fought, and the cavern shook when Anak smashed her skull against the side of the cavern.

At last, though, the wyrm queen cornered the Slaughterlord and struck him a true blow. A stone fouled Anak's step as he tried to leap away from her lunge, and he stumbled. The bulk of the queen's weight slammed on top of him, and he only managed to just get his goreblade pointed up.

The queen screamed in mortal agony as her weight thrust her onto the goreblade, driving it deep within her core and finally tearing through the column of nerves snaking through her body.

Then Anak began to cut.

The queen took eight minutes to die, thrashing around the chamber and shrieking in ungodly furor. Gouts of flame burst from her mouth, and Ursus was forced to find cover, lest the frantic blasts find and kill him by accident.

In the end, the queen shivered like a dying fish, a last gasp of chemical reek exhaling from her mouth. With the clamor ended, Ursus could hear the sound of sawing within.

When Anak finally emerged from the rent he carved in the queen's side, Ursus nearly did not recognize his father. All his hair had been burned off. The yellow white of exposed bone shards poked through his shoulders, arms, and legs. Acid had stripped his skin away and left his eyes milky white with blindness.

Ursus staggered and knelt beside him. The Slaughterlord fell into a fit of coughing, hacking up bloody phlegm and spitting it onto the stone floor.

"Ursus..." Anak breathed.

Ursus gripped his hand. "Father," he answered.

Anak gripped the handle of the goreblade and slowly passed it to him. "This is yours now."

Taking the sword in his hand, Ursus shook his head in denial. "No, lord. You will—"

"—not recover," Anak finished for him. "The wyrm has stolen all feeling from my legs, and the clan cannot be led by one who is both lame and blind. Our enemies would fall upon us in moments once they learned of such weakness."

Ursus took a deep breath. "The goreblade can only be taken in combat, lord."

Anak chuckled. "And so I, Anak, Slaughterlord of the Tor Kayn, accept your challenge, Ursus...Skulltaker, I think. You took the skull of a firewyrm by might alone. It is a good name for you."

For the first time in his life, tears stung Ursus's eyes. "I do not want this."

Anak grunted. "None who should lead do. But our clan deserves to led with strength, and I am no longer strong."

Ursus searched for words, but words were not his gift. There was nothing to say.

Anak reached up with his great, scarred hands, and gripped Ursus by the back of the neck. "Now fight me, boy. My life has been full. I have seen you grow to a man the gods will fear, and I am glad to be ended by the most fearsome warrior in Sinai."

Ursus stood, feeling the weight of the black greatsword in his hands. Slowly, he raised it above his head, his eyes never breaking from his father's gaze.

His voice shuddering, Ursus promised, "I will make you proud."

A smile touched Anak's scorched lips. "It is far too late for that."

The blade fell.

The temple of Bel Farak swarmed with the loathsome servants of Mammon. Bagral of the maksai pushed his way through the mob. He saw many he recognized: the seer Etrigan, the Consort, Gowbron the Feastmaster.

He made his way to these three. Gowbron saw him first and gestured him over. "Bagral!" the frog-headed warlord gushed in his warbling tones. "I hear celebration is in order!"

Bagral snorted. "Too long to happen," he growled. "My Herd lost many to Tor Kayn. It good Anak dead."

Ja'a fingered her flute of wine. "Mammon will not miss such a heretic from his forces. We are closer to purity now."

Etrigan shrugged. His body was thin to the point of starvation, and his eyes gleamed with madness. "You are welcome, lord of the maksai."

Bagral inclined his head. "My thanks, seer. Without word for where wyrms nest, death of Slaughterlord not possible."

Ja'a snickered and lounged back in her seat. "And now, what to do with the rest of his savages?"

Etrigan smiled. "There is talk of enslaving them for breeding purposes. Mammon is displeased with their rates of reproduction, and how they insist on training their young as an entire clan."

Gowbron chuckled. "A hard fight that will be, to put those monsters in chains."

Ja'a glared. "If the Faminefather commands it, it shall be done."

Bagral opened his mouth to acknowledge the sentiment, but gasps from the crowd cut him off. Cries of alarm rose up, and something heavy smashed into the floor of the cathedral, overturning tables and spilling wine. Guests and warlords leapt back from the tumbling object, swearing and screaming in equal measure. Once it came to rest, it became visible as a monstrous skull of a leering drake, all flesh scoured from the bone.

Bagral's eyes turned to the entrance of the temple, and his heart froze in his chest.

A goliath stood in the entry way, flanked by even more. The entirety of the Tor Kayn clan stalked into the temple feast, looming above the various warlords and mortals within.

Two of them hauled two more skulls on their shoulders, smaller but clearly also belonging to firewyrms. They were known to the warlords as Arla Hornripper and Jabal Skysinger.

The Tor Kayn at their head, Bagral almost recognized.

At first, he thought it Anak, returned from the dead. He wore his iron armor, the famed goreblade sheathed upon his back. His presence commanded the room, the sheer brutality of his every movement eliciting terror.

Yet Bagral knew it could not be his rival, because the newcomer clutched the skull of Anak in his giant fist.

Without a word, the giant in the Slaughterlord's armor stalked to the bronze gates of Mammon's sanctum. He made no obeisance to the images at the gate. He shoved the gate open and walked in, brazen and unannounced.

Beside Bagral, Ja'a hissed, "The effrontery!"

Etrigan stood to his feet and asked loudly, "Who does that oaf think he is, to barge in on Lord Mammon and disturb his repose?"

The one called Arla turned to him, her death mask inscrutable. "That is the Slaughterlord of the Tor Kayn, false seer. Is your sight blinded here, as well?"

Gasps rose at the insult. Yet another of the Tor Kayn, Jabal, continued speaking. "Know his name, slaves of Mammon. He is Ursus Skulltaker, the son of Anak, Slaughterlord of the Tor Kayn."

Bagral saw Arla turn the fury of her demon-head mask on him. Dread gripped his soul at the unremitting gaze, and Etrigan sputtered, "This is irregular! No warlord may ascend to command without Mammon's blessing! What are his qualifications? What virtues of command does he possess?"

Jabal set his skull down and sat on it, the relaxed nature of his repose no mask for the sheer lethality seeking to burst from him. "Fearlessness. Strength. Cunning. But we'll tell you what virtue he does not have."

"What?" Bagral snuffed uncertainly.

A predator's smile infected Arla Hornripper's voice as she answered with a satisfied snarl, "Control."

ASHES

Unlike most others of its kind, the door did not open to the small party huddled before it, trying to escape the gritty wind.

It told them to leave.

Talion scratched at his salt-and-pepper beard and commanded the guide, "Read it again. Perhaps you got it wrong."

Plep nodded obediently and turned back to the cuneiform slithering up the doorposts of the great stone door barring their path. Plep was a little gray man, his skin and that of all his kind tinted so by the desert in which they dwelt. The wind-swept expanse of the Onyx Desert threatened to stain all of them before they escaped it.

Plep muttered to himself, tracing a finger across the swirling lettering. One thing Talion had to give the little man; he was thorough. Talion told him to read it again, and the man read the entire thing again.

Finally, the guide gave a little honk and said in his nasal voice, "Oh, yes, yes. Um, this is tomb of Aj-Ardur, and um, it's cursed really badly, so, you know, you need to leave and not disturb the treasure within."

Behind Talion, one of his swords-for-hire grunted. He turned to face the young man with his steely gaze. "You have something to offer, Kel?"

The young ranger checked the edge of his dagger with his thumb before he answered. "I think you should beware of the natives' biases twisting the information they give you."

Plep screwed up his face in offense and stomped toward the mercenary. "Hey, we are Bobagan. We don't lie. We know this land well, for our ancestors lived here. We are Bobagan."

Kel glanced at Talion. "And that should tell you everything you need to know."

Talion gestured sharply at the ranger to fall silent, and the man complied with a small bow. "Spellcaster. Open it."

An exasperated sigh exploded behind him, and Bekla's voice filled his ears. "Daaaa," she whined. "Let us just go home. No one wants to be here except you."

Talion gritted his teeth for an instant, but forced himself to calm. "Once Marduk gets the door open, my pet, we'll get you out of the wind and sand."

He turned to see her pout a bit. "Fine," she relented. "But there's probably nothing here. Some *other* grave robbers probably got here first."

He leveled a finger at her. "Treasure hunters, daughter. Treasure hunters. And we but restore the glory of past civilizations to their descendants."

"For a price," Farim put in, his dark eyes glittering with avarice. The stocky ex-soldier remained entirely too close to Bekla for Talion's taste, but he managed to keep her out of his hair, so Talion suffered the proximity. Besides, Farim commanded the trio of guards, and it paid to stay in his favor.

Talion inclined his head toward Farim. "For a price. So, esteemed Marduk, do as you have promised, and open the Pyramid of Aj-Ardur for us."

Marduk walked up the steps, passing the diminutive Bobagan guide on his way up. His hands slipped within his robes, seeking the secret pocket that held the priceless Eye of Aj-Ardur. He pulled it out and relished the gasps at its revelation as its full beauty glittered in the light of the torches. The jewel weighed two pounds of flawlessly cut sapphire, and it shone as if lit from within when light touched it.

He heard Talion's entitled brat whisper to her father, "Da, I want that. Give it to me when we're done."

Her father shushed her, and Marduk smiled grimly. As if he would allow this thief and his spawn to possess what was rightfully his.

He approached the door and examined it. The entire edifice of the pyramid had been cut from sandstone and blackened by the Onyx Desert's winds. The door, however, was dark iron, and would be nearly impossible to break through. The ancient lords of this land intended their tombs to be accessed only by their kin.

The door held a large indentation in its center, almost a mouth with spines reaching out of its border. Marduk recognized it from the books he had studied to prepare for this expedition. "And now, lord," he announced to Talion, "my promise is kept."

He pressed the Eye into the mouth. Something clicked, and Marduk only just managed to snatch his hand away before the spines *snick*ed into place over the gem. A burst of blue light snaked across the surface of the door, like bolts of lightning, and disappeared into the sandstone of the black pyramid.

With a crack as hidden gears broke from their inactivity, the door sank into the floor, taking the Eye of Aj-Ardur with it. Marduk snatched at the gem with a curse, but it was not possible to break the jewel free of the spines before the priceless artifact vanished into the floor.

"Daaaaa!" Bekla shouted. "He lost it!"

Farim put a comforting arm around her shoulders and snapped, "What's the matter, wizard? Did they not cover this subject at your school, or did you fail out *before* you reached that class?"

Marduk ground his teeth, but kept back a fiery retort, well aware that Talion might consider his usefulness at an end now. It was the ranger who interceded for him.

"Peace, Farim. I am certain the kings intended to enter this tomb more than once and had a method of reclaiming their key. We shall discover it in due course."

Kel unslung his short bow and put an arrow to the string. "Now, however, we must survive the tomb of Aj-Ardur."

Talion grunted. "Survive it? What makes you think it's trying to kill us?"

Marduk nodded. "He's right, lord. This crypt is likely to contain the relics and knowledge of Ardur, the ancient prophet that turned this land into the onyx wasteland it is now."

"His name was just Ardur?" Farim cocked his head. "What does the Aj stand for, then?"

Marduk turned away and stepped into the shadow of the interior as he answered, "It was a title adopted by the lords of this land. The prefix *Aj* signifies that one is a lord of the Everlasting Dark."

The party moved past the threshold into the pyramid. Almost immediately, the howling of the wind outside cut off, and every breath and cough could be heard echoing throughout the dim interior. Their feet kicked up a carpet of dust several inches deep.

Kel crossed the threshold last. He paused by the doorway, examined a short column there, and pressed something atop it. Immediately, the door lifted back from the insert in the floor, sliding into place with the sound of stone grating on stone. A dull boom announced its arrival, and several cracks sounded from within the walls as locks clunked into place.

The Eye of Aj-Ardur now hung on this side of the door. The spines snapped outward from the gem, and Kel pulled the artifact free of its resting place in the door.

He tossed the priceless jewel to Marduk. "As I said."

Marduk caught the Eye and secreted it back into his robes, jealous that another had even touched his possession. His eyes narrowed to slits as he regarded the mercenary.

Soon, all offenses would be balanced.

Farim surveyed the corridor in which they found themselves. Cuneiform embroidered the walls, looking much the same as the inscription covering the doorway, but looping over and over again. Other than that, no decoration could be found.

"Where is the treasure, lord Talion? Have others beaten us here?"

Talion stepped forward, peering around. "No, this place is different. There are no plinths to hold jewelry, no chests broken open, not even any means of hanging anything on the walls. This is not like any tomb of the ancients I have ever entered."

Farim kicked at the ground. "The sand is undisturbed, and the wind cannot penetrate within. We are the first to be here, I think."

"Unless the sand was swept," Kel commented.

They glanced at him. The bowman shrugged. "The gate opened smoothly. There are no treasures to greet the entrance of kings, which does not fit the narcissism of those ancient despots, yet this purports to be the tomb of fabled Aj-Ardur. This place feels like a trap."

Talion glared at him. "Then it is good I have hired swords here to protect us. Go use your keen judgment to find those traps you speak of."

Kel touched his first knuckle to his forehead in salute and moved off into the darkness of the pyramid, leaving them to watch him go.

"I don't like him," said Bekla.

"Then I shall kill him for you, and serve you his head," answered Farim.

The girl sighed. "You always know just what to say."

Marduk raised an eyebrow, but made no comment. This would be Talion's problem. "Shall we proceed, lord?"

Talion shot a glare at Farim, but visibly made an effort to ignore the soldier's conversation with his daughter. "Yes, we go. Farim, you shall lead."

Bekla pouted as Farim released her hand and made his way to the front of the party, hand on his scimitar. He called out orders as he walked.

"Salim, Felden, stay near the lord. Zayz, take the rear."

Salim and Felden answered crisply and shifted to their positions.

Farim glanced back and snapped. "Zayz? Answer!"

The wind howled outside like a lost soul.

They found the body by the doorway, near the column Kel used to close the portal behind them.

Farim lifted his man's head and let it fall back. "His neck has been broken."

Talion let out a breath through his gritted teeth. "How was he killed so that none of us could hear it?"

Farim's dark eyes narrowed in fury. "Perhaps you should ask the tracker you hired. He was the last to stand here."

Talion laughed. "Kel? And what reason would he have to kill us? He doesn't get paid until we arrive back in Athrenad. Maybe your man tripped and fell."

Shooting to his feet, Farim stabbed his finger at Talion. "Zayz has been with me since home, you thieving— "

Bekla stepped between Farim and her father and put a finger on Farim's lips. "Mm-mm, not now, sweet Farim."

Talion released the hilt of his own scimitar. "I don't care how many of you die, so long as my daughter and I leave this place with the treasure. Take care of your own lives and don't blame me for carelessness."

He turned back. "Now where is Plep? Plep!"

The little gray man shuffled forward. "Yes, lord? I am Plep."

Talion gestured toward the corridor. "Your people have the most experience with these tombs. Please lead us to the primary burial chamber."

Plep beamed at him. "We are Bobagan!"

"Ah, yes. The chamber, if you please."

The journey did not take long. Plep led them through a sandy corridor that seemed to inscribe a series of squares on the interior of the pyramid. When they finished traversing a square, an entry way led them deeper into the bowels of the crypt.

Footprints marred the sand before them, evidence of Kel's passage. They found toxin-tipped darts embedded in the walls, spears sprung from the ground and pits gaping at them from the ground.

They did not find a drop of blood.

"Your man seems remarkably skilled," Marduk commented as he gingerly stepped over a line of spring-loaded traps filled with iron teeth.

Farim nodded, for once his insolent tone bordering on respect. "The guilds in Athrenad said Kel has no equal. I'm starting to believe them."

Talion scowled, hiking up his robes to prevent them catching on the iron teeth. "His fee has no equal, either. Why all these traps, for so little treasure? If we don't find something, we're going to take a serious loss on this venture."

Bekla shrugged. "Maybe Ardur just wanted to be left alone?"

Before them, Plep halted. "Here you are, most excellent masters. The resting place of Aj-Ardur."

The anticipation of the party rose to a fever pitch. They shoved and pushed past one another as they hurried to enter.

The scene within took their words away.

There was little in the great chamber. The black stone walls slanted toward the ceiling, ending in a point far above their heads. In the center of the room, a sarcophagus with a carved lid stood above a large black stone circle on the floor. The image of a somber man in repose rose from the sarcophagus, forged with exceptional craftsmanship.

Four other statues, images of faceless men and women in dark robes, stood around the circumference of the circle with the sarcophagus. Hands carved from onyx reached from the sarcophagus toward it, mirroring the hands of the statues.

They seemed to press down, holding something in.

After half a minute of gaping, Farim turned to his master and hissed, "There's *nothing in here!*"

Talion could not speak. Most burial chambers of the Onyx Desert abounded with treasures and artifacts, as the ancient kings surrounded themselves with wealth to take to the afterlife. This chamber held... nothing.

Marduk walked toward the sarcophagus and the black circle. His eyes were wide as he took in the cuneiform carved on the sarcophagus, the edge of the circle, the perimeter of the walls.

It was *everywhere.*

Talion glared at him. "What is it, wizard?"

Marduk cleared his throat. "I have seen nothing like this. This place... it lacks any treasure on purpose."

"What do you mean?" Farim growled.

Marduk pointed. "Look. The runes tell the story."

He indicated the walls of the room. "It says that Aj-Ardur, Lord of the Everlasting Dark, and eight acolytes embarked on a journey to the desert to find an object that fell from the sky. Somehow, they had warning of it, some kind of prophecy among the followers of the Dark."

"Now, here, you can see that they found it. But," Marduk squinted at the writing, "they did not find what they thought they would find. They found only death, and at significant cost to themselves, sealed it away rather than risk it being found."

Talion furrowed his brow, staring at the statues holding the black circle down. "What was it?"

Marduk traced his hand across a swirling band of lettering. "The writing is strange. There are spaces where there should be words, as if the carver were forbidden from writing the thing's name. Voids...."

He gasped suddenly.

"Not voids. The Void."

His eyes darted around, falling on the lettering on the black stone circle. "It is not possible," he whispered.

"What isn't possible?" Farim barked.

"This place," Marduk breathed. "It isn't just the tomb of Aj-Ardur. This is the crypt-prison of Aj-Kenaz."

Plep ducked his head and mumbled something, fingering a string of beads, while everyone looked at him. Finally, Bekla asked, "Who?"

Marduk pinched the bridge of his nose. "In the libraries of the Scion, the oldest books tell of a sorcerer who traveled to the Darkness beyond the stars, a man named Kenaz. He is recorded as the first Lord of the Everlasting Dark, the first of the Ajen. Thousands of years ago, he performed an immense sacrifice, slaughtering thousands of his subjects to gather the power for his journey. It is believed that the Onyx Desert is actually the residue of his ritual."

"Aj-Kenaz sought the great dragon of the Void that prowls beyond the Light of the stars, the ancient serpent of chaos, Tamath. He told his servants, those that would become the Ajen of the Dark, to expect his return, for he would bring with him a weapon able to snuff out the Light that prevents Tamath's return."

Marduk drew in a shaky breath. "Aj-Ardur must have found Kenaz, but instead of serving him, he sealed him away. Here."

Marduk gestured about him. "That is why there is no treasure. Ardur wanted nothing that would draw anyone to this place, nothing that might accidentally free whatever he found."

He pointed at the black circle. "This must be a coverstone for a second crypt beneath the Tomb of Aj-Ardur, a seal to keep the dark lord in. It must be that the Tomb of Aj-Kenaz lies beneath, along with whatever it was he brought back from beyond the barrier of the stars."

"What did he bring back?" Bekla asked.

Marduk squinted at the carvings again. "I am uncertain. The phrasing is metaphorical, and the meaning is difficult to determine. Cloak, perhaps, or skin? Something to coat the wearer in the deep Dark and protect them from Light."

Talion glanced at him, shrewd calculation in his gaze. "Would that be valuable?"

Marduk blew out his breath rudely. "Of course, you cave-dwelling rock-pounder! There would be nothing else like it in all the world. Even the starswords could not compare with an artifact from the Void!"

At the mention of the starswords, everyone's eyes lit up. Marduk gritted his teeth and tried to calm his speech. "Whoever has this artifact can ask the wealth of nations and expect to receive it. It is beyond price."

Farim pressed his lips together. "Then we should go now and retrieve it."

One of Farim's men, Salim, pointed at a section of wall, covered in recurring glyphs. "Wait. This one all says the same thing. What's it mean?"

Marduk peered at the wall section. "As far as I can tell, it is a single imperative, pitched in the most direct tense the language has."

"Yeah?" Farim said. "And what's it say?"

"Uh, it says '*Get out.*'"

Beklah blew her breath out rudely. "Please. They would say that, just to keep us from getting the treasure."

Felden shook his head. "That warning's carved, woman. Someone thought it was real enough to waste time etching it into a wall over and over again."

Farim glared at him. "So?"

The soldier glanced at Salim for support. "So, maybe we should listen. Nothing about this place has been like a normal tomb. And we still don't know who or what killed Zayz."

Talion walked toward the black slab. "Captain, get control of your men. We're not going anywhere until we have what we came for."

"We should hurry," Marduk said.

He pointed at the sand before the coverstone. "By the footprints, it looks like your man Kel's already entered the second tomb."

It was an act of simplicity itself to find the lever Kel had used to open the crypt. Marduk pushed the arms of Aj-Ardur's sarcophagus back, and the coverstone transformed with the sound of scraping rock into a stairway, descending into the blackness beneath.

Farim made to take a step down, but Talion stopped him with a hard palm to his chest. "I think not. This treasure is mine."

Farim's eyes glittered in anger, but he stepped back, allowing Talion to shuffle down the stairs. He exchanged looks with his men, then Bekla.

Marduk did not miss the silent message passed between them.

Bekla pulled out a dagger from her belt and quietly stepped down after her father.

The darkness above had been oppressive. Down here, it was a physical thing weighing on Talion's heart. He could feel it pressing on him, crushing him as though he walked on the floor of the ocean. He found it an effort to draw the stale air into his lungs. Even the sound of the others descending the staircase behind him seemed muted and hushed.

As his eyes adjusted to the dim light, Talion saw narrow hallways like black mouths in the walls. There was no light source other than the weak illumination from above. They would need torches to explore this crypt.

Talion heard the scrape of a soft shoe on the ground just behind him, and a sharp intake of breath he recognized. He turned back, arm lifting to take his daughter in an embrace.

That likely saved his life.

Bekla's dagger plunged into his side, but she was no assassin. Talion's voluminous robes fouled the blade and drove it upward to scrape along his ribs, leaving a gash of fiery pain. Talion swore and shoved her back.

"Bekla! What the devil is this!"

She swayed before him like a snake, her dagger held out in front of her. "I'm tired of waiting for you to die, old man. I'm tired of these endless treks into god-forsaken deserts. I want my inheritance now, before you spend it all on these stupid ventures."

She lashed out again, and Talion stumbled back, avoiding the blade. Anger and pride flared in him, and he kicked at her. "You ungrateful whore! I gave you everything!"

Bekla sneered at him. "'Everything' is less than it used to be, you toothless old man."

Talion saw Salim and Felden march down behind Bekla. He had been a thief for decades, and he knew the glint of murder when he saw it in a man's eyes.

All right, then. Let's see if the young can beat an old man's tricks, then.

His foot dipped into the sand at his feet, and he lashed out with his foot. Black grit exploded from the ground, blinding the three would-be killers, and Talion wheeled about and sprinted into the crypt, hand pressed to his side, grimacing at the pain.

Farim stalked down the stairs and saw Bekla and his men coughing and spitting. Talion had vanished.

"Where is he?" he growled.

Salim gestured to Bekla. "She let him get away."

Fury, hot and overwhelming, reddened Farim's face. "You *what?* How stupid could you be, you spoiled brat? How much more simple could it have been than stabbing an old man in the back?"

Bekla recoiled from him. "Don't you dare speak to me like that! I did my best!"

Farim clenched his fists and gritted his teeth to keep from screaming. "Every step of the way, you make this more difficult than it has to be."

She scoffed in disbelief. "Me? If you'd killed Da back in Athrenad, like I said, then we wouldn't be here right now."

"If I'd killed him in Athrenad," Farim snarled, "then we wouldn't have known where to find this pyramid supposedly filled with treasure!"

She glared at him, then her face softened. "Look, all we have to do is find a bleeding old man down here, finish him, and take whatever artifact there is down here. Then we can go back to civilization, and we can finally be together."

Farim's eyes narrowed, and he said, "I don't think we need you for any of that."

He snapped his fingers at Felden, and Bekla's breath exploded from her as his knife punched up through her diaphragm into her lungs.

"I needed you to secure this contract with Talion. Besides, you insolent witch," Farim hissed, "I'm already married."

Felden shoved her forward, and Bekla collapsed into the sand, her mouth working silently, like a fish out of water.

Disgust screwed up Farim's face at the sight of the repugnant woman, and he turned back to his men. "Find the old man and finish him, too."

He turned to see Marduk standing behind him. "This a problem for you, wizard?"

Marduk shrugged. "You saved me the effort of doing it myself."

Farim eyed him, then turned away. "Let's find this artifact of yours and get out of here. It's hard to breathe down here."

The sound of stone rasping against stone froze the two of them in their tracks. Both men looked back to see the coverstone sliding back into place, sealing them in the darkness.

The titles of Plep were many.

He was the Un, the wandering exile, the preparer of the Way, the bringer of harvest. The Bobagan people honored him greatly for both his calling and his steadfast dedication to it. He stood over the Great Seal now, watching as twenty of his tribe pushed it back into place, sealing the infidels within. The expression on his gray face was solemn, but his eyes gleamed with excitement.

As the stone slid over the gap in the floor, the Un raised his stubby arms in benediction. *"Khaz akay kolo atem. Bitala maka'a'telem, wutim Bobagan dilak."*

The unbelievers have taken the bait. The Great One will feed on their souls and walk among the Bobagan once more.

Gone was the fawning nasal tone used to project subservience to prey. In its place, the booming growl of a predator.

The three dozen Bobagan around the circumference of the room ducked their heads within their black robes and intoned, *"Jeel ack utim sut."*

May He walk among us again.

Plep snapped a quick gesture of command, and without further discussion, the cult broke apart and vanished into the darkness.

The Gathering had begun.

"Was that some kind of mechanism?" Salim asked.

Unease twisted Marduk's guts as he stared up at the immense

coverstone burying them within the pyramid. Beside him, Farim's men shifted to cover the doorways leading into the chamber they stood in. Marduk had to praise their discipline. Even sealed in the alleged tomb of a mythical sorcerer, they behaved as professionals.

For all the good it had done them so far.

Farim stepped away from the stairway first. "It doesn't matter," he barked. "We finish the mission, then we worry about getting out. Keep your eyes up. Find Talion."

He glanced at Marduk. "Keep that jewel handy, almost-wizard. Maybe it will get us out of here."

"Captain, what if we find Kel?" Felden asked. "What do you want us to do?"

Farim shrugged. "He's Talion's man. Kill him."

Salim and Felden glanced at one another, and Felden muttered, "And what if he finds us?"

Farim glared at them. "There are four of us, brother. I think we can handle one ranger."

The mercenaries remained silent, but Marduk could feel their doubt lingering.

Taking a deep breath, Farim said, "All right. Let's go get the old man."

He stepped over the body of Beklah toward the hallways where Talion had disappeared, following the depressions in the sand.

Salim sighed and said, "It wasn't a mechanism."

Farim hesitated. "What?"

Salim pointed at the stone above them. "I can hear chanting."

Jeel ack utim sut.

Jeel ack utim sut.

Jeel ack utim sut.

The drone almost masked the sound of a dart lancing through Salim's neck. The man's head snapped to his shoulder as the bolt punched through his spine and dropped him convulsing to the sand.

"Down!" Farim roared, as more bolts hissed through the air. He and Felden fell immediately to deep crouches and scrambled for cover, blades held forward. Salim's eyes stared at them in mute terror as his life drained into the black sand, and Farim cursed silently. First Zayz, now Salim.

Talion had much to answer for.

Shafts sliced through the air toward Marduk, but the wizard muttered a few arcane words, moved his hand in a complicated symbol, and the darts ricocheted from an invisible ward.

Figures in black robes ducked within the hallways, popping up to loose their shafts from spring-loaded crossbows. They were short, and on more than one occasion, Farim caught sight of grey skin.

"Plep," he snarled. A bolt clanged from the stone next to his face, and he jerked back.

"Wizard!" Farim shouted. "Can you do something?"

Marduk nodded, his face lined with strain as more and more shafts slammed into his ward. "Shield your eyes!" he growled, and light exploded from his outstretched hand. The shadows fled the chamber as though they were sentient entities, and Farim saw the same cuneiform engravings covering every inch of the chamber's walls.

Get out.

Farim bolted for the hallway with Talion's footprints. Behind him, he heard Felden scream, "Captain!"

As he reached the temporary safety of the hallway, he looked back and saw Felden on the ground, a Bobagan strangling him from behind while three others held down his limbs.

Jeel ack utim sut.

"Help me!" Felden choked out, struggling to keep his throat from the Bobagan's forearm.

A blade glittered in the black, and Farim cried out, "Felden!"

The blade flashed down. All four black-robes released their prey and began stabbing the body in a frenzy.

Marduk grabbed Farim. "We have to get out of here!"

Farim snarled at him, "Not without my men!"

Marduk pulled at him, yelling, "They're already dead. Let's go!"

"Get off of me!"

Soldiers.

Marduk shoved Farim away and took off into the darkness. If the brute wanted to die beside his men, let him. Marduk did not intend to die today.

With a thought, he summoned small lights to orbit him and light his way. The last thing he needed was to survive an ambush, only to trip on a stone and crack his skull open.

Behind him, he could hear Farim roar in anger, and the clash of blade on blade. The squeals told him that Farim actually did possess some level of skill, though it would not alter the likelihood of his survival.

With each death cry, though, the whispers in the back of his mind grew in intensity.

Since the death of Zayz, Marduk had felt a susurration in his consciousness. It had been subtle, like wind moving through trees at a distance, or silk sliding across silk. Yet as the deaths mounted, the hushed voice had become an intense whisper, demanding Marduk's attention.

Suddenly, a command gripped Marduk's brain.

Karmen util bildi'al dalek.

Marduk's mind parsed the ancient language and translated it into a message of welcome.

Come to me, chosen.

It entranced him. As though in a dream, Marduk navigated the halls of the crypt, turning almost at random, guided by the harsh voice in his thoughts.

Karmen util bildi'al dalek.

At last, as he turned a corner, he saw it.

A simple garment of mail draped over an obsidian statue set in the center of a great hall. Plates as black as the dark beneath the mountains sheathed a simple coat of equally black links. The light did not glint off the edges of the metal; it either avoided the mail completely or was devoured before it could escape.

Towering statues, robed and cowled, stood against the walls, maintaining silent vigil over the artifact.

The scholar in Marduk noted their positioning. *Likely representatives of those who sealed this armor here. They stand as far away from the relic as possible, as though they feared it might pollute them even through their likenesses.*

The whisper in his mind drowned out all other thoughts.

Karmen util bildi'al dalek.

"You found it."

Marduk whipped around at the voice his ears could actually hear, and he felt a strange rush of guilt. He found that absurd. It was as though his conscience knew he had been listening to a voice forbidden to him.

Kel stood behind him in the chamber's entrance, arrow set to the string of his short bow. The lower end of his tunic was striped with blood where he had wiped his blade to clean it.

Marduk looked around. How had he crossed the room to the plinth? He did not remember stirring from the doorway.

The tracker did not seem bent on murder. He stood entirely relaxed, arrow angled toward the floor.

Marduk readied a spell and held it in his mind. If this mercenary dared...

Kel cocked his head. "Relax. I have no intention of stealing your prize. It is yours, as you are its."

"Back away, dog!"

Marduk twisted to see Talion stumbling in one of the doorways. He still held his side in pain, but clutched a hand crossbow in the other, aimed at Marduk. His hand trembled only slightly.

"That treasure," the old thief spat, "is *mine*. I lost my daughter to this venture. I deserve it. Now get on the ground!"

Slowly falling to his knees, Marduk glanced at Kel to see his reaction. To his surprise, the mercenary seemed not to care about his employer's entrance. If anything, he looked *bored*.

"What's the matter with you?" Talion hissed. "Did all the time in the dark steal your sense?"

Kel held up a finger in the universal command for *wait*. Talion looked puzzled for an instant, then gasped as all air exploded out of his lungs. He stared down at his chest, incredulous at the length of iron protruding from his sternum.

The mercenary offered his hand toward the transfixed thief, as if presenting him at court. "And there we have it."

Talion fell to his knees, revealing Farim behind him. The soldier panted, his body and face nicked and bleeding, but his expression contorted with fury as his victim toppled before him.

"That... is all you deserve, you old dung beetle!"

Farim stepped over the dying man and reached down to pick up his hand crossbow. He stood back up, aimed the crossbow at Marduk once more, and said, "Now, get away from that thing, if you please."

Karmen util bildi'al dalek.

Marduk blinked at the force of the sending, but felt the whisper's attention receding, turning to this newcomer. This strong one, able to overcome ambushers, murder his lord and threaten a sorcerer. Perhaps his body would be the better choice...

Marduk shook his head, trying to free whatever parasite it was that thought with his own mind. Kel stepped past him, an expression of mild impatience on his face. "Just put the armor on, wizard. I'll take care of this one."

Farim scoffed. "And what will you do, way-sniffer? Track me to death?"

Neither Marduk nor Farim even saw Kel move. In one instant, Kel was walking forward, bow angled down. In the next, a shaft leapt from the mercenary's bow and shattered the crossbow in Farim's hand. Farim dropped the weapon with a shouted curse and staggered back, massaging his injured hand.

Kel looked at him, his eyes cold. "That is, of course, your choice. If you would rather run to death like a horse than die in combat, then I can arrange that."

Karmen util bildi'al dalek.

Kel glanced back at Marduk. "Put it on. Your new master awaits."

Marduk's eyes went in and out of focus, but he reached for the link armor. As he did, he could hear dozens of Bobagan in the corridors without, droning their mindless chant.

Jeel ack utim sut.

Jeel ack utim sut.

He caught sight of Plep watching him from a doorway, his black eyes wet with tears. The diminutive traitor held a hand to his breast.

Marduk lifted the mail above his head and let it fall across his shoulders.

"No!" Farim shouted, and he rushed forward, shoving at Kel. The mercenary twisted like a snake, gripping Farim's wrist and tripping him with a savage kick. The blow knocked Farim off-balance, sending him tumbling forward toward Marduk and the plinth.

His balance was righted for him by a vise around his throat.

Farim choked, but nothing would pass through his lungs. The iron grip constricted his neck and squeezed, nearly causing the blood in his head to burst from their vessels.

Farim's feet left the floor, and he looked down at what had once been Marduk as the man lifted him from the ground with one hand.

If the ghost screaming in the back of this thing's eyes was any sign, Marduk was not in control anymore.

Marduk's face had become imperious and cold. His eyes were black upon black, and his dark veins spread like a poisoned web beneath his paling skin.

This was Farim's last sight in the realm of the living.

The last word he heard was, "Pathetic."

Aj-Kenaz, First Lord of the Everlasting Dark, let the limp body of the soldier fall from his grip, and looked upon his prison with eyes of flesh for the first time in centuries.

He saw the Faithful standing without. He could sense the heat of their bodies, hear the rush of excitement in the hot blood sloshing through their hearts. He saw the Un, the Primus of the Bobagan, the one banished from his own people to bring suitable vessels for

Kenaz's return. It was his solitary journey that had engineered this resurrection.

"Un." The word was a dread rasp.

The diminutive Bobagan crawled forward, not even daring to lift himself from his knees. He shuffled to a stop before the dark lord. "My Aj."

Aj-Kenaz looked down on him. "You have done well, slave. Your days of exile are over. No more will the Bobagan require that one of their number walk the Outlands alone to hunt their prey."

The servant quivered before him in ecstasy.

"Is that what 'Un' means? Lonely hunter?"

Now the dark gaze fell upon one who dared speak without leave. "And who is this?"

A man stood before him. He did not kneel in his presence, nor did he grovel at the majesty of the First Lord. He stood by, an arrow in one hand, a simple bow in the other, looking up at Aj-Kenaz with polite indifference.

Aj-Kenaz loomed over him. Already, his power was overwhelming the figure of the Sacrifice brought to him, and his physical frame swelled to contain it. In the back of his mind, the worm who had been Marduk shrieked, his voice heard only by oblivion.

The Un lifted his head, so as not to mumble his answer unclearly into the black sand. "This is Kel, my Aj. He is an Onyxian hunter who helped to bring the Sacrifice here."

The Dark Lord looked down on Kel and considered him. "And is he one of the Faithful, my Un?"

"I... am not sure, my Aj," the Bobagan said. "He has aided the Bobagan in your return and slain those who might have prevented it."

"Hm," Aj-Kenaz growled. "Interesting."

Kel stood before him, no evidence of fear or trembling in his demeanor. Aj-Kenaz found this almost unsettling.

"I have studied the writings of the Ajen. This is how I knew to find you in the Pyramid of Aj-Ardur."

Aj-Kenaz's lips pulled back from his teeth in a snarl. "Ardur," he spat. "That blind insect. He and the rest of those simpering fools claimed to serve the Lady of the Dark, but faltered when the time of their service had come."

Kel cocked his head. "I find the writings vague, as most one-sided accounts are. They allege that you traveled to the void beyond the star barrier. That you entered the court of the Dragon."

Aj-Kenaz closed his eyes, remembering. "Yes. I remember. It took the death energy of one hundred thousand slaves to make the journey. There, in the Everlasting Dark itself, I gained audience with mighty Tamath herself, and she bestowed on me this gift."

The Dark Lord indicated the black mail sheathing his body. "Dark-mail. Armor forged where no Light might reach it. It stands proof against all weapons forged in Light. She commanded that I use it to darken the way for her return."

Kel considered him. "But it cost you."

Aj-Kenaz nodded, almost weary. "To make the journey beyond the barrier of stars took the passage of centuries. By the time I received the gift of the Dark, I stood at the farthest limit of mortality. I was old, yet my mission remained. I would not allow Death to prevent my triumphant return."

Nodding, Kel said, "So you used your own death energy."

Aj-Kenaz smiled without humor. "You are quick-witted, Kel of the Onyxians. Yes, I sacrificed my body to generate the energy required to make the return journey, and bound my soul to Tamath's gift."

Kel chuckled. "Then you arrived, and the Ajen locked you away."

"They refused to provide a vessel suitable enough for my resurrection," Aj-Kenaz hissed. "Those traitors preferred to use the power of the Dark for their own advancement, rather than prepare the way for Tamath to darken Creation. Ardur sealed me within this prison and erased all mention of me from your civilizations. If not for the Bobagan tribes, I might never have been found."

Kel gestured. "Yet, at last, you have manifested on Avalon once more."

Aj-Kenaz nodded. "Indeed. And my vengeance will be swift indeed on all those who dared falter in their allegiance to me."

Kel smiled up at him. "Ordinarily, I would wish you the best in that pursuit, Kenaz. Unfortunately, I have other plans."

Aj-Kenaz's wrath ignited, and dark flames sprouted from his shoulders. "You dare blaspheme against me, worm?"

Kel chuckled. "I think you have taken yourself too seriously for some time now. I only allowed you to take poor Marduk's body to get you out of the darkmail. I require it for my own purposes, and I would rather not deal with a passenger."

Aj-Kenaz struck him. A bolt of pure Darkness lanced from the revenant's palm and transfixed the insolent man in the chest.

It only knocked him to one knee.

Aj-Kenaz's eyes widened. That bolt should have peeled the human like an apple. "H-how...?" he stammered.

In the wake of the blast, Kel no longer looked the same. The glamor cast over his features stripped away, blowing off like leaves, and he looked up at Aj-Kenaz now with eyes that glittered with the frozen hue of ice. His hair was white and straight, hanging lank and loose about his face. A terrible blade hung across his back, and Aj-Kenaz, so long accustomed to spiritual perceptions, recoiled from the horror of the sword's existence.

Most important of all, the Dark radiated from every pore of his body, and it was fueled by a will that staggered even Aj-Kenaz.

Kel drew the sword from his back, and faint screams sounded from its edge. "I'm taking the darkmail now. I suggest you take it off, before I shuck you out of it back into the Void you escaped."

Contempt drew an awful smile across Aj-Kenaz's face. "You little fool. No matter how much power you may possess, you cannot pierce the gift of the Lady with your pathetic weapons. No weapon touched by Light may harm me."

Kel smiled. "As it so happens..."

Faster than sight, Kel rammed the blade just above Aj-Kenaz's collarbone. The Dark Lord gasped, staring in shock at the impossible sight as cold flooded his stolen body. The darkmail had provided no resistance; the links actually parted to permit the blade's entrance.

"...I came prepared," Kel hissed.

He twisted, and Aj-Kenaz felt a dark sentience in the blade tearing through his soul as the edge sliced open his body. His spirit lost its grip on Marduk's body, and with a final wailing scream lost to the voidblade's hunger, Aj-Kenaz vanished into outer darkness.

Kel pulled Acherlith from the Dark Lord's body once the spasms receded.

There is no sense in carelessness, I suppose.

Kel reached down and peeled the failed lord's eyelid back. No life remained in those black orbs, and the Dark leaked out of the corpse like wine from a split cask.

"So much for the First," Kel murmured, and with that eulogy, he summoned a fire to incinerate the corpse.

Within seconds, only the darkmail remained. Kel lifted it over his head, and without ceremony, dropped the armor over his shoulders.

It fell across his body, clinging to him perfectly like a second skin. Gauntlets of dark chain wrapped his hands, light and flexible, yet harder than adamant. Furthermore, the Dark within the essence of the armor bonded with the energy within him, and Kel felt his power expand exponentially in that moment.

The sensation was intoxicating, overwhelming, and Kel therefore rejected it. Ironclad discipline fell into place, and Kel opened his eyes to see Plep, the Un of the Bobagan before him.

The little gray man had tears of a different kind in his eyes now. "What is your command, my Aj?" he asked shakily.

Kel furrowed his brow slightly. "I beg your pardon?"

Plep fell to one knee. "We are Bobagan. We serve the Aj."

Kel considered him for a moment. "I prefer to hunt alone in the wastes for worthy prey, not waste my time with plays for power. I suppose I am closer to an Un than an Aj."

"Now that is just hurtful."

The voice came from the doorway, and Kel twisted to see a familiar robed female striding toward him. Her voice was soft, her eyes gleaming with humor above her midnight-blue half-mask. "After all," she teased, "you're not alone if you've got *me*."

Kel smiled at her, wry humor in his expression. "*Now* I have you. I notice you waited until after the First had been banished."

Gath waved that away, then looked him up and down brazenly. "I could get used to this look. I think I need a matching set."

"Feel free to breach the barrier of stars, then."

She ran her hands across his chest. "Seriously, though, I think you should take the title. You killed an Aj. By the Dark, you killed the First! I think that deserves some commemoration."

Gath put a finger to her lips. "Aj-Kel. No, let's go with the southern pronunciation, Ash-Kel. Hm, that still feels wrong. It feels like it's missing something."

Kel glanced down at the Un on his face, then looked back at Gath and raised an eyebrow.

Her mask distorted as a mischievous grin crossed her features. "Un-Kel? Really? You want to go back to the Ajen as Un-Kel?"

Kel crossed his arms and waited patiently.

"Fine." Gath groused. "I suppose *Ashkelon* rolls off the tongue better, anyways."

"I knew you'd see it my way."

"I'm still calling you Un-Kel, though. Makes our relationship... *spicy.*"

The ice in his eyes thawed as he reached out and took her hand. Together, they stepped past the cowering Bobagan and back into the corridors.

As he and Gath sealed the gate of the Tomb of Aj-Ardur, trapping the Bobagan within, Gath looked at him. "Hey, Un-Kel. What do you think of the pyramid idea? Should we get our own, someday?"

Ashkelon considered the black edifice. Finally, after a moment's pause, he shook his head and answered, "Not if I were the last man on Avalon."

ACKNOWLEDGEMENTS

Pride of place has to go to my beautiful wife Amanda, for all her support, advice, critiques and endless patience. You cannot imagine how many times this remarkable woman has suffered through me saying, "Okay, it's done now! Wait...." Thank you so much for everything, babe.

Thanks to my brilliant artist and illustratator, Louie Roybal III. Without Louie's genius and constant questions, we may never know what Gideon actually looked like, or kept track of the scenes in which he was wearing a helmet. Thanks for coming on board, Louie.

To my mentor and coach, Thomas Umstattd Jr., muchos thanks for all the advice, courses and admonishments that made this project successful. From his course on crowdfunding to the free information in the Novel Marketing Podcast to the mastermind group he moderated, I have reaped a tremendous wealth of knowledge from Thomas's in-depth industry knowledge. Live long and prosper.

This book might not have gotten anywhere without my best friend and alpha reader, Mark Smith. You cannot imagine the hours we spent arguing the philosophies and argumentation used by the characters in this novel. Thank you for all your help, man. (Also, you're still wrong about Tom Bombadil. Dude is absolutely worthless.)

And then there's you guys, the Kickstarter backers who made all this possible. When I saw that the project had been funded to 358%, I couldn't believe my eyes. It was amazing for my narcississm, let me tell you. Without further ado, here is the list of Kickstarter backers who made this project a reality.

Aaron, Adam C. Rodgers, Allen Fredericks, Allyson West Lewis, Andrew Baerlocher, Andrew Corliss, Andrew Nakamura, Andrsong, Andy, Andy Salas, Arnan Heyden, Austin Gardner, Author Media, Bailey Kielek, Becca Woodson, Brian Griffin, Bryan Timothy Mitchell, Carlos, Cassandra Janson, Chad Cargill, Charelshe and Adrian Enosaran, Chautona Havig, Daniel Cooley, Dakota Jacques, David, David Weis, Dort Goodman, Eugene Wheeler, Fiona Aubian, Flora Pearce, Francesco Tehrani, George Kerwood, Gerome Frei, Gregory, Hannah, I'M A NINJA, Inkprint Press, Jared Leroux, Jeff, Jen, Jennifer Goodwin, Jeremiah, Jeremy Shuerger, Jill Hermanson, Jon Shuerger, Jonathan Fuller, Jonathan Ruland, Jordan Edwards, Joshua Francis, Juliane Purves, Justin Peterson, Karen Shuerger, Kate, Katie Clarahan, Kati Pilz, Kelly Wilson, Kevin, Kyle Meyer, Lawrence Adams, Leah, Leslie Clave, Lexie, Logan Bankston, Logan Edwards, Louie, Mandy Ray, Mark Smith, Melissa Huss, Micah Pilcher, Michael Johnson, Michael McClure, Nathan Jensen, Nicholas Liffert, Nicholas Reitz, Paul, Paul and Deissy Paquin, Peter DeHaan, Peter Last, Peter Younghusband, Petra Wilkes-Edwards, Rachel Strehlow, Rafael Campos, Raina and Robert Meginley, Romeo McClarry, Ruben Marquez, Ryan, Sean McClure, Shannon, Shelleen Weaver, Sheri Herum, Sterling Bancroft, Sunmi Ejiwunmi, The Creative Fund, Timothy Allen, Vincent Araujo, Zachary Dale, Zhaxtbrecht, kwl168, and Matt.

Thank you all so much!

ABOUT THE AUTHOR

Jonathan Shuerger is a Marine Corps veteran and author with a passion for telling stories and making people laugh. His first book is *The Exorcism of Frosty the Snowman*, released in 2017. He lives in Tucson, AZ, with his wife and three daughters, who moonlight as domestic terrorists in their free time. Jonathan wargames, DMs tabletop RPGs, and slays it at Smash Bros. and Mario Kart, like every dad should.

You can follow Jonathan on Facebook, Instagram, Twitter and Patreon.

Get updates on Jonathan's next release by signing up for his newsletter at creativegrumbles.com, and get a free story!

CPSIA information can be obtained
at www.ICGtesting.com
Printed in the USA
FSHW011154151020
74758FS